ExMormon

ExMormon

WRITTEN AND ILLUSTRATED BY C. L. HANSON

MORMON ALUMNI
ASSOCIATION
Gone for Good

PUBLISHED BY THE MORMON ALUMNI ASSOCIATION
SALT LAKE CITY, UTAH

Printed in the United States of America

Typesetting, cover, and interior design by John Hamer.

Contents

I. Young Women's

April

1. Thursday Evening

"OH NO! Bobby will be here any minute!" shrieked Annette, playing her Barbie-doll Patty. "I can't let him see the house like this with the walls all splattered with green jello! I'm so embarrassed!"

"Yeah, we should have known better than to try to make Jennifer's special exploding jello for company—the recipe's just too complicated!" said Lynn for her doll Tuesday.

To think that Lynn was already twelve years old and in Young Women's at church. For ten-year-old Annette to still want to play Barbies was already kind of borderline. But I supposed it wasn't too embarrassing if they just did it at home with nobody else around.

It was so annoying that Mom and Dad insisted I set up my drawing table and paints in the toyroom where Annette kept her elaborate doll house! I got to have the joy of listening to two giggly little sisters while trying to concentrate on creating my masterpiece graphic novel.

"Uh-oh, he's here now!" said Annette, driving a Ken-doll up to the house in a red convertible.

"Quick!" said Lynn's doll Tuesday, "Let's go outside and pretend like we're locked out of the house!"

"Okay, I've locked the door," said Patty.

"Hurry! Hide the keys in your bra!" said Tuesday.

I managed to get the various watercolors placed just right to create an iridescent effect on Wyxetta's wings despite having to listen to this vulgar scene. Wyxetta was the beautiful fairy princess who was the heroine of my story. In the cover design I was painting, she was lazily reclining in a red tulip, blissfully unaware of anything but her own daydreams.

"We're so glad you could make it, Bobby," said Lynn's doll Tuesday, as Lynn took the Ken doll out of the toy car. "Let's go straight to the pool around back." The pool was actually a basin for washing dishes.

Then Lynn switched to an exaggerated male voice for Bobby's reply: "Okay, but I'm kinda thirsty. Can I go to the kitchen first to get a drink of water?"

"No!" exclaimed Annette's doll Patty. "We have a cooler full of pop by the pool. Come with us, we'll go straight there."

I moved on to painting the flesh tones of Wyxetta's slender, elegant leg that she was dangling down between the petals of the flower. Her head was resting gently on her arms on the curved portion of another petal.

"Ah, that hit the spot," said Lynn in her Bobby voice. "Now I have to go to the bathroom. Can I go in the house?"

"No, just go in the bushes," said Annette's doll Patty.

"I don't want to," said Lynn's ridiculous Bobby voice, "and besides, that's not polite when you're a guest at someone's house. Why can't I just go inside?"

I was working on adding the sun-rich highlights to Wyxetta's blond hair—spilling across her arm and onto the flower petal—as Annette continued as Patty. "We can't let you in because we're locked out."

"Then I'll break the door down!" said Lynn as Bobby.

Switching to her Tuesday voice Lynn assumed a shocked tone "What? That's even less polite than peeing in the bushes!"

"Well how did you get locked out anyway?" asked Lynn's Bobby voice.

"We lost the key!" said Annette as Patty.

"Where did you see it last?"

"I accidentally dropped it in my bra," said Annette's Patty voice, "and now I can't find it anymore!"

Lynn laughed. Then continuing in her Bobby voice she said "I'll help you find it!"

"Bobby, stop it! That's so naughty!" said Annette as Patty.

"Lynn!" I called. I looked up from my painting to see Lynn putting the Ken doll's hand up Annette's Barbie doll's shirt.

Lynn looked up nonchalantly. "Could you maybe go paint in another room?" she asked. Then she went straight back to her Bobby voice. "Hmmmm, what's in here?"

Just then we heard the front door open, which meant that Dad was home from work. That was enough to make Lynn stop. "We'd better just open the door," said Lynn's doll Tuesday.

Next I started sketching Wyxetta's friend Adrianna. Adrianna was flying upright near Wyxetta's flower, right where Wyxetta would see her if only she were to look up from her daydream.

Adrianna was balancing a leaf on its point on the tip of her nose while hovering perfectly still in midair. Adrianna was a bit of a tom-boy, but she was as beautiful as Wyxetta. I was so entranced by sketching her that I lost track of Lynn and Annette's game, which had moved on to some silliness about trying to keep Bobby from going into the kitchen.

Adrianna had her long, fine arms outstretched. One leg extended straight down all the way to the point of her toe, and the other was slightly bent, like a ballerina. Her wings fluttered behind her. I was working on her curly, black hair and her pointed ears when I heard Mom calling all of us to the dinner table.

Lynn and Annette reluctantly put down their dolls and stopped by my drawing table to admire my work on their way to dinner.

"Wow, she's pretty," said Annette, pointing to Wyxetta.

"Is that one a boy?" asked Lynn, pointing to Adrianna.

"No, she isn't," I replied.

"Well, what do the boy ones look like?" asked Lynn.

I went through my pile of pages of my novel and pulled out one that had a picture of the fairy king.

"Oh," she said, looking at it. Then pointing to my painting she said "I think you should add a boy one here, hiding behind this tree, watching the girls and thinking of coming over to talk to them."

"Yeah, that would be cool," Annette agreed.

"That's not in the story," I said. "This is the cover to the novel, and it illustrates a scene from the story."

"Oh, okay," said Lynn, and she and Annette set off for the kitchen.

Ugh, little sisters! Everything with them was boys, boys, boys! Boys and boys' adventures seemed to matter more to both of them than the fun adventures girls might have on their own! Neither one of them was ever likely to be much of a feminist.

After dinner I went back to my drawing table. Lynn and Annette went straight back to their Barbies, so it was impossible to ever get a chance to paint in peace.

Now Patty and Tuesday were sitting on the edge of the pool dangling their feet in when Ursula approached. That was the name they had given to a ratty old Barbie doll that they had cut all the hair off of.

"Hi guys, can I go swimming in your pool?" asked Lynn, giving Ursula an annoyingly nasal voice.

"Oh no! Who invited her?" whispered Annette's doll Patty.

"I sure didn't," whispered Lynn's doll Tuesday. "She just comes around without being invited."

"Yeah, who would ever invite her anywhere? She's such a geek!" said Annette's doll Patty.

"Look, she's picking her nose and scratching her butt!" said Lynn, laughing.

"We'd love to swim with you," said Annette's doll Patty in a fake-sweet voice, "but we just remembered that we have to go to the television studio because we're going to be in a commercial."

"Yeah," said Lynn as Tuesday. Then she switched to her Ursula voice and said "You don't have to leave right away, do you? Let's swim a little." She then plunged Ursula into the pool.

"Yuck! The water's turning all brown!" exclaimed Annette's doll Patty.

"Oh yeah, I forgot," said Lynn's Ursula voice. "I have a can of root beer in my pocket. I was going to share it with you guys. I only drank a little. Want some?" Annette and Lynn both laughed.

"Um, no thanks," said Lynn's doll Tuesday.

"Let's ditch her!" whispered Annette as Patty, and Annette and Lynn had Patty and Tuesday run off laughing, leaving Ursula alone in the pool.

Since there was clearly no way I could concentrate on my painting with this nonsense going on, I got up and went back to my room. I sat on the bed and read *The Hobbit* until Mom came around to tell us to start getting ready for bed.

I brushed my teeth and put on my pajamas, then I grabbed my copy of the *Book of Mormon* and went to Mom and Dad's room for our nightly family scripture reading.

As usual, Lynn and Annette were dragging their heels and moaning and groaning about being made to read the *Book of Mormon*. When they'd taken about ten times as long as necessary to brush their teeth, I heard Mom sternly say to them "You two had better be ready in two minutes, and I don't want to hear any more complaints!"

Mom had a frustrated look on her face as she came into the room where Dad and I were already sitting with our books open. Dad walked up to her and hugged her and kissed her on the forehead.

"They're just kids," he said. "They'll thank you someday, and you know I appreciate the effort you make for us to follow the prophet's advice and read the scriptures together as a family."

Actually, I wasn't too keen on reading the *Book of Mormon* myself, but I didn't want to upset Mom like my little sisters did, and besides I knew that it was an important book for all of us to be studying.

Finally Lynn and Annette appeared and opened their books to the right chapter. As usual we went around in a circle and had each person read a verse until we got to the end of the chapter.

Our chapter for the day was Ether 6.

Mom began: "And now I, Moroni, proceed to give the record of Jared and his brother."

Then it was my turn. "For it came to pass after the Lord had prepared the stones which the brother of Jared had carried up into the mount, the brother of Jared came down out of the mount, and he did put forth the stones into the vessels which were prepared, one in each end thereof; and behold, they did give light unto the vessels."

As the story continued, I imagined doing a painting of Jared and their group, with all of their animals, traveling across the ocean in their submarine-like barges. I thought about painting the scene where the brother of Jared brought the stones to be touched by the Lord to give light inside the barges. But I couldn't think of how to portray the shot of the brother of Jared seeing just the Lord's finger in a way that was reverent and not silly.

It was kind of funny that one of the most important prophets of the *Book of Mormon* was referred to only as "the brother of Jared" instead of by his name, but my dad had once explained to me that the prophet Joseph Smith had had a revelation that the brother of Jared was actually named "Mahonri Morincumur" and that the *Book of Mormon* authors just wrote "the brother of Jared" as shorthand to save space on the gold plates.

I decided the scene I'd paint would be the people gathering their things and loading up the barges. Then I imagined Mom and Dad looking at my painting proudly and hanging it on the wall. I was so lost in my little fantasy that Mom had to get my attention to remind me that it was my turn again.

"And it came to pass that when they were buried in the deep there was no water that could hurt them, their vessels being tight like unto a dish, and also they were tight like unto the ark of Noah; therefore when they were encompassed about by many waters they did cry unto the Lord, and he did bring them forth again upon the top of the waters," I read.

Lynn went on and took her turn, reading about how they were being driven towards the promised land. Luckily we were near the end of the book – we were already on the second story of the righteous crossing the ocean to the promised land of the New World.

To make up for my earlier inattention, I paid close attention to the rest of the story of how the people of Jared arrived safely in the New World and chose themselves a king. Then it was time for our family bedtime prayer. Dad called on Annette to say it.

"Our Dear Heavenly Father," she began, "We thank Thee for our many blessings. We thank Thee for our happy home and family. Please bless us to sleep well tonight and to have a good day tomorrow. We say these things in the name of Thy Son Jesus Christ, Amen."

We all repeated the "amen" and went off to bed.

2. SUNDAY MORNING

AS SOON AS I woke up on Sunday morning, I went to look at my painting again. It was beautiful! Wyxetta and Adrianna had such a perfect life in their little fairy kingdom.

Saturday had been a productive day since Lynn and Annette had decided to spend the day at the mall and then the library. I'd gotten the chance to add lots of colors and details to finish the scene. I hated to put it down when Mom came up to tell me to start getting ready for church.

I heard the door downstairs, which was undoubtedly Lynn getting back from her paper route, so I went down to the kitchen to have breakfast with her. I poured myself a bowl of cereal as Lynn took off her hat, scarf, and mittens and placed them on the drying rack, hung up her coat, and put her boots on the mat.

"Snowing?" I asked.

"As usual lately," said Lynn, sitting down to take off her wool oversocks and her outer pair of pants. "Fortunately it isn't too deep. As it is I had to knock the snow off the wheels every twenty feet. It's bad enough pushing a cart full of Sunday papers in the Summer, but in the Winter it's a real pain."

Of course if it had been much worse, Mom or Dad would have helped her in the car. Still, the thought made me glad I'd given up my paper route even though I missed the extra spending money.

Lynn was getting out a bowl for herself when Dad came in all dressed in his suit and tie. "You're finally back just now?" he asked Lynn. "We have to be out the door in half an hour, and you haven't even started getting ready! You either!" he said, turning to me.

"I'm sorry," said Lynn, "the snow slowed me down."

"Here," I said, quickly scarfing down the last of my cereal. "I'll go take my shower while you have your breakfast, then you can go after me."

"Thanks," said Lynn, pouring the milk on her cereal.

On my way up the stairs, I passed Annette coming down. She was yelling "Mom! I don't have any clean dresses!"

"What?" Mom called back from downstairs.

"Or underwear!" continued Annette.

I heard Mom saying "If it's not one thing it's another in this house! Couldn't you have said something yesterday? Come on, we'll find you something."

I left them to deal with their problem and got in the shower. A hot shower always feels good on a cold day. Of course the house was heated and insulated, but still it was always a little cold in the winter, especially with people coming in and out. So after walking barefoot on the cold kitchen floor, it was nice to warm up in the shower.

Sunday morning was never really the time to savor a shower though since we had church first thing in the morning, and everybody needed a turn. So I turned off the water as soon as I was clean enough but long before I was warm enough. As I went back to my room, I called down to Lynn to tell her the shower was free.

Of my three church dresses hanging up in my closet, I chose the dark blue one with little white flowers. Since I'd learned to button and tie it behind my back, I was able to get ready by myself in a matter of minutes. Once I had my nylons and dress shoes on and my hair combed, I went to Mom and Dad's room to see if Annette needed any help.

In Mom and Dad's room, Mom was curling Annette's hair with a curling iron. Annette was wearing one of Lynn's dresses. I didn't ask what she had done for panties, but I imagined it was something similarly improvised.

It looked like they didn't need any help, so I went back to my room and sat down to admire my painting some more. Adrianna was perfect, but the more I looked at it, the more I got the impression that one of Wyxetta's legs was longer than the other. Oh well, it was too late to fix it now.

"We're getting in the car now!" called Mom from downstairs. "April! Lynn! Come put your coats on!"

I put down my painting and started going down the stairs. Lynn followed, still wearing her bathrobe and holding a dress that was the same as mine only in green.

"Lynn, you're not dressed!" exclaimed Mom. "We're on our way out the door!"

"Mom, I can't wear this dress, it's horrible!" said Lynn, throwing the dress down on the living room couch. "It's the ugliest dress on the planet! I'll look like hell!"

"Lynn Hanson!" said Dad, shocked. "This behavior is totally unacceptable. You march back upstairs this minute and put that dress on."

So Lynn grabbed the dress and stormed back upstairs. We all waited in the foyer except Dad who went out to the garage to unplug the heater in the engine of the car and to start the car running. In a few minutes Lynn was back downstairs wearing the dress and a huge scowl.

The seat was cold as the three of us girls took our place, with Annette in the middle and me and Lynn on either side. Once everyone was settled and belted in, we set off.

"Great!" said Lynn, still in a foul mood, "You have on my barrettes too! Is there anything of mine you didn't take?"

"Shut up!" replied Annette.

I turned to Lynn and said "Don't make trouble. It's already your fault we're going to be late."

"It's not my fault, it's Annette's for taking my good dress!" With that she gave Annette a shove.

"It's not my fault!" cried Annette. "It's Mom's! She made me wear this!"

"Well you could have gotten ready faster anyway," I said to Lynn.

"And you could stop being a jerk all the time!" she snapped back.

"Girls!" said Mom. "We're on our way to church! I will not have the spirit of contention in this car!"

"Let's sing a song!" said Dad. Then he started singing *"I'm a Mormon, yes I am!"*

The rest of us forgot about our fight and joined in singing with him. *"So if you want to study a Mormon I'm a living specimen! Maybe you think I'm just like anybody else you see, but trust in my word, you'll quickly observe, I'm different as can be..."*

When we finally arrived at church, of course Sacrament Meeting had already started. So we had to take a seat in the foyer and partake of the sacrament there. Actually I would just as soon have stayed in the foyer for the whole meeting if I could have, since in the foyer you can more easily get away with talking or drawing or reading. But we didn't have a good excuse to stay there—not having any unruly toddlers in our family—so as soon as the sacrament was over we went in the chapel.

There was an empty stretch of pew way up in the third row that apparently Mom and Dad had decided to go for, so the whole ward saw us come in late as we walked up to the front. Since we were one of the established, active families of the ward, it wouldn't do for us to slink into one of the back rows of the chapel even on Sundays when we didn't manage to make it to Sacrament Meeting on time.

Just across the aisle from us, occupying three whole rows of the smaller side pews as usual, was the Grant family. They'd moved here to Minnesota from Idaho a few years earlier, and always talked about how much it strengthened their testimonies to now be living out in the "mission field." With their eight kids ranging in age from teenagers to young primary kids, they were the largest family in the ward. Some of the other important families had five or six. We were in the next tier down with only three.

The meeting got back underway as Sister Shumway got up to give a talk on missionary work. I discretely took out my copy of *The Hobbit* and started reading. After reading a whole chapter, I looked up to see that Sister Shumway's talk was still going strong. She was now reading excerpts from letters from her son who was on a mission to Mexico. Annette and Lynn were playing the dots and squares game on their program. Mom and Dad seemed to be paying attention although I got the distinct impression that Mom was kind of half-participating in Lynn and Annette's game. Up on the stand, one of the Bishop's counselors seemed to be dozing off. It appeared that it was going to be a long meeting, so I went back to my book.

I had gotten to the part where Bilbo Baggins meets up with the dragon when the first few notes of the closing hymn brought me back to reality. I reluctantly put down my book and grabbed a hymn book and sang along. Once the closing prayer was over, we got up to go to our Sunday School classes.

Lynn immediately went off to find her best friend Amy Thomas. I followed to meet up with Amy's older sister Alexandra, who was my best friend at church.

When I found Alexandra, I said hi to her, but as usual I didn't have all that much to say to her. I caught myself feeling a little jealous of Lynn as she and Amy ran off laughing together. Alexandra was nice enough, but she wasn't much for conversation. It was funny that the two sisters could be so different: Amy so full of jokes and fun, and Alexandra so dull. She and I sometimes had fun together, but it was never like Amy and Lynn.

There wasn't much to be done about it though since there wasn't much of a selection to pick church friends from. The only girl in the ward besides Alexandra who was around my same age was Claire Miller, the bishop's daughter. Claire was above speaking to me and Alexandra because she was friends with Isabel Denton, who was an older girl, already in the Laurels class. So my choice of best church friend was effectively made for me.

As a consequence, I wasn't all that disappointed that I hadn't quite turned fourteen yet and hence was still in Amy and Lynn's Sunday School class with the twelve and thirteen-year-olds. Even Sarah Grant, who was kind of friends with Amy and Lynn off and on, was more lively than Alexandra.

In class I chose a seat next to Amy and Lynn and Sarah. Lara Snyder sat with Claire's sister Kimberly on the other side of the room, surrounded by boys. The two of them were Claire's counterparts in Lynn's age group, and hence only spoke to other popular girls or to boys.

Our teacher, Brother Trent, called the class to order and had one of the boys say the opening prayer. Then he started on a lesson about the great faith of the early Latter-day Saints as they crossed the plains to the lands the Lord promised them in Utah territory.

Reading from the manual, he told a story of a young pioneer boy who strayed away from his camp one night. Then Brother Trent looked up from the book and asked, "And there, in the moonlight, what do you think he saw?"

"His cousin?" asked Amy. Both Amy and Lynn broke out in hysterical laughter as Sarah blushed. I laughed a little myself.

The whole cousin thing was a bit of an inside joke. Sarah and her family had recently traveled back to Idaho for a big family reunion. She came back with stories of a boy she had met there, and how she had held hands with him and kissed him in the moonlight. Amy and Lynn both insisted that Sarah had made the whole story up, probably because they couldn't bear the thought that Sarah—the geekiest girl in the ward—had been kissed by a boy and they hadn't. They kept saying Sarah's story was a lie until I instead made a joke about "kissing cousins." That was a big hit. Amy and Lynn loved that idea, and immediately switched to teasing Sarah with all sorts of incest jokes. Sarah didn't talk about her new boyfriend much after that, so for all we knew maybe he really was her cousin.

Laughing back and forth about our little joke, we completely missed the point of the teacher's story, and didn't pay much attention to the rest of the lesson either. Then it was time for a quick pass by the ladies' room for everyone to check their hair, and we were off to Young Women's.

As the girls filed into the room and took their seats, the adult leaders were already there waiting, including my mom who was the first counselor in the Young Women's presidency and was also the teacher of the Laurels class.

After the opening song and prayer, Sister Denton, the Young Women's president, called the meeting to order. She explained that in honor of the women's broadcast we had attended this past Wednesday, we were going to have a special testimony meeting instead of dividing into our separate classes as usual.

"What?" whispered Lynn. "It's bad enough we have to endure 'open mike day' with the ward on Fast Sunday, and now we have to do it here?" I shushed Lynn as Sister Denton called her daughter Isabel to the front to bear the first testimony.

Isabel stepped to the front of the room and placed her Gucci purse on the table beside the small podium as she began.

"I'd like to bear my testimony that I know this church is true, and I know with all my heart that Joseph Smith was a true prophet of God who restored the true gospel and the priesthood for the saints in these latter days to prepare for Christ's second coming." She went on to talk about the broadcast we had seen and its theme, which was "love". She told us that all the talks on love reminded her of how she loves each and every one of us. Then she described how strongly she felt the spirit throughout the broadcast.

I remembered going to the Stake Center with all of the other women of all the wards in our stake to watch the broadcast, and I had to admit that I didn't feel the spirit there at all the whole time. To me it was just talk after talk after talk about the fact that our divine role as women was to serve in the home as good wives and mothers in Zion to build up the Kingdom of God in righteousness. I wasn't about to question Heavenly Father's plan, but still it always kind of annoyed me that the boys were encouraged to pursue all sorts of dreams and ambitions while we girls were always reminded to put marriage and family first and to pursue other interests only as a back-up, if at all.

When Isabel had finished, Sister Johnson, the new teacher of the Beehive Girls class, stood up to bear her testimony. Sister Johnson was the main reason I was looking forward to graduating from the Beehive Girls class to the Mia Maids class. She was twenty years old and hence barely out of the Young Women's program herself. Mom had told me a bunch of times how she and the rest of the Young Women's presidency were glad to have Sister Johnson there to set a good example for the girls, having recently gotten married in the temple.

In keeping with her role as "good example", Sister Johnson spent a portion of the class time each week talking about how fun and exciting it was for her to be setting up her new household with her wonderful husband. As far as I could tell, the other twelve and thirteen year old girls (including Lynn) were enthralled by her "happily ever after" lifestyle and couldn't stop asking her for details on her table settings or on how she arranged and decorated this or that room in her apartment.

I wouldn't admit it to anyone, but personally I found Sister Johnson vapid and her stories unspeakably dull. So while she was successfully inspiring most of the girls to focus on the goal of a temple marriage, she was having exactly the opposite effect on me, making me dread my future role as wife and mother.

As I expected, after the usual remarks about Joseph Smith and the church, Sister Johnson started bearing her testimony of temple marriage and of eternal families. After that she started talking about how much the women's broadcast had meant to her, since love was such an important part of her life. She told us that a wife's love for her husband is as divine and sacred as the love we as children of God feel for our Father in Heaven. Then she closed in the name of Jesus Christ and sat down.

After Sister Johnson's testimony, Claire, Lara, and Kimberly each took a turn and bore testimonies that were essentially repetitions of Isabel's, about how they loved all of us, etc. Then some older Laurels bore their testimonies as did some more of the adults, followed by Alexandra.

I started to realize—to my horror—that we were actually going around the room and taking turns bearing testimonies in a systematic way instead of following the usual testimony meeting practice of allowing each person to stand and speak if and only if they felt inspired to do so. This time I would have no choice but to stand and bear my testimony.

I dreaded doing it because even though I obviously believed the church to be true, I felt like I still had some work to do before reaching the level of having a sure knowledge. But it was clear that I couldn't get out of it, and I could hardly stand up and say "I'm not sure the church is true" or really anything other than "I know this church is true," so I went ahead and recited the right words with all of the sincerity I could muster.

My one consolation was that Lynn's testimony was even worse than mine. She went up right after me and perfunctorily said "I'd like to bear my testimony that I know this church is true and it was a very spiritual and inspiring women's broadcast, in the name of Jesus Christ, amen." Then she sat down.

After Lynn, Amy and Sarah each bore ordinary testimonies, and then we closed the meeting with a song and a prayer and were dismissed.

In the hall after the meeting Alexandra caught up with Claire, who was talking with Isabel.

"Claire?" asked Alexandra.

"Yes?" responded Claire, apparently surprised that Alexandra had addressed her.

"That was a really good testimony you bore in there," said Alexandra.

"Thanks," said Claire.

"Did you mean it?" asked Alexandra.

"Of course," said Claire, seeming a bit annoyed.

"That's really cool," said Alexandra, "because my sister and I are having a slumber party at our house on Friday, and you can come if you like."

Claire thought about it for a bit and said "I don't know... I don't think I can make it." Then Isabel whispered something to Claire, and they both laughed and walked away.

"Don't worry about those jerks," I said to Alexandra. "We'll have a great slumber party without them."

"Yeah," agreed Alexandra half-heartedly.

When I got home from church, I went to my room and started thinking about that testimony meeting. I felt like it was wrong that I didn't have a real testimony to bear as I should. I decided to set a goal right then and there to try to gain one.

The first step was to try to be more righteous in general. I got down my journal off the shelf. It was a pink hard-bound volume that was about a third of the way filled. But when I saw that I hadn't written in it in over a year and a half, I decided that I need to start fresh, so I got out a blank spiral notebook from my parents' study and started writing.

On the first page I wrote the date and my list of long-term goals: a temple marriage, and eventually to be worthy to enter the Celestial Kingdom. Then I started listing my short-term goals to get there.

I thought about feeling angry at Claire and Isabel at church, so the first goal I wrote was "1. Be more forgiving." Then I thought some more and wrote "2. Obey my parents willingly," and "3. Love my sisters (don't fight with them)." Continuing, I wrote "4. Study the scriptures, 5. Write in my journal regularly." I underlined "regularly" three times.

Then I wrote the most important goal of all: "6. Pray for a testimony."

Fast Sunday was coming up in two weeks. I set a goal to be ready to stand up in front of the ward and bear my testimony.

It was a pretty ambitious goal considering that on some level I'd been trying to gain a testimony my whole life. But I figured that putting a concrete time frame on it would help me focus and really get there. I was sure to succeed.

FRIDAY EVENING rolled around, and with it came Alexandra and Amy's big slumber party. After dinner Mom dropped Lynn and me off at their house. It turned out that the only guests other than me and Lynn were Sarah Grant and a girl named Melissa that Alexandra introduced as being her best friend from school.

Normally I wouldn't mix school friends and church friends like that myself despite what we're told about how every member should be a missionary and make sure that all of our non-member friends hear about the gospel. I wasn't sure if Alexandra had invited Melissa in order to show her how much fun Mormons are in hopes of converting her or if it was just a way of filling out the guest list a little since it was hard to have a big party with just the girls from the ward.

Whatever Alexandra's reason, I figured she had done the right thing by inviting Melissa. From the minute I saw her, I knew she was going to be a lot of fun. She had long, wavy red hair going in every direction and a perpetual smile. She was a little taller than me—which wasn't hard since I'd always been small—and she was a little more stocky and athletic than the rest of us. Instead of wearing a preppy sweater like the girls at my school usually did in January, she was wearing some sort of rugby jersey over her faded jeans.

I talked to Melissa a little and asked her about her school and such as we all gathered our things into Alexandra and Amy's family room. Once we had banished their little brothers, we were ready to start the first activity of the evening: "killer Uno." Lynn wanted to play "I doubt it" (which was the polite name for a game called "B.S."), and Amy suggested that since it was a slumber party it should be "strip I-doubt-it," but we all agreed that we should at least pretend to be good girls until the rest of the family was in bed.

Melissa had never played "killer Uno" before, but she got the hang of it right away. She seemed to be enjoying the fun of making everyone draw as many cards as possible, and rather than getting uptight about winning or losing, she laughed when she had to draw a big pile of cards herself since she was psyched to get some new good cards she could use later to make other people draw. She was in the middle of drawing twelve cards (and joking about how many draw-two's and draw-four's she was getting to zing us with later) when Alexandra's mom came in and brought us some popcorn and pop.

"What fun!" said Alexandra's mom Sister Thomas. "I remember how much I used to love slumber parties when I was a girl! I almost wish I could join you." Amy laughed, but Alexandra looked worried, as though her mom might actually join us if we accidentally invited her out of politeness.

Once Sister Thomas had handed us all napkins, she said "Well, your father and I are going to bed, so you can start whispering about your secret loves now without worrying that we'll hear you." Then she gave us a big smile and a wink and left.

We played a few more rounds of killer Uno to make sure the family had plenty of time to fall asleep before we chose our next activity. Sarah suggested "Monopoly", but that was unanimously rejected right off the bat. None of us wanted to get stuck playing some boring board game all night that would just put us to sleep.

Amy suggested that we should play dress-up. I wanted to reject that suggestion as well for being too babyish until I saw the box of dress-up clothes Amy went and brought out. There were all sorts of strange-looking dresses and other costumes. Alexandra said that her mom had made a lot of them and collected the rest second-hand for road shows and Halloween parties. There were a bunch of things that looked fun to try on.

"Your mom must really be just a big kid at heart," said Sarah, pulling some sort of royal robe out of the box. "She likes to play dress-up, have slumber parties, swap secrets about boys..."

"Don't I know it," said Alexandra, grabbing a shimmering silky black dress.

"If we'd have let her stay, she'd have been the first one to suggest that we play the game where we go around in a circle and say which boys we like!" laughed Amy.

Once we all had our dresses on, we started doing each other's hair and make-up. For the make-up we had loads of fun giving each other an exaggeratedly glamorous look with bright colored lipstick and eye shadow and lots of glitter. Melissa drew a little purple star on my cheek.

The only exception was Lynn, who had found an old tuxedo jacket and a top hat in the box and thought it would be funny to dress up as a man. She had Amy draw a mustache on her and dark eyebrows.

The last step was for all of us to do each other's hair. Lynn just pulled her own hair back into a ponytail and tucked it into the back of her collar and watched the rest of us. Amy seemed pretty skilled at doing hair. After curling up Alexandra's hair with a curling iron and accessorizing it with ribbons and little sparkly clips, she gave Sarah an appropriately regal hairdo with some straight parts and some small braids draped around her head in different ways.

Doing up Melissa's hair, I tried to copy Amy's style to go with the green velvet Renaissance-style dress she was wearing. I started by carefully brushing her long red hair to gleaming. I gathered it up in my hands and made most of the back part into a series of braids. After pinning up some loops of braided hair in back, I took the curling iron and framed her face with little ringlets.

When we were done, we all looked beautiful yet hilarious. Melissa seemed to get the biggest kick out of the whole thing of any of us. As soon as she got in front of a mirror, she about died laughing and couldn't stop.

"I have to get a picture of this!" she said. "I have to show this to the guys I play hockey with! They'll laugh their asses off!" She ran off to get her camera out of her bag and gave it to me to snap her picture.

After I'd snapped a few good shots of her, Lynn insisted on getting into the act. She made a huge production of getting into a theatrical pose on bended knee to kiss Melissa's hand. Melissa tried to put on an expression of mock rapture, but she couldn't stop laughing long enough, so I just got what pictures I could. They were pretty funny.

I couldn't help but want to join in the fun, so I was pretty happy when Melissa had me give the camera to Lynn and beckoned me over and put her arm around me to do another funny pose. Maybe it wasn't quite as funny as Lynn's but I was sure we looked great together as I pulled her in close for a split second for the shot.

I was wearing a very simple sparkling silver lamé dress that looked so much like something a fairy princess might wear that I promised myself I'd paint the same dress on Wyxetta, the main character in my graphic novel, for her next portrait. I couldn't see putting my other main character Adrianna in Melissa's green velvet renaissance dress, but I was tempted to paint her in a rugby shirt, even if it wasn't very fairy-like.

I started thinking about how cool it would be to have someone like Melissa as a church friend instead of Alexandra, but I just couldn't picture Melissa as a Mormon. Or really, it was more like I didn't want to imagine her that way, all proper and reverent dressed up for church.

I wanted to see her in what I imagined was her natural habitat, on a hockey rink playing rough and wild against a bunch of boys.

After the pictures of me with Melissa, we got some of Melissa with Alexandra and then of the three of us, and then of all of the various combinations of Lynn, Amy, and Sarah. Actually it kind of increased my respect for Alexandra to see that of all the girls in her school she would choose someone like Melissa as a best friend.

Once we were done taking pictures, we had gotten to the point in the night where there was really only one clear choice of what to play next: truth or dare! The official name of the game was "Truth, dare, double-dare, promise, or repeat", but since "promise" and "repeat" weren't interesting and "double-dare" was essentially the same as "dare", each player had only two real options.

Alexandra decided that since it was her party, she should be the one to select the person to go first and come up with that person's challenge. She picked me, and I decided to go with "truth".

"Ask her who she likes!" suggested Lynn. "I think I know who it is."

Everyone laughed and seemed to like that suggestion, so Alexandra decided to go with it and ask me to say who was my secret love. I was beyond being surprised to see that everything always came back to boys eventually.

"And it's not fair to name someone from your school that we've never heard of," said Sarah. "Tell us who you like of the boys in the ward!"

"I don't like any of the boys in our ward," I said. "They're all disgusting."

At that the girls all burst out in laughter and groans of "Yeah, sure!"

"I know who it is," said Alexandra. "It's Andrew Denton."

I wasn't sure how to respond to that. It was true that if I were forced to pick one out of all of the boys in the ward it would be Andrew. He was always sweet and friendly and fun to hang out with.

"Aww, she's blushing!" said Amy. "Looks like you guessed it!"

"Well, he likes you, that's for sure," said Sarah. "And it looks like the feeling is mutual."

"Okay, who's next?" asked Lynn. "April, you get to pick somebody."

"Pick Alexandra!" suggested Melissa. "Get her back!"

"Okay, Alexandra," I said "Truth or dare?"

Alexandra looked a little nervous for a second, and then gathered up her courage and said "dare!" The girls all laughed with anticipation.

"Make her roll around naked in the snow!" said Melissa, laughing.

"No, come on guys!" said Alexandra. "That's no fun! I'd get hypothermia! I could die!"

"Okay, okay," I said. "Just barefoot, then. Take off your socks and go touch the maple tree in the very back of the yard."

Alexandra didn't have a good reason to refuse that one, so she took off her socks and put on her coat, and we all watched by the light of the back porch as she ran barefoot all the way to the end of the yard and back.

"Yow, that's cold!" she said as she rushed back inside to rub her feet in front of the heating vent.

"Now you get to pick someone again," I said.

Alexandra didn't seem too interested in looking up from her task of warming her feet, but she absently glanced over and said "Amy."

Amy also chose "dare" so we all started racking our brains for ideas of what Alexandra should make Amy do. Sarah suggested we should make her stick her hand or her toothbrush in the toilet, but that one was such an old stand-by for truth-or-dare that we were bored of it.

Finally Alexandra came up with the idea that Amy should have to take off her bra and wear it as sunglasses and let Melissa take a picture. She was probably hoping to embarrass Amy about wearing such a big bra at her age, but Amy didn't seem to be embarrassed in the slightest. She had fun making faces in her unusual sunglasses as Melissa snapped her picture. Obviously it would have been more embarrassing for me to show off my small bra, and worse for Lynn, who wore a training bra even though she was still totally flat at twelve years old.

Amy then decided that it was time to get Melissa back for all the help she'd given on the other dares. Of course Melissa chose "dare". Amy thought for a minute and then told Melissa that she had to kiss every girl in the room.

Melissa laughed and said "That's nothing!" Then, not only did she kiss everyone, but she kissed them all on the lips, making a show of getting into how funny it was.

By the time she got around to Lynn, her little act had become pretty exaggerated. We were all still wearing our costumes, so Melissa started by giving a curtsy and asking "Will you kiss me, handsome gentleman?" before going after Lynn.

I laughed and said "Aw, come on!" as I kicked her foot.

Melissa looked up from kissing Lynn and jokingly said to me "Don't worry, you're next!" Then she laughed at making me wipe my face after she gave me a wet, sloppy one.

"Now it's my turn to choose!" said Melissa. "I choose... Lynn!"

Lynn actually looked a little worried about what Melissa might make her do, so after a very short hesitation she said "truth."

"Aw, what a wimp!" teased Melissa. "Kidding! We'll just have to think of a good one for her, won't we?"

"Let's ask her who she likes!" said Amy. Amy and I both knew very well that Lynn's secret love was Sarah's older brother Rodney, but that she didn't want to admit it in front of Sarah for fear she'd tell him. Personally I thought Lynn had terrible taste to like him. He was an awkward and strange boy, but I supposed that the draw was that he was an older boy—almost sixteen—but was willing to pay attention to her occasionally. It was embarrassing the way she would go find him to flirt with him between meetings at church or follow him around at church activities.

There was no way anyone was in the dark about Lynn's secret, so it seemed like asking that question would be letting her off way too easily. Especially considering her tone of voice when she protested "Aw, you don't want to ask me that." It made me think that she was actually hoping for an excuse to spill the beans to Sarah in hopes of enlisting her aid or getting her opinion of her brother's feelings.

"Come on, that's so ordinary, asking who she likes!" said Melissa. "And besides, I don't even know any of these stupid boys you guys know anyway! Doesn't anyone have something that will really get her?" And with that Melissa lunged forward to tickle Lynn, who jumped out of her reach laughing.

It was at that moment that I was struck with an idea—a wonderful, terrible, awful idea!

"I know," I said. "Ask her when was the last time she played Barbie dolls."

Lynn froze and turned as white as a sheet.

"Ooh! That's a good one!" said Melissa, roaring with laughter. The other girls joined in laughing as well. "All right, let's have it. When was it?"

"I don't know," stammered Lynn. "I don't remember. It was a long time ago."

"Truth?" I asked raising one eyebrow as the girls laughed some more.

"Ha ha, Lynn and her Barbie dolls!" teased Alexandra.

Lynn glared at me with such intense hatred in her eyes that I thought she would have pounced on me and scratched my eyes out if there weren't so many people around.

"Okay, okay, I guess we'll accept that answer," said Melissa, winking at Lynn. "So now you get to pick someone."

"I'm the only one left," said Sarah, "so you have to pick me."

"Hmm," said Lynn, regaining her smile as she made a show of trying to decide. "I'll pick... Sarah!"

"I know!" said Melissa. "If she picks 'truth' let's ask her if that boyfriend of hers really is her cousin!" and she burst out laughing as did the rest of us. I was impressed—in the space of just our card game and dress-up, Melissa had already picked up on our inside joke about Sarah's cousin.

Sarah looked slightly miffed and huffily said "I choose double-dare!"

"Ha ha!" said Alexandra. "She doesn't want to have to admit it! That means it must be true! She wouldn't be embarrassed to answer otherwise!"

"Nuh-uh!" said Sarah. "I just want to do a double-dare for fun."

"Sure you do," said Amy, patting Sarah's arm and smiling. "We understand. Sometimes those cousins can be temptingly cute!" Everyone laughed.

"Will somebody tell me what my dare is?" asked Sarah.

"Ideas?" asked Lynn.

"Oh, I've got the perfect thing!" said Amy, and she ran off to her room and came back with a small paper packet. "I found *this* among the free samples when I was helping Mom sort the coupons that came in the mail."

We all looked at the tiny treasure. It was marked "Folgers".

"Amy!" exclaimed Alexandra.

"Oh, it's just for fun!" said Amy.

"That's perfect!" said Lynn. "For your dare, you're going to drink some coffee. Come on, let's go heat up some water."

"Come on guys, that's not funny!" protested Sarah, but we were all on our way to the kitchen already, so she could do nothing but follow us.

Amy got out a kettle that they normally used to heat water for hot chocolate, and she filled it with water and put it on the stove.

"Why the hell is this a dare?" asked Melissa.

"Because coffee is a sin for Mormons," explained Amy.

"It is?" asked Melissa, making a confused face. Amy and Lynn both laughed, but I felt a little embarrassed.

"Come on guys!" said Sarah. "You can't ask me to go against the commandments and break the Word of Wisdom."

"It's a *dare*," said Amy. "It wouldn't be a dare if we were making you do something you didn't mind doing."

"It'll just be one sip," said Lynn. "If Heavenly Father gets on your case about it on Judgment Day, just blame it on us."

Looking at Sarah's worried face, I couldn't help but remember my goal to be more righteous. I'd done a good job all week of being nice to the other kids at school and obeying my parents. I even felt like I might be starting to feel the spirit witnessing to me during my personal prayers. And now here I was destroying all that progress by helping the other girls to pressure someone to sin. And worse, I had really hurt Lynn by embarrassing her in front of the other girls with that Barbie doll question. I started to feel ashamed that I was unable to live up to simple goals like being kind to my sisters.

As soon as the kettle started to whistle the tiniest bit, Amy took it off the heat so as not to wake anyone. Then she poured it into the mug where she had already placed the instant coffee powder. We could see the brown water churning with the slightest foam on top as the dangerous aroma of coffee filled the air. The image of going out to breakfast in a restaurant while on vacation with my family suddenly came to mind.

Amy picked up the mug and held it out for Sarah.

"A dare, huh?" asked Sarah, looking at the mug. Then she started singing: "*Dare to do right. Dare to be true. You have a work that no other can do.*"

I immediately realized that Sarah was right. I joined in with her on the next line. *"Do it so bravely, so kindly, so well, angels will hasten the story to tell."*

Alexandra, Amy, and Lynn all looked annoyed by Sarah's little song, but they seemed to realize we were right. Amy poured the coffee down the sink, and with a resigned expression, she and Lynn sang the rest of the song with us. I couldn't bring myself to look over at Melissa.

Just as we were finishing the last line, Alexandra's dad burst into the kitchen. "What's with all this noise?" he asked. "There are people trying to sleep in here!"

"Sorry Dad," said Amy.

"Keep your sorry," he said. "Just get in bed—all of you—and not another sound!"

At that point we had no choice but to put our pajamas on and unroll our sleeping bags and get in bed. I set up my sleeping bag next to Melissa's. She was wearing her rugby shirt as a nightshirt. I was too embarrassed about the song to say anything, so I just gave her an apologetic look. She returned a smile that told me that she understood that I had only done what I had to do.

As soon as the lights were out, Lynn said "How about some ghost stories?"

"Lynn!" I whispered back, exasperated.

"Wooooooo!" Amy howled softly with a little laugh.

"Shut up, goddammit!" said Melissa, and with that no one said another word until morning.

When I woke up to a bit of morning light coming in the window, I saw that Lynn, Amy, and Melissa were all already awake, sitting on their sleeping bags reading. Sarah and Alexandra were still asleep.

"What are you reading?" I asked Melissa softly.

"It's called *Punch and Cookies Forever*," she replied. "It's pretty funny. It's a bunch of stories about Mormons falling in love and getting married and shit."

"I lent it to her," said Amy. I could see that Amy was also reading a collection of Jack Weyland's short stories: *The First Day of Forever*. I asked Lynn what hers was and she showed me the cover. Lynn's book was simply titled *Forever*, by Judy Blume.

"Where'd you get that book?" I asked Lynn.

"It's Melissa's."

"And you just started it this morning? You're pretty far in it!"

"We got up early," said Melissa.

"Yeah, it's cool that Annette is subbing my route for me this morning, but I can't seem to shake this habit of waking up at five," said Lynn. "That and I'm skipping around, just reading the good parts."

"It's my sister's book," explained Melissa. "She underlined all of the dirty stuff."

"What?" I asked.

"It's amazing!" said Lynn, turning to Melissa. "I can't believe your mom let you read this!"

"Yeah, she read it and said it was okay for my sister and me."

"Wow, your mom is a lot different from my mom!" said Lynn.

"What's in that book?" asked Amy, starting to look curious.

"It's a story about a girl who's a virgin who's going to have sex with her boyfriend for the first time. But on every date she keeps telling him not to go too far because she wants to take it slow."

"Really?" asked Amy. "Why?"

"Not sure," said Lynn, looking a little confused. "That's the part I can't figure out, actually."

"Maybe because it's a sin," suggested Alexandra, who had apparently woken up as we were talking.

"Nah, she's not too concerned about that since she's not religious," said Lynn.

"Can I read it after Lynn?" asked Amy.

"Sure, no problem," replied Melissa.

I was getting out my backpack to look for my own book when Sister Thomas came in to ask us if we wanted blueberry pancakes or chocolate-chip. Lynn's book seemed to catch her eye.

"What are you reading?" she asked Lynn.

"Oh, just a Judy Blume book," Lynn replied, kind of hiding the cover.

Sister Thomas snatched the book out of Lynn's hands. She seemed to recognize it. "This is pornography!" she exclaimed.

"How can it be pornography, Mom?" asked Amy. "It's just a book."

Sister Thomas looked sternly at Amy and then turned back to Lynn. "Where did you get this, young lady?"

"It's mine," said Melissa. "My mom bought it for my sister and me."

Sister Thomas looked surprised and horrified as she took the information in. "Well, I'll hold on to it for you until it's time for you to go." She took the book with her as she left the room.

"Well, so much for that," said Lynn. Then turning to Amy, she asked "Do you have any more of those Jack Weyland books?"

"Yeah, of course," said Amy, going to the bookshelf and grabbing a copy of *Charly* for Lynn. Lynn immediately opened it and started reading.

I found my own book and opened it as well. I had started reading *The Annotated Alice*, which was a special edition of *Alice in Wonderland* full of footnotes explaining what everything meant. After reading it with the notes, it amazed me that anyone could read it without them given that so much of the humor was based on inside jokes and parodies of poems that were popular at the time.

Actually it was Lynn who had lent me the book in the first place. She apparently really liked it and had read it several times. I was happy to see her getting involved in a girl's adventure for once. It was a little disappointing (but not too surprising) to see her go straight back to romance novels just like that.

When I got home, my first thought was to go to my drawing board. I wanted to start on the painting of the Jaredite barges that I had planned to do. After that slumber party, I felt like I was farther behind on my goals than I had been a week earlier, and now there was only one week left before before the day I planned to bear my testimony for the ward. Painting a scene from the *Book of Mormon* seemed like a good way to get myself back on track.

I got out a clean sheet of paper and started sketching the barges. Then I added figures to indicate where the various people and animals would go—all doing different things to prepare for their voyage. In the center I sketched the brother of Jared raising his arms to heaven.

After setting the scene and adding all of the details I could think of, I glanced down at some of the pages of my graphic novel. Without thinking, I grabbed a clean sheet of paper and put it over the first. I first sketched Wyxetta wearing my sparkling dress from our game of dress-up. Then I drew Adrianna in the foreground, dancing and laughing. I drew her elegant features and her short, curly hair. But this time, instead of coloring her hair black, I prepared my paints to color it a little bit auburn.

4. Sunday Morning

THINGS STARTED LOOKING brighter as soon as I woke up on Sunday morning. It was a sunny day, and we all managed to get ready and get to church on time without fighting. I even listened to all of Sacrament Meeting without reading a book. Lynn read *Charly* through the whole meeting—which I thought was pretty funny since it's a Mormon story that should be teaching her to be good—but I didn't judge her for it.

On Sunday afternoon and for the whole week I made progress on my *Book of Mormon* painting. It helped inspire me to do a good job on my other goals like helping my mom and obeying her willingly and being kind to my sisters. I felt like I should apologize to Lynn for telling the other girls that she played with Barbies. After all, apologizing and making amends are steps in the repentance process. But things were going well between us, and I was worried that bringing it up at all—even to apologize—would just cause trouble.

Every night I prayed a long personal prayer asking for a testimony. At the end of each personal prayer I would pause to listen for the still, small voice. It seemed like I was getting some sort of warm feelings and promptings, but I couldn't really tell if these feelings meant I'd finally reached the point of receiving messages from the Lord or if it was still just my own thoughts.

After dinner on Friday Lynn came over to admire my work as I was adding some color to my drawing of the Jaredite barges.

"Wow, you sure are righteous," she said.

"No, not really," I said, laughing.

"I try to be righteous too," said Lynn, "but I can't help but feel like I'm just not good at it."

"It's not a question of being good at it," I said. "I mean, I suppose it comes more easily to some than to others, but the Lord expects all of us to strive for perfection."

"What's this thing the little girl is holding?" asked Lynn, pointing at a little girl in the foreground of the picture.

"It's one of the illuminated rocks to light the barges with," I replied.

"You know what would be funny would be if all the kids took one of the barges and steered it off course on purpose to go exploring!" Then Lynn started speaking in a funny mock-scripture voice: "And it came to pass that I, Anita Bandita, being of badly parents, therefore I did sneaketh into the barges by night and did changeth around all of the place-cards so that all of my friends would be of one barge with no adults therein to call us to repentance. And none save it were to rejoice in naughtiness was among us."

I laughed and continued her little story. "And it came to pass that our parents did awaken on the morrow and they were sore amazed by the great confusion of the many place-cards in the barges. 'It must needs be a sign from on high,' sayeth Jared."

Then Lynn broke in, laughing. "And it came to pas that Jared sayeth unto himself 'It must needs be that I shall ask my brother if it be right, for he is a mighty man of God, and he will know if it be so.' But it came to pass that the brother of Jared was in the bathroom and could not be disturbed. Therefore Jared sayeth unto himself 'Verily I say unto myself, it must needs be that the place-cards are rearranged by angels, as a sign.'"

Still laughing, I rushed to grab a notebook and started writing down the story we had so far. We then continued the story in the same style, telling how Anita Bandita and her first mate Chiquita Bandita steered their barge off course on purpose and pretended it was an accident. Then they lassoed a whale and had it pull their barge so that they could escape from the grown-ups' barges more quickly. Anita and Chiquita let the boys come with them, but only if they agreed to do all of the cooking and cleaning.

We were having so much fun that we didn't want to stop for dinner. We scarfed down our food as quickly as possible so we could get back to work. Mom and Dad asked us what we were working on, and we told them that it was a story and they could read it when it was done.

Then we got back to giving our heroes more adventures such as one where the whale swallows the magically illuminated rock and Anita wrestles him to try to get it out, but in the end they decide it's a good thing because it makes light shine out of the whale's eyes like headlights to light the way so they can travel even at night. The kids were about to arrive in Candy Land when Mom told us to get ready for bed and family prayer and scripture reading.

Fortunately the chapter we had for that night was a really short one. We were almost to the end of the book, so we were at the part where Moroni is the last of his race and he's wandering around with nothing to do but compile records (like the story about the Jaredites) until he dies. For tonight's chapter Moroni had written out the sacrament prayer on the water. Of course the book said "wine" but everyone knows that water is used for the sacrament.

After the prayer, Lynn and I were about to go back to our story, but Mom said she wanted us to go straight to bed so we'd be ready for the youth service project we were doing the next day. So I put the notebook on my bookshelf to finish later and went to bed.

I was pretty excited about the service project—it seemed like just the thing that would help me prepare to bear my testimony the following day. Plus I was really hoping that Alexandra would bring Melissa along again so we could hang out some more.

The service project was a canned food drive that was organized by one of the older boys in the ward as his Eagle Scout project. The whole morning Mom drove me, Annette, and Lynn around the neighborhood collecting cans. Annette was still in Primary, but Mom decided she should come along anyway. So we all put on our coats and hats an mittens, and Mom kept the car warm at each stop as Annette, Lynn, and I knocked on doors asking for canned goods.

Then, after going back home for lunch, Mom dropped off Lynn and me at the food bank where the youth of the ward were gathering for the next stage of the project, which was to take inventory of all of the cans we and other people in the community had collected.

Just as we arrived I saw the Dentons' van drive up. Isabel got out of the driver's seat dressed in an outfit that was casual yet somehow absolutely perfect. Her brothers Andrew and David weren't quite at her level of fashion, but they were dressed nicely for boys. Then I was surprised to see the Grants—Rodney, Jonathan, and Sarah—getting out of the same van. Their parents must have arranged for the Dentons to give them a ride. All three looked like they were wearing second-hand clothing. Isabel seemed to be pretending not to know them. She made a beeline for the bishop's kids, Marc, Claire, and Kimberly, who were just getting out of Marc's BMW.

A bunch of other kids from the ward arrived as well, and Brandon Carlson, whose project it was, started organizing people. I was thrilled to see that Alexandra had brought Melissa, and since it turned out that there wasn't that much work for us to do, the three of us sat off to the side near the window to hang out. We could see that Amy and Lynn were among the boys supposedly helping them, but obviously more

interested in carrying on an animated conversation with Rodney and Jonathan Grant.

"They work fast for little kids, don't they?" asked Melissa, looking over at Amy and Lynn.

"That Lynn!" I said, rolling my eyes.

After a while, Andrew got bored of his task and came over to sit by us.

"Hi April," he said. "I don't think you've introduced me to your friend."

"Andrew, this is Melissa," I said. "Melissa, Andrew."

"Actually, she's *my* friend," said Alexandra.

"Nice to meet you," said Andrew.

"Likewise," replied Melissa, absently. Then looking out the window at Marc's BMW she said "That's a pretty sweet car, huh? Are your parents going to give you one like that when you turn sixteen?"

Andrew laughed. "I don't know. I guess that would be pretty cool, wouldn't it?"

"My mom says she's dreading the day I learn to drive," I said. "She's afraid something bad will happen."

"She'll change her tune next year when you start attending early-morning seminary," said Andrew. "Once she gets a taste of getting up

at five every morning to warm up the car in the dead of Winter, she'll
be begging to give you the keys. I know my mom was pretty happy
when Isabel learned to drive."

I smiled in response.

"Andrew, you're not done here!" called Brandon.

"Oops, duty calls," said Andrew. "It was nice meeting you," he
said to Melissa, and he got back to work.

Melissa watched him as he left, sizing him up as if he were a piece
of meat. "He seems pretty nice," she said. "I can see why you like
him."

I gave a sigh of exasperation. "I didn't say I like him."

"Yeah, sure," said Alexandra.

"What about you?" I asked Alexandra. "You haven't told us who
you like."

"Oh, I don't know," said Alexandra, a little dejectedly. I followed
her gaze and saw that she was looking at Steve Shumway, who was
talking to Claire.

Melissa looked across the parking lot at the mall in the middle of
the next block. "This totally blows," she said. "Let's go to the mall."

Isabel seemed to have a similar idea. She and Claire and Kimberly
and Lara were heading towards the door as we spoke. As Isabel opened
the door to leave, Sarah suddenly noticed and ran up to her.

"Are you guys leaving?" she asked.

"Oh, you can find a ride home with the other girls, can't you?"
asked Isabel. The only other girls that had come were some older
Laurels who had already gone home, so obviously Isabel was talking
about us.

Sarah immediately turned to her brothers. "We have scouts after
this," said Rodney. "Brandon's taking us."

Sarah then looked to us. Melissa and Alexandra both looked really
annoyed, but I gave her a sympathetic smile, so she came over and sat
near us as Isabel and her friends left.

"Let's go," said Alexandra, getting up. Melissa followed and so
did I.

"Hey, where are you going?" called Amy.

"To the mall," replied Alexandra.

"Well, wait up," said Amy, and she and Lynn grabbed their coats
and rushed to join us. Sarah followed behind as we crossed the parking
lot.

"God, those other girls are real stuck-up bitches," said Melissa.

"Yeah, they think their fancy clothes and cars make them better than us," I agreed.

"And they think *we're* in the same league with *Sarah*," said Alexandra disgustedly. I hoped she hadn't said it loudly enough for Sarah to hear. I looked back at Sarah and felt kind of bad for her, but not bad enough to try to invite her into our circle.

Melissa smiled at me and seemed to understand what I was feeling. "It was nice of you to stick up for her the other night during her dare. Me and Alexandra were talking about it, and we know you were just being nice. But that was really gay of her to sing that dorky song to get out of one little sip of coffee."

I laughed uncomfortably. I wasn't sure what to think.

When we got to the mall, we started by looking for clothes. After a while, Melissa wanted to go look at skis, so we gathered up our little group to go and discovered that Sarah was missing. She must have wandered off or something.

"She probably left," said Lynn. "She can call her parents for a ride home as easily as we can."

"Besides, we're not responsible for her," said Alexandra. "It's not as if we invited her to come with us."

We looked around at the sporting-goods store for a while and a few other stores when all of the sudden we saw Sarah come running up to us.

"I'm so glad I found you guys again!" she said. "My parents can't come pick me up today because of car troubles."

"Why did you wander off?" asked Melissa.

"I'm sorry," said Sarah. "I saw some shoes I liked in another department near where you guys were looking at dresses, and when I was done trying them on, you guys were gone."

"That's okay," said Lynn. "Just don't do it again." She then got a little smile on her face as if she were plotting something.

"I'm hungry," said Amy. "Let's go get some fries."

So we went and found a fast-food place, and sat down at a table. Alexandra had brought some money, and Lynn had a little from her paper route, so the two of them bought some large orders of fries for all of us to split.

While we were eating, Sarah started telling us about how her brother Rodney had just gotten a puppy. This topic seemed to help

Melissa warm back up to Sarah a bit. It turned out that Melissa's dog was only a year old, so she had a ton of funny puppy-training stories. Lynn was pretty interested in the conversation as well since she was thrilled to talk about anything that involved her beloved Rodney.

Everything was going great until Melissa told a story where she did a funny impression of her dad saying "Did that damn dog crap in my shoe again?"

Sarah immediately cut her off and said "You know Melissa, you really shouldn't swear all the time."

That set Melissa off. She screwed up her face and sarcastically repeated "You shouldn't swear all the time." She continued talking to Sarah about dogs after that, but kind of half-heartedly.

When we were done eating, Lynn and Amy wanted to go with Sarah to the pet shop to get some stuff for Rodney's dog, but Melissa wanted to check one more thing on the skis she was thinking of getting. So Lynn suggested that we split up and meet back at the usual place in a half an hour.

Our usual place was the clearance furniture section of J. C. Penney, which was way up in the top floor in a low-traffic wing. Lynn and I had noticed that that department was kind of out-of-the-way and rarely had any salespeople or customers—just a big collection of sofas and armchairs where we could hang out and no one would find us or bother us.

Once we were done looking at skis, I took Alexandra and Melissa to our secret meeting place. When we arrived, we saw Lynn and Amy sitting on one of the couches playing cards.

"Where's Sarah?" I asked.

"We ditched her!" said Amy.

"We waited until we were sure she couldn't see us, and we ran away!" said Lynn. Then they started laughing and so did Melissa and Alexandra.

"But she doesn't have a ride home!" I protested.

"Oh, don't get your panties all in a bunch!" said Amy, "We'll go find her again."

Sure enough we had no trouble finding Sarah again since she was obviously looking for us. She was standing at the balcony overlooking the main open court of the mall. Lynn walked straight up to her and with an exaggerated expression of concern in her voice asked "Where

were you? We looked all over for you! We told you not to wander off!"
Melissa was having trouble hiding her laughter.

Sarah looked a little confused and said "I'm sorry, I guess I wasn't
paying attention."

"Well, don't let it happen again," said Amy. "We were really
worried!"

But sure enough, we had hardly been shopping for twenty minutes
when Melissa tapped me and whispered "Quick! Run! Now!" and ran
away.

I didn't want to get ditched myself, so I ran off with Melissa, and
the two of us ran off to meet up with the other girls who were all at
the meeting point laughing. Lynn and Amy thought the game was so
funny that they couldn't wait to go back and do it again. I might have
expected Alexandra and Melissa to be a little more mature, but they
were as excited about the game as Amy and Lynn.

We found Sarah in the same place as before. Amy walked up to her
this time and said "There you are! We keep telling you not to wander
off!"

Sarah looked really angry this time. "This isn't funny anymore. I
think we should go home."

Since Sarah wasn't going to be a good sport about it, we all kind
of agreed that we might as well head back, so Lynn and Amy went off
to call our mom and Amy's. Alexandra, Melissa, Sarah, and I went and
sat down on a bench near one of the entrances to wait.

Sarah was still angry, and as soon as she sat down she started
yelling at us. "I know you were ditching me on purpose! You guys are
all jerks!"

"It was just a game," said Melissa. "It's not like we were going to
leave you here."

"Yeah, not like Isabel, who ditched you for real," said Alexandra.
"We invited you to our party and we shared our fries with you. And
now you're going to get all huffy over a little thing like this?"

"You guys are mean and nasty all the time!" said Sarah. "I hate
you!"

"Oh, come on!" I said.

I was starting to get annoyed at Sarah. Sure what we had done
wasn't very nice, but it wasn't that big a deal. She was being a real
baby about it.

"I don't care what you say because soon it won't matter," said Sarah. "I wasn't supposed to tell anyone until it's all settled, but I'm going to anyway. My whole family is moving back to Idaho, and I won't have to put up with your meanness ever again!"

"Won't that be nice for you?" I said sarcastically. "You'll get to see your cousin every day." Melissa and Alexandra both burst out in laughter.

Amy and Lynn came running up and sat down with us. "We're in for it now!" said Lynn. "Mom is really mad that we left that activity and didn't tell anyone where we went."

"Our mom is mad too," said Amy. "We're in deep doo-doo."

We all sat and silently waited for the punishment that was coming. We saw our car drive up first, so I quickly went to say goodbye to Alexandra and Melissa. Melissa was sitting on the bench kind of looking down. I touched her shoulder and gave her a worried smile as if to say "I hope I'll see you again under more pleasant circumstances." She put her hand over my fingers briefly as she returned my look. Then Sarah, Lynn, and I went out to the car.

Sarah went to the driver's side and asked my mom "Can I have a ride home, Sister Hanson?"

"Of course you may," said Mom politely, though she was clearly pretty mad.

We rode in silence until we dropped off Sarah. Then Mom let us have it.

"How could you? Why didn't you call and tell us where you went? Your father and I were worried sick not knowing where you were! Do you know there's going to be a blizzard tonight?" It was already starting to snow. "And we didn't even know if you were outside or lost or what! We called everyone in the ward, and no one knew where you were!"

"I'm sorry Mom, I wasn't thinking," I said.

"You weren't thinking?" asked Mom angrily. "April Hanson, I expect more responsible behavior from you than this! As your punishment, both of you are going to bed without supper. You can sit alone in your rooms and think about what you've done. And you're getting off easy since you should be starting your fast tonight anyway."

I felt horrible. I already felt bad enough about the fact that I had been so irresponsible and made my parents worry. Then she had to remind me that the next day was Fast Sunday. I didn't see how I could possibly have messed up my goal worse than this. I was ashamed to see that I couldn't follow through on such simple goals. I couldn't even manage to honor my parents and be kind to the other girls in the ward for a couple of weeks.

When we got home, I followed Mom's instruction to go to my room to think. There were no two ways about it—I'd screwed up big time. I thought about how inconsiderate I'd been of my parents' feelings, and then I thought about how mean we'd been to Sarah, who had a hard enough time already. The fact that the popular girls were mean to us was no excuse. If anything, that made us more guilty since we knew what it felt like to be treated like dirt. We should be kinder instead of taking it out on the next person down on the popularity ladder.

Then I thought about Melissa. On some level I wanted to blame her for this, but I couldn't. I pictured her carefree smile. I couldn't help but want to be her friend—maybe her best friend if possible. She wasn't really bad, she just didn't have all of the light and knowledge of the gospel that we had. I should have been setting a good example for her instead of hiding my light under a bushel. Actually, it seemed like Melissa hadn't been any worse than the rest of us even though we had more truth.

It hit me that the worst part was that I hadn't made any progress at all towards my goal of gaining a sure knowledge of the truthfullness of the gospel. I didn't see how I could stand up in Fast and Testimony meeting the next day and bear my testimony for the whole ward. But I didn't want to just throw in the towel.

I decided to pray. I prayed like never before. I started by repenting of all of the things I'd done wrong that day, and then started pleading with the Lord to give me a testimony by the next day.

When I got in bed, I wasn't really sure if I felt better or worse. I still felt kind of guilty and apprehensive. I knew we weren't supposed to test God by asking for a sign, so I couldn't tell if it was righteous or unrighteous of me to ask Heavenly Father to manifest Himself to me before the next day. I figured it was probably the wrong thing to ask for because on some level I was sure that it wasn't going to happen.

When Lynn's alarm clock went off in the next room, it woke me up. It didn't normally, but I had slept so fitfully that night that the slightest thing disturbed me. I tried to go back to sleep for about a half an hour, but it was no use, so I got up and went downstairs.

Lynn was already dressed to go out, and my dad was up putting on his winter gear as well.

Dad looked happy to see me. "Oh good, you're up," he said. "The snow's piled higher than I've seen it in a while, and it's still coming down. Can you help us with Lynn's route?"

"Are there any papers to deliver?" I asked.

"Yeah, there are," said Lynn. "I don't know how the delivery guy got his truck through this, but he did. So I guess we can take them the rest of the way."

"Okay, I can help," I said, "no problem."

Dad and Lynn went out and got the papers and brought them in to stuff them in the house. By the time I was dressed, they had all of the piles of papers set up to stuff the comics section and the middle section into the front section.

Reading the headline aloud, I said "Blizzard."

"Yeah, no duh," said Lynn. "But I guess we have to get this important news out to our customers anyway."

Mom came down in her robe and slippers and made us some peanut-butter-and-jelly sandwiches.

"Mom, it's Fast Sunday," I said.

"If you're going out in this weather, I don't want any danger of any of you fainting," said Mom. "Fast Sunday will come again next month."

Dad didn't feel like it was worth the effort to try to do the route by car since we were sure to just get it stuck somewhere. And since we obviously wouldn't be able to push the cart of papers through the snow-covered roads, Dad had us pile the papers on sleds and pull them through the snow.

It was slow going because we sank into the fresh snow past our knees with each step. Fortunately we had good boots and snow-pants. In the end it was kind of fun. The snow put a clean blanket of white over everything. Plus, it wasn't cold enough to make us grow icicles from our scarves or to freeze our eyelashes together or anything.

When we got home, we were greeted by the smell of a full breakfast cooking. Mom was cooking hash browns and bacon and scrambled eggs, and Annette was up helping her.

"What's all this?" asked Dad.

"Well, since we're not fasting anyway, I didn't see any point in fasting halfway or something. We'll do it right next month."

Dad seemed satisfied by that explanation, so he called on Lynn to say a prayer on the food, and then we all sat down and ate. "Since we've got the sleds out and all this snow," said Dad, "what do you say we go sledding? We haven't done that in years."

"Aren't we going to church?" I asked.

"Through this snow?" asked Dad, looking out the window. "Better not risk it."

Annette and Lynn both cheered. Mom gave a bit of a disapproving look, but ended with an understanding smile.

As soon as we were done with breakfast, we put our snow gear back on and pulled our sleds to a nearby hill. We all had a great time sledding down the hill like little kids, even Mom and Dad.

I wasn't sure what this meant for my goal. It looked like the Lord Himself had let me off the hook. I figured it was probably His way of telling me that I needed to give myself more time.

CHARACTERS IN YOUNG WOMEN'S

The Hansons

April   *Lynn*   *Annette*

The Hansons   The Thomases

Sister Hanson   *Brother Hanson*   *Alexandra*   *Amy*

The Grants   The Millers

Rodney   *Jonathan*   *Sarah*   *Claire*

The Dentons   Others

Isabel   *Andrew*   *David*   *Melissa*

II. Youth Conference

Lynn

5. THURSDAY AFTERNOON

T HE VERY FIRST THING I heard upon arriving at Youth Conference was a dirty joke.

Somewhere behind me in the long line of kids walking from the buses to the registration tables a boy's voice said "Why did the condom fly across the room?—because it was pissed-off!" Not very funny, really, but it made me smile to myself. It seemed like a good omen for how the conference would go—hopefully not one hundred percent goodie-goodie. Not that I objected to religious education in principle—heaven knows I had a lot of work ahead of me if I wanted to make it to the Celestial Kingdom one day. It was just that for this event the prospect of spiritual growth was hardly my real reason for attending.

I was sure most of the other kids felt the same way. We came for the fun of spending the weekend in a college dormitory with five stakes worth of Mormon kids—practically all of the Mormon teenagers in all of Minnesota.

After registering, Amy and I grabbed our dorm keys and rushed to check out our room. It was nothing to look at—two beds, two desks, two dressers, and an ugly vinyl curtain covering the one window—but it was fabulous! This was the life!

"In another few years we'll be living in a room like this at BYU," Amy said, "you and me."

"Yeah, that should make a nice change over sharing a room with Annette," I replied. "Which side do you want?"

"Whichever, they're the same," she said and threw her stuff on one of the beds. "C'mon, let's see where the other girls are staying."

It wasn't hard to find our sisters and other friends. All the girls from our ward were grouped on the same stretch of hallway so that our chaperones could easily keep an eye on us. The rooms were all the same, but we had fun comparing them anyway.

We started with Annette and Jenny's room, then checked in on Amy's older sister Alexandra who was sharing a room with her best friend Cookie. Cookie's real name was Caroline, but everyone always called her Cookie, even her family. Then we went to see my older sister April. April was seventeen and good friends with Alexandra and Cookie, but since there wasn't a fourth girl among our friends in that age group, she was sharing a room with a fourteen-year-old named Tammy. Tammy was okay, but she was maybe even a bit more of a geek than the rest of us.

Once we were done gushing over how fabulous all of the rooms were, we were off to dinner. We didn't visit the rooms of the girls from our ward's "in" group, but it was no big loss because they were undoubtedly the same as all the others. They were along the same hallway intermixed with our rooms. Kimberly and Lara, who were just a little older than Amy and me, were sharing the room next door to ours. Then on the other side of our room was Claire, Kimberly's older sister, with a girl she had invited named Tina. Tina, in fact, attended my high school, but I hardly knew her as she was a senior and a cheerleader. I was surprised that she had come to Youth Conference at all since her family wasn't active in the church and she almost never attended the Sunday services.

After dinner and the opening welcome program, we rushed back to our rooms to prepare for the big event of the night: the dance.

The rule with Mormon boys and girls is that when you turn fourteen you can go to dances and when you're sixteen you're allowed to date. I was looking forward to turning sixteen in a few months and the prospect of dating. Not that I actually had any prospects. So far the only guy who had thought to ask me out was the nerdiest guy in my school, a guy so undesirable that even I didn't want to date him, and normally I would be willing to set the bar pretty low for this sort of thing. Yet not only was this guy remarkably funny-looking, he was also a bit strange. He seemed to believe that his dog understood human speech as well as any human and that she spoke German. He was always on about his dog except when he was bragging about his grades or test scores, so I found that I couldn't tolerate speaking to him for longer than the six minute breaks between classes. In that case the excuse that I wasn't old enough to date yet came in handy. And I figured that hopefully in the time leading up to my sixteenth birthday I'd be able to convince the love of my life to notice me, or failing that I hoped to at least find an acceptable substitute. So you see my real motivation for attending Youth Conference.

My little sister Annette was pretty excited about meeting people at the dances as well. She had just turned fourteen two weeks earlier, so she just barely made the age requirement to attend this year's Youth Conference. She had really lucked out on the scheduling. Tonight's dance would be her first, and she was thrilled about it. After this, the usual monthly dances with just one stake of maybe six wards of kids might be a disappointment.

As we were working on our make-up and hair and comparing dresses, Annette was ecstatic. We all gave her special attention and advice. Amy did Annette's hair up in a style that looked fabulous, and we all complimented her on it. Our discussion while getting ready was generally a profusion of compliments: how the color of Jenny's lipstick perfectly flattered her complexion, or how Tammy's dress was so gorgeous that you could hardly tell she had made it herself.

In truth we were all reasonably attractive for teenage girls. I was a little short and Amy could probably have stood to lose a few pounds off her butt, but we weren't too bad. Once we'd made ourselves as beautiful as we were going to get, the eight of us were off to the dance.

When we arrived, the hall was already set up with streamers and other decorations. The punch was on one side, the chairs were set up all around the edges, and the mirror ball was spinning millions of polka-dots of light all over the floor and walls of the darkened room. The stereo speakers were already booming out a dance beat even though no one was really dancing yet.

So our little group did what we always did at the start of a dance: we went out into the middle of the dance floor and stood in a circle and started dancing. Not that it was particularly interesting to dance in a circle with a bunch of other girls. As soon as we started dancing, as usual I began to wonder if this wasn't perhaps kind of nerdy of us, a bunch of girls just dancing together like that. After all we weren't particularly good dancers—we just moved our arms and legs randomly more or less in time with the music. But the idea was that if we were out there dancing on our own we would look like maybe we were having fun instead of projecting the look of desperation we would have had if we stood or sat on the sidelines staring at our shoes waiting for boys to ask us to dance. So we danced, and soon a few other circles of nerdy girls were occupying other parts of the dance floor. Some couples started dancing, but these were probably established boyfriend-girlfriend pairs since there was still plenty of time before the DJ would be moving on to slow songs, and people rarely asked people they didn't know to dance a fast song.

After a few songs out on the dance floor, Amy and I had completed our opening penance, so we slipped out of the circle and off to the sidelines to scope for boys. Obviously we each had someone in particular that we were on the lookout for, but our respective favorites hadn't arrived yet (and undoubtedly wouldn't be looking for us anyway when they arrived), so we started checking out the other possibilities. As usual, the girl-boy ratio appeared to be about three to two. In some theoretical sense the boys were supposed to be the ones to ask the girls to dance, but in practice that was rarely the case. They didn't need to put themselves out since every guy from the hottest to the most undesirable would be approached frequently by a variety of girls. So unless you were one of the most popular girls, you didn't just wait around to get asked unless you didn't want to dance with boys at all.

"What do you think—do you see anyone promising?" I asked Amy.

"Those two guys over by the corner of the punch table look interesting."

I looked over to check out who she was talking about. There were two guys standing there: one taller, a bit chubby wearing sneakers with his dress pants and his shirt half-untucked, the other quite short wearing a full suit and tie and glasses with thick, dark frames. They both looked nervous and shy, which was a good sign if we wanted to attract them. There were of course already plenty of guys around the perimeter who looked cool and confident, perhaps athletic and/or very well dressed, but those guys didn't even show up on our radar—they were for girls like Kimberly and Lara and Claire. Amy and I weren't going to spend our time and emotional energy on guys that would never give us the time of day. But we might have a reasonable chance with the two Amy had spotted.

"A big one and a little one—like us. Not bad," I said.

"Well then I guess it's time for us to go get some punch," said Amy.

So we ambled nonchalantly over to the punch table and took up a position, not right next to the two guys, but close enough that it would be difficult for them not to notice us. We each grabbed a cup of punch, and Amy started telling me a funny story about some things that she and her sister had done at the mall. It didn't matter what we were talking about really because the guys couldn't hear our conversation over the music—we were just making a show of talking and laughing so that they could see that we were having fun.

But glancing over Amy's shoulder from time to time, I could see that the two guys really weren't paying any attention to us—they were looking rather intently across at some popular-looking girls on the other side of the hall. In fact it looked like they might be looking at the popular girls from our ward. Oh, well. So we set off for the bathroom to check our make-up, making a point to walk right past the two guys while appearing to be engrossed in the most hilarious and fascinating conversation ever and pretending that we hadn't even noticed them.

We arrived in the bathroom and found that it was already crowded with giggling girls. We squeezed our way into a little spot by the mirror and pulled out our lipsticks and hairbrushes.

"So far no luck," Amy commented.

"Yeah, why do you think that there are always so many more girls than boys at every youth activity?" I asked.

"I don't know. I don't see any reason why Mormon families would produce more girls than boys, so it must be that boys are more rebellious and more likely to refuse to go to church things and become inactive."

"That must be it," I said, "I can't think of any other explanation for it. Anyway, it's still early. Y and Z haven't even shown up yet."

"That reminds me," said Amy, "I have something planned for them that I forgot to tell you about. Let's go somewhere where we can talk privately."

Just as we were gathering our things to leave, Annette walked in giggling with Jenny and Tammy.

"Hi guys, what's up?" I asked.

"Did you get a load of those two girls with the rhinestone-studded glasses out in the hallway?" asked Jenny.

I thought about it a minute and replied "Oh, yeah, I think I saw them. Not a pretty picture those two, huh?"

"Already, what kind of baby thinks it's cool to dress up in sparkly things?" Jenny continued, "and these two look like their goal in doing it was to maximize their ugliness." Annette burst into giggles again, and Amy peeked her head out the door of the ladies' room to see who they were talking about.

Amy closed the door again, and exclaimed "Wow, jeez, that one girl has the hugest nose on the planet! Why in heaven's name would she want to draw attention to it by framing it with bright purple jewels?"

"Maybe she was trying to draw attention to her eyes so people won't notice how big her nose is," I suggested. "She'd be better off doing really dramatic eye make-up though."

"Yeah, but the other girl is so much worse!" Jenny said, and Annette could not contain her laughter.

"It's so true!" Annette squealed.

"Her face is covered with zits," continued Jenny, "and she deliberately puts these sparkly red fake rubies on her face to complement them! Is she completely insane? You have to look twice at the one on the bridge of her nose to see that it's a jewel and not a giant zit ready to explode all over everyone."

"Seriously, you really have to wonder what could possibly have been going through her head when bought those glasses," I added. "Did she honestly look at herself in the mirror with them on and say 'Oh, yeah, this looks really good'?"

"Well, there are plenty of fashion retards in this world," Amy commented.

Then Tammy, who had been silent this whole time, broke in. "C'mon you guys, it's not nice to make fun of people like that."

"Why not?" I asked, "There's no harm in discussing 'fashion don'ts'."

"Anyway, all they had to do is not dress like that," Annette pointed out.

"Then you would just make fun of someone else," Tammy said. "We're here to dance and have fun, not say nasty things about people. How would you like it if people were talking about you behind your back like that?"

"Maybe they are—what of it?" responded Amy, and Jenny kind of rolled her eyes and looked over at Tammy as if to say that they'd had to put up with this all evening so far. I was guessing that Jenny and Annette would be finding a way to ditch Tammy in the near future.

"Anyway, we're on our way back into the dance," I said, "We'll see you guys later."

As soon as we were on the other side of the door, Amy said "What's with Tammy? She's such a goodie-goodie!"

"I don't know," I replied. "I have to admit that I really can't relate to her. She's so into all of these homemaking and child-rearing things—and more than once she's said that her mother is her best friend. Isn't that kind of odd for a teenage girl?"

"That is a bit strange. Anyway, let's find a secluded corner—I want to tell you about something I have planned—it's a secret."

We stepped out of the building and found a low brick wall that we could sit on with no one around.

"Well?" I asked.

"I've brought a little present that I was thinking we could give to Y and Z. I baked them a batch of delicious heart-shaped cookies."

"What?!? Are you crazy?! Can you imagine the embarrassment of giving them something like that?!?! We'll look like the biggest geeks on the planet! Don't you think that we should stick to more subtle tactics?"

"We'll give them anonymously," Amy explained. "They'll find the cookies and eat them and all the while they'll be wondering romantically about the girls who thought to give them this little gift. It'll be perfect! Anyway, my mom always says that the way to a man's heart is through his stomach."

"And how to you propose to give them anonymously?" I asked. "We can't just drop the cookies off on their doorstep—the boy's dorm is off-limits to girls. And even if it weren't, I wouldn't dare drop them off myself—I'd be mortified by the thought that someone would see us and tell them who did it."

"We'll have Mindy do it," Amy said. "As a chaperone she's allowed in the boy's dorm, and she would never betray our little secret."

I considered the plan for a second. "You have this whole thing thought out, don't you? Well, okay, but we'll have to tell her to be sure no one see her dropping them off, because people know that she's our teacher and our friend, so if they see her they'll figure out pretty quickly that it was us."

"Of course she'll be careful. She does this sort of thing all the time to try to catch the attention of her karate teacher, doesn't she? Now all we need to do is find Mindy to ask for her help and then write something on the card."

"Mindy's sure to be chaperoning in the dance hall, so we might as well go back in there and find her."

When we got back to the dance hall, we saw Mindy on the sidelines keeping an eye on people. She was supposedly ensuring that the dancing couples weren't dancing too close—the boy and girl were supposed to be far enough apart that you could put a *Book of Mormon* between them—but Mindy wasn't the type that would embarrass people by enforcing that rule. Enough other chaperones would, though, to keep people in line.

Of course almost before we noticed Mindy, we noticed Y and Z over on the edge of the room by the wall. Their names were really David and Peter, but we always referred to them as Y and Z when talking about them in case anyone overheard us.

David (a.k.a. "Y") was the most beautiful guy I knew. He was taller than average, but not too tall, and he was extremely thin. He had very fair skin and dark hair with a natural wave to it and the most beautiful light brown eyes you can imagine. For the dance he was dressed simply but nicely with a plain white dress shirt and a tie, and pleated dress pants. Amy's true love Peter (a.k.a. "Z") was an exceptionally tall boy with bright red hair and kind of a round face. I didn't find him all that cute, but Amy swooned over him. And so we had divided them up among ourselves. Everything would be perfect if only we could get them to agree to the arrangement.

Not far from them stood Y's older brother Andrew and my own older sister April. This was what was so galling about the fact that Y refused to pay any attention to me: his own older brother was my sister's boyfriend! My sister was fine for Y's brother, but somehow Y thought that he was too good for me. It didn't make any sense.

Amy and I immediately decided that it was a good time to chat with April and see how she was doing. So we walked straight up to April and asked her and Andrew what they thought of Youth Conference this year and how they thought it compared to the college we were at last year and all that. Without directly looking at Y and Z, we used our peripheral vision to make sure that they had a good view of our respective good sides and that they could see that we were having an animated and witty conversation with Y's own brother. Y and Z were just far enough away that they couldn't hear our conversation over the music, but they could undoubtedly see that we were charming and having a good time.

After about two or three minutes, though, Y and Z suddenly started walking away, and took up a spot by the wall on the far side of the hall. As far as anyone could tell by looking at us, we didn't even notice that they had left, but in reality it was a harsh blow to see that they would rather walk away to go stand in another place for no apparent reason instead of joining our pleasant conversation. We continued chatting for a few minutes so it wouldn't look like we lost interest just because Y and Z were gone, but it wasn't long before we remembered that we wanted to talk to Mindy, so we excused ourselves to go find her.

We took Mindy aside and asked her if we could all go somewhere and talk privately.

"Well, I'm on duty," she said jokingly, "but there are plenty of other chaperones here, so I can probably get away with a short break."

So we took her outside to our private spot on the brick wall and let her in on our secret. Mindy was twenty-six years old, but at heart she was as much a schoolgirl as we were, so she was at least as excited about the whole secret project as Amy was. We easily got her to agree to drop the package off in front of the door to Y and Z's room during the night so that there was no chance of her being seen.

"Ah, what fun!" she said, "This reminds me of when I was at BYU!"

"You anonymously gave heart-shaped cookies to guys when you were at BYU?" I asked, astonished.

"Well, not that in particular, but we used to do that sort of thing," she replied. This amazed me since I thought that it was already a bit childish for fifteen-year-olds to be doing such a thing, so I couldn't imagine what kind of college students would think that this was a good idea.

"It must be easier to attract guys at BYU than at an event like this, though," I protested, "so you shouldn't have had to resort to this kind of silly tactics."

"Oh, no, no, it's much worse," Mindy said. "It's true that when I was there there were more male students than female students, but that was just because the girls would usually drop out when they got married. In the singles wards, the girl-boy ratio was something like three to two."

"Why do you think that is?" I asked.

"Everyone knows that even though the holiest people—the prophets and General Authorities and such—are men, the spiritual duds that go inactive and leave the church tend to be men too. Women are more faithful and spiritual on average. It's kind of like how in school the genius and the flunk-out stoner are usually both boys while the girls all bring home B's and C's and end up having a higher GPA on average than the boys. Plus the boys that are the top students are really focused on their careers, so even good Mormon boys will often choose another university over BYU if it has a really good program in this or that specialization. The girls just want to get married, so they go where the boys are. Sure they outnumber the available guys by quite a lot at BYU, but that's still the place where you'll find the highest concentration of faithful, marriageable Mormon guys, so we all go there to try our luck."

Mindy's luck must not have been all that good since she graduated from BYU with her degree in "family science" (i.e. Home Ec.) and came back just as single as when she left. I couldn't bear to agree that there was any truth to her characterization of girls and boys. In my school I was one of the top students, and I liked to imagine that I was as focused on my future as the boys were—and not just on earning my "MRS" degree, as they say.

Amy agreed with her, though. "It's true," she said. "My mom told me that she and her roommates used to do laundry and ironing for lots of guys in their BYU ward for nothing, just to get noticed."

"I never went that far," Mindy said, "but I definitely heard about girls doing that. The competition is fierce, so if you're not Miss Utah, you have to go the extra mile to get a guy's attention. I used to cook a big dinner at my apartment every Sunday and invite a whole group of guys from my ward. I knew that college students couldn't say no to free food, and you know what they say about how the way to a man's heart is through his stomach." (Here Amy nodded vigorously.) "Unfortunately, it didn't work out for me with any of those guys, but I didn't mind doing it because I like cooking anyway."

"Ah, maybe you should have gone with the laundry after all, then," Amy piped up. "My mom is always telling me about how my dad was the handsomest returned-missionary in her ward, and she managed to steal his heart away from a real beauty queen by ironing his shirts just right."

This whole conversation was starting to frighten me just a bit. Not that I had never heard such stories about Mormon girls and their husband-hunting activities—far from it—these sorts of things were well known. But it was a bit upsetting to hear my friends so readily embracing such an attitude, and—worse—admitting to it! Personally I hoped to have a bit more dignity than that, but who knows what would happen to me when I got the chance to taste the "fierce competition" at BYU first hand. Still, I wasn't sure I really wanted to win the heart of a guy who would be so attracted to fine ironing. Despite all of our plans, I was starting to think that it might be more fun to go to an ordinary university...

"Let's get back to the dance," I said. "We're not going to meet any cute guys out here. Can you meet us in our room tonight to pick up the package?"

"Sure, no problem."

As we entered the building, off at the end of a darkened hallway Mindy noticed a guy and a girl sitting on the floor engaged in what appeared to be a rather intimate conversation.

"Excuse me, ladies, chaperone duty calls," said Mindy as she went off to chastise and separate the naughty couple. So Amy and I went back into the dance hall. Since there was a fast song playing and since we had nothing better to do, we rejoined the dance circle of girls from our ward.

As always, dancing in a circle with other girls was kind of lame, but there wasn't much else to do during the fast songs. The only one who seemed to enjoy it (instead of just pretending to enjoy it) was Tammy. With all of her interest in cooking and sewing, it seemed like seeking out a husband should be her top priority rather than dancing with us, but she probably figured that her superior ironing skills would snag her a husband at BYU so easily that she hardly needed to worry about finding a boyfriend now. And anyway, a boyfriend you find at fourteen or fifteen is unlikely to end up as your husband (although in Y's case I could dream). Even so I couldn't help but feel that it would be fun to have a romance and a boyfriend now.

My reverie was interrupted by the switch from a fast song to a slow song. Jenny turned to Annette and appeared to say "Let's go ask some boys to dance." They walked towards the outer edge and as far as I could tell selected the first two boys they encountered and started dancing with them. I figured that I should do the same if I didn't want to go the whole dance without dancing with a single boy, but there was only one that I really wanted to dance with, and I hadn't gotten up the nerve to ask him yet. So I found a chair along the sidelines and sat this one out.

The next song was another slow song, and this time it was *Lady in Red,* which was the song I had chosen for myself and Y as our song.

"We can't sit this one out," said Amy. "We've got to ask Y and Z to dance, it's now or never."

I was a bit nervous, but willing. We started walking over towards them, but we'd hardly gone a few steps when we saw that someone else had beaten us to the punch. It was none other than the two girls with the sparkly glasses! They approached Y and Z and led them out onto the dance floor. Amy looked shocked, but I could see from the looks on their faces that Y and Z weren't too thrilled about their partners. People tend not to say no when asked to dance because it's impolite. The preferred strategy when pursued by someone undesirable is to avoid them and hide.

"Ugh! Our song is ruined!" Amy said.

I shrugged. "We can ask them for a different song, or if we don't, they'll play this one again at tomorrow night's dance."

All of the sudden we were surprised by two guys coming up to ask us to dance—none other than the big guy and the little guy we had noticed at the beginning of the night. Things seemed to be turning around. It was always a good sign to get asked to dance rather than the reverse, and these guys apparently noticed us without our even having to follow them around or make eyes at them or anything!

I got the short one, of course, being the small one myself. We walked out onto the dance floor and he put his hand on my waist while I put my hand on his shoulder, as is the usual custom, and with our other two hands clasped together we sort of swayed back and forth.

"What's your name?" he shouted over the music.

"Lynn," I replied, "and yours?"

"Tom."

"Which stake are you from?" I asked him.

"Well, I'm not really from a stake since I'm not a member of the church yet, but I was invited by someone from the Minneapolis stake."

It was a bit of a strain to communicate over the music, but this was good news to hear that I'd actually met someone from the twin cities rather than meeting someone from the far north that I could never hope to see again.

"I'm from the Minneapolis stake too," I said.

"I know," he said. "You're from the Morningside ward, aren't you?"

This amazed me. This guy had taken all of this trouble to find out who I was! I figured he must be really interested in me, and I had hardly noticed him!

"That's right, how did you know?" I asked.

"In fact it was a girl from your ward who invited me and my friend to this conference, and she pointed out all the kids from her ward to us. You must know her, her name is Lara."

Upon hearing this my heart sank. Ah, yes, Lara. I knew her. She was probably the prettiest and most popular of all of the girls in the ward. I could see her across the room dancing with some really cute guy I'd never seen before. Our little small talk went on, but it was unfortunately peppered throughout with little references to Lara. He made a point to explain that, although as a good Mormon girl Lara was not supposed to get too serious with any one guy at her age (which was supposedly why she was dancing with every cute guy in the room), still she had promised Tom the last dance (which he emphasized was the most important one).

Great, he just asked me to dance in order to kill time until his fabulous dance with Lara. I wanted to go crawl under a rock, but I consoled myself with the fact that this dance meant that at the end of the night at least I wouldn't have to tell the other girls that I hadn't been asked to dance at all.

When the song ended, I went and found Amy to ask her how her dance went.

"Great," she said, "his name is Greg, and he seems to like me. He said that his friend who was dancing with you is in love with Lara, though."

"Yeah, I noticed," I said.

"Oh, well, there are plenty of other guys here."

Greg then walked up to Amy with two cups of punch and handed her one. I could see Tom bringing me one, too, but since he was undoubtedly just doing it out of politeness since his friend was interested in Amy, I wasn't too impressed by the gesture. I accepted the punch gracefully, but at my earliest opportunity I slipped away saying I had to check my hair in the bathroom. Tom was gazing across at Lara and didn't try to stop me.

April was in the bathroom with Alexandra and Cookie, all three of them discussing some guy from Ely that Alexandra had met and danced with. I gave my hair a quick once-over and then asked the other girls to tell Amy that I was tired and had decided to leave early.

"I'd tell her myself, but she's with some guy she she seems to like, and I'm avoiding the guy's friend," I said.

"Ah, she ran off and stuck you with the ugly one, huh? Poor abandoned Lynn!" said Cookie.

"Something like that."

"Don't worry, you'll find someone tomorrow," April said encouragingly.

"Whatever. In the meantime, just tell Amy I'm turning in. See you tomorrow."

"See you," they all replied.

On my way back out, I peeked into the dance hall one last time. There was Y off in a corner talking to Z as usual, not even dancing with any girls.

Someday, I thought to myself walking back to my dorm room. Maybe tomorrow night... It wasn't as if he was with someone else, so why not me? I tried to convince myself that maybe it wasn't that he didn't like me—maybe he was just shy. But I could see that this was just wishful thinking since I often started up conversations with him, and his response was always to escape as quickly as possible. Yet he would converse willingly enough with Claire or Kimberly when they found time for him. There were no two ways about it really, he just wasn't interested.

I got back to my room and immediately got out my photo of Y. The photo was a present from April since she suspected that I liked him. Even though April and I had always been close, I insisted to her that I most certainly had no interest in him. I was mortified at the thought that April would tell Andrew who would tell Y himself, and I would be ridiculed. Already I had been worried by what she might have had to say to have gotten a hold of that picture, but it turned out that it was nothing suspicious. Andrew had merely given her a discarded family portrait one time, and April had cut out Andrew for herself and David for me and then had discreetly thrown away the rest of the family. So I accepted the photo while assuring her vehemently that I had no need of a photo of this person, and then I promptly hid it away for private contemplation.

Alone in my dorm room I gazed at the photo. I started to go through my usual fantasy of somehow supernaturally giving him a dream in which he finally sees how beautiful I am. In the dream, my hair is gorgeous and my dress is perfect (I had mentally designed three fantastic red dresses just for this dream), and he can't help but want to ask me to dance. The song playing in the background of the dream is *Lady in Red*.

In my mind I went through the song and imagined it playing stanza by stanza, *"I have never seen that dress you're wearing, or the highlights in your hair, they catch your eyes—I have been blind,"* and all that. And then I imagined how he would wake up thinking about me and want to see me.

In the middle of this fantasizing, a knock came at the door. Ah, it must be the other girls returning from the dance with stories of their conquests, I thought.

But when I answered the door I saw that it wasn't. It was Mindy. Of course, the cookies—I had forgotten.

"Amy's not back yet," I said, "and I don't know where the package is. Besides, now that she's found a new boyfriend, maybe she'd rather give the cookies to him."

"No, no," said Mindy, "I've already talked to her. She just stayed late to help clean up, but she told me to swing by your room to get the cookies. She said that she still wants to give them to you-know-who and you-know-who, and that they're in a box in her suitcase near the top."

We looked in her suitcase, and sure enough there was a box wrapped in shiny pink paper and a little pink envelope taped to it. I handed the box to Mindy.

"You have to write something on the card," she said taking the card out of the little envelope and giving it to me. Thankfully the card was just a blank pink rectangle and not something covered covered with hearts or love poetry or worse. I wrote on it simply "To Peter and David" trying to disguise my writing as well as possible. Not that either one of them knew my writing, but I would hate for the card to be used as evidence against me later.

I was actually grateful that Amy had stayed behind and let me write the card myself since I was sure that she would have insisted on writing something embarrassingly cutesy like "from your secret admirers" or "from: guess who?" and then she would have covered the whole thing with hearts. It was probably wishful thinking on my part to imagine that I had lent some dignity to this whole misguided endeavor by avoiding that level of ridiculousness, but at least I was doing my best not to let the thing get too out of hand.

"I'll put it in front of their door around 4 or 4:30 a.m. so no one will see me," Mindy said taking the package.

"Thanks, that's nice of you to be willing to get up in the middle of the night for us like that."

"All in a day's work," she said, sighing. She then concealed the box in a huge tote bag that she was carrying and took it with her.

I got back to my picture of Y and was about to maybe start writing in my journal when Amy finally arrived.

"So how'd it go?" I asked her as soon as she was inside with the door closed. "Are you in love?"

"Not like with Z," she replied, "but I'm starting to like him. After you left, there were only three more songs, so you hardly needed to leave early. Tom would have left you soon enough to claim his dance with Lara."

"I know," I said. "It's a tiny little gesture, but I kind of wanted to reject him first. So tell me about Greg."

"You were wise—I didn't get off so easily. Shortly after you left, Lara stopped by to encourage Tom with a few words before rejoining her other admirers, and when the last dance was announced, Tom immediately rushed to her side. She remembered her obligation to dance with him, and as a treat to Greg, she convinced Kimberly to ask him to dance the last dance with her. From what Greg was telling me, he and Tom go to the same high school as Kimberly and Lara, and Kimberly and Lara are two of the most popular girls in the school, so of course he couldn't pass up his opportunity to dance with Kimberly. I was left with the fun of being a wallflower for the last dance of the night."

"So they're both non-members?" I asked.

"Yeah, but they've met with the missionaries and they're taking the discussions. Apparently Greg is a little leery about the whole thing since he's an atheist, but he says that Tom has been terribly enthusiastic about it. He's told Greg that he's starting to feel the truth of the message, but it seems suspiciously linked to the fact that Lara gives him the time of day exactly when he's talking about how interested he is in the church."

"Well, she's clearly taking her 'every member a missionary' calling to heart. But if Greg's not interested, why did he even come to this conference?"

"He said that Tom convinced him that it would be fun. He says that he's having fun so far. And he seems to like me—or at least he did until he wandered off with Kimberly."

"He'll be back as soon as she starts ignoring him again. She's not going to waste too much of her missionary zeal on a guy who's clearly never going to join the church."

"True, but I should probably stick to good Mormon boys myself."

"Yeah, but a non-member is better than nothing, which is what we have now."

"We'll see," she said, "maybe our little present will have the desired effect."

"Hope springs eternal," I replied. "Let's get some sleep."

As soon as I got into bed, my thoughts turned to Y again. This time I imagined us together at the end of a dark corridor like that couple we saw at the dance. I imagined him touching me, and I pictured him doing a little more than maybe we were supposed to do. They say that boys are even more preoccupied with dirty thoughts than girls, and I wondered if he had imagined such things and if he could possibly be tempted. Of course it was a sin to even fantasize about sinning, but despite all of my prayers for help, I couldn't stop these sorts of thoughts from coming to me. So for this time I silently gave in to them. Once this business was finished, I drifted off to sleep.

6. FRIDAY MORNING

THE NEXT MORNING over breakfast we compared notes on the dance. This didn't take too long since no one had really met any serious prospects. The ones that were closest to finding a romance were Amy with Greg and her sister Alexandra with this guy Matt who was from Ely. But neither one of these was particularly promising since Greg was a non-member and Matt lived way on the other side of creation where Alexandra could hardly hope to see much of him. Plus he seemed like a bit of a hayseed. So when they had finished their stories, I recounted to them the whole situation with Tom and how Lara was leading him on just to get him to join the church. The other girls agreed that it was pretty pathetic of him to fall for such a thing, but that on the other hand if it got him to convert to Mormonism, his soul would be saved, so at least some good would come of it. Then, since no one else had had more than one or two dances with any one guy, we moved on to comparing our class schedules to see if we had any classes together.

We each had received a schedule of classes in our registration packets, just like a real college class schedule supposedly. They appeared to have been randomly generated by computer, but they were personalized and the teachers would be taking attendance, so we couldn't get away with just ignoring them and all going together to whichever classes we wanted. It was unfortunate because none of my classes looked even mildly interesting, and Amy and I didn't have any classes together at all for the whole day.

My two morning classes were "Ordinances of the Gospel" (yawnsville) and "Treasures from the *Pearl of Great Price*." Hardly anyone ever spent time studying the *Pearl of Great Price*, so I figured that that class would be given by someone who was really into in-depth analysis of obscure scholarly boredom and Mormon trivia. Not that any of the scriptures were particularly interesting. I consoled myself with the idea that it could hardly be worse than study of some of the more obscure books of the *Old Testament*. Then after lunch I had Gymnastics. I supposed that this was meant to be a pleasant break from all that theology, but Gym had never been my strong suit, so I wasn't looking forward to it. Then the last class on my schedule was the most horrifying of all: "Sexual Purity."

Looking at the other girls' schedules for the day, I saw that no one was in my Ordinances class with me, but that Cookie and Annette would be in my *Pearl of Great Price* class, Tammy was with me in gymnastics, and April, Alexandra, and Jenny would all be attending my "Sexual Purity" lesson. As it turned out, the four of us weren't the only ones who had the misfortune of learning about sexual purity. Every single schedule had some class on it somewhere with a title like "Chastity" or "Holy and Unholy Types of Intimacy."

"Wow, they really don't want us to miss that chastity message, do they?" remarked Cookie.

"Well they probably figure that by putting all these boys and girls together on one campus hormones will be running high, so we have to be reminded of what not to do," said Alexandra.

"I don't think we're likely to forget what it is we're not supposed to do," said Jenny.

"But they want the message to be fresh in our minds when temptation strikes, and they're right to do it," interjected Tammy. "It's mostly for the boys anyway. They don't have as much to worry about from us girls. They're just making us attend the same lessons out of fairness and to specify where we should be drawing the line when a boy gets all kissy and like that."

I winced a bit at Tammy's childish expression, and I really had no desire to enter into this conversation at all, so I gathered up my tray and suggested that we start heading for our morning classes.

I took my time getting ready, and then it took me a while to find the right room for my first class because the building had a strange numbering system that I couldn't quite fathom. When I finally arrived, who should I see but Y, himself, sitting right there in the middle of the classroom! What luck!

Y didn't look up as I came in the room, which was just as well. I took a seat behind him. Not immediately behind him, but rather at an angle that I calculated would work out so that I could gaze at him for the whole hour while appearing to be looking at the teacher or at the board. This was a really good omen. We were together for our first class of Youth Conference! I took it as a sign that something good would happen between us before the end of the weekend.

A few more kids filed in after me, and then the teacher entered. He opened with a prayer, and then started right in on the lesson without taking roll. So I could have gotten away with skipping this class, but I was glad I didn't.

The teacher started by asking what were the first principles and ordinances of the gospel. That was an easy one since he was obviously asking for the fourth Article of Faith, which everyone had memorized because it was usually set to music. Six or seven hands shot up—not mine or Y's though. I figured I'd sit back and not put too much effort into this. The teacher called on a guy in the front row.

The guy responded by quoting the fourth Article of Faith verbatim: "We believe that the first principles and ordinances of the gospel are first faith in the Lord Jesus Christ, second repentance, third baptism by immersion for the remission of sins, and fourth laying on of hands for the gift of the Holy Ghost."

"That's exactly right," the teacher said. "Let's talk a little bit about baptism and about the laying on of hands and why these ordinances are necessary for our salvation."

I could tell that this was going to be a long lesson. I started staring at the back of Y's head. He really had beautiful thick wavy hair. His ear was perfect in size and shape as far as I could tell. Then I looked at his hands. His fingers were long, slender and graceful. He was absently doodling on the corner of his paper, but I couldn't tell precisely what he was drawing. It looked like it might be an airplane if it was anything at all. He was slouching a bit in his chair and resting his feet on the rack under the chair in front of him. Even his ankles and feet were slender and graceful in his worn sneakers. All in all I had to admit that he was quite a beautiful specimen.

In the background I could hear the teacher was still droning on about ordinances. "Now, who can tell me why we go to Sacrament Meeting every Sunday?" he asked.

That's an easy one, I thought to myself: because our parents make us go.

The teacher called on a girl in the second row. "Because our parents make us go," she said laughing. The whole room burst into laughter, and I even saw Y chuckle to himself. At that point I was really kicking myself. That was my line! I thought of it before she said it! If only I'd raised my hand, I could have impressed him with my wit! Darnit!

The teacher brought the class back to order and found someone to give the "real" answer, which was of course that when we partake of the sacrament we renew the covenants we made at baptism. But I couldn't help but think that my answer was also a correct answer. As I went back to gazing at Y, I started thinking about the Sunday services and how they were sufficiently unpleasant to require some temporal motivation to go along with the spiritual motivation. Or anyway some of us required extra motivation.

Probably Tammy would say that she enjoyed going to church because the spirit there made her feel close to Heavenly Father or something like that. She might even really mean it, too. I figured that that was a level of spirituality I should probably be striving for even though I found it kind of hard to comprehend. Personally I had a hard time seeing past the droning boredom of it all, and I found that I was slipping more and more into the habitual sleeper category. And my sister April generally read a book (*not* the *Book of Mormon*) throughout all of Sacrament Meeting. But it would be a sin not to go, so we showed up every Sunday more or less willing to participate or at least tolerate it.

I thought about how we Mormons pride ourselves on not having a paid minister to give a sermon but rather just have ordinary members of the ward give inspiring messages every week. Still, after being lulled to unconsciousness so many times by the same repetitive talks, I couldn't help but think that having a professional speak to us might not be such a bad idea. The faces changed from week to week, but about ninety percent of the time the talk would start with "The bishop called me up last week and asked me to give a talk on [insert topic here: faith, charity, tithing, etc.], so [this morning] I looked it up in Webster's Dictionary, and here's what it said." I added "this morning" as an aside because people wouldn't really say that, but it was pretty much understood that nobody prepares a talk very far in advance. Or, if the talk followed a musical performance, then the speaker would get a free opening line because it was unofficially obligatory to start by saying how inspiring the musical number was. The musical performances in Sacrament Meeting tended to be about the same caliber as the talks, but it was always necessary for the following speaker to say how good the singer/pianist/harp player was because the performer never gets any applause as it would be disrespectful to clap in the chapel. After the standard opening, the speaker would read some poem or anecdote on the assigned subject that they found in a church manual and which you would already have heard a million times, then the speaker would end with "in the name of Jesus Christ, amen."

My impressions of the of the efforts of my fellow imperfect children of God shouldn't be taken as intentionally unkind. To me, this was reality. This was how it was possible that I found it so difficult to concentrate on something that Heavenly Father clearly wanted me to be there listening to. Already I was at a disadvantage because I had to get up at five to deliver newspapers, so I would normally be there in a sleep-deprived state. Then a couple of repetitions of "Here's a scripture on faith that I found by looking up faith in the index of my *Bible*" and I would be out like a light.

Fortunately I wasn't one of those people who snores during the meeting (at least I hoped not—no one had ever mentioned anything to me to that effect) but it was really tricky to avoid doing the head-bobbing thing. You know what I'm talking about: It's when you start dozing off and your head starts to droop, and then you wake up a little and it suddenly snaps back up. The only remedy I had found was to rest my chin on my palms and my elbows on my knees and just give in to the call of sleep. This, by the way, is not at all a comfortable sleeping position, especially in the winter when the building's so cold. The church apparently designed the meeting houses for California and/or Utah and then decided to use the same floor plan for churches all over the world. I didn't know how well this design worked elsewhere, but in Minnesota eight months out of the year the classrooms could be used as freezers, and the chapel, the warmest room in the building, wasn't much better. But none of the minor discomforts (or even the spiritual rewards) proved sufficient to counter a sleep-inducing agent as powerful as Sacrament Meeting.

Usually the high point of Sacrament Meeting is the sacrament itself. I knew that partaking of the sacrament every Sunday was a commandment, and hence was supposed to be the primary reason for coming to church: to renew our baptismal covenants as mentioned earlier. I usually tried to think about that if I'd been reminded of it lately, but that wasn't really why I thought of the sacrament as the high point of the meeting. The real reason was that the sacrament was prepared, blessed, and passed by the boys from ages twelve to seventeen. The "priests" (sixteen and seventeen year-olds) sat in the front of the chapel to give the blessing. The "teachers" (fourteen and fifteen year-olds) prepared the sacrament. I wasn't sure precisely what this entailed since it took place behind a barrier nor why they were called "teachers" since the job certainly didn't require any teaching. The "deacons" (twelve and thirteen year-olds) distributed it. It wasn't so interesting back when Y was a teacher because the teachers' task is not visible, but since he had graduated to the priests' quorum, he sat up in the front of the chapel where I could shamelessly ogle him for the whole of the sacrament when it was his turn to be one of the two giving the blessing.

The sacrament was always taken care of right at the beginning so as not to interrupt the napping part of the meeting. And if only Sacrament Meeting were the whole of our Sunday services, it wouldn't be so bad. After all, it was only one hour out of the whole week. But sadly that was not all. Following Sacrament Meeting there was an hour of Sunday school and then an hour of Young Women's.

Sunday school had approximately the same advantages and drawbacks as Sacrament Meeting. The drawbacks were freezing to death and listening to someone read an unprepared lesson out of a dull and repetitive lesson manual. The advantages were theoretical spiritual uplift and gazing upon the love-object since the Sunday school classes were divided by age and not by gender. But the spiritual uplift was really very theoretical except for those especially righteous people who had a special talent for being inspired, and the love-object gazing had been completely eliminated for the moment until I would turn sixteen and move up to being in Y's class again.

After Sunday school, it still wasn't over because we had to go to Young Women's. This part was normally the boringest part of all. It started with "opening exercises" with all of the girls aged twelve to seventeen together for some more singing and praying (this after the five or six prayers we had already endured during the first two hours of our church meetings), and then we divided into classes to hear more readings from lesson manuals without even any boys around to attempt to flirt with.

This year, however, my Mia Maid class had been saved from the usual pit of boredom by our fabulous teacher, Mindy. (Mindy was a real teacher who teaches things, not a fifteen year old boy holding the office of teacher.) As I said, Mindy was single, twenty-six years old, and more of a friend than an authority. She knew how to make class fun. She gave us the gist of the lesson from the manual—sort of skimmed it so that we weren't completely without spiritual edification—and then got right to the good stuff.

The good stuff was the latest installment in the soap opera of her pursuit of her karate teacher whom she was in love with. Mostly this involved accounts of things he said to her during karate class and the possible ways of interpreting his remarks so they might mean that he was interested in her. One week, she gave him a gift that he really appreciated. Another week she had some important karate business to discuss with him so she took him out for a milkshake after class, which was almost like a date! The best one though was when his mother was in town visiting and stopped by class and met Mindy. Mindy felt like she'd made a really good impression on his mom, and with his mom on her side, he was bound to notice her sooner or later. It turned out that the mom was LDS even though the karate teacher himself wasn't (or at least wasn't active). So the mom would certainly be really happy to see her son settled with a good Mormon girl.

Normally a Mormon girl wouldn't want to consider marrying someone who wasn't Mormon since the church teaches that you need to have a temple marriage to a worthy spouse in order to enter the highest degree of the Celestial Kingdom and become a god or goddess of your own world in the next life. But Mindy figured that once he fell in love with her he'd start coming to church again. Plus, she couldn't afford to be too picky. Not to be mean to a friend or anything, but to be honest and blunt, Mindy was fat. *Really* fat. And everyone knows that while a Mormon man would be the best, fat girls have to take what they can get.

Actually, that was part of the tragedy of her whole story with her karate teacher: realistically speaking he didn't even fall into the category of someone she could get and settle for. She'd shown us pictures of him, and he was a normal guy—even handsome and muscular. He could have an attractive girlfriend. For all I knew, he probably did have an attractive girlfriend. But doomed unrequited love was something we could definitely relate to in the Mia Maids class (me, Amy, Tammy, Jenny, and now Annette), so we were all very happy to spend the class period discussing and analyzing the karate teacher's every word, and we were sincerely rooting for Mindy in this even though deep down we know where it was heading. It made it like a slumber party every week. There was really no comparison between that and listening to some lesson out of the manual.

The end of the ordinances lesson put an end to my little daydream. Despite the subject matter, I felt like my little hour with Y was over far too soon. I bid him goodbye (to myself, of course, outwardly I didn't pay him any more attention than he was paying me), and then I set off for my *Pearl of Great Price* class.

When I arrived, Annette was already there saving me a seat, and Cookie joined us shortly after I came in.

"I don't know why they're giving us a *Pearl of Great Price* lecture," Cookie said taking her seat. "That's one of the books we covered this past year in seminary."

"Yeah, but it was hardly covered—they just squeezed in a couple of lessons about it at the very end," I replied. "Besides, probably what happened was that the person who volunteered to teach it has a particular interest in the *Pearl of Great Price* for some reason. I'm guessing that to some degree they have to offer the lessons that they can find people to teach."

The teacher started by calling on one of the kids to give a prayer, and then he took the roll, so it was good that we didn't try to skip this class. The teacher was a short little guy with thick glasses and a nasally voice, but the class turned out not to be too dull since he decided to go over the whole section about the planet Kolob, which we normally didn't cover too much. The Kolob part of the *Pearl of Great Price* is fun because it's kind of ridiculous, but of course since it's in the scriptures, it's true. Basically the idea is that God lives on or near the planet Kolob, and that when God talks about "days" in the scriptures, he really means Kolob days and not Earth days. That's why one day for God is a thousand years long: one day on Kolob is a thousand years on Earth. Well, why not?

I turned a couple of pages in my *Pearl of Great Price* to look at some of the Egyptian drawings and hieroglyphs that the prophet Joseph Smith had copied and interpreted. I'd heard some strange rumors about these, but I was a little vague on the details. Some people said that the original papyrus that Joseph Smith had translated the book from had been lost and maybe destroyed in the great Chicago fire. But then I'd also heard that the papyrus was later found and that modern scholars translated it and declared Joseph Smith's interpretation to be completely wrong. If this was true it was a bit worrisome. On the other hand, I seemed to recall someone saying that maybe Joseph Smith didn't really *translate* the *Pearl of Great Price* from papyrus, but rather the papyrus inspired him to receive the text of the book as a revelation. Or possibly the papyrus that was found was incomplete and the part that he had translated really was lost. Or, who knows? Maybe the modern scholars were the ones who were wrong.

Anyway, I told myself that there was no sense worrying about it since we know the church is true. Plus, it wasn't as if the *Pearl of Great Price* was the most important of the Mormon scriptures. The most important one was of course the *Book of Mormon*, which Joseph Smith translated from gold plates that were never found again because they were taken back into heaven as soon as he was done.

"Psst, Lynn," Cookie whispered to me.

I looked up, "yeah?"

"Look at facsimile number two."

I already had my book open to that very page. "I'm looking at it," I whispered back. It was a circle divided into lots of different sections and covered with hieroglyphs and Egyptian drawings.

"One of the hieroglyphs in it is a picture of a penis," she whispered.

"Really?" I whispered back.

"It's a little hard to make it out, but it's in the outer ring, right there next to the picture of a bull."

I looked at the character she was pointing at. It was really small and not very clear, but it was possible that it could be a picture of a penis.

The teacher rapped on his desk irritatedly and said, "Ladies, please, save your conversations for after class."

"But we were just talking about the lesson," I said.

"Oh, were you now?" he said. "Then perhaps you'd like to share your insights with the rest of the class."

So Cookie perfectly nonchalantly said "I was just pointing out to my friend that one of the hieroglyphs in facsimile number two is a picture of a penis."

The whole class erupted in laughter.

"It's true," she said. "My brother showed me a book explaining the facsimiles which gave details about all of the characters drawn on them. And one of the characters is a penis."

At this point the teacher looked really annoyed and the class was still snickering.

"It's true, I swear," she continued. "My brother bought the book about it in the BYU bookstore!"

"We do not swear in class young lady," the teacher said sternly, "and here we're interested in the messages written in the facsimiles, not the shapes of the particular characters used. Now why don't you gather your things and go sit on the other side of the classroom—away from your friends—where perhaps you'll have an easier time keeping quiet."

So Cookie picked up her book and walked calmly to the other side of the classroom. So much for doing extra research on your own and sharing your findings with the class! I looked at the picture again. It could be a penis, but it wasn't obvious. I could see that a lot of the other kids were examining facsimile number two very closely as well. After a bit more of the lesson, the class ended and we went to lunch.

As we were entering the cafeteria, Amy came rushing up and pulled me aside, away from the other girls.

"Well?" she asked.

"Well what?" I asked.

"Has your sister said anything to you?"

"About what?" After a second it hit me. "Oh, the cookies." I had completely forgotten. "I haven't seen April since breakfast."

"Well, we've got to ask her if she's heard anything about them!" Amy insisted.

"No way!" I said. "I forbid you to mention anything about this to her! If you say anything that makes her start asking Andrew questions that will lead him to say something suspicious to his brother, I swear that I will personally strangle you!"

"But don't you want to know what their reaction was?" Amy asked.

"Not enough to risk them finding out it was from us! Look, if April says something about it at lunch, we'll listen as though we know nothing about it. If she doesn't, we'll cut our losses and just be grateful that we haven't suffered any massive humiliation from all of this."

"But what if we don't hear anything? I worked hard on those cookies, and I want to know if Z liked them."

"What do you think that April is going to say? 'Z just got a box of the most delicious cookies he's ever tasted, and now he's looking for the girl who baked them so he can propose marriage to her'? Get real. If we don't hear anything, it just means that they liked the cookies so well that they didn't tell any of the other boys about them because they didn't want to have to share them, and so much the better for us."

"You're right, of course," Amy said. "I still hope we hear something, though. Let's go get our lunch."

We took our lunch with the other girls, and April didn't mention anything at all about anyone receiving any anonymous packages. Fortunately Amy behaved herself and didn't ask any suspicious questions, but I could tell that she was dying for news. Then we all set off for our various classes.

Tammy and I went to the gymnasium and found the gymnastics room. I was a little apprehensive, but it turned out to be a lot more fun than I expected. The teacher didn't structure that class period at all (we didn't even open with prayer!) but instead she just let us play on the gymnastics equipment however we pleased. I was amazed that the college where we were staying would allow this, but I supposed that the church had paid a fee for use of a few of the buildings, and this one happened to be included. When our hour was up, I was sorry to see the class period end. And I was doubly sorry when I thought about what was next on my schedule...

7. FRIDAY AFTERNOON

IN MY NEXT CLASS, "Sexual Purity," they were bound to take attendance, so I couldn't very well just not show up. I thought a bit about what the consequences might be if I were to skip one of my classes, but in the end, since I knew that some of my friends would in there with me, I decided to just bite the bullet and attend.

When I arrived at the classroom, sure enough April, Alexandra, and Jenny were already there saving me a seat. The classroom was a bit bigger than the others had been. Undoubtedly they were more concerned about giving this lesson to as many kids as possible than they were about getting us to read the *Pearl of Great Price*. Each of the desks had a Mini Reese's Peanut Butter Cup sitting on it, but it was written on the board in big letters that we were not to eat them.

I noticed that Claire was sitting in front of us with Tina, the less-active member who went to my school. They seemed to be giggling about something, so I strained a little to try to make out what they were saying. It seemed that if I understood correctly Tina had skipped her morning classes and had snuck a boy into her dorm room! She very clearly said "It was an 'uplifting' experience for him," and then she and Claire both burst out laughing.

I couldn't believe it! Here at Youth Conference? She had decided to sneak a boy into her room to do precisely the sort of thing we weren't supposed to be doing! And on top of that, she was bragging about it in this class of all classes! I was amazed that it was possible.

Shortly, the teacher came in and, as expected, called on a kid to give the opening prayer and then took attendance. I looked around and noticed that the desk immediately next to mine was vacant. At this point no one else was likely to come in, so I reached over and took the chocolate off that desk and ate it.

"As this is a bit of a sensitive subject," the teacher began, "we're going to start with a short video." He then dimmed the lights and started it up. The video was all about the evils of pornography. Basically the idea was that there was this teenage boy who started looking at pornography and then became addicted to it. He later repented and Heavenly Father forgave him, but he could never completely get the dirty images he had seen out of his mind. So even though you can always repent, you shouldn't count on a strategy of "sin now, repent later" when it comes to pornography because it can have permanent consequences even after you've repented. The whole video was less than ten minutes long, but it got the point across with no difficulty.

I began to relax a little because it seemed clear that Tammy was right: they were mostly aiming this lesson at the boys.

The teacher started off by explaining how we might think that there's nothing wrong with our sexual desires because they're natural. But he told us that in fact, that's one of the main reasons we need to fight them because as it says in the *Book of Mormon* (Mosiah 3:19) "the natural man is an enemy to God." He said that we needed to be on a higher plane than the natural, we needed to be spiritual instead.

Then he moved on to a concrete example: masturbation. This froze me because I had never heard it mentioned by name at a church function before. He explained that just because masturbation is not mentioned explicitly in the scriptures, that doesn't mean that it's not a sin. It is a sin, he told us emphatically, a terrible sin. He backed this up with the verse from the *New Testament* (Matthew 5:28) where Jesus says "whosoever looketh on a woman to lust after her hath committed adultery with her already in his heart." And he explained that the same goes for fornication. So if you lustfully imagine committing adultery or fornication, to Heavenly Father it's as if you had done it for real.

And he reminded us that adultery and fornication are the worst sins you can commit short of murder and apostasy (Alma 39:5).

Listening to this lecture, I felt like I was maybe starting to turn a bit red. I glanced over at the other girls to see what kind of a reaction they were having, but they looked completely blasé. It was as if this message meant nothing to them and was meant for someone else. I started thinking that maybe it's not normal for a girl to be imagining these sorts of dirty things. Maybe I was the only perverted one. I tried to look as casual as possible in hopes that no one would see that this message was making me nervous.

The teacher then shifted the discussion to the evils of homosexuality. Only then did I relax completely. Whew, no problems there! The teacher mentioned Sodom and Gomorrah and lusting after "strange flesh" and such like that, but it rolled right over me. You could put me in a room full of naked women and girls (like at the locker room at the pool, for example), and my thoughts would be as pure as an angel's.

But then he started moving back into dangerous territory. He started telling us a story about a teenage boy and girl who had to go to their bishop to repent because they had committed the grave sin of fornication. When asked to explain, the teenagers said that it just happened all of the sudden. But as the bishop started posing them more questions, he found that they had deliberately gone to a secluded place where they would not be disturbed or discovered. And then they proceeded to cross more lines that you aren't supposed to cross by deep kissing and heavy petting. So when they ended up committing fornication, it wasn't really "all of the sudden." He used this story as an illustration for why unmarried people shouldn't be making out and for why they certainly shouldn't be petting.

I hated it when teachers used the word "petting." It made it sound like something you would do with a dog. Maybe there wasn't really any dignified way of saying "don't touch each other's naughty parts." On the other hand, maybe they deliberately wanted us to feel embarrassed and repulsed by the whole thing.

At the end of his discussion of petting, the teacher told us that now we were allowed to eat our Reese's Peanut Butter Cups.

"See, aren't you glad you waited?" he said. "It's a little like waiting for marriage." Then he told us that we were free to go.

April turned to the rest of us and said "What? Waiting until the end of class is like waiting for marriage? That doesn't make any sense

at all! If I had eaten my candy at the beginning of class I'd have been glad I was eating it then, and by the same token, if I save it for another ten minutes after class is over, then while I'm eating it I'll be glad that I waited another ten minutes so I could enjoy it right then."

"Yeah," I agreed, "I took one off an empty desk and ate it at the beginning of class, and I was glad I did it. It hasn't detracted in any way from my enjoyment of the one I'm eating right now."

Then Jenny piped up. "Yeah, he's come up with a pretty stupid metaphor here. Mini Reese's Peanut Butter Cups are a dime a dozen. They're not like something that is better eaten at a particular time. If you want to you can buy bags and bags of them and eat them all day and share them with all your friends. So if you apply the logic of candy equals sex to that, you get precisely the opposite of what he was trying to say."

"Oh, well," I said. "I don't think that anyone expected that this lecture was going to be the high point of Youth Conference. What's the next thing on the schedule now that we've finished our classes?"

"We have to go out to the main lawn and sit with our wards because they're going to divide us into teams for sports and games," said Alexandra.

Oh great, more fun, I thought. The four of us followed the rest of the slow-moving mass of kids out onto the main lawn. Outside, April spotted Andrew sitting with his friend Dan a bit off to the side on a little hill, so we all went and sat by them.

"Are you having fun?" Andrew asked April.

"Not really," she replied. "We just finished our 'Sexual Purity' class where the teacher gave a really lame metaphor equating sex and candy."

"Yeah, it was really retarded," I said. "It was that saving yourself for marriage is like saving a Reese's Peanut Butter Cup for the end of class."

"Ah, you guys should have been at the 'Sacred Within the Bonds of Holy Matrimony' class with us this morning," Andrew said.

"Yeah, we got a food-sex metaphor, too," said Dan, "but ours was really graphic."

"And disgusting," added Andrew.

"What was it?" asked April.

"Well, the teacher picked one of the girls to stand up at the front of the class and had her hold up a glazed donut," Andrew began. "Then he picked two guys and had them stand on either side of her. He told one of the guys to lick all of the glaze off the donut while the girl just stood there holding it. Then when he was done, the teacher asked the other guy if now he would like to eat the donut. Of course he didn't eat it, but we got to see the look on his face as he thought about it."

"Eeeeeeww!" shrieked Alexandra.

"That's horrible!" said Jenny.

"Yeah, it was really revolting," said Dan, "but it got the point across."

"Well, I for one am glad I didn't have to attend that class," said April.

"Think of that poor girl who had to be in that demonstration!" I said. "She probably had no idea what the teacher was going to make her do, otherwise she would never have agreed to it."

"Well I didn't make it up," said Andrew, "I'm just telling you what I saw."

Just then Mindy came by with a big sack of t-shirts and a clipboard. She checked each of our names to be sure to give us shirts of the right size and color. Andrew and Dan got yellow, April and I both got blue, Alexandra got white, and Jenny got orange. The t-shirts had this year's Youth Conference logo and motto on them which was

"Standing Tall for Righteousness." Jenny wasn't at all happy with her color, but we all put our t-shirts on over our other clothes and started moving towards the places where the variously-colored teams were gathering.

Amy and Tammy were already wearing their blue t-shirts and sitting with the blue team. Apparently the organizers of the conference at least had everyone be on the same team with their roommate even though the wards and stakes were split up. I looked around and found Y and Z over on the red team. The red t-shirt actually went pretty well with Z's red hair, and Y of course looked fantastic in any color.

The blue team leader (one of the adults) told us that today was going to be a getting-to-know-you day for the teams and that the sports where the teams compete against each other would be tomorrow afternoon. So she had us all sit in a circle and tell our names and something about ourselves. I wasn't sure which I felt was worse: playing sports or sitting in a circle and telling something about ourselves, but it looked like we weren't going to have much choice in the matter.

I had a hard time thinking of what I might possibly say about myself. I could say "I'm short, but good things come in small packages." That would be sufficiently lame and geeky for this exercise. Or perhaps I could say "I'm almost sixteen years old, and yet last night I anonymously gave a box of heart-shaped cookies to the boy I'm secretly in love with." But seriously I had to think of something quickly because it was coming around to my turn soon.

Amy was just before me. "My name's Amy," she said, "and I like to bake cookies." Now there's a good Mormon girl hobby for you, I thought to myself. At least she didn't mention her specialty in heart-shaped ones. Then, unfortunately, it was my turn.

"My name's Lynn," I began, "and..." Here I paused for a really long time. "...and I can't think of anything to say about myself."

"Aw, c'mon, you have to say something," the team leader said encouragingly. "What's your favorite subject in school?"

"Math," I said.

"Okay, that's Lynn and she likes math," the leader said summing it up. Then it was Tammy's turn.

"My name's Tammy, and I like to knit, sew, cook, can fruits and jams for our year's supply, and help my mom take care of my little brother and sister. I'm working on a patchwork quilt right now for my hope chest, and I brought it with me to Youth Conference to work on in my spare time."

"Wow, you can't beat a list of homemaking skills like that!" exclaimed the team leader. "Boys, you should all be making a note of this one." Tammy blushed.

Then it was April's turn. She said something about how she was writing a graphic novel. I couldn't help but notice that of the four of us she was the only one who said something remotely reasonable and didn't end up looking like a fool.

After that we continued going around the circle and the other kids listed off their names and hobbies. I hardly listened to them since I had always been terrible with names so I wouldn't remember them even if I were paying close attention. Then we had to sing a couple of camp songs, and the leader asked everyone to try to make up a team cheer for our team for tomorrow, and then mercifully we were free to go to dinner.

* * *

After dinner, while getting ready for the second dance of Youth Conference, I resolved that I was going to seriously make an effort to meet someone good this time. Otherwise I would be down to my last chance on Saturday night. I looked at my dress closely in the mirror and couldn't help but feel that it just wasn't right. I wasn't unattractive, and there wasn't anything specifically wrong with my look, but I felt that I somehow lacked a certain *je ne sais quoi* which would attract the boys to me like they came to Lara for example.

In the background, I could hear Amy talking on the phone to her mom. I wasn't really listening as they were discussing which dress she should wear to that night's dance and which one she should save for Saturday night. But then a shift in the topic caught my attention.

"No, we haven't heard any news," Amy said and then paused. "Well, we were thinking that it was probably just that they liked them so much that they didn't tell anyone anything so that they wouldn't have to share them with the other boys."

She didn't! I couldn't believe she had told her mom about the cookies! I was never going to hear the end of this! As soon as she got off the phone I confronted her about it.

"How could you tell your mom about the cookies?" I asked her.

"Well, I didn't so much tell her, really. Actually the whole thing was her idea to begin with. And anyway, who's she gonna tell?" I couldn't really argue with that logic, so I decided not to worry about it. We finished getting ready, and then set off with the other girls to the dance hall.

The decorations they had put up were exactly the same as they had been the previous night. We got into our usual dance circle formation, and this time instead of worrying about how foolish we might look, I decided to really focus on scouring the room to find someone— anyone—who might look promising. There were some chubby guys over in one corner who looked available, but I felt like I hadn't quite gotten to the point where I wanted to settle for someone fat. I wanted to be at least a little bit attracted to my boyfriend. Then along another wall was a guy standing all by himself. His hair was a mess, and his face had a few more zits than optimal, but he could be worse. Okay, that's the one, I decided. He wasn't the most attractive guy I'd ever seen, but he fell into the acceptable range. I resolved to approach him for the first slow dance.

I also looked around the dance hall to find Y. He wasn't that hard to spot—he was talking to Z, as usual. If only I could get up the nerve to ask him to dance, then maybe I could be with someone who's actually desirable. But it wasn't as if he hadn't had ample opportunity to notice me. I'd started conversations with him tons of times, and he always just got this pained expression on his face and found some excuse to slip away. If I were to ask him to dance, he probably wouldn't say no, but it would likely just be awkward and painful. I figured I shouldn't waste this opportunity to meet some boy who might actually return my interest. It was the story of my life: I couldn't really expect to attract Mr. Right, so I should count my blessings if I managed to snag Mr. Better-Than-Nothing.

It wasn't long before a slow song came on, and as soon as I heard the first few notes I walked directly towards my chosen quarry. The opening formalities passed smoothly: I asked him to dance with me, he said okay, and we walked out onto the dance floor together. Not far away, I saw Greg walking towards Amy and Tom following behind.

Good, I thought. Tom will see me dancing with another guy. Maybe when he realized that Lara wasn't the only one who could play a little bit hard to get, he might start being interested in me. And if he didn't it was no big loss.

In accordance with the standard custom, I started by asking my new partner his name. He replied, but I couldn't hear what he said.

"What was that?" I asked him a little more loudly.

"Bob," he said. This time I heard him, but it was still pretty faint.

"I'm Lynn," I said. Then there was a long pause. It didn't appear that he was going to say anything further on his own, so I figured it was up to me to continue the conversation.

"So, how do you like Youth Conference so far?" I asked him, making a point to speak up over the music. He replied, but again I couldn't make out a word he said. Oh great, I thought, he's one of those really quiet talkers. That would make this difficult.

Looking a bit to the side, I noticed that Y was dancing with Kimberly. I wondered precisely how that had happened and who had asked whom. Well, it hardly matters, I thought. Even though I theoretically wasn't supposed to be leading, I kind of steered Bob around to block my view so I would be spared this spectacle.

The song seemed to just keep going on and on as usually is the case when the conversation is a little difficult. I asked Bob a few more questions just to avoid the awkward situation of saying nothing at all, but I tried to stick to small talk where it wouldn't matter if I didn't hear his responses. That way I avoided the annoyance of having to yell "What?!?" all the time.

The following song was a fast song, and for once I was grateful to be getting back to my little circle of girls. So I thanked Bob for the dance and got back to my friends.

I ended up just dancing with the other girls for a long time, and then I went for a walk by myself outside to assess the situation. The fact that Bob was a bit hard to hear didn't rule him out completely as a prospect, I reasoned. For all I knew, he might be a nice guy, even interesting. I figured that maybe I should try to talk to him in the hallway or the foyer where there was less noise. So I came back in to try to find him.

I didn't see Bob right away, but I saw that Amy was still talking to Greg and Tom, and it looked like the three of them were headed for the door. They probably had decided to go somewhere quieter to talk too, so I went to join them. It would work perfectly: that way if Bob were to wander by as we were talking, I could try to draw him into the conversation.

I caught up with Amy, Greg, and Tom just as they were sitting down on some couches in the foyer. Fortunately the foyer would make a good strategic location to watch for people since anyone who wanted to go outside to get some air would have to pass through.

"Oh, hi, we were wondering where you went," Amy said looking up.

"Well, here I am," I said as I took a seat next to her on the couch. "What's up with you guys?"

"Greg was just telling us why it's foolish to believe in God, and we were explaining to him why it's foolish not to," Tom said.

An interesting topic, I thought. Good, I figured that while I was sitting around waiting I would have the opportunity to earn some stars in heaven by doing missionary work.

"Well, I didn't exactly say it's foolish," Greg said, "I was just saying that the evidence just isn't there."

"Yeah, but do you have any evidence that there isn't a God?" Amy asked.

"No, no, it doesn't work that way," he said. "You're all saying that the universe works a certain way. I'm not saying I can prove that it doesn't, I'm just saying convince me."

"But you're proposing that the universe is a certain way, too, namely God-free," I said. "So we just want to know what evidence you're basing that supposition on."

"Oh great," he said, "you really want me to review all of science for you from Geology to Physics to Astronomy to Biology? Don't you guys go to high school?"

"Okay, I'll grant you that there's not much evidence for the existence of God, and that if I didn't know the church was true, looking at it objectively I might say that it seems pretty reasonable to conclude that there is no God," I said. "But it's not really a question of logical proof, it's a question of faith."

"Well then this is the point we disagree on," Greg said. "As far as I can tell, faith just means believing in something that you have no good reason to believe in."

"I wouldn't say 'no good reason,'" Amy said. "If you pray sincerely, God will tell you in your heart that it's true."

"And since He's God, you'd better listen when He tells you something," said Tom.

Just then my little sister Annette walked through towards the dance hall from outside, and she was holding hands with a boy! And what's more, he was cute! A little short maybe, but I had to say that she had done pretty well for herself at her very first Youth Conference. She smiled and waved to us as she walked by, but she didn't stop to chat. I made a mental note to ask her for all the details later. It wasn't fair—even my little sister had better luck than I did!

While I was watching my sister go by, Greg responded with something about how you couldn't really be sure that the feelings you get when you pray are really messages from God.

"When you feel it you just know," Amy said.

So she's one of the lucky ones who's righteous enough to be receptive to God's messages, I thought.

"And what if it turns out that it is true?" Tom asked. "Do you really want to risk suffering for eternity? You might as well believe in God just to be on the safe side."

"I've heard that one before," Greg replied. "But how do I know which religion I should pick to be safe? Maybe if I pick Mormonism I'll die and find out I was supposed to be a Muslim, and I'll end up burning in hell anyway. Or maybe it'll turn out that there is no God after all, and I'll have wasted the only life I have following some stupid bullshit that I had no reason to believe in in the first place."

At this point Claire and Tina walked through towards the outside followed by Kimberly and Lara and some popular girls from another ward.

"Hey Lara," Tom called, "your friends here have been trying to convince me to join the church, but I still have some questions."

"Oh, I can help out," she said. The other girls in her group kept on walking, but Lara said hi to each of us and took a seat. "What was your question?"

Here Tom clearly had to think fast to make up a question that he could pretend had stumped us. "Well," he began, "we were talking about faith, and I was wondering how you could tell if that burning feeling you get when you pray is God telling you that the *Book of Mormon* is true."

"Oh, it is," she said, "it most certainly is. So you've been getting a burning feeling when you pray about the *Book of Mormon*?"

"I think so," he said. "I haven't quite finished reading the whole book yet, but I feel like God may be telling me that it's true."

"Why don't we go back in and get some punch, and I'll tell you about my testimony," Lara said, and they left together.

"Well, whatever else you can say about her, she's quite a missionary," I said.

"Maybe we should get back to the dance, too," suggested Amy.

I agreed to this since it looked like Bob wasn't going to pass through anytime soon at this rate. But just as we were about to walk into the dance hall, by chance Bob came walking out.

"Oh, hi Bob," I said, "how's it going?"

"Fine," he said, and the shy way he said it was so cute that it made me want to talk to him some more. Amy and Greg waved bye and continued on into the dance hall.

"I just wanted to ask you about what you were saying about..." Here I regretted starting a sentence without thinking it all the way through to the end since I sincerely hadn't heard a word he had said aside from his name, so there was no way I could come up with a good follow up question.

"...about my computer?" he offered.

"Yes, exactly," I said. "What was it you were telling me that you were doing with your computer?"

"Well I was just saying that a friend of mine sold me a used CPU. It's only a year old, so it's not really out of date yet, and I'm installing it in a new box."

I was pleased to discover that I could hear him clearly when there was no background noise, but since I didn't know a lot about the inner workings of computers I wasn't sure I really followed him even with the sound.

"So you're building a computer from parts?" I ventured.

"Well essentially that's it, yes," he said, and he immediately launched into a detailed explanation of the motherboard and all of the different pieces and how they fit together. He made sure to list all of the different giga-this and kilo-that, and I followed it just enough to occasionally ask a question that seemed reasonable, or failing that, at least to nod at appropriate pauses. We moved over to chat on the sofa as he continued by telling me about the two other computers in his network and the different special options he used when installing the system on each one. I began to regret that I had started this conversation, but I didn't see a good way to get out of it. So I continued to act interested in hopes that he would eventually run out of steam and I could steer the conversation to another topic.

When finally he came to a long enough pause that I figured he might be done describing his network, I asked him if he had any other interests besides computers.

He thought about it for a moment and said, "I like to read science fiction."

Ah, science fiction, I thought. It wasn't my best subject, but I could surely do better on that topic than I could on the technical details of putting together a computer network from scratch. So I mentioned a couple of books I'd read and asked him what he thought of them. The discussion continued in two-way mode for some time, which I felt was a real breakthrough.

I was surprised when I heard the DJ in the other room announce the last dance since I didn't think that we had talked that long. "Oh, wow, it's already the last dance," I said.

"Would you like to go in and dance with me?" he asked.

"Sure," I said.

So we went back into the dance hall and danced together. This time I didn't really even try to talk to him over the music. We'd already talked quite a bit at that point so it wasn't too awkward to just dance

without talking. At the end he walked me back to the door of the girls' dorm. Fortunately there were a lot of people around when we arrived, so we didn't have to deal with the ticklish question of whether or not he might try to kiss me goodnight.

"Well, g'night Bob," I said.

"Goodnight," he said. "Oh, and by the way—my name is Bill, not Bob."

"Oh, sorry!" I said. "See you tomorrow."

"See you," he said.

Amy was already waiting in our dorm room when I arrived.

"I see you've finally met someone," she said. "So, give me all of the details."

"Well, he's really into computers, and when you get him started on that topic it can get a little dull. On the other hand I think he's kind of cute. What do you think?"

"He's very cute," she said. "So do you like him?"

"Yeah, I guess so," I replied.

"Better than Y?" she asked.

"No. There's no comparison. But we'll see. Maybe once I get to know him better he'll start to grow on me. And what about you? Are you making any progress with Greg?"

"Progress, no," she said. "In fact he pulled exactly the same stunt at this dance as he did at the previous one. He acted interested all night, and then when Kimberly asked him for the last dance, he went off with her!"

"Jeez, that's not very nice of him. She's not even giving him the time of day, but at the drop of a hat he's ready to snub a real girl for her."

"I know," Amy said, "and I'm wondering what I should do about it. I can't very well just put up with it as if it were nothing."

"Well, let's sleep on it, and maybe we'll think of a good way to get back at him tomorrow," I said.

Once we were in our beds, I said to her "By the way, I have something personal that I was meaning to ask you about."

"What?"

"Well, today in one of the lectures they were talking about how it's a sin to even think about having sex."

"Oh, yeah, I had one of those lectures too," she said.

"I was wondering: Do you ever imagine touching the boys and doing those sorts of things with them?"

"Sometimes," she said. I was really relieved to hear it.

"But it's a sin to even think about fornication, isn't it?" I asked.

"Well, yes, but here's how I get around it. I start by imagining getting married in the temple. I go through the whole fantasy of the beautiful dress I'll have and the reception and all of that. And then after all that is finished I imagine the wedding night. So then I'm not imagining fornicating, so it's not a sin."

"Hmmm, that's an interesting idea," I said. "Good night."

"Good night," Amy said.

I thought a little more about her solution. I couldn't really find a hole in her logic, but somehow it seemed like that was cheating. I couldn't put my finger on what was wrong with it, but I also couldn't quite believe that that technique would make it okay...

AT BREAKFAST ANNETTE was ecstatically telling everyone about Tony, her new boyfriend. She recounted how she met him and how she'd asked him to dance and all that. It turned out that he was in the Crystal second ward, so he wasn't too far away even if he wasn't right next door. And they'd already exchanged phone numbers so that they could keep in contact after the end of Youth Conference. We all congratulated her and gushed about how very cute he was. At this point I had no reason to be jealous since I had met someone too.

Not to be outdone, as soon as her story started to wind down a bit I launched into my narrative about Bill. I skipped the parts about not hearing him and about computer networking and went straight to telling them about how cute he was and how much he seemed to like me. All the girls who had seen him agreed that he was very cute.

On the schedule for that day we had two morning classes, and then the entire afternoon was set aside for team sports. Since I hated sports, and my two classes didn't look too interesting either ("Journal Writing," and "Prayer and Faith"), I figured it was going to be tough to pass the time until that night's dance. Comparing with the other girls, I found that Amy would be in the journal writing class with me. We were happy to have a class together, but we weren't too thrilled about the topic. How much is there to say about keeping a journal? And to make matters worse, we had just had a lesson about journal writing two weeks earlier in Sunday school.

The Sunday school lesson had been all about how Nephi had been commanded to keep a journal, and how his journal became the first part of the *Book of Mormon*, which is the most important book of scripture. Likewise, our journals might be used as scripture by angels in heaven if they're really good. Then to illustrate how hard it was to write scripture and to show the kind of effort required for such a journal, the teacher had had us each try to write a scripture ourselves.

In fact I had found the exercise pretty easy. I'd already had a little bit of practice writing scripture since once when we were younger April and I had written something of a parody of the *Book of Mormon*. We hadn't really meant it as a parody. What had happened was that our mom had been having us read a chapter from the *Book of Mormon* together as a family every night. So one day when April and I had the

idea to write a funny story, we did it in the style of the *Book of Mormon* because that was something that was fresh in our minds. We were so proud of it that as soon as we were done, we took it straight to our mom to show her how clever it was.

Her reaction, however, wasn't quite what we were hoping for. Basically she was angry with us because she felt that our response to her sincere efforts to edify us spiritually was to mock the holy scriptures. This of course was her punishment for raising clever children: the dim-witted ones don't cause you this kind of grief. We really hadn't meant to upset our mother, but maybe was just that the *Book of Mormon* was written in an unusual and challenging style that we wanted to try for ourselves. We wouldn't have done it if we'd found the *Book of Mormon* completely uninteresting, like Mark Twain who mocked it by calling it "chloroform in print," and joked that without all of the repetitions of "and it came to pass" the book would be a pamphlet.

So in the end, Amy and I decided to just skip our morning classes since we figured that they weren't going to do anything bad to us on the last full day of Youth Conference. We went outside and found ourselves a nice spot where we could sit down under some trees and chat. The sky was starting to cloud over a bit, but it was still nice out. We were discussing the situation with Tom and Greg when Mindy came over and sat down with us.

"Ah, I didn't think I'd find you two among the people I have to chase back to class," Mindy said.

"So during the day you have to play truant officer?" I asked.

"Yep," she replied, "a chaperone's work is never done."

"You're not going to make us go back to class are you?" Amy asked.

"Well maybe not this first one since I know you're good girls. Not like what I've found while patrolling the dorm rooms."

"What have you found in the dorms?" Amy asked.

"As always, girls in the boys' dorm and boys in the girls' dorm, usually up to no good."

"Tina," I said absently, and then I caught myself because I hadn't meant to tell on her.

"Yeah, she was one of them," Mindy said. "That girl! I had to throw this one boy out of her room twice yesterday! After the second time, we called his parents and sent him straight home."

"But Tina didn't get sent home?" I asked.

"Well you know she's inactive," Mindy said, "so we figured that she'd be better off staying here where she might be inspired to start coming to church more regularly. And since this sort of thing is usually the boy's idea anyway, we were thinking that with his bad influence gone she'd behave herself."

"Are you really sure that it was mostly his idea?" I asked. From what little I had overheard of her conversation the other day, she had seemed pretty enthusiastic about it.

"Obviously you can never be sure," replied Mindy, "but that's the way it usually goes. A girl wants a boyfriend so badly that when she finds one she usually goes along with what he says, just to please him. And that means that a lot of times girls let themselves get into situations where they can get taken advantage of. Like they were talking about in that 'Sexual Purity' lesson."

"You were in the sexual purity class?" I asked.

"I sat in on one of the sessions," Mindy said, "and it's really true that part at the end about how things just happen when you let yourself get into a bad situation. My only complaint was that in the story the teacher just assumed that the blame should be shared equally by the boy and the girl, when that isn't always the case."

"But it must be that sometimes the girl is just as willing as the boy, or even more, don't you think?" I asked. I couldn't help but think about how if I got into a "bad situation" with Y, I would hardly be an unwilling participant.

"Maybe," Mindy replied, "but really it's almost always the boy. After all, because of the way hormones work, the boy wants it more. And the girl has more to lose because she could get pregnant."

I had to agree with that last bit at least about pregnancy. If the couple used a condom of course there would be no problem, or at least a lot less risk of one. But how could you possibly have a condom with you unless you were *planning* to have sex? Obviously you couldn't set off on a date with the intention of committing a grave sin. So in fact when push comes to shove, a lot of those stories like the one the sexual purity teacher told us probably ended with the girl refusing, or at least trying to. And if fornication is already the worst you can possibly commit short of murder, how much worse could that make it in the guy's mind if the girl wasn't one hundred percent willing at the last minute?

"Anyway, enough about all this nasty business," Mindy said. "Did you guys get any news about how your little boyfriends liked the cookies?"

"No, we didn't hear anything," said Amy, "but we were thinking that they just didn't tell anyone about them so that they wouldn't have to share them."

"Ah, yeah, that's probably what happened," said Mindy.

All of the sudden we noticed that a bunch of kids were streaming out of the building and milling around. Mindy looked at her watch. "Oh, look, the first class period's over. Now I want you both to go to your next class, and don't let me catch you playing hooky again because I won't be so forgiving the second time."

After Mindy's admonition I couldn't very well skip my next class, so I went to the classroom and took a seat in the back. After a minute or two, Tom came in and took the seat next to me.

"Hi, Lynn," he said. "This is quite a coincidence. Here we are having a 'Faith and Prayer' class when we were just talking about this same subject last night."

I didn't think that it was very much of a coincidence since faith and prayer were obviously topics that are bound to come up frequently at a religious conference, but I didn't bother to contradict him. I figured I would stop beating around the bush and ask him directly the question that was on everyone's mind.

"I was wondering," I began, "not to ask you a personal question or anything, but are you really serious about joining the church, or are you just pretending so that Lara will like you?"

"I'll admit I'm interested in her," he replied, "but I really mean it about feeling that the church is true."

"That's good news," I said. I wasn't sure I believed him. Or more precisely I wasn't sure that he really believed what he was saying. If he was in love with Lara, and she wanted to convert him to Mormonism, then that would present a very powerful motivation for him to convince himself that he was really feeling the spirit.

The lesson turned out to be exactly what I expected it would be. The teacher focused it around the scripture in the *Doctrine & Covenants*, section 9, verse 8: "But, behold, I say unto you, that you must study it out in your mind; then you must ask me if it be right, and if it is right I will cause that your bosom shall burn within you; therefore you shall feel that it is right." She told us that although this message appears to be directed to converts, really it is directed to all of us because even lifetime members need to convert themselves and work on building and strengthening their testimonies. She then challenged us each to read the *Book of Mormon* thoroughly and prayerfully, and promised us that then Heavenly Father would give us a sure knowledge that it was true.

I felt frustrated by this message. I'd read the *Book of Mormon* carefully and intently, all the way through, and I had certainly prayed diligently. And yet Heavenly Father kept witnessing to everyone else and not to me. Didn't He love me? Was I not strong enough spiritually to receive His message?

The teacher continued by reading to us Moroni 10:4 from the *Book of Mormon* about how we should approach the question, namely "with a sincere heart, with real intent, having faith in Christ." She said that to have the proper spirit in our hearts, we needed to free ourselves from the cares of the world and come to God in purity, having repented of our sins.

I started to have a sinking feeling. It's because of my own weakness, I thought. If I were more righteous, I'd be receiving the message like everyone else. Even Tom has received the "burning in the bosom." I was the one that was deluding myself, not him. I resolved to study the *Book of Mormon* more thoroughly and pray harder and repent better. Then I knew I would receive a sure knowledge of the truthfulness of the gospel.

"Wow, that was a powerful message," Tom said at the end of class.

"Yeah," I replied.

"I could really feel the spirit when she spoke, couldn't you?" he asked.

"Yes, the spirit was very strong," I said.

"Well, I'm going to tell Lara that I've finally decided. I'm ready to pass through the waters of baptism," he said. "See you later."

"Good for you," I said. "I'll see you around."

* * *

Our lunch group this time was down to me, Amy, and Tammy. Annette and Jenny were sitting with Tony and some boys from his ward, and April, Cookie, and Alexandra were all sitting with Andrew and Dan. Since it appeared to be 'eat lunch with the boys day' I looked around for Bill, but I couldn't find him. I saw Y and Z off at a table by themselves, but we weren't exactly invited to go sit by them. Then I looked for Tom and Greg, and saw that they were sitting with Kimberly and Lara.

"Well it looks like we've been abandoned," I said.

"Yeah, and I'm absolutely furious about it!" Amy said. "If that Greg thinks that he can be with Kimberly whenever she's free and then come running to me whenever she's not, then he's got another thing coming! He's not so cute to be worth putting up with treatment like that!"

"Yeah, you're better off without him," I said. "We probably were never going to see him again after Youth Conference is over anyway."

"How come today all of the sudden they're having lunch together?" Amy asked, still clearly annoyed.

"It's probably because of Tom," I said. "He was in my last class with me, and he said that he's decided to go through with it and get baptized. So Lara's undoubtedly putting in an extra effort to encourage him in his decision."

"Jeez, what a fool!" Amy said. "Can't he see that she's not interested in him? He's a nerdy guy and she has a million totally hot boyfriends. The second he's been baptized she's gonna drop him like a hot potato!"

"Amy!" Tammy interjected. "We should be happy for him that he's come to see the truthfulness of the gospel!"

Amy grumbled something in agreement and then didn't really say anything for the rest of lunch.

"I'm really not looking forward to the sports this afternoon," I said to break the silence.

"Well then your prayers have been answered," said Tammy. "Look outside." I looked across out the window and saw that it was pouring rain. It was really coming down.

"Wow, I guess my prayers *have* been answered," I said. "Or at least they would have been if it had occurred to me to pray for rain."

"Well, probably some other kid who hates sports thought of it," she said. She seemed to be kidding, but I wasn't sure.

An announcement came over the loudspeaker that because of the rain the games would be held in the main gymnasium. We were told to all meet back there and bring our scriptures.

"Well, if we have to bring our scriptures it's probably not going to be sports," I said, but I couldn't help but feel that that was a bad sign for what the activity might turn out to be.

So we went back to the dorms and grabbed our scriptures and put on our t-shirts, and then we went to the main gymnasium and found our team. I looked all around the room to see if I could spot Bill.

"I still can't find Bill," I said to Amy.

"Yeah, I haven't seen him since last night," she said.

"I wonder which team he's on," I said, looking around some more.

Amy looked a little surprised by this. "But, he's on our team," she said. "Don't you remember him introducing himself yesterday?"

"Really? He's on our team?" I asked. "Wow, I must not have been paying very close attention! I didn't notice him at all."

"I think that that guy's his roommate," Amy said pointing to one of the other guys on our team. "Maybe he knows what became of him."

So we went over and asked the roommate if he knew where Bill was.

"Oh, he had to go home early," the guy said. "He had a really bad asthma attack this morning."

"Oh, no, that's terrible!" I said.

"It happens every now and then," the roommate said. "You shouldn't worry too hard about it, he'll be okay."

I looked across the room and saw Annette flirting with her new boyfriend Tony. This is just great, I thought. My little sister meets someone wonderful, and all I can attract is a sci-fi-computer nerd with bad asthma!

One of the adult leaders then took a microphone and announced that this afternoon's activity would be a scripture-chase tournament, and he put up a big piece of poster-board with a tournament tree drawn on it indicating which teams would be playing which other teams. Our individual team leaders had us set up chairs in various parts of the room.

The announcement of a scripture-chase wasn't too bad of news. It wasn't my favorite thing in the universe, but I'd rather be playing that than soccer or (heaven-forbid!) volleyball. In my early-morning seminary class, I was reasonably good at scripture-chasing.

The idea of the game was that we learn a set of really important scriptures from the book we're studying that year, the teacher gives a clue for one of the scriptures we've learned, and we race to find the correct scripture in the book. The tournament would undoubtedly be on the *Doctrine & Covenants* and the *Pearl of Great Price* since that was what we had studied this past year. All of the kids in the church studied the same book the same year on a four-year cycle: *Old Testament*, *New Testament*, *Book of Mormon*, and *D&C & PoGP*.

The very first team that my team was scheduled to play was the red team, which meant that our first match would be against Y and Z. I did okay at finding some of the scriptures, and Y was at about my same level. I looked wistfully over at him while we were playing—he was so cute while scripture-chasing! Z, on the other hand, was a master of scripture-chasing (as I already knew from seminary), and he kept finding the scriptures first over and over. To make matters worse, there was also a girl on their team who was essentially just as fast, so the competition ended up being between the two of them rather than between their team and our team. They beat us easily and moved up to the next level of the tournament.

In the next round, we played the purple team, who had also lost their first round. It wasn't clear to me whether this was supposed to be a double-elimination tournament or whether they just had us keep playing to keep us busy. It hardly mattered, as the purple team also beat us.

The third round was already the championship round since there were only eight teams to begin with. It ended up being the red team versus the orange team. For this match they put the two opposing teams in the center of the room and just had the rest of us watch. Annette and Jenny were on the orange team. Annette looked especially nervous because she hadn't attended seminary this past year since she had just finished the eighth grade and seminary doesn't start until ninth grade. So she really didn't know any of the scriptures at all. But it didn't matter because her team had some people on it who were like lightning, so no one noticed that after each clue Annette was just flipping through her book pretending to look for the right scripture.

The real contest was between the two champs on the red team and three star players on the orange team. But Y was holding his own, and got a couple of them first for his team. He was of course the one I was watching most closely and rooting for. The teams ended up being very evenly matched and were neck-and-neck right up to the end.

After some time, the teacher announced that the next clue was the tie-breaker that would win the tournament. The clue was "your bosom shall burn." I know that one, I thought. After what seemed like less than a second, Y flipped to the page and raised his hand. When called upon, he showed them *D&C* 9:8. Y had won the tournament for his team! The whole gym applauded, and I did most of all. This'll give me something to say to him at the dance tonight, I thought. I'll be sure to find him and compliment him on his masterful performance in the scripture-chase.

* * *

For that night's dance, the last dance of the conference, Amy and I were more resolved than ever to talk to Y and Z and dance with

them. This would be our last chance of the conference to get together with our true loves, and besides that our other prospects hadn't really panned out.

The beginning of the dance didn't offer us any more obvious openings than the previous two dances had. We realized that we didn't really have much choice in the matter: if we wanted to talk to them, we were just going to have to get up the nerve and walk over to them and start talking. It shouldn't be so hard! People just walk up to other people they know and start conversations every day. Why couldn't we bring ourselves to do it?

We figured that some compliments about the scripture chase would be a good place to start, but before approaching them we decided to try to prepare some clever and witty comments that we could have on hand. Unfortunately even after a good chunk of the dance had passed, we still hadn't thought of anything witty.

After a while we noticed that we couldn't find Y and Z in the dance hall anymore, so we went out into the hallway to look for them. When we discovered where they were, we realized that our luck had changed. Y and Z were sitting out in the foyer having a conversation with Dan, Andrew, April, Cookie, and Steve (another guy from our ward). This was perfect because there was no reason at all why we couldn't just walk up and join right into their conversation.

So we walked in and sat down, and everyone said hi to us. Y and Z even sort of nodded to acknowledge our presence. We found that they were all talking about plans for what we might do for this year's road show, which was something that April and I had already started brainstorming on a few weeks ago.

April was describing how we had been thinking for our ward's skit in the road show we might do something along the lines of the "Fractured Fairy Tales" from the classic *Rocky & Bullwinkle* cartoon shows. Y said that he thought that that was a good idea, and April told him that I was the one who had thought of it (which was true!).

He responded by kind of smiling and nodding to me as he said "ah." I was in heaven. This couldn't be going any better!

Everyone started throwing out ideas for different fairy tales and how we could fracture them and how we could combine them into one coherent skit. Z offered to be the "Mountie" Dudley Do-Right and ride in at the end. Y got out his notebook and started taking notes on what people were saying and also started drawing some preliminary sketches for the sets. His rough sketches were fantastic, and his long slender hands were so beautiful as he drew them. I didn't want it to end—this was going to be the best road show ever.

But of course we couldn't spend the whole evening in the foyer, and after a while April and Andrew decided to go back into the dance. That kind of broke up the whole party, so we each went our separate ways. Amy and I could barely contain our excitement. We rushed to the ladies' room to fix up our hair and compare notes.

"This is so fantastic—they're finally starting to notice us!" I said to her.

"I know! I can't believe it!" she gushed.

We took the time to get our hair and make-up absolutely perfect to be extra-gorgeous when we got back out into the dance hall. We then set ourselves up way off to one side of the room to avoid being asked to dance by any other boys. Not that there was much danger. Tom and Greg were dancing with Lara and Kimberly, and we hadn't really met anyone else. We knew that we needed to cross the room and go ask Y and Z to dance, but even after that fabulous exchange in the foyer, we were still too nervous to approach them.

All of the sudden, the DJ announced the last song of the night. And what's more, it was our song: *Lady in Red*. We had to go immediately and ask them to dance.

Then tragedy struck. Y and Z walked straight up to two girls that were standing near them—two girls that we had never seen before—and asked them to dance! We had never seen them ask any girls to dance before, and they had to choose our very last opportunity of Youth Conference to do it! We were crestfallen. We didn't know what else to do, so we just slipped back to our little corner of the dance hall and watched.

Everyone we knew was dancing the last dance with someone. Tom and Greg were still dancing with Lara and Kimberly. Annette was dancing with Tony, and it looked like Jenny had taken up with one of Tony's friends. April was with Andrew of course, and Alexandra was still with Matt from Ely. Even Tammy and Cookie had found boys to dance the last dance with although we didn't know precisely how or when that had happened. We couldn't stand it anymore, so we just headed back to our dorm room without even offering to help with the clean-up.

Back in our dorm room, we managed to get our spirits back up a bit. So we hadn't succeeded in dancing with our true loves. But at least we were making progress! We'd shared a whole conversation with them! True, Y hadn't said anything directly to me except "ah" the entire time, but it was a start! They were on the road to falling in love with us, we were certain of it. So we fell asleep with sweet dreams of our beautiful future boyfriends in our heads.

* * *

The next morning after breakfast a huge Sacrament Meeting had been set up for us in the room that had served as the dance hall. The organizers felt that since many people would miss church that day as some had come from places six hours away or more, we should all have a Sacrament Meeting before setting off. But fortunately in the interest of time they didn't plan us a session of Sunday school or Young Women's. Also in the interest of time, they had us check out of our rooms and pack all of our things into the buses before the meeting.

Amy and I lost track of time chatting, so we got to the meeting late and slipped into the very back. There weren't enough chairs back there, so we had to kind of just lean against the back wall. It turned

out that Y and Z were sitting right in front of us in the very back row of chairs with Y on the aisle and Z one chair in.

The meeting was probably as dull as Sacrament Meeting usually is, but I didn't know because I didn't hear a word of it. I was too busy watching Y and daydreaming. But I perked up a bit during the closing remarks. After thanking everyone who worked so hard on the conference, the bishop who had directed the organization of the conference announced that he wanted to award a prize to the team that had done such a fantastic job of learning the *D & C* and had won the previous day's scripture chase. The prize was a little enameled pin for each member of the team, which he handed to a team representative at the head of the room to distribute to his teammates.

This was my big chance to say something to him. I took a few steps forward, put one finger on Y's knee, looked straight at him and said, "You really earned that for your team David, getting the winning scripture and all."

Y just looked at me, then he looked at my one finger, and then he looked back up at me. He did not say a single word. He just had this shocked expression on his face as if to say, "What are doing? How dare you touch me?"

I slowly backed up, and then I slipped out the back door and down the hall into the ladies' room. I breathed deeply and tried to regain my composure. Do not cry, do not cry, I told myself, you have to get on the bus any minute, do not cry. After a few more deep breaths, I was ready to go back out. I could hear them singing the closing hymn which signaled that it was almost time to go, so I started walking towards my bus.

Soon all of the other kids started streaming out of the building and moving towards their buses. I stood by the bus and waited for Amy. Mindy walked past me with a big smile on her face and said, "Another great year at Youth Conference, huh?"

And we got on the bus and went home.

Characters in Youth Conference

Laurels

April

Alexandra

Cookie

Tina

Claire

Lara

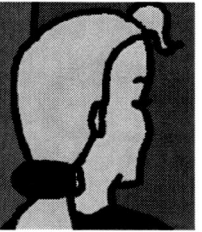

Kimberly

Miamaids

Lynn

Amy

Jenny

Annette

Tammy

Boys from Lynn's Ward

Andrew   *Dan*   *Peter, "Z"*   *David, "Y"*

Other Boys

Tom   *Greg*   *Bill*

The Chaperone

Mindy

III. Saturday's Warrior

Jill

9. THURSDAY AFTERNOON

"WELL, HERE IT IS—jumping-off point, and here we are one breath away from a sick world that's been crying out for what we can give it: truth! freedom! salvation!"

He was perfect for the part. I watched as Walter and Jake stood around the piano singing their number and Pinky played. Walter sang his part with gusto. He seemed to be happy to have been cast in this role, but really it was more that the production was lucky to have him than vice-versa.

There were so many male singing roles in the play that Pinky had had trouble filling them all. Basically any guy that was willing and able to sing and dance on stage was welcome to do so. I knew this because when Pinky called me up to tell me about my part, she asked if my older brother Rex would be willing to play one of the kids in the gang. I figured she must have been pretty desperate to get more guys in the chorus if she was to the point of offering parts to people like Rex who had two left feet and couldn't sing a note. Since he would have to bring me to the rehearsals anyway it made sense that he should participate, but he was more interested in the technical stuff so he offered to do the lighting instead.

It was so lucky for us all that Walter was back from his first year of college and wouldn't be setting off for his mission until after the production was over. He was born to be in the spotlight. In my mind I could picture him basking in it on stage. Plus he seemed pretty excited about his upcoming mission, so it was cool to have him playing the part of a missionary. Even his first name—Walter—was the same as the character's name, Wally. Really it couldn't have been more perfect.

"Okay, one more time from the top," said Pinky. "Oh, and I know a lot of us learned these songs from listening to the original cast recording, but really you don't have to rehearse the spoken part over the intro this time."

Everybody laughed at that as Pinky started to play again. Walter laughed at himself along with everyone else. He knew he liked to ham it up and wasn't ashamed to admit it. The eyes of every girl in the room were on him. Even with Pinky's big flaming red hairdo and bright-colored clothing and million bangles, she seemed drab and uninteresting next to Walter. I imagined that all of the other girls were probably as in love with him as I was. How could they not be? With his gorgeous smile and his playful manner....

Of course I had no shot with him outside of the realm of fantasy. He could have his pick of any girl, and I couldn't think of anything I could do that would make him notice me over the others. On the other hand, there had been some pretty serious competition among the girls for the parts in the play, and I hadn't done too badly there.

I was proud to have been chosen for the role of "Alice." It wasn't that important a character, but I got to be in a bunch of fun musical numbers such as *Daddy's Nose* and *He's Just a Friend,* plus I had a solo verse in the song *Pulling Together.*

There weren't that many girls' roles that were more important than mine—just the roles of Pam and Julie, and in our production Pam actually had two people to play her. Pinky had given the part to both Laura and Linda Hobbs who were identical twins. Pinky must have figured that she couldn't choose just one of them for the part without the other one going ballistic, so she told them they'd have to have identical hair and costumes and let them divide their stage time among themselves.

In theory Pinky might have solved the problem of Laura and Linda both wanting roles by having one of them play Pam and the other play Julie. But that was out of the question since the role of Julie obviously had to go to Charlene Brooks, who was by far the best singer and dancer in the school. Apparently Charlene had even been in a beauty pageant once and hadn't done too badly according to a conversation of Laura and Linda I had overheard in the bathroom during the auditions. They had been saying that Charlene's talent entry for the pageant was a song and dance routine that was so fantastic that she surely would have won the pageant if only she had lost a little weight.

Charlene didn't seem fat at all to me—she was thinner than Laura and Linda, for example—but I supposed that they had different standards for this sort of thing in the beauty pageant world.

As soon as Walter and Jake were done with the second run through of their number, Pinky gathered the chorus of kids in the gang around the piano to sing *Summer of Fair Weather.* This wasn't really a formal rehearsal. Since it was the very first rehearsal, it was more a fun getting-to-know-you thing.

Walter walked away from the piano and stood over by the retractable vinyl accordion-wall that separated the main part of the room from the baptismal font. The entire production would be taking place here in this stake center where a lot of people had their ordinary church meetings every week. Seeing Walter unoccupied, Laura and Linda both immediately rushed over to him to compliment him on his singing. I was hoping to talk to him myself as well, but I knew that Laura and Linda wouldn't welcome me into their conversation.

I could hear Walter thanking them sweetly and politely for their compliments. It sounded like he was trying to be humble—after all, the song he'd been doing was called *Humble Way*—but it was clear that he was in his element with this type of attention.

Before the rehearsal broke up I got to do a run-through of one of my numbers as well, but I didn't get a chance to talk with Walter. The best I got was that at one point he noticed me smiling at him and responded by winking at me. That made me happy as it seemed like a promising sign for the future. Of course he probably didn't even know who I was—I mostly only knew him from observing him from a distance. Still, we were both in the number *He's Just a Friend*, so I figured we'd have plenty of opportunity to get to know each other better over the course of the next several weeks of rehearsals.

As Rex and I were getting into the car to go home, I noticed a lady sitting on the grass just outside the stake center, smoking a cigarette.

"Look, that lady's smoking right outside the church building!" I said to Rex.

"What?" he asked. He looked over at the lady and then back at me with a puzzled expression. "That's Jake's mom. Don't you remember Pinky introducing her? She's involved in Pinky's community theater group and she's going to be acting as the assistant director for this play."

"Won't that be a little weird?" I asked. "I mean, doing a church play in a church building, and the assistant director sneaking out for a smoke all the time?"

"Well, aren't you little miss judgmental today?" asked Rex. "In fact, she's a really nice lady, and she's tried to quit smoking a million times. Attitudes like yours are the very reason she never goes to church. According to Jake, she gets really upset about the way everyone in her ward looks down their noses at her when they catch the slightest odor of tobacco on her clothes, so she can't stand to attend Sunday services. Then he says she ends up not bothering with any of the other commandments, which just makes the ward gossip about her worse, and the whole thing becomes a vicious cycle."

"That's too bad," I said. I felt kind of guilty judging her like that exactly the way the people from her ward had done, but I didn't know what else to say about it.

At dinner Mom wanted to know all of the details of what had happened at the rehearsal and which of our friends had been cast in which roles. I felt sorry for my little sister Joy here because she had tried out for the part of Shelley and hadn't gotten it. But that really wasn't my fault, and I couldn't help but want to tell my mom all about the production and how excited I was about it.

My part of telling Mom about my friends' roles was pretty short since none of my friends had gotten parts. I was the only person from my whole grade who had gotten any part other than just being cast in the chorus, either the angel chorus or the chorus of rebellious kids. Rex however had plenty to recount since practically all of the starring roles had gone to kids from his grade, that is people who had just graduated from high school this past Spring.

Rex's two best friends, Ben and Jake, had both gotten important parts. In fact Ben had landed the starring role of Jimmy. Ben's girlfriend, Paige, had gotten a speaking role as one of the kids in the gang. Her part had vocal solos in both the songs *Zero Population* and *Summer of Fair Weather* even though her character didn't have a name other than "first girl."

Mom said that it seemed appropriate for Paige to play one of the bad guys since she could hardly play one of the wholesome kids with her outlandish "goth" look. Rex didn't comment on that, but I felt a little less guilty about having been judgmental earlier since it was clear where I'd gotten it from if my mom was doing it too.

"I suppose Jake's in the gang too," said Mom. "Let me guess— they cast him as the gang leader, Mack. Right?"

Rex laughed. "Nope, you're not even close. Jake got cast as one of the two missionaries."

Mom's eyes widened. "Really?" she asked. Then she laughed sardonically. "So he's going to ride up to the theater on his motorcycle and take off his leather jacket and trade it in for a missionary suit and tie?"

"Yeah, I guess so," said Rex in a perfectly serious tone.

"How did that happen?" asked Mom.

"I don't know," said Rex. "Maybe his mom wanted him playing a missionary. She's the assistant director of the production and surely helped out with the casting."

"Jake's mom wanted him to play a missionary?" asked Mom. "Now I've heard everything! Is this the same Jake's mom that smokes and drinks and swears like a sailor?"

"Mom," said Rex, annoyed. "Jake's mom is happy for him that he's taking more of an interest in the church these days. You know very well that he's going to be attending BYU this Fall."

"I wish you would go there too, Rex, like Kathy, since all your friends are going there," said Mom.

Rex closed his eyes for a moment, in exasperation. "Not this again," he said. "Mom, I've lived my whole life here in Utah Valley looking at these same mountains. Do you have to begrudge me my opportunity to get out and see the world?"

"You'll see the world when you're off on your mission," said Mom.

Dad sat back and folded his arms across his chest. He didn't intervene, but we'd had this discussion enough times that I knew what he was thinking. Dad felt that with Rex's grades and test scores it made sense to send him to a serious university. But I imagined that he was refraining from commenting because he didn't want to get into yet another debate with Mom about whether or not BYU was really "the Harvard of the West" as people liked to say it was.

Rex just looked at Mom for a second and then apparently decided to drop it and go back to their earlier discussion. "What were we talking about again?" he asked. "Oh, yeah, so Ben is playing Jimmy, and Jake is playing Elder Greene."

"And to play Wally they found a guy who's actually named Walter," I piped up.

"Another friend of yours from school?" Mom asked Rex.

"Not really. He was in the grade between my grade and Kathy's so I don't know him all that well." Turning to Kathy, he asked "Do you remember him? Walter Smith?"

"Oh yeah," said Kathy. "Cute guy. I didn't really know him personally, but I remember that he was pretty good-looking."

Hearing that, I felt pretty stupid for being so attached to him. After all, if he was known far and wide for his good looks, how could I imagine that there was even the remotest possibility that he would be interested in some plain, shy little fifteen-year-old kid like me? To think I'd allowed myself to get my hopes up on the strength of one wink. I resolved then and there to try not to like him so much.

"So who did they get to play Mack if it's not Jake?" asked Mom.

"Andy Ross," replied Rex. "You don't know him. He's a nice guy. He says he's going to grow a goatee for the part so he'll look more evil." Rex laughed a little at that. "Let's see, who else is there? Oh yeah, Pam is being played jointly by a pair of identical twins, Laura and Linda Hobbs. Oh, and get this—this is funny—Todd and Julie are being played by Noah and Charlene Brooks! Can you believe that? Brother and sister, and they have to sing all of these love duets to each other!" Everyone laughed at the thought of that.

"It kind of makes sense, though," said Kathy. "They're probably the two best singers in the school, and those are the two most important singing roles."

"True," said Rex. Then with a smile he added "Sometimes I'm glad I can't sing actually."

"Mom, I'm done, can I go play?" asked my little brother Jared.

"Okay, honey. Don't forget to clear your plate," said Mom.

Jared put his plate and cup and silverware in the dishwasher and ran off.

"Is that everyone?" Mom asked Rex.

"I think so," Rex replied. "The parents and the other kids in the family are being played by people from Pinky's community theater group. I don't think you know them."

Joy then got up and cleared her plate as Jared had done and left. I felt bad for her that she had had to sit through this discussion all through dinner after not getting a part herself, and I knew she'd be hearing a lot more about it in the weeks to come. I cleared my own plate and went up to the bedroom I shared with her.

Joy was on the bed reading *Godel, Escher, Bach*. I had just finished reading the book myself on Rex's recommendation, and I'd in turn told Joy about it and suggested it to her. It made me smile to see she'd listened to my advice.

"I guess you'll have to pass that book along to Jared next when you're done with it," I said.

"Are you kidding?" Joy asked. "Jared would never read a book like this one. The kid's as dumb as a post. I don't know how he ended up in the same family with you and me and Rex."

"So what do you think of the book so far?" I asked.

"Seems pretty interesting," she replied. "Of course I've only read the first few chapters. I liked the dialog between Achilles and the Tortoise."

"There are dialogs like that all through the book," I said. "The Zen stuff is cool too." Joy didn't respond.

I wanted to make Joy feel better, so I invited her to come along on the babysitting job I had lined up for the following evening. We occasionally did babysitting jobs together just for fun, even though it meant splitting the money. Our plans seemed to cheer her up a bit, so I figured everything was okay.

10. Friday Evening

THE BABYSITTING JOB that I was splitting with Joy was at the house of the Jensens, who were non-members. It was fun having Joy along for a job like this one since it was one where the kids went to bed right off the bat, and all we had to do was hang out and be there to make sure nothing bad happened to them while their parents were gone.

This was a fantastic task since the Jensen's house was full of tempting delights. I almost would have been willing to pay to spend the evening there if I weren't being paid to do it.

First and foremost, the Jensens had cable. Our family could have afforded cable, but my dad hated TV on principle—he was always telling us how it rots our brains whenever he caught us watching it— so he certainly wasn't going to pay to have more television options piped in. I didn't care so much for TV that I was terribly disappointed about not having cable in general. What interested me was that in the evening cable meant the forbidden pleasure of R-rated movies.

At church they were reminding us practically every other week about how watching rated R movies is a sin, particularly ones that are full of nudity and sex, which were the only ones I wanted to watch. So on some level I felt like I shouldn't be doing it. But the opportunity didn't arise every single day, so on those occasions when I had the opportunity, I couldn't bring myself to pass it up.

Also, I felt less bad about it knowing that Joy was the same way. She was always willing and ready to join me for this sort of entertainment.

As soon as the kids were in bed, we put on a promising-looking movie. The film itself looked pretty stupid actually, so we just kind of ran it softly in the background waiting for the good parts. In the meantime, we started in on Mrs. Jensen's stack of back issues of *Cosmopolitan* magazine.

It seemed like every single issue of Cosmo had at least one article about sex. They were mostly various types of advice and suggestions. I couldn't really judge whether the advice was any good or not, but I learned quite a lot about how the whole thing worked by piecing together tidbits from the different articles. Plus the sex articles were full of amusing sexual anecdotes. I hardly cared what point this or that

anecdote was supposed to illustrate. As long as it was kind of erotic, it was interesting.

The other marvelous wonder they had at the Jensen's house was this book called *The Joy of Sex*. If there were any gaps left in the sex education Joy and I were getting from Cosmo and nudie flicks, this book certainly went a long way towards filling them in. It amazed me that such a book could even exist. It was basically full of diagrams of people having sex in all sorts of positions. I figured it wasn't really pornography since it was just drawings. Every one was fascinating, and I'm sure I would have been happy to look at the book all day given the chance.

When the movie got to the good part, we turned up the volume and watched. It turned out that it was about some boys off at camp who snuck over to a nearby girls' camp and attempted to spy on the girls in the shower, etc. Some nonsense, really, but I found it riveting and arousing. In fact it was quite a standard fantasy. When we were at girls' camp there were a number of camp songs centered on this same theme that the girls would sing when there were no adult leaders around to make us stick to the wholesome songs. Unfortunately in all my years at girls' camp there'd never been a boys' camp nearby enough for such an excursion. Just a bunch of girls sitting around talking about boys and giggling.

Later the Jensens came home and paid us and Mrs. Jensen took us home. It wasn't much money to split, but we'd had fun. Anyway, for spending money I also had my gardening job at Sister Sanderson's house.

When I got into bed of course I reviewed the images from the movie and from the magazines in my head. That's not to say that these non-members had corrupted a pure little Mormon girl with their free access to dirty materials. Babysitting jobs like this one simplified the matter, but you can always find interesting information if you're on the lookout for it. For example my own mother sometimes bought some fashion magazines for old married ladies that weren't quite on par with *Cosmopolitan* but still had some decent sex articles. Plus my parents had various medical and anatomy books which—while they couldn't compare to *The Joy of Sex*—still had some pretty good diagrams and articles.

One time for fun years earlier I had even looked up "sex" in the encyclopedia. That article was where I first learned the word masturbation. Actually it kind of shocked and embarrassed me to read it because up until that point it had never occurred to me that there was a word for it, yet I knew immediately what it was. It was at that moment that it really hit me that it must be a sin, although I had kind of suspected it all along.

There was one troubling thing that I had learned in Sunday School about repentance, namely that in order to work it had to be completely sincere, and that therefore falling back into the same sin would undo earlier repentance for it. I was always sorry, but I was never able to attain the level of sincerity necessary to completely reform. Even going a full week took more resolve than I could usually muster.

The only hope I could see on the horizon was that in another five years or so I would be old enough to get married, and then it wouldn't be a sin to have all of sex for real. That would finally cure this problem and I would be free to become righteous enough to fully live the gospel as Heavenly Father intended.

* * *

When Tuesday rolled around, I was really psyched to go to my rehearsal. This time we were going to get down to business on learning the musical numbers and dances for real.

Right off the bat we broke into small groups to practice the various numbers in different rooms. I went with the other family members to practice the number *Daddy's Nose* and Walter and Jake went to a different room to practice *Humble Way*.

I was actually kind of glad to be off doing something interesting away from Walter so that I wouldn't be tempted to just watch him and think about him. I was serious about wanting to be less in love with him since it was hopeless that anything would ever come of it.

Learning the dance to *Daddy's Nose* worked like a charm to take my mind off him since the dance was so elaborate. Fortunately I'd taken dance classes since I was a kid—both modern and ballet—so it was no problem for me to learn the steps. The girl who played Shelley was having a lot of trouble, though, which kind of annoyed me because I couldn't help but feel like my sister Joy, who had taken dance classes with me, would have done a better job. But then I figured that it wasn't really this girl's fault that she had been chosen over Joy, so I determined to be patient with her and to try to help and encourage her as much as possible.

Jake's mom had worked out all of the choreography for the number. She showed us what to do. It turned out that Rex was right that she was a really nice lady. I felt bad that my first reaction had been to judge her for her "Word of Wisdom problems" (i.e. smoking) the way the people from her ward and my mom had done.

I learned that Jake's mom's name was "Ms. Lawrence," which was interesting since Jake's last name was Winchester. Of course it wasn't too surprising that Jake and his mom didn't have the same last name since I knew that Jake's parents had gotten divorced when he was little.

Ms. Lawrence had us all call her by her first name, Grace. She probably did it to be like Pinky, who always had everyone in all of her productions call her by her first name. Pinky was a teacher at the high school, so in theory people were supposed to call her "Ms. Pinkerton," but that wasn't allowed during rehearsals of any production either by the high school drama club or by the local community theater.

When we were done rehearsing *Daddy's Nose*, Pinky wanted to start on practicing the number *Will I Wait for You?* in which Walter played the guy leaving on his mission asking his girlfriend if she would wait for him and not marry someone else while he was gone. Charlene played the girlfriend, Julie. None of my scenes were being rehearsed at the moment, so I watched their number for a few minutes.

Jake's mom showed Walter and Charlene and the others the dance they were supposed to do. It was interesting, but watching Walter flirting with the beautiful Charlene between takes was too much for me, so I went off to try to find Rex.

Rex was in the room where the kids from the gang were practicing the number *Zero Population*. This was the song where the bad kids try to convince the Mormon kid Jimmy (played by Ben) that people really shouldn't have too many kids. It was one of Paige's two big numbers. For the moment, the kids were taking a break from performing the song and dance number and were working on blocking the scene that led up to it.

I sat down next to Rex on the orange industrial-carpet floor and leaned back against the whitewashed cinder-block wall. Paige seemed engrossed in reading her copy of the script.

"This is really wild!" said Paige, looking up. "This scene is completely different from the way I remember it from watching the video."

"Really? In what way?" asked Ben.

"Well, I've only seen the video a couple of times," said Paige, "but the way I remember it, the kids in the gang were telling Jimmy that the reason people shouldn't have big families is because that way they have less money to spend on themselves. I specifically remember them mentioning Porsches more than once as something you have to sacrifice in order to have a lot of kids. But I don't see anything like that in this version of the script."

"I've seen the video too," said Andy, "and now that you mention it, I think you're right that in it the gang was basically championing small families as being the way to go for the selfish and materialistic."

"Yet what's written here is exactly the opposite," said Paige.

"No Porsches?" I asked.

"Not at all, listen to this." Paige started reading, "First boy: Well, if we, the enlightened generation fail to save America, who will? Jimmy: America? First girl: Yeah, from sea to shining sea... heard of it?

Second boy: Once America the beautiful, now America the polluted! The depleted! First boy: The crowded! Mack: her slums crawling! Her suburbs sprawling! Second girl: Her voice calling 'help! Save me!'"

Paige looked up. "Isn't that strange? There's nothing in here about materialism at all. The gang's reasons for promoting 'zero population growth' are completely altruistic concerns about being responsible for future generations!"

"Well the video is more recent than this version of the script," said Andy, "so they must have changed the scene."

"Not surprising," said Ben. "It's kind of hard here to tell who's supposed to be good and who's supposed to be bad."

"I think that that may be one of the reasons nobody performs this play anymore," said Rex. Then with a smile he added "except us."

"You may be right," said Paige.

"Of course I am," replied Rex. "People like this play because the music is catchy, but in reality the story is an embarrassment to the church. The bad guys are good and the good guys are awful! This scene is only the most flagrant example, but the whole play is like that.

"Think about it," he continued. "This guy Jimmy—he's what? Eighteen or nineteen years old? All he does is go on a road trip with his friends to San Francisco or something, and his parents completely flip out! They're about to disown him and write him off as a failure, and he hasn't even really left the church or anything.

"Then there's the Mormon family with their seven kids. Of course the parents don't give the kids individual attention, and the kids are always fighting and picking on each other. I don't know if that's supposed to be comedy or realism or what. And the supposedly faithful Mormon girl who is waiting for her missionary dumps him! Twice! The second time taking up with the one guy that her missionary converted to Mormonism. Again the play is too honest here about the cruel realities of the church."

It was true actually that Charlene's character dumped Walter's character twice in the course of the play and wound up in the end with Todd, the convert played by Charlene's brother Noah. Even though it was fiction, I felt kind of bad for Wally getting dumped like that while he was just trying to serve the Lord. Then I thought about how—since I was playing the younger sister of the girl who dumped him—I would logically be in the best position to catch him on the rebound...

As the kids went back to blocking the scene, I looked at Paige, all dressed in black from head to foot as usual, including her hair and lipstick. I wondered if she did it to be rebellious or just to get attention. If it was to get attention, it seemed to have worked since she had managed to land herself a hot boyfriend.

It was getting to the end of the time scheduled for the rehearsal, so Pinky gathered us all into the gymnasium to tell us some general stuff about how things were going to be organized. While we were all standing around listening to her, completely out of the blue Walter walked up to me with a big smile and quietly said "Hey Alice."

"Hi Wally," I replied in the same tone.

"I know your name's not really Alice," he said. "It's Jill, right?"

"That's right!" I said.

"See? I'm getting to know the cast here," he said. "You're the sister of the guy who's doing the lights, aren't you?"

"That's exactly right!" I said. I was a little surprised that he had taken enough of an interest in me to find all that out.

"Cool," he said, still speaking softly enough not to disturb the others from listening to Pinky. "Maybe next time we'll practice the number *He's Just a Friend* that we're both in together. That'll be fun." Then he flashed me the most beautiful smile I'd ever seen.

I couldn't believe it! My mind was racing trying to think of something clever to say back to him. But before I could come up with anything, Pinky finished her discourse about whatever it was she was talking about, and Rex came around and said "Let's go."

"Bye," I said sweetly to Walter.

"Bye, see you next time," he replied. Rex kind of nodded to acknowledge Walter and brought me back to the car.

On the way home in the car I was beside myself with joy. Any resolve I had had not to love him was shattered. He had spontaneously come over to chat with me! He was looking forward to seeing me again at our next rehearsal on Thursday! It was too good to be true!

* * *

During rehearsals over the course of the next few weeks, I had at least some individual attention from Walter essentially every time. I couldn't really be sure that that meant I was making progress with him, though, since he seemed to take time out to talk to each of the girls in turn during each rehearsal. Basically whenever he wasn't actively rehearsing a scene, he would go find some girl or other to flirt with.

Walter seemed interested in Charlene most of all, but Laura and Linda each got their allotted attention from him, plus he had several favorites among the girls in the chorus. He even sometimes appeared to be flirting with Pinky or with Jake's mom. I figured that it must just be that his regular personality was like that.

One thing that was clear was that he didn't have one particular exclusive girlfriend. It was probably just because he was about to set off on his mission, so he didn't want to get too attached to any one girl only to have her dump him while he was away like what happened to his character in the play. That was fine with me since it was really no problem for me to wait until he got back from his mission before starting a serious relationship. After he got back I would still only be seventeen.

Meanwhile it looked like Rex was starting to develop an interest in Laura. He would hang out and watch her perform her scenes and then chat with her whenever she wasn't chatting with Walter.

The funny thing in my mind was how he would specifically seek out Laura and not Linda. Now that they had started doing their hair alike for the play, I could barely see any difference between them at all, and as far as I could tell they both had the same personality as well. So it wasn't clear to me why Rex would prefer one over the other. To be funny sometimes Laura and Linda would try to trick him as to which one was which, but he was very good at telling them apart so they never succeeded.

All this time I was still kind of half-heartedly trying to convince myself not to be in love with Walter. After all, I knew in that in reality there was no chance I would ever be his favorite. I wasn't as pretty as Charlene nor did I have big breasts like her. I didn't know if the latter was a consideration for him, but it was something I had noticed myself. Still, the fact that he paid attention to me so sweetly when we talked and the fact that I was treated to this attention at least twice a week made it difficult if not impossible for me to put him completely out of my mind.

Between rehearsals I would think of him constantly, particularly when I was doing my gardening job at Sister Sanderson's house. It was a solitary task, so I had plenty of opportunity to go over all of the adorable things he said to me and analyze them in my mind and plan other conversations to have with him. I thought of him during the day at home too and particularly at night.

At rehearsals I allowed myself to get into this bad habit of always keeping one eye on where Walter was and what he was doing, even when it was flirting with other girls, which was most of the time. One fateful Tuesday, however, he wandered off and I kind of lost track of him. As soon as the scene I was working on broke up, I walked around the building to see if I could find him.

When I got to the second foyer of the building which was on the side that I didn't normally go in by, I found him. He was asleep on the couch with his head on his folded jacket. His legs were bent as the couch wasn't long enough for him. Some light was coming in through the glass doors, but it was still somber because we weren't on the sunny side of the building.

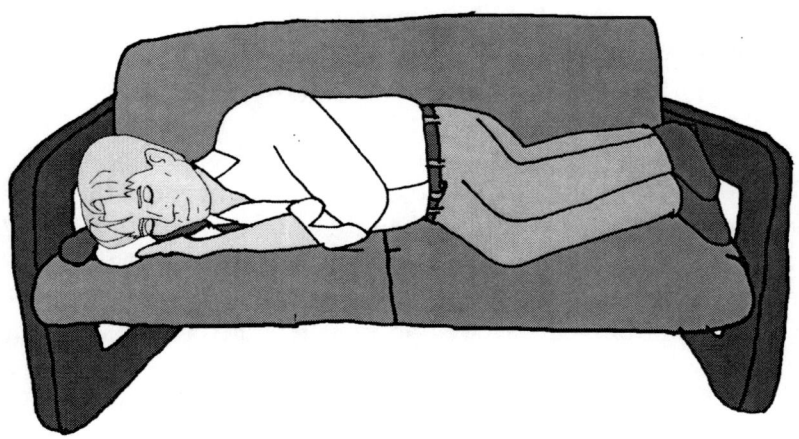

I was thrilled to have this unique opportunity to gaze at him. He was beautiful from one end to the other. He had straight sandy-blond hair framing his perfect face. He had long, dark eyelashes, which is a lovely quality for a man to have since nice eyelashes bring out one's eyes even for men, but of course men can't get away with faking it with mascara. His eyes were closed at the moment, but even like that they were pretty. His other features were exquisitely perfect as well, his cheekbones, his nose, his lips, even his ear and the line of his neck. He was a rare beauty—in all seriousness the type of person who could easily be a movie star or a model.

I took in the shape of his body, his exposed forearm and hand. I knew that Walter wasn't quite as tall as my brother Rex, but while Rex at eighteen still had the build of a scrawny teenager, nineteen-year-old Walter had the build of a man. He was neither excessively built-up nor remotely fat, but rather solid and athletic. Even his feet reminded me that he was an adult, wearing unadorned leather shoes instead of sneakers as most of the boys wore.

I knelt down beside him and was thinking of touching his face when he started to stir and opened his eyes. I jumped back, startled, which made him laugh a bit as he sat up.

"Hi there," he said. "I wasn't really asleep, I was just resting."

"Oh," I said, not really sure how to explain why I had been watching him so closely.

"I imagine you were thinking of playing a prank on me, like drawing on my face or putting my hand in water or something," he said laughing.

"Oh, no, I wouldn't do that."

"Come here and sit by me," he said, indicating the spot next to him on the couch. He didn't have to ask twice. I sat down on the couch, and he immediately put his arm around me and pulled me close to him. I was amazed and delighted by his affectionate action as I had never before had any real indication that he might be interested in me at all.

"You're such a pretty girl, Jill," he said. "I've always thought so, and I know that you've noticed me too." He put his other hand around the back of my neck with his fingers through my hair.

Then he moved forward and began kissing me on the neck on the other side near the jawline. I put my arms around him as well. I could smell the faint, pleasant smell of his warm skin. It was pleasure beyond description to be held by him after having wished for it for so long.

With his hand that was around my waist he started to touch the skin of my back directly, under my shirt. He leaned in closer to me and started kissing me on the lips. That was when I started to feel something rubbing against my leg. I knew it couldn't be his hand because I could feel where both of his hands were. It could only be one thing. It so surprised me that I immediately pulled away from him and stood up.

He took my hands in his hands and looked up at me innocently. "Is something wrong?" he asked.

"No, of course not!" I said. I gave him another squeeze and a kiss on the lips and said, "But we have to get back to the rehearsal. People will come looking for us!" Then I ran off down the hall. I went all the way around the building—past all of the rooms where people were rehearsing various scenes—and went into the ladies' room on the far side.

I looked at myself in the mirror. I couldn't wipe the grin off my face even though I had already started kicking myself for running away like that. Why had I run away instead of enjoying the pleasure of the moment? Now I wished I was back in his arms. It was just that the whole thing was so new that it was hard for me to handle it all at once.

In the first place, I'd never been kissed by a boy before at all except for an awkward experiment with a neighbor boy when I was just a kid. So that alone was something new to be excited about. On top of that, it was Walter, who was my heart's one desire. I was thrilled that he had noticed me and was interested in me. Then to discover such concrete evidence that he was really attracted to me was this wonderful surprise that I hadn't even anticipated. Of course I'd read about guys getting erections, but finding out about it in the real world was a completely different experience from just fantasizing about it.

I figured I'd better come out of the bathroom, otherwise people really would come looking for me, so I went out to see if I was needed somewhere. The rehearsal was breaking up, and fortunately I hadn't been missed. I wanted to look around for Walter to say goodbye to him, but I ran into Rex first. Rex was ready to leave, and I couldn't very well ask him to wait around to give me a chance to go see Walter again, so I just left with him.

The next morning I went to my gardening job at Sister Sanderson's house as usual. She was an elderly neighbor who had had a passion for gardening her whole life, but was too frail to do it herself anymore, so she hired me to come by for an hour a day to work on her garden for her.

Part of Sister Sanderson's garden was a vegetable garden of course. She wasn't really interested in the vegetable garden though. It was clear that she only maintained it because it was a commandment to do so. The part she really loved was her rose garden.

When I arrived, I gave the vegetable garden a quick once-over and then set up the sprinkler. The sprinkler was fine for the vegetables, but Sister Sanderson liked me to water her rose bushes by hand with a watering can. This was a non-trivial task, so I got in some weight-lifting exercise while earning my pay.

The whole time I was gardening I couldn't stop thinking about what had happened the previous day. I could hardly believe it had really happened. Maybe I had been the one who had been asleep and dreaming.

I brought the heavy watering can over and carefully watered the first few rosebushes, inspecting them for new buds and shoots. The bush of white roses had two new buds, and one of the buds I had noticed the other day was starting to open. I knew it hadn't been a dream, though. He liked me, or at least he felt some attraction to me.

I wished I hadn't run away. I wished I was still there with him on the couch of the unlit foyer, holding him in my arms and caressing him and being caressed by him.

I inspected the leaves of the next rosebush for fungus. There was still a little, but it was getting better. I would probably have to put some more fungicide on it again today. I went back to fill the watering can again. All I wanted to do was to try to arrange another opportunity to be alone with him, to continue what we had been doing and more.

I watered the next rosebush and again inspected for new buds. It had a beautiful, perfect pink rose on it, just in the early stages of opening. I smelled its natural perfume as I imagined him running his hands over me. The funny thing was that I didn't feel at all guilty for wanting this. Logically I should be ashamed to want and to imagine such a thing, but I wasn't. I discovered that I wanted his touch so badly that I really didn't care if it was a sin or not. The fact that he seemed to desire me was what made all the difference.

As far as I knew I'd never been desired sexually by anyone before. I had only know desiring others. The idea that someone who was so much older and more beautiful could want me was amazing. I was certainly not as mature and developed as some of the other girls. But the fact that he had shown some attraction to me made me feel attractive.

I started trying to think of ways to get him alone again. The simplest would be just to go out on a date with him, but even if he were to ask me out, my parents wouldn't let me go since I wasn't sixteen yet. I could try to convince him to go off somewhere with me during a rehearsal, but there was nowhere private we could go where we wouldn't be discovered in the stake center. I thought perhaps we could arrange to secretly meet somewhere at another time, but I wasn't sure where or how to suggest it to him.

I then realized that I had finished watering all of the rosebushes without really being aware of what I was doing. I looked over at the back porch of the house and saw Sister Sanderson coming out and slowly walking towards her beloved rosebushes, leaning on her cane with each step. I went over and took her arm and let her lean on me.

"Thank you, dearie," she said, as I led her to the garden. She inspected the rosebushes one by one and commented on them, giving me additional instructions as to which branches to prune and which plant products to apply to which ones. Then she had me cut some roses for her to enjoy inside the house, and I led her back. I carried out the instructions she had given me, and then I put away the sprinkler from the vegetable garden and went home.

At Thursday's rehearsal, I was breathless with anticipation to see Walter again. He greeted me with a warm smile, but in fact it wasn't that much different from usual. I had made a point to wear a shorter skirt and a tighter blouse, and a few times I could have sworn I caught him looking, but I wasn't sure. He took time to chat with me between takes, but not any more frequently or affectionately than he ordinarily did.

I got the impression that that whole incident at the previous rehearsal really wasn't that big a deal for him. It was crazy that it was such a fixation for me. I absolutely had to come up with a way to get him alone again.

11. Sunday Evening

A S IF OUR USUAL three-hour services weren't sufficient, after dinner on Sunday Rex, Joy, and I had a youth fireside to attend at the bishop's house. Logically Rex shouldn't have been required to attend since he was eighteen and hence no longer in the youth program, but Mom insisted that she wanted him to go. Actually none of would have gone if we'd had a choice. So naturally we dragged our heels a bit getting there and arrived late.

When we got there it had already started. All of the couches and chairs in the living room were filled with kids. I waved to my friends Michelle and Alison, but there wasn't room for me to go sit by them.

The bishop's wife brought in some more chairs from the kitchen for us and set us up near the entry to the room. Fortunately our arrival didn't cause too much of a disturbance.

The speaker didn't interrupt his talk for us. By bad luck, his topic was morality—exactly the subject I least wanted to hear about. It probably wasn't that much of a coincidence actually since it seemed like this was a subject they were always harping about. By "morality" of course they meant sex, and how young people shouldn't be having it.

The speaker was explaining the importance of not getting too serious about one person when you're too young. He talked about how when you're sixteen and old enough to date, you should go mostly on double dates with a variety of people and do clean, wholesome activities like miniature golf. He explained how this was the best way to avoid being tempted while dating to do the things we shouldn't be doing.

This was really the last message in the world I wanted to hear. All I wanted was to date Walter seriously and exclusively and perhaps maybe do a few of the things we weren't supposed to be doing. I certainly had no interest in waiting until I turned sixteen and then going on a bunch of double-dates with a series of random guys I cared nothing about doing some nonsense like playing miniature golf.

On the other hand, I thought that perhaps that was why Walter was always flirting with all different girls rather than getting too serious about just one girl. This lesson came up all the time, and he was following it better than I was. It seemed that in addition to his beauty and charm he was also righteous.

Then the speaker started in on how a date shouldn't be about kissing and making out and certainly shouldn't be about "petting" or worse. Listening to this discourse I started feeling completely detached from the ideas I had grown up with. I'd heard all of this a hundred million times, but I no longer agreed with it. Sin or no sin, all I wanted was to hold him in my arms and to touch him and especially to be touched and desired by him. It was so forceful and present in my mind that I was ready to suffer for eternity to pay for it.

It didn't even phase me or change my resolve when the speaker read from the prophet Spencer W. Kimball's book *The Miracle of Forgiveness*, quoting the prophet David O. McKay as saying "Your virtue is worth more than your life. Please young folk, preserve your virtue even if you lose your lives."

Then, so as not to exclude the kids who had no sexual experience at all from feeling bad, the speaker started talking about how sinful it was to even think about sex. He told us we shouldn't allow Satan to tempt us to look at pornography or watch rated R movies and allow our minds to be filled with impure thoughts. He reminded us that our bodies are temples that should be clean places that we would be happy to invite Jesus to dwell in.

I looked all around the room. Essentially everyone looked at least a little bit uncomfortable to be forced to listen to such an embarrassing and intimate message. Even the bishop himself was kind of forcing a smile. His wife was the only one who was smiling sincerely and nodding enthusiastically. I felt kind of sorry for him and their kids.

I looked over at Rex and Joy and noticed that they looked as embarrassed and uncomfortable as the rest. I knew that Joy had watched rated R movies with me so I understood why his message might be making her feel ashamed. Since Rex was older and a boy, I figured that he had probably done worse although of course I didn't know the details. Personally my only real experience was that fleeting moment on the couch with Walter, but still I felt knowledgeable and experienced. Oddly, although the message seemed calculated to make kids feel ashamed of any sexual experience they might have, I still felt pleased and proud of mine.

When I got home from the fireside, I got the idea that it might be helpful to talk to my older sister Kathy about the whole thing since she was sure to know more about sex and all that than I did.

In truth I wasn't as close with Kathy as I was with Joy or even with Rex for that matter. It was probably mostly because of the age difference, but it was also because she and I had kind of different interests. She was into all sorts of crafts and homemaking and such which I found kind of pointless and uninteresting. Every so often an activity at church would inspire me to want to try out needle-working or quilting or some other handicraft, and when that happened Kathy was always the one to help me. Then we'd have some fun and laughs together, but such occurrences were pretty few and far-between.

Also it didn't help that she had her own room. She was the only person in the whole family that had her own room. I had to share a room with Joy, and Rex had to share a room with Jared, and of course Mom and Dad shared a room. We had a pretty big house, but since Mom and Dad each had to have their own individual study there weren't any extra bedrooms. Since Kathy was the oldest, she'd had her own room as long as I could remember. We didn't even get to free up some space when Kathy started college since she decided to go to BYU which was right nearby, and the expense of moving her into her own apartment didn't seem justified.

I knocked on Kathy's door and found that she was in. She was sitting at her desk writing a letter to her missionary Bob. Bob was coming home in just a few months, and Kathy was thrilled about it. Every letter these days was filled with wedding plans. So not every girl was like "Julie" from the play. Kathy and Bob had gotten engaged before he had set off, and Kathy hadn't dumped him even once the whole time he was gone. Except a few double-dates "just for fun," Kathy hadn't dated anyone else in the whole two years even though she was a pretty girl and probably could have if she'd wanted to. Now she would soon be reaping the rewards of her fidelity.

I sat down on the bed as Kathy finished up her letter. Then she turned to me and asked "What's up?"

"Nothing really," I said. "Just the usual topic: boys."

"Ah, yes, that's the big sister's job, isn't it?" She said it with a huge grin, and in her faraway look I could practically see that she was picturing herself in her white wedding dress, hand-in-hand with Bob.

"So fill me in!" she said. "What are the details? Are you in love?"

"Unfortunately I think I might be," I said. "I say unfortunately because I'm sure he's not as into me as I am into him. I know he's at least a little bit interested though."

"Tell me about him!" said Kathy enthusiastically.

"Actually, I more wanted to ask you a question about sex."

Kathy seemed somewhat less thrilled about that but said okay.

"Did you and Bob do anything naughty before he set off for his mission?" I asked.

"We certainly didn't have sex, if that's what you're asking."

"Well maybe not all of sex," I said, "but..."

"But what?" asked Kathy.

"Don't make me spell it out," I said. "All of the words are so embarrassing. Just—if you're okay with telling me—how far did you guys go?"

"We made out a few times."

"What kind of making out?" I asked. "Could you feel his... you know..."

"What?" she asked, shocked. "Of course not! Perish the thought! He was just about to set off for his mission when we started dating. As you know, a missionary needs to keep himself morally clean."

"But did you want to?" I asked.

"Jill!" she said, "What kinds of questions are these? Of course I didn't want to. Bob is my eternal companion, not some sort of plaything of the Devil! We love each other with a pure, spiritual love."

"So you're saying that you've never found it difficult to avoid impure thoughts even though you're in love with him?"

"A little, but not really. I care more about being worthy to go through the temple with him than I care about sinning. Why are you asking this? Are you having some sort of morality problem? Is some boy pressuring you to do more than you're comfortable doing?"

"No, no, I was just curious. Sorry to bother you," I said, and I left the room.

So that settled it. I was sick and depraved and needed to try harder to be a good girl like Kathy if I wanted to be worthy to go through the temple and eventually to the Celestial Kingdom. At least Joy liked to watch rated R movies with me, so she'd probably be down in the Telestial Kingdom too to keep me company for eternity.

I was actually tempted to go ask Rex if he knew anything about sex, but I thought better of it since asking my sister about sex was one thing, but asking my brother about sex was quite another.

* * *

Tuesday's rehearsal passed like the previous Thursday's, with no particularly special attention from Walter. I was getting desperate and felt like I had to do something.

At our next rehearsal on Thursday, Rex brought the school's videocamera and some special lights to do video footage with. Rex had a job working for the school district's media and technology services. According to Rex, during the Summer it was primarily doing inventory work on new items purchased by the school district, but it also involved various other tasks such as editing videos produced by the school.

Since our production was partially sponsored by the school's drama club, Rex had gotten special permission to make a video of the production for the school, and he wanted to include some footage of the rehearsals for fun.

Notably, he filmed my favorite number *He's Just a Friend*, where Julie, Shelley, and I sing about how Julie was dumping Wally for another guy and Wally and Greene (played by Jake) were singing about how upset they were about it. He also filmed the song *Voices* where Todd (played by Noah) sings about being tempted by various things such as "books and learning" as the chorus of bad kids does a dance acting out the various temptations.

Of course Rex filmed Pam's big number *Line Upon Line*. That was the one where the really spiritual crippled girl Pam tries to convince her twin brother, Jimmy, to be more interested in the church just before her tragic death. Obviously Rex waited until a take where it was Laura singing the part of Pam before he started filming. Actually in the course of filming various scenes it seemed like Rex got an awful lot of footage of Laura. At one point I could have sworn I heard him say to her "The camera loves you, babe," which only went to show that even Rex was willing to make a fool of himself for love or perhaps for the hope of sex.

He also got a fair amount of footage of Pinky's little eight-year-old niece who was playing the part of "Emily." Emily was the youngest child of the big Mormon family in the play, and her birth at the end was one of the main subjects of the play. The character spent the whole play looking down on her intended family from the pre-existence.

Pinky doted on her niece during rehearsals, so she was happy that Rex was giving her attention by filming her. People said that Pinky herself had been in a big production of *Saturday's Warrior* when she was younger, and that that experience was what had inspired her love of the theater. She was thrilled to have her favorite niece in the same play, and everyone suspected that that was the whole reason that Pinky had wanted to produce *Saturday's Warrior* in the first place. Even though the play was old-fashioned and an embarrassment to the church, Pinky loved it and wanted to relive her early theater memories vicariously through her niece.

Near the end of the rehearsal I went to the bathroom, and out of habit I checked the door in the back of the bathroom that led to the baptismal font. Normally this door was locked at all times, but every now and then someone would forget and leave it unlocked. When that happened while we were at church in our own ward building, Joy and I would sometimes go into the baptismal font with other girlfriends because it was kind of a cool, hidden place to hang out.

Today, by luck, it was unlocked. I went through the door into the ladies' dressing room and checked the door on the other side. It was unlocked as well, so I could go all the way into the font itself. I stepped into the font and crossed it and went back up to check the door on the men's side. It was locked, but, as I knew, I could unlock it by hand from this side.

I crossed back over to the ladies' side of the font. There was no noise coming from the other side of the vinyl retractable accordion-wall, so I supposed that there was no one in the adjoining room. That divider was closed and locked as usual, so even if there had been people in the room, they wouldn't have been able to tell there was someone in the font unless I made a lot of noise.

The fact that the door was unlocked was an incredible stroke of good fortune, and it was just the opportunity I had been looking for. I immediately thought of Walter. The baptismal font was one of the few places in the building where we would have complete privacy. And the fact that it was amusing that it was unlocked in the first place was excuse enough to ask him to come with me to see it.

As I walked back to where people were rehearsing, I wondered to myself precisely what I hoped to do with him there. I wasn't really sure. Probably some making-out, as they say. Maybe even some "petting" to use the awful word they taught us in church for it—I didn't know any other. I thought perhaps I would even be willing to go all the way with him if I had a condom. I hadn't thought to get one, but I figured that that level of sexual adventure was still far enough in the future that there would be time to cross that bridge later.

When I got to the cultural hall, I found that they were just getting started at rehearsing the number *Pulling Together*, which was one that I was in. Walter wasn't busy with any of his scenes at the moment, so he was sitting on the edge of the stage watching. As I passed him, I told him I had something that I wanted to show him privately after our number.

"What is it?" he asked.

"It's a surprise," I said with a sly smile.

"Sounds interesting," he said, complicitly returning my look.

We were almost done with our first run-through when Rex appeared in the doorway. As soon as the music stopped he asked "Jill, are you ready to go?"

Rex's question hit me like a ton of bricks. Of all the days for him to want to leave early! What rotten luck! I was sure that someone would discover that the font was unlocked between now and next Tuesday, and my window of opportunity would be closed.

"We only need to run through this number two more times," said Pinky. "Can you wait?"

"No," said Rex. "I have all of the video stuff loaded up in the car, and I have to get it back to the school before Ron locks up and goes home. I'm already pushing it as it is. We have to go now."

"I can take her home," said Walter. "I have to stay to lock up the building here anyway, so it's no trouble."

I was absolutely elated by his offer! Not only did it make my little plan possible, but it meant that he found the plan interesting enough to want to make an effort himself to help carry it out without even really knowing what it was.

Rex raised an eyebrow warily at Walter, and then looked with displeasure at my expression of obvious delight. Still, he didn't have the authority to forbid me from staying with Walter nor did he even have a good reason to ask me to leave early with him. So he grumbled an okay and left.

Once we had finished our two run-throughs, our little group started breaking up and Pinky went off to give some last-minute instructions to another group that was finishing up a scene in another room.

I went over to Walter, and he smiled and asked me what the surprise was.

"Come with me," I said, and I led him towards the doors to the bathrooms, grabbing my jacket along the way.

12. THURSDAY AFTERNOON

I STOPPED IN FRONT of the doors to the bathrooms.

"The surprise is here?" asked Walter.

"Not precisely here," I said. "Go into the men's room and wait by the door in the back."

He laughed. "You have the key to the baptismal font?"

"No, I just happened to find it unlocked today on the ladies' side."

"Cool!" he said, "What fun!" and he went into the men's room.

I went into the ladies' room myself and went through the door in the back into the dressing room. I locked the door behind myself and turned on the light. Then I went through the other door to the font, leaving it wedged open so that there would be some light.

I went down the stairs into the font and crossed to the other side and back up and unlocked the door to the men's dressing room and went through it. I then unlocked the door to the men's bathroom and opened it. Walter was waiting right there on the other side.

"This is so sneaky," he said as he came through the door and locked it behind. He put his arm around my waist as we walked towards the font. It seemed like he already had the idea of what I had in mind.

We walked down the steps hand-in-hand and sat down on the tile floor of the font, leaning our backs against the tiled wall. I put my folded jacket behind my back, but it didn't help much to make the cold, hard tiles any more comfortable.

Walter immediately put one arm around my back and the other hand behind my neck and started kissing me. I put my arms around him as well.

He paused for a moment and said "This is so naughty! We shouldn't even be in here at all! I'm so impressed that you thought of this."

He kissed me again, and then he pulled back and got a mischievous grin on his face. "You know, speaking of naughty, I've heard that some girls can take their bra off without even taking off their shirt. Can you do that?"

"Of course," I said, and I immediately demonstrated.

"Wow," he said, seeming impressed and pleased. "I imagine that since you're wearing a skirt it would be super easy to do the same with your panties."

I laughed. I figured he thought he was cleverly tricking me into something. Still this idea was deliciously erotic that he would know that I was uncovered underneath while still not being able to see anything, so I obliged willingly.

That seemed to excite him, and he started kissing me more passionately than before. I touched his soft hair and caressed his beautiful face. As I ran my fingers along his jawline, the sand-papery feel of it reminded me again that this was an adult man.

He repositioned me so that I was lying on the floor of the font with just my head on my jacket. I could feel the cold tile floor against my butt. He laid down on top of me and started kissing me in this position. Through his pants I could feel his penis hard against my pelvic bone as he started making something of a thrusting motion with it.

If I had had any doubts as to whether he might desire me, they were certainly gone now. It was abundantly clear that if nothing else he at least found me sexually attractive. It was a rush to sense his intense and passionate desire for me. I felt like this was exactly what I had brought him there for.

I ran my hands up under his shirt and touched the warm skin of his muscular back, feeling the individual bones of his spine. For his part, he ran one hand up under my shirt, almost to my breast.

He didn't touch the breast itself but rather put his hand over my ribcage outlining the shape of the breast, as if he wanted to touch it but hesitated. I found his reticence amusing, and I wondered if it was that he wasn't sure if I would object or if it was that there was a line that he himself was reluctant to cross.

"It's so hard to resist temptation," he said. "I've been trying to overcome my desire to sin, but it's too powerful. I'd thought I was making real progress this last time. It had been more than a week..."

"Since what?" I asked.

"Never mind," he replied. Then I thought that perhaps he was talking about masturbation.

He then opened his pants "to be more comfortable." This was a bit of a worrisome development because the next thing I knew I felt the head of his penis pressing against exactly the place it shouldn't be. There was some moisture there as he continued kissing the side of my face and neck, and I could feel him starting to push it in just a little. It hurt some, but more than that it frightened me.

"Walter, I don't think we should be doing this," I said.

"I know, it's terribly wrong..."

"No, I mean it," I said. "I think we need to stop now and get out of here."

"Of course you're right," he said. He pulled out, but he was still kissing my neck, and I could still feel it right there at the threshold.

"Imagine," he said, raising himself up on his elbows. "I'll have to wait another two years. More than that really. It hardly seems possible."

After a short pause, he said "Perhaps you'll at least let me look at your breasts, just a little."

"Are you sure that's a good idea?" I asked, but he was already unbuttoning my shirt when he said it.

Then he opened my shirt and looked. I felt his hands warm over my small breasts and sensed that he was starting to breathe more heavily. He put one had behind my neck as before and kissed me just below my ear on the other side.

Then I felt him enter as before, only more deeply this time. I could feel his breath on my neck as he began thrusting in and out. I didn't protest. When I felt his motion become more powerful and rapid and then felt him begin to relax, I knew he had reached his climax.

He stood up and went to the door. He paused for a moment and said, "My God, what have I done?"

Then he went through the door and immediately came back with a huge wad of toilet paper, which he handed to me, and he left again. I wiped myself and put my bra and panties back on. Then I wiped the blood off the floor of the baptismal font.

I went out of the font through the ladies' room, turning out the light in the dressing room. I threw the toilet paper away, and paused to look at myself in the mirror. I was so overwhelmed by what had just happened that I had no idea what to think.

When I came out, I saw that Walter was waiting for me by the exit. He looked a little sad, but he didn't say anything. As soon as I had passed through the door, he followed me out and locked it.

His car was the only one left in the parking lot. We both got in and he asked me my address. After I told him, he drove silently for a little while, and then without looking at me he said, "I suppose you think I'm a terrible person and you hate me now."

"No, of course not," I replied.

"Why not? It's true, I'm a terrible person. I don't know why I don't have any self-control. I try so hard." He breathed a breath of disappointment. "It's just that sometimes I'm completely overcome by lust. It's my biggest weakness."

"I understand," I said.

"You do?" he asked, kind of surprised.

"Yeah, why do you think I brought you there in the first place? Actually I kind of wanted to do it too even though I know it's bad and I got scared at the last minute."

He smiled a little tiny bit and said, "I'm going to repent, though, and try to do better. I know that that probably sounds stupid since how many times can you try to give up a vice and fail? But I have to do better if I want to go on a mission."

"Of course," I said.

"Actually, it's probably stupid of me to even imagine that I should be going on a mission. I'm obviously not the sort of person the Lord wants to have representing His true church. But I can't help but feel like if I spent two years completely focused on serving the Lord that maybe it would help me to become a better person, and I might even do some good in the world."

"Of course that's what the Lord wants you to do," I said. "He'll forgive you and everything will be okay."

"You think so?" he asked.

"Absolutely."

"Then maybe let's not go to our bishops about this, okay? I'm supposed to enter the Missionary Training Center in a month, and if my bishop finds out about this he might not let me go."

"Of course," I said. "I don't think it's always necessary to confess this sort of thing to the bishop. Individual repentance should be sufficient."

"Thanks," he said as we arrived at the house. "I'll see you Tuesday, Jill."

"See you," I said, giving him one last parting smile before going into the house.

When I got inside, I went straight to my room and sat on the bed. Fortunately Joy wasn't around so I had some time alone to think.

I was still essentially in shock about what had happened. I didn't know what to think. First and foremost I was terrified. After all, Walter and I had definitely had unprotected sex, which could have dire consequences. If I was unlucky, I might end up with a very big problem. Still, there was a good chance that I would be lucky, so I tried to put that fear out of my mind for the time being.

Aside from the fear of pregnancy, however, I was surprised to discover that I actually felt kind of excited and happy about what had happened. I thought maybe I was completely crazy to feel that way.

By logic it seemed like I probably ought to have agreed with Walter that he was a terrible person. Still, he seemed so genuinely sorry about what he had done. He wasn't a bad person really. I knew he hadn't really wanted to hurt me or to force me against my will. It was just that his desire was so powerful and intense that he couldn't help himself. That was why I felt happy about it. It was incredible to be the object of such a ferocious passion on the part of someone so beautiful.

Being honest with myself, I found that I wanted to do it again, only under different circumstances. In a proper bed, for one thing, and with a condom or some other contraception. But of course that would be impossible.

I felt kind of evil for secretly wishing to ruin Walter's resolve to improve himself for his mission. I was tempted to imagine that he and

I could have one date and one night of passion and then we could both repent afterwards.

It would be so beautiful. I couldn't see it as evil and dirty in my heart even though I knew Heavenly Father felt otherwise.

I figured I should get down to business on repenting, but I didn't feel like letting it sink in to myself just yet how wrong my experience had been. I wanted to be alone with my pleasant memory of it just a bit longer.

Could I really love a man who would do something like this?

It didn't make sense, but I did.

1 3 . SUNDAY MORNING

A T SACRAMENT MEETING, I wondered if perhaps I shouldn't take the sacrament. It had been three days since the incident with Walter, and I hadn't even started repenting yet. I knew that you weren't supposed to take the sacrament if you had some big sin on your conscience that you hadn't repented of.

On the other hand, I figured that if I didn't take it, my parents would notice and they would ask me what was up. That was a question I really didn't want to deal with. In the end I figured that my big sin plus unworthily taking the sacrament didn't really amount to all that much more than the big sin alone without unworthily taking the sacrament, so I just took the sacrament as usual.

I wondered if Walter was having the same dilemma in his own ward at church. Of course he was probably clever enough to have already started repenting by this point, so he probably didn't have to worry about it.

When Walter saw me at Tuesday's rehearsal, he looked startled at first and flushed red. Then he immediately got a hold of himself and was back to his usual friendly manner. At least he was almost all the way back to his usual self. He seemed like he wanted to be as friendly and flirty with me as always, but he was a little off. He gave the impression that he was ashamed of the memory that my presence brought to his mind.

I hoped that at some point we would talk about what had happened so that we could work it out. I didn't want this to prevent us from ever having a relationship at any point in the future. I wished I could have some sort of affectionate reassurance from him—nothing sexual, just a hug or something—but I didn't see how that would be possible. I didn't dare suggest to him that we should go somewhere to talk privately because I was afraid he might think I was trying to tempt him again.

Over the next week or so, I managed to put myself into complete denial about the very real danger of pregnancy. It was such a terrifying prospect that I couldn't bring myself to hold it in my mind. Until the day my period was due, I could tell myself that certainly it would come, and that it was foolish to think otherwise.

That is, I managed to tell myself that until the day it was due and it didn't come. Nor did it come the day after nor the day after. This threw me into a state of panic. I had never felt more terrified in my entire life, and this new terror was nonstop from morning until night with no hope of recovery on the horizon.

One thing I knew was that if I really was pregnant, there was no way I could carry it to term. I was only fifteen for heaven's sake! I was an honor student and had a brilliant future ahead of me. I cared about my education, and I didn't see that it would be possible for me to just continue to go to school like that. I would have to be sent away somewhere getting heaven-knows-what kind of substitute for schooling, and my education would probably never recover.

To get final confirmation, I managed to bite the bullet of my embarrassment and go out and buy a pregnancy test.

Of course it came out positive.

This dashed my last tiny shred of hope. I was like a zombie as I went to my gardening job that morning. As I got to working, I found that I just couldn't stop crying. I was glad that Sister Sanderson didn't happen to come out that day and see me.

On my way home from work I took a long detour to an anonymous garbage can to throw away the remains of the test and the wrapper where no one would find it who would trace it back to me.

By afternoon, I figured I was okay to go to my Tuesday rehearsal as usual. It seemed like it was hardly worth doing anything at all at this point since my life was over, but I continued going through the motions out of inertia.

In the car Rex noticed I was upset, but I didn't feel like talking to him about it. Actually, I wasn't really sure who I could turn to for help. It seemed like Rex would probably be a good choice since he was usually pretty understanding and wasn't as judgmental as a lot of people. Plus I knew he cared enough about his own education to understand how I felt about just throwing it away, and I knew he cared enough about me to try to help. Still I was reluctant and ashamed to tell him about my problem.

I wasn't able to enjoy the fun of the rehearsal as I usually did. I tried to put on an act and hide my feelings, but it was hard to disguise my despair. I noticed that Walter was watching me from a distance with a sad and worried look in his eye. He didn't try to chat with me, though. He seemed terribly afraid to approach me.

At one point it just became too much for me, so I went outside and hid around the backside of the building and cried. Jake's mom, who had come out for a smoke, noticed me. She had just finished up her cigarette when she saw me. She came over to see what was wrong.

Actually I was relieved to see Jake's mom approach because I felt like maybe she was one of the few people I might feel comfortable talking about my problem with. She was judged by everyone for being a sinner, so she might understand and be able to help me.

"Are you okay?" she asked.

"No, not really," I replied.

"What's wrong?"

"It's nothing."

"This doesn't sound like nothing," she said. "It's about Walter, isn't it?"

"Kind of," I said.

"I know how it is when you're young," she said. "You get so attached to someone who is older and outgoing, and then it kills you to see him paying attention to other people and not to you."

"It's not that this time," I said.

"What is it then?"

"The problem was more when he did pay attention to me, and then something bad happened."

"I don't like the sound of that," she said.

I became worried that perhaps she would condemn me for this after all. "I told him to stop," I said. "I asked him not to do it, but he couldn't resist the temptation, and now I have a big problem."

"So are you going to press charges?" she asked.

"What?!" I asked.

"He raped you, right?" she asked. "I mean, that's what you're saying, isn't it?"

"No, of course not," I said. "I brought him to a private place where we could be alone. I locked the door myself. Really it was my fault."

"That's your brainwashing talking," she said. "I mean, no offense to the church or anything, but that's your brainwashing talking. Jesus, he's nineteen years old, and you're what? Fifteen? Shit, even if it weren't regular rape, it would at least be statutory rape."

I looked down and started crying again.

"Well, let's not worry so much about what has happened as about what we can do about it," she said. "I imagine you must be pregnant. That's the big problem you mentioned, isn't it?"

"I just took the test this morning, and it came out positive," I said.

She put her arm around me. "It's not the end of the world. There are clinics around here you can go to."

I looked up. I started to feel the first glimmer of hope that I'd felt in days.

"Of course you'll be required to tell your parents," she said.

Her statement dashed my hopes anew.

"I can't tell them," I said. "They would never understand. They're really strict Mormons. Nothing like this has ever happened to anyone we know. They would never forgive me."

"I don't know about that," she said. "You'd probably be surprised. Still, I personally don't really agree that you should be forced to tell your parents about this. One thing you can do to avoid having to tell them is to go have it done in Nevada instead."

"But how could I get to Nevada?" I asked.

"Well, it looks like this is your lucky day and you've come to the right person," she said beaming. "My little Jake was saying just the other day how much he wants to go on a road trip to Vegas, but he doesn't have a lot of money or a girl to go with him. I offered to go myself, but for some reason he didn't want to take his mom. Maybe he could be persuaded to take you, though. Do you have any money?"

"I have several hundred dollars in savings," I said.

"Good, you'll need them," she said. "I can get an advance from work and lend Jake some more money just in case, but remember that we're not made of money at our house. I'll arrange the appointment and talk to Jake about making the trip. Don't worry, everything will be fine."

I felt the most incredible sense of relief. I was going to be saved from the worst thing that had ever happened to me in my life. "Thank you so much Grace, I don't know how to thank you enough!"

"It's okay," she said. "I know what it's like to be in trouble and terrified. I'll help out any way I can. Now all you need to do is gather your money and come up with an excuse to tell your parents for where you'll be for the weekend."

I started to panic again. "I have no idea of what to tell them!"

She smiled. "Here, maybe I can help you out on that one, too. If you're too embarrassed to tell people, I can talk to Jake about it and have him talk to Paige. She can probably cover for you."

"Could you have him tell Rex, too?" I asked.

"You can't bring yourself to talk to your own brother?" she asked. "Oh, alright." She smiled at me. I felt so relieved. It wasn't over yet, but I felt like a huge weight was lifted off me.

I thought for a second and said, "I know I'm in no position to ask you any more favors but... what I've said is in confidence, okay? Please say you won't tell the rest of the cast about me or about Walter either."

"Of course I'm not going to spread your secret around behind your back!" she said. "As for Walter, though, I think that he should be made to understand that this sort of thing is not okay."

"Oh, he understands!" I said. "He's *really* upset and sorry about what he did."

"Well, okay, I'll leave him alone then if that's what you want. But if I see another girl like you that I think might be getting into a risky situation, I can't promise not to give her a gentle warning."

That seemed reasonable, so I thanked her again, and we went back into the rehearsal.

The next morning, after Rex and I had both finished our respective jobs, I asked Rex to take me to the bank. He agreed.

Jake's mom must have done her job pretty efficiently because as soon as we were in the car and moving, Rex asked me why I didn't feel like I could come to him directly about my problem.

"I wanted to," I said, "but I was too ashamed. I was afraid you'd be angry with me."

"I'm not angry, I understand how these things happen," he said. "Still... " he paused for a second. "Well, I guess I don't need to give you a lecture about condoms that you'll probably be getting a million more times before this is over."

"Oh, I've learned my lesson there," I said. "I'll be more careful next time."

"I could drive you to Nevada myself," he said. "I don't see why you need Jake to do it."

"Oh no, Rex, it would look suspicious if we both go. Mom would immediately get the idea of sending Kathy along or turning it into a full-fledged family vacation! If that happens, I'm done for! It's better for me to just go with Jake."

"You're probably right," he said.

"Have you talked to Paige? Is she willing to provide an alibi?"

"Yeah, no problem. She said she'll say her family is going away for the weekend and that they've invited you along."

"That's wonderful!" I said.

"She also said to tell you that she has a cousin that adopted a baby through LDS Social Services, and that you should maybe consider that as an option, but that she's willing to respect your decision on the matter."

I became upset and worried again. "I really could never do that! I'm only fifteen!"

"I know," he said.

"Is that what you think I should do? Carry it to term?" I asked.

"No," he said. "Anyway, it's your business."

When we got to the bank, I withdrew everything from my bank account except for the minimum balance. I was grateful that my parents had always taught me the value of saving money. Of course most of what was in that account had been gifts which were intended to be saved for the future. I really wasn't supposed to just take it all out like that, but it was an emergency. Hopefully I wouldn't need to spend it all, and I would have some left over to put back later.

After dinner Rex took me aside to speak privately. "Jake just called," he said. "He says to be ready because you're leaving first thing tomorrow morning."

That was pretty fast. I had only told Jake's mom about my problem the day before, and already everything was arranged for tomorrow. I was beside myself with gratitude to her. It meant I would miss one Thursday rehearsal, but that was no big deal considering the situation.

I gathered up a few items of clothing to pack in a small backpack. I put in the money I had withdrawn from the bank. Then I went to the box in my drawer where I kept the money I'd been setting aside to pay to the church as tithing. I figured I'd better take that money too, just in case.

Then I asked Joy to cover for me at Sister Sanderson's, and I told Mom and Dad about how I was going to spend the weekend with

Paige's family. They had no problem with that, and in fact didn't seem even remotely suspicious.

Going to bed, I allowed myself to indulge in one dangerous fantasy. I imagined what would happen if I chose to keep the baby. I imagined getting a little apartment with Walter where we could raise it. There were a couple of pretty moments in this image, setting the table for dinner at home, the baby playing sweetly on the floor.

But it took only an instant of looking at this picture for the dark side of it to appear. Two teenagers with no skills sacrificing our youths and our future for a set of responsibilities we weren't ready for. As much as I felt I loved him, I couldn't bring myself to want to walk this path even for a second.

I went to sleep thinking of my plans for the next day's voyage.

14. THURSDAY MORNING

IN THE MORNING Rex dropped me off at Jake's house. Jake already had his motorcycle out in the driveway and was working on it with some tools. I hoped that it was just some last-minute adjustments and not that something was wrong.

"Thanks for doing this, man," said Rex.

"No problem," said Jake. "Like I said, I was planning to ride to Vegas one of these days anyway."

Then Rex turned to me and sighed. "Good luck," he said. "And try to... try to have some fun on this trip if that's at all possible."

"Thanks," I said.

"Don't worry about Mom and Dad," said Rex. "I'll take care of damage control on the home front if anything happens." Then he got back in the car and left.

Jake gathered up his tools and put them away in the garage. Then he came back out and walked around the bike, looking at it from all angles. It was really quite a beautiful motorcycle, although I couldn't claim to know much about them. Jake took out a white cloth and polished it until it was gleaming in the morning sun.

I looked over at the porch and noticed that Jake's mom had come out and was standing there smoking a cigarette and watching.

"How are you holding up, honey?" she asked.

"I guess I'm okay," I said. "I'm a little nervous."

"Well, you can't wear that light jacket on a trip like this. Here, I'll lend you mine." She went in the house and came back with a black leather jacket. She handed it to me with one hand, still holding her cigarette between two fingers of her other hand.

I took off my backpack and my jacket and tried on Jake's mom's jacket. It was heavy and a little too big for me, but I figured it would be okay.

"You look great," said Jake's mom. "Like a real biker-chick! Now all you need are some tattoos!"

I smiled and laughed. I knew she was just humoring me. Jake laughed too. "Are you ready to go?" he asked.

"I guess so," I said.

"Good," he said, handing me a helmet and straddling the bike. "Hop on."

"Wait, I don't know what to do," I said. "I don't even know how to put on the helmet."

Jake laughed. "The helmet is pretty self-explanatory. As for what you have to do, just hang on!"

So I put on the helmet and got on the bike just behind Jake and put my arms around him. Before I was even expecting it, we were moving. Even at low speed the turn at the end of the driveway was already a little scary. As we rode away, I looked back and saw Jake's mom at the end of the driveway, smiling and waving with her cigarette-hand.

Driving through town was exhilarating but scary, the turns especially. Everything seemed to be coming at me so fast, and I had no control at all. All I could do was hold on tight and trust Jake.

It wasn't long before I started feeling a little queasy. As soon as we got onto the highway, it seemed like it should be better, but it wasn't. The road was now smooth and straight, but the mild vibration of it was making me downright nauseous.

I started frantically tapping Jake's arm and pointing at the side of the road. Jake pulled over and stopped, and I managed to get the helmet off just in time to avoid puking into it.

Jake took off his own helmet and asked "Are you okay Jill? Do you need to take a break?"

"I'm okay," I said. "I'm starting to feel better already. Anyway, if we start taking breaks every few minutes from the very beginning, we'll never get there."

"Okay," he said. "Have you been getting sick like that a lot lately?"

"No, that was the first time," I said. "I'm sure I'll be okay."

He got out a water bottle and had me drink some, and then we got back out onto the highway. I started to feel a lot better this time.

I was already starting to get used to the sensation of riding, and could just enjoy the feeling of motion and watching the scenery go by.

Actually, going south on I-15 wasn't the most picturesque way to leave Utah Valley. Compared to the canyons, this stretch of slowly meandering highway was almost desolate. Occasionally my gaze would follow a small bush as we passed by it. It was almost hypnotic.

I couldn't help but feel like it was a little bit sexy riding behind Jake pressed up against him like that. There was something undeniably masculine and powerful about his control over the bike.

It was kind of funny to be in this position. As a kid I had always been interested in Rex's friends whenever he invited them over to the house. Rex was such a nice brother that he would occasionally let me hang out and play games with him and his friends if his friends didn't mind. Of course the bigger boys weren't interested in me at all, but that didn't stop me from fantasizing that I might attract one of them.

I remembered how years ago Rex would make these elaborate Lego cities with Jake and Ben. They were always kind enough to set aside a plot or two for me and some bricks so that I could have a house or building or something in their city.

Actually back then I probably had a little more of a crush on Ben than on Jake, but at that age I would have gladly taken either one had one been interested. Now I wasn't so sure how I felt anymore. Certainly Jake was attractive, but not like Walter.

Walter was so exceptionally beautiful and charming. Of course it was clear that his uncontrolled passion could have disastrous consequences. But I imagined that going on a mission would help him grow spiritually and maybe teach him some self-discipline. I thought that perhaps on his return his desire for me would be transformed into a pure, spiritual love like my sister Kathy's love for her missionary Bob.

Around noon Jake pulled into a gas station to fuel up the bike and I went in and paid. As we walked around and stretched a bit, Jake suggested that we get some lunch at the diner next door.

We went in and took a booth off away from the other people who seemed to be mostly clustered around the counter. I just ordered two eggs and toast. Jake ordered a hamburger and fries and coffee.

It seemed normal for him to be ordering coffee since we were on a road trip and it's always important for the driver on a road trip to stay alert. Even my parents did the same thing. Still I imagined that at Jake's house his mom probably made coffee all the time, so maybe his taking coffee today wasn't just a special exception.

"So, are you having fun so far?" he asked.

"Yeah, it's great," I said. "I mean, it's kind of scary, but it's exciting."

Jake smiled. "This is the life. The open road..." He kind of looked off in the distance as if thinking about it.

Once our food arrived and the waitress was gone, I asked Jake if he knew where it was that we needed to go.

"Oh, yeah," he said. "I have the address and phone number and the time of the appointment and everything. Don't worry, my mom gave me all the info."

"Good," I said.

"Can I ask you a personal question?" he asked.

"Okay," I said.

He looked around conspiratorially and then leaned in and quietly asked "Who was it?"

"Your mom didn't tell you?"

"No," he said.

I figured he deserved to know since he was going through so much trouble for me. "Promise you won't tell anyone?" I asked.

"Of course," he replied.

"It was Walter."

"Walter?!" he asked, "Walter Smith? That guy's an asshole!"

"Ssh! keep it down," I said. "And anyway, he's not an A-hole, he's very sweet." I paused a second and added "and righteous."

"Righteous?" asked Jake. "Is that supposed to be some sort of joke? And anyway, if he's so sweet, why isn't he the one who's helping you take care of this... little problem?"

"I haven't told him," I said. "I didn't want to worry or upset him."

"Oh, no, we can't have that," said Jake sarcastically. "So you can tell me and not him?"

"I didn't tell you," I said. "I told your mom. She was the one who said you'd help."

"Humph," said Jake. "All I know is that that Walter leads a pretty charmed life. All he has to do is flip back his perfect hair and flash that perfect smile, and he has people lining up to clean up his messes for him."

I didn't say anything to that.

"Jeez, I would have warned you to steer clear of that guy if I'd had any idea. But it didn't occur to me. I would never take advantage of a kid like you, and he's a year older than I am! But I guess my warning is a little late now."

"Yeah," I said, looking down. "He's sorry, though. He's repented."

"Yeah, I'll bet," said Jake.

"He's determined to be good. He's entering the MTC in two weeks, right after the big production is over."

"Oh is he now?" asked Jake. "I suppose that that means that he hasn't told his bishop about this little indiscretion."

"No, and don't you tell either."

Jake looked annoyed and exasperated. "I just hope you don't think that you're his only girlfriend," he said, "because you're not."

"I know," I said looking away. Then I turned back to Jake and said, "You know, in every one of your scenes in our production you play his sidekick. Yet I would never have guessed that you dislike him so much."

"It's called acting, my sweet," he said. "And I am a master of it. Anyway, I figure there's no sense making trouble with other members of the cast whatever my personal feelings about them may be. But you may have noticed that I'm not exactly buddy-buddy with him either."

Jake picked up the check and looked at it. I remembered his mom telling me how lack of money had been one of his reasons for not making the trip earlier. "I'm treating," I said, taking the bill. I didn't know how much money Jake had brought for the trip, and I hoped that between the two of us we had enough for everything.

Getting back out onto the road, I thought about how Jake had said that he wouldn't take advantage of a kid like me. So he still saw me as a kid. It figured. Of course he wouldn't be attracted to some little kid. He was just bringing me on this trip as a favor for a friend because his friend's kid sister had gotten into trouble. If it weren't for that, he would never have had any interest in making a trip like this with me. I was kind of hurt by that realization even though I didn't have any intention of taking up with him romantically. Jake was an adult and I was a kid. So be it. At least Walter saw me as a woman.

At our next pit-stop Jake seemed less interested in talking about my condition and my love-life. We walked around a little and stretched and then as we sat down on the ground he started telling me some of the technical details about his motorcycle. He probably thought he was dumbing his discussion down enough for me, but I really had no idea what he was talking about as he described the various modifications and restorations he had done to the bike. All I picked up was that it was some sort of Harley. But the gleam in his eye and his warm, heartfelt tone made me want to listen to him all day, even if he were speaking Chinese.

I followed him better when he started telling me the story of where the bike came from. It turned out that had belonged to his grandfather, and that Jake's grandpa had left it to Jake's mom when he died because she had loved riding it with him as a kid. It was kind of fun to imagine Jake's mom as a young girl riding on this same bike with her dad. Less sexy perhaps than this trip, but sweet. But Jake's mom didn't have the mechanical knowledge necessary to keep it running nor the time and interest necessary to learn, so she had given the bike to Jake, who had passed countless hours fixing it up.

Then Jake came to the sad part of the story where he talked about how he was preparing the bike in anticipation of possibly having to sell it. It turned out that he and his mom had had some unexpected emergency expenses that he'd ended up having to clean out his savings to pay for. Then since he hadn't succeeded in getting any grants or scholarships and his mom was barely getting by as it was as a waitress, it looked like there was a chance that he might have to sell the bike in order to have enough money for tuition and college expenses.

I hoped for his sake that it wouldn't come down to that because it would be a tragedy for him to have to give up his motorcycle given his obvious love for it and his love of the open road. I felt sure that he was resourceful enough that he would find a way to avoid having to sell it, or if he did end up selling it, he'd find a way to buy it back or perhaps another like it one day.

As we got back out onto the highway, I held him as before, but perhaps more affectionately this time. With my whole heart I felt like I wanted him to succeed since he had come so far on the strength

of his own determination given so few material advantages. He had something special in him, that was for sure.

Perhaps it was just this stupid fascination I had for the male of the species. I was sure that he had his own doubts about himself, but I believed in him completely.

The rest of the trip went like a dream, and in no time it was late evening and we were in our little cheap hotel room. We were too tired to see the sights or go out to eat, so we just picked up some takeout Chinese from a little place nearby. We sat on the one double bed and laughed together as we ate it.

Soon there was no denying that it was time to go to bed. We hadn't discussed what the arrangement would be, but logically since the one bed was big enough, we would both be in it.

I excused myself to the bathroom and put on my nightshirt. I had just brought an ordinary nightshirt like I might wear to a slumber party with a bunch of girls—nothing sexy. Jake hadn't specifically brought anything to wear to bed, so he just stripped down to his boxers. I tried not to look too closely, but of course I couldn't help but look a little bit. In the past, Rex had brought Jake swimming with the family a few times, so it wasn't the first time I'd seen him with his shirt off, but the current situation made it a little different.

We both got into the bed on our respective sides, and Jake turned out the light. I was lying on my side with my back to him when I felt him caressing my arm with his hand. How could he help it? The situation was just a little too erotically charged to ignore.

I took his hand with my hand and pulled his arm across me, effectively pulling us closer together. He responded by moving closer yet so that he was right up against me. I could feel that he had an erection. This sort of thing was no longer a mystery nor a surprise to me. Still I felt a little nervous and apprehensive. But I imagined that this was the way it was with men, and I shouldn't expect it to be any different.

Even though Jake was clearly attractive and we were having a nice time together, I wasn't sure how I felt about turning our relationship into a sexual one just like that, especially given that it had been an almost familial relationship for so many years up to that point.

Still, it seemed reasonable that I should offer him some sort of reward or payment for the trouble he had taken to bring me here. It hardly made sense to worry anymore whether it was a sin considering what I had come to Las Vegas to do. And there was no further worry about getting in trouble since I was already in trouble. And besides that, knowing Jake's mom I imagined that she would have insisted that he bring along a condom, just in case.

This whole sordid affair was going to require some major repentance anyway, so I figured I might as well go ahead with it.

"Do you want me to do something for you?" I asked him softly.

He thought about it for a long time. "I don't know," he said. "I mean, what kind of guy would I be to pass up this kind of opportunity, right? But still I feel like it's not right, not like this."

"If you want to, I will do it," I said.

"Of course I want to, badly," he said "but that's not the only consideration."

He rolled onto his back as he continued. "The thing is that you know I'm going to be starting at BYU in the fall. Nobody thought I could do it, given the way my mom raised me. The whole ward is proud of me. My uncle is proud of me. I've already passed my worthiness interview with the bishop. I'm not sure I want to turn that into a lie at this point unless... unless I'm sure that this is going to be a serious relationship, and I'm not sure that it is."

I held his hand in my hand and squeezed it. "It's your call," I said.

He took a deep breath and got out of bed and went over to the bathroom. He was in there for some time, and then he silently came back and got into the bed on his own side, facing away from me.

I put my arm around him and held him. I kissed him once on the neck just below the ear and once on the forehead. Then I went back to my own side of the bed and went to sleep.

15. FRIDAY MORNING

WHEN I WOKE UP, Jake was already in the shower. I rested in bed listening to the water and gathering my strength.

Jake came out of the bathroom in his boxers and started getting dressed. "Well? You'd better get up and take your shower," he said. "You've got a big day ahead of you."

In truth I was terrified even after Jake explained that this morning's appointment was just the warm-up.

I got myself ready, and we got on the bike and went to the clinic. The building wasn't too impressive. It was a squat little rectangular one-story building. More than anything else it reminded me of the veterinarian's office where we would take our cat. Of course it wasn't the same. I saw the place as somehow cold and sinister even though I knew intellectually that they were there to help me and I was lucky to have them.

As we got off the bike started walking up to the building, Jake put his arm around me as if to support and protect me. I could just imagine what this must look like—a biker tough in his leather jacket and black boots escorting a young girl into this sort of place. To most people it wouldn't look like anything good. Yet Jake put himself in this position despite the fact that it wasn't his responsibility at all. No one had ever before given me such a strong impression of manliness and courage.

When it was time for my appointment with the counselor, she started in immediately on explaining to me the importance of using a condom. I felt really stupid and humiliated because of course I knew I should have used one, and I couldn't bring myself to lie and say that it was just that the condom had broken or something. I felt almost on the verge of tears, but I tried to be as normal and nonchalant as possible as she gave me some condoms and demonstrated how to use one by putting it on a banana. In truth, I had never done it, so if I hadn't felt so emotionally distraught by the whole thing, I would have been grateful for the instruction.

When my session was over, they had me sign some forms and pay my money, and they gave me a card with the time of my appointment the next morning and an envelope full of some sort of pamphlets. That was it for that appointment, so Jake took me back to the hotel.

I felt so shaken already and was so filled with dread for the next day that I found that all I wanted to do was lie down on the bed.

"Well, that didn't take too long," said Jake. "And now we have a full day to have fun in Vegas. Let's go hit the casinos."

"I don't know," I said.

"Come on. It'll take your mind off of all of this, and we'll have some fun. Remember, your older brother specifically instructed you to have fun," he said smiling.

"Jake, you know I'm only fifteen," I said. "If I go with you, I'll just get us both thrown out of any casinos we visit and you know it."

"Well, what do you want to do then?" he asked.

"I think that you should go enjoy visiting the casinos, and I should just hang out here at the hotel and rest."

"Leave you here all alone all day to sit and contemplate your situation?" he asked. "I don't know that I can do that. Look, if you don't feel up to going out, I can stay here with you, and we can do some calm, non-stressful things like take a walk around the neighborhood."

"No, now it's my turn to veto this idea," I said. "I know you had your heart set on seeing some of the casinos here, and as bad as I feel right now, I would feel a hundred million times worse if I felt like I had kept you from having fun here after you've gone to all of this effort and expense for me. Seriously, I'll be okay here by myself."

Jake looked like he was torn between wanting to go out and have fun, and yet not wanting to leave me alone to be overtaken by dark brooding.

"I think I may have just the remedy for this situation," he said. "I've brought something from my mom's cabinet that perhaps I shouldn't have." He went to his bag and pulled out a bottle of vodka.

I gasped. "Alcohol," I said. I didn't know why, but somehow that seemed like going too far. Here I was in sin city committing every kind of sin possible. I wondered if there would ever be any hope for me to recover after this.

Jake seemed to understand what I was feeling. He came over and sat down on the bed and put his arm around me. "Think of this weekend as your grace period," he said. "Nothing you do this weekend counts for or against your eternal salvation."

I was still a little worried.

"Now," he said, "I'm your doctor, and this is your medicine. This will help you to relax and survive this one difficult day. There's a convenience store next door. I'm going to get you a sandwich and some chips. What would you like with your medicine? Orange juice? Cranberry? Something else?"

"Orange juice," I said.

"Okay," he said, standing up. As he went to the door, he noticed the envelope and picked it up. He looked over some of the materials inside and shook his head. "I can't in good conscience leave you alone with this," he said. "It'll just make you crazy." Then he left with it.

When he got back a couple minutes later, he had a sack from the convenience store, and he didn't have the envelope anymore. He set the sack down on the table by the bed and pulled out a bottle of orange juice. He then poured some vodka into the bottom of a glass and filled the rest with orange juice and handed it to me. I sat there and held the glass in my hand and looked at it.

"I'm not going to leave until you drink this," he said.

I took a swallow. It had a sharp, strange taste to it and a bit of an after-bite.

"Good," he said. "Now, if you'll drink that and settle in and watch some good old-fashioned mindless television, I believe you'll be okay." He turned on the TV and started flipping through the channels. As he hit one with an old Scooby-Doo cartoon on it, I laughed a little.

"Ah, this is just what you need," he said, leaving it on faintly in the background. "Now drink up."

I drank some more of my drink and took the chips out of the sack.

"Good," he said. "Now how do you feel? Do you want me to stay here with you? It's no big deal, I will. I can come back to Vegas anytime."

"No, no, go, seriously," I said. "I'm okay. I'll have fun relaxing and watching these ridiculous old-time cartoons. In fact I've even brought some mindless reading material." I went to my bag and got out the latest issue of *Cosmopolitan* which I had bought the other day and hadn't even started reading yet.

He laughed. "Good, you're already one step ahead of me," he said.

"Exactly," I said. "I'll be fine."

"Okay," he said. "Actually, there's one more thing." He paused, looking a little sheepish. "I've counted my money, and without digging into my mom's advance on next month's paycheck, I have enough money for the hotel balance and gas and provisions for the way back, but just barely..."

I took the hint and grabbed my bag. I pulled out a hundred dollars in twenties and gave it to him. "Here," I said. "You don't need to pay me back."

"Thanks," he said. "I'll pay for the rest of the trip then." He put the money in his pocket and looked up. "This isn't all the money you have left is it?"

"No," I said.

"Good," he said. "I'll be back in a few hours, and then we can go out to dinner together, and after that cruise the strip to see the lights." He gave me a little hug and said, "Take care of yourself. Drink your medicine and try to relax." Then he left.

I felt a twinge of fear upon hearing his motorcycle speeding out of the parking lot. I settled back against my pillow and watched the nonsense on TV and took another gulp of my drink. I started paging through the glossy pages of Cosmo one by one. The colors of the photos in the make-up ads in the first few pages of Cosmo were always so striking that I liked to page through them slowly and study each one.

My next instinct was to try to find the sex article, but given the circumstances, I didn't really feel like it today. I poured myself another does of my medicine and then I sipped it and munched on the sandwich as I turned to the horoscope.

Obviously I didn't believe in astrology or think that it had anything useful or relevant to my life, yet I found it amusing to read the Cosmo horoscope. It was kind of a fun game to show how any horoscope could be applied to anyone's life at any time if you spent a little mental effort finding an appropriate interpretation. I was disappointed to see that my horoscope for this month didn't say anything about a voyage, which was a very common theme in horoscopes, and here I was on a voyage. It was as if the horoscope writer didn't even know I was here! I was starting to feel the effects of the alcohol enough to think that that was a clever observation.

I drank some more as I paged through some fluffy articles and half-watched a rerun of "The Brady Bunch" that I found. It wasn't long before I'd made a sizable dent in the bottle of vodka.

When I finally heard the door open, the sound seemed distant. I was lying on my back on the bed looking at the ceiling enjoying the ride.

I was happy to see him again even though between the alcohol and the mindless entertainment, I'd managed to get to the point where I'd forgotten to miss him. And since missing Jake was the thing I was trying to put out of my mind, I hardly even noticed that not a single thought had crossed my mind with respect to that other subject that I was trying not to think about.

Jake came in and sat down on the bed. "How do you feel?" he asked.

"How do I feel? Hmmm, how do I feel?" I wasn't sure.

Jake laughed, probably because I'd done as instructed and had gotten drunk.

"Did you have fun?" I asked.

"Yeah, it was great! You wouldn't believe some of the crazy stuff they have here. It's like some giant amusement park for grown-ups."

"Yeah, I imagine," I said. "How'd you make out?"

"Well, since I'm not twenty-one yet, I had some trouble getting into some of the casinos, but I managed to get into Caesar's Palace. It's really wild, all done up like the decadent days of ancient Rome."

"Did you win anything?" I asked.

"Well, I won a little on the slots, but I ended up losing it all on Blackjack. Sorry."

"That's okay. The point is you had fun. The money you set aside to gamble is like an admission fee for your fun time out."

"Exactly," said Jake. "If you look at the money you take into the casino as just the entry fee for an amusing game, then it's like it's not really gambling—which technically I'm not supposed to be doing. Anyway, even though it was fun this once, I don't think it was interesting enough to make a habit of it."

I laughed.

"What's so funny?" he asked.

"Really you got lucky," I said. "It's good to lose big on your first try. That way you won't get hooked."

Now he laughed. "That's a good way of looking at it," he said. "So in the grand scheme of things I won big!"

"Yep!" I said.

"There was one little glitch, though, actually."

"What?"

"Well, when I was at Caesar's Palace, I saw one of my uncle's business partners. I know the guy recognized me, and I know this guy well enough to know that he's going to for sure tell my uncle that he saw me in a casino."

"So?" I asked. "What's your uncle going to do? Tell your mom on you? She knows you're here—she arranged the whole trip!"

Jake laughed. "Another good point. You're pretty sharp-witted tonight for being so drunk! Still, I hate to disappoint my uncle. He and his wife couldn't have any children of their own, and so he's helped me a lot growing up since my dad really isn't in the picture. Never really has been in the picture, actually. So my uncle's opinion is important to me. He's a really strict Mormon though, and he won't be happy to hear that I went out gambling."

I wanted to say something comforting, but I couldn't think of anything.

"Oh, well," he said. "I guess it's not that big a deal. So how about we go get some grub? You're sober enough to hang on, right?"

"Yeah, no problem," I said.

"Cool. You know a lot of the casinos have these great inexpensive buffets in order to draw in people to gamble. I'll bet we can sneak you into one of them. Some of the older casinos are more lax because they have trouble competing for customers against the new, flashy ones."

I got up out of bed and we got on the bike. I still felt drunk enough to be only half-aware of my surroundings. Jake found us an appropriate casino buffet, and not only managed to get us in, but also managed to somehow get us some real drinks. It was interesting to look out of the buffet area to see the main part of the casino with its rows of slot machines and tables for playing cards. It looked exactly the way casinos look in movies except perhaps this one was a bit older and shabbier. We had a lot of fun hanging out there and chatting.

When we were done it was dark out, and Jake suggested that we should go cruise the strip. This was apparently the traditional main road for casinos although it wasn't where all the biggest, newest ones were because there wasn't room. Merely driving down this street itself part of the entertainment. The whole experience was spectacular: holding Jake and riding through the evening air that was just starting to cool, seeing the endless stream of bright lights of all colors and shapes against the black sky still with my vague, lingering feeling of intoxication. This alone was worth making the trip for.

It wasn't until we were back in bed that I was struck with the memory that this wasn't just a pleasant weekend vacation. I started feeling nervous and afraid again thinking of the next morning's planned events.

"Can I ask you a question?" I asked Jake quietly.

"Sure," he replied.

"Do you think I'm a murderer?"

"Of course not," he said. "If I thought that, then I would think that I was an accomplice or an accessory or something. I wouldn't bring you all the way here to commit a murder."

"But that's what people say," I said.

"Look," he said. "No one knows when the spirit enters the body. Look at the play we're in. In it, the spirits don't go down from the pre-existence until birth. At one point in the play, the mom has a miscarriage of the body that was intended for little Emily, yet Emily is okay to try again later. I know that seeing it in a Mormon play isn't the same as it being doctrine, but at least it shows there's some leeway for different interpretations."

"That's a good point," I said.

"I don't know all of the theology behind it," he said, "but on a gut level I just can't see this as being the same thing as killing a person, especially at this very early stage."

"Thank you," I said. His words made sense, but I couldn't escape the feeling that I was somehow fallen and tainted and evil and that no amount of repentance would ever restore me. My mind was full of darkness and monsters as I fell asleep.

When we got up in the morning it was time for the appointment, the real one this time. It turned out to be less of a big deal than I'd expected. the clinic was now familiar, and the doctor himself was sympathetic.

He gave me a pill to take and some water. He said that that would render it "non-viable" which seemed to be a nice technical euphemism for killing it.

I thought to myself how I'd already decided and it was too late to change my mind now as I took the pill. I repeated to myself that this was my grace period.

Then the doctor gave me some pills to insert twenty-four hours later and a rubber glove to do it. He also gave me some painkillers to take on the same day. After that, the counselor came in to check on me one last time to make sure I was okay, and that was it, we were free to go.

We had already checked out of our hotel, so from there we set straight off onto the road back home to Orem. Jake told me his mom had explained that it was necessary to work it out to drive back the morning of taking the first pill since that day would be okay whereas the next day it would be impossible to travel, particularly by motorcycle. I was a bit scared of what was in store for me for the next day and feeling kind of overwhelmed with conflicting emotions about what I had just done.

I actually kind of wished I had some more vodka to keep the bad thoughts away. One nice thing about going home by motorcycle was that I had an excuse to hold Jake in my arms for hours on end. I couldn't think of a single other circumstance that would permit such a thing. It was still vaguely sexy, but more than that it was comforting and familiar. I couldn't help but feel like Jake was kind of like Rex only with a leather jacket and a harley instead of glasses and a math book.

This is my grace period, I told myself again. Grace. It's a word that hardly exists in our Mormon vocabulary. We're more likely to hear that "faith without works is dead," and "the kingdom of God is righteousness." It is by righteousness that one attains the Celestial Kingdom. Since no one except Jesus is perfect, some grace is necessary in the form of His atonement allowing us to repent of our sins. But that grace is something that comes after you have done everything you can do.

I figured that theologically Jake's idea that this was a grace period was completely wrong, but I hated to let go of it. I couldn't imagine that it would be possible to repent and be forgiven of this. When I thought about it, I knew that I would never be innocent again.

Fortunately the rhythm of the road helped the pleasant memories from the weekend drown out the bad ones as we sped home.

16. SUNDAY MORNING

I INSERTED THE PILLS the next morning as instructed. Even though the counselor had explained what would happen, I didn't know exactly how it would go. It seemed to me like it wouldn't be a good idea to go to church, so I got back into bed and asked Joy to tell Mom and Dad that I wasn't feeling well.

Surprisingly, Mom and Dad were perfectly okay with me staying home. Mom just came in to check on me briefly to see if I was okay and that was it. I guess I figured that since this whole weekend was such an incredibly wrenchingly big deal for me, that they should somehow be suspicious about it. But since I had always been a good girl and had never given them that much of a hard time about not wanting to go to church, they apparently were willing to take my excuses at face value and trust me.

Once the family was gone, the cramps and bleeding started as expected. I took the painkillers and tried to relax. This was the first part of the whole experience that was actually painful, but in fact it wasn't as bad as the terror and emotions of the earlier parts. At this point I was so emotionally drained that I could hardly feel anything more about it. It seemed like this stage was more housekeeping than anything else, and all I could bring myself to feel was relief that all of this would soon be over. Essentially I felt like I'd dodged a bullet.

Alone in the house and calm, I felt like it was finally time to start the repentance process. Not including the usual family and church prayers I hadn't prayed once since that first incident with Walter. Now it was time.

I got down on my knees as best I could with the cramps. I prayed earnestly and sincerely for forgiveness for all of the terrible things I had done. Then I pleaded with my Heavenly Father to give me the strength never to do any of that again nor even to want to.

In then end, I was pretty sure it didn't work. How could Heavenly Father ever forgive me for all of that? I figured I would just have to resign myself to the fate I had earned.

* * *

Tuesday's rehearsal was the first complete run-through of the whole play. The dress rehearsal was scheduled for Thursday night, and then the big production would be performed for two nights: Friday and Saturday.

I didn't get a chance to talk to either Walter or Jake before the run-through on Tuesday night began. As always, it began with the various characters in the pre-existence talking about the things we would do during our future lives on Earth. First Todd and Julie sang about their love and about how they would find each other and marry one day. Then Todd went down to earth and Julie stayed as all of the other kids joined her to sing about how they would pull together as a family. This was of course my first number. After that, it was time for Jake and Walter, or Wally and Greene, as it were, to sing about how they would be LDS missionaries and bring people to the gospel.

I watched their number from backstage. In some ways it was painful to see it, but I couldn't look away. Jake did his best to perform his comic scene, but he almost seemed to be doing it through clenched teeth. His every smile for his missionary companion seemed painfully forced. Walter was oblivious. He reveled in his own charm, in his gorgeous face and smile, his light and witty manner, and his beautiful singing voice. He performed his song about spreading the gospel with joyous abandon.

Of course there was no audience, but when they finished their number I clapped enthusiastically from the sidelines. Walter turned to me with a big satisfied smile and winked. Jake looked shocked by my reaction and seemed genuinely upset to see me so quick to go back to showering affection on Walter. He seemed to hate him all the more watching his innocent pleasure after what we had been through.

Still, I felt like Walter could hardly be blamed for not taking care of a problem he hadn't known about. I wanted him to stay the way he was—happy and light-hearted—and not see him hurt and broken by this whole thing.

During the scene with the number *He's Just a Friend* that Jake and I were both in with Walter and the girls, Jake seemed to do a better job of putting his feelings aside and having fun with it.

Between my scenes I went out to sit by Jake's mom, who was sitting as the lone person in the audience.

"How are you doing, honey?" she asked.

"Okay," I said.

"Jake says the trip went smoothly," she said.

"Yeah."

"And after?" she asked.

"It wasn't too bad."

"That's good," she said. "I'm glad." We sat and watched together silently until my next scene.

Throughout the rehearsal I didn't get much chance to talk to Walter since the other girls were monopolizing his attention. I didn't go out of my way to seek him out because I didn't really feel like talking to him again just yet. We exchanged a few smiles though.

The dress rehearsal on Thursday night was exciting right from the beginning. This time we had a real audience in a sense because they'd brought in a bunch of old people from various retirement communities to come watch it.

There was a big room in the basement that had been set up as the dressing room with a long table in the center with chairs and mirrors where all the make-up was to be applied. We had to wear a lot of stage make-up so as not to look too pale under the strong lights. The dressing room had two separate annexes that were curtained off for the men and the women to change costumes separately.

Walter and Jake had both gotten their hair cut in the super-short missionary style. It wasn't becoming on either one of them, but as far as I could tell the standard missionary haircut was never becoming on anyone. Of course Walter was still drop-dead gorgeous. Not even a missionary haircut could put a stop to that.

While we were all downstairs changing from our spirit robes of the pre-existence to our normal Earth clothing, I saw Walter alone off to the side of the dressing room holding a single rose. He beckoned me to come over to him.

"I would like to try to make things right between us if possible," he said. "I've brought you this small token which I hope that you will accept." He handed me the rose.

"Thank you," I said, taking the rose. I was happy to see that he was finally willing to address what had happened and was interested in trying to work it out.

"I know we haven't had much chance to talk these past few weeks," he said. It's not that I've forgotten you, it's just that I feel bad about what I did, and haven't really been able to figure out how to deal with it."

"I understand," I said.

"Well, now I have some idea of what I'd like to do. I would like to take you out on Tuesday night if you're willing. Not like what happened that other time, but rather a pleasant, chaste evening. We can go out and have a nice dinner and talk privately about what happened and about the future."

"Of course I would be happy to," I replied.

"That's wonderful, Jill. It makes me very happy. We can arrange the details tomorrow night."

I took my rose back to the ladies' changing area and put it with my things. Again I thought I was perhaps crazy for wanting this, but I couldn't deny feeling thrilled that he wanted to try to make things right and particularly that he wanted to talk with me seriously about the future. I was also happy to be the only girl in the entire production that night to have received a rose.

On opening night a lot of the ladies received full bouquets of roses, including Jake's mom and Pinky. Charlene in particular received several bouquets.

Walter had brought a rose for every single girl in the entire production, including one for Pinky's little niece who was playing Emily. The little girl was thrilled to receive it because it was the only one she'd gotten, and she seemed pleased to be treated like one of the big girls and get a gift from such a handsome and popular guy. She gave him a big hug and kiss in return. For my part, with my rose from the previous night, that made two rose from him for me, which was one more than he had given any other girl.

Rex brought a dozen long-stemmed roses for Laura, which she accepted gracefully. He then proceeded to ask her out for the following weekend. This was not at all surprising considering that they'd been flirting since the beginning of rehearsals.

Bizarrely, though, Laura seemed surprised by his offer. She thought about it for a minute and then said "Yeah, when I decide I want to go out with one of the guys from the *school A.V. club*, you'll be the first one I'll call." And then she walked away.

I was about to die seeing poor Rex shot down like that. Fortunately there hadn't been too many people around to hear, but I imagined that it must have taken him a lot of courage to ask her out given that he'd waited until the very end of the production to do it, so that rejection must have really hurt. There was no time for tears, however, as the production was about to begin, and Rex needed to go take his place like everyone else.

I came up to listen from backstage as the female soloist opened the piece:

"Who are these children coming down
coming down like gentle rain through darkened skies
with glory trailing from their feet as they go
and endless promise in their eyes?"

Then the angel chorus came in:
"Who are these young ones growing tall, growing strong
like silver trees against the storm
who will not bend with the wind or the change
but stand to fight the world alone?

"These are the few the warriors saved for Saturday
to come the last day of the world,
these are they on Saturday.
These are the strong the warriors rising in their might
to win the battle raging in the hearts of men on Saturday..."

It was so thrilling to be finally on stage performing our scenes for real. It was the culmination of all of our efforts over the past few months. Looking out at the audience, I saw Mom and Dad sitting with Kathy and Joy and Jared. I also saw the video camera that was filming us. Rex had helped to set it up, but another guy who worked for the school's media and technology services was operating it because Rex was backstage sitting on a stool beside the lighting panel.

After all of our efforts over such a long period of time, the actual production went by surprisingly quickly. We went through our scenes the first night and the second night, and the next thing I knew it was over and it was time for the cast party.

The cast party was held right there in the stake center after the performance. The refreshments were set up in one of the larger meeting rooms—in fact it was the very room that adjoined the baptismal font. The party was a big enough deal that Pinky had had caterers bring in some fancier treats in addition to the standard fare of chips and punch.

My first thought was to go find Walter, but of course he was surrounded by other girls. It seemed like half the cast wanted to get in one last evening with him before he set off for the MTC. As soon as he saw me, he smiled and waved and beckoned for me to come over, but really he looked pretty occupied. One of the girls from the chorus was sitting so close to him that she was practically in his lap. I figured that there was no sense trying to squeeze into that scene, especially since I'd have him all to myself on our date a few nights later.

My next thought was to look for Rex, but he was nowhere to be found. I didn't see Jake or Ben or Paige either in fact, so I figured they'd all gone off somewhere. I looked all around the building, and then outside.

Finally I saw them. Rex, Jake, Ben, Paige, and Andy Ross were all sitting on the grass on the far side of the parking lot. When I approached them I noticed that they were all drinking beer. This completely shocked me.

"Rex, what are you doing?" I asked.

He laughed. "What, this?" he asked, indicating the beer. "It's nothing, it's just beer."

"But you're breaking the Word of Wisdom," I said.

"I'm not sure that's the case," he said. "I've been reading the Word of Wisdom more closely, and I'm convinced that not only is beer not forbidden, it's actually recommended."

"It's true," said Jake. "He showed us, and it's pretty convincing."

"Do you want to try one?" asked Ben.

"No I don't think so," I said, but I decided to sit and hang out with them anyway. Of course I'd had alcohol when I was in Las Vegas with Jake, but that was during my grace period, and I didn't want to undermine my repentance by falling back into sin.

I listened to their conversation for a while, and as soon as I got the impression that Rex was a little detached from it, I moved closer to speak to him privately.

"Are you having problems with sin too, like me?" I asked.

He laughed derisively. "Sin? What's sin?"

I was surprised by his question. "It's when you break the commandments, of course."

"Look, I'm probably the wrong person for you to talk to about this whole thing," he said. "The truth is that I've been having a lot of very serious doubts lately, like I'm not really sure anymore that the church is true."

I couldn't believe my ears! "You of all people!" I said. "You've always been the great scriptorian. You know the *Book of Mormon* and the *Doctrine & Covenants* better than anyone else I know. How could you be having doubts about the church?"

"Actually, I think that that's exactly the problem," he said. "I feel like I'd be able to believe it more if I knew it less."

Upon hearing that, I felt like I was really alone and had no one left to turn to for support. On the one hand I had Kathy who was Molly Mormon and could never understand what I'd been through, and on the other hand I had Rex, who from the sound of it was practically an apostate! At least I still had my little sister Joy who was a faithful sinner like me. She and I would be probably be together in the Telestial Kingdom while Kathy went with Mom and Dad and possibly Jared to the Celestial Kingdom and Rex went off to outer darkness with the apostates.

At the end of the party I was hesitant to ride home with Rex because he had been drinking. He laughed at my fears and told me that he had only had two beers the entire evening and was certainly not drunk. Still, I suggested that since I had my learner's permit maybe I should be the one to drive. "Whatever," he said, handing me the keys.

On the way home Rex told me that he was planning to edit all of the videos of the production over the weekend and asked me if I would like to watch them with him and his friends on Tuesday night. I told him that I would like to except that I had a date.

"What do you mean you have a date?" he asked. "I thought you weren't allowed to date until you turn sixteen."

"Well, I've talked to Mom, and she's letting me make a special exception this one time because I won't turn sixteen until after he leaves on his mission."

Rex looked surprised. "Please don't tell me you're going on a date with Walter Smith," he said.

"What's wrong with that?" I asked.

"Well, isn't he the guy that...? you know..."

"Yeah," I said. "So what?"

Rex looked at me like he thought I was completely insane. "Just bring a condom this time," he said.

"Rex, it's not like that!" I said. "He's repented and reformed. And so have I."

"Whatever," he said. "Just humor me and bring a condom with you. Do you have one?"

"Yes, as a matter of fact I do, and I'm planning to bring it, but I won't need it!"

"Fine with me," he said. "I hope you have fun." We rode the rest of the way home in silence.

17. TUESDAY EVENING

T UESDAY WAS A BIT of a strange night for a date, but I was sure it wasn't easy for Walter to schedule in all of the things he needed to get done before entering the Missionary Training Center on the following week. Actually I vaguely suspected that he was saving the choice nights of Friday and Saturday for dates with other girls, but I put that thought out of my mind and told myself that it was just that he had tons of stuff to do and scheduling it all in was tricky.

Mom was pretty happy for me that I would be going on my first date with a boy who was about to set off on a mission. She was perfectly willing to overlook the fact that I wasn't quite sixteen yet, although Dad wasn't too thrilled about it. Mom patiently explained to him that we needed to make a special exception this one time because if we waited until I turned sixteen, Walter would already be gone.

"I don't think that that's a good reason to be making a special exception," said Dad. "I don't know that she should be dating a boy who's so much older."

"But he's about to set off on his *mission*," said Mom. "Our missionaries need to be encouraged by the support of girls back home." She said it as if I were doing some altruistic thing to advance the spreading of the gospel, but the gleam in her eye as she helped me get ready said that she was proud that her daughter was on the road to snag such a desirable guy.

"I don't like it," said Dad. "I hope that this 'last date before going on a mission' isn't like the proverbial 'last date before going off to war.'"

"Sweetheart, what a terrible thing to say," said Mom. "This Walter is a fine, upstanding, righteous boy who is about to sacrifice two years of his life to serve the Lord. The least we can do is believe in him and encourage him."

"I'm still not happy about it," said Dad. "If you insist on allowing this, I won't try to stop you, but I'm not going to be a part of it." He went into his study and closed the door. I supposed that that meant that he wasn't going to come out and insist upon meeting Walter. So much the better, really.

"Don't worry about Dad," said Mom. "He'll come around. Now let's work on getting your make-up and hair just right..."

* * *

Walter arrived in his suit and tie since the plan was to go out to a fine restaurant. Dressed like that and with his haircut, he looked like he was on his mission already. With his gorgeous looks and friendly manner, it was clear that he would have no difficulty approaching people and convincing them to be receptive to his message in the two years to come.

We spent most of dinner talking about how excited he was about his mission. As I already knew, he was being sent to the Florida Jacksonville Mission. That part was a bit of a disappointment because, like everyone else, he had been hoping for a foreign call. But some people were needed to spread the gospel stateside, and it was important to go where the Lord called you and needed you.

When we got back into the car he told me that he wanted to take me somewhere special and show me something that he had never shown anyone. I agreed a little nervously.

Noting my unease, he laughed in a friendly manner. "Don't worry," he said. "It's nothing bad. In fact, it's exactly the opposite— it's something very, very good."

He started driving up into the canyon. It was already dark out.

"You see," he said, "I've been doing a lot of thinking and praying and struggling with my conscience in order to prepare for my mission. I want to do what the Lord wants me to do, and I'm sure that this mission is it."

"Of course it is," I said.

"Now I know I should have gone to the bishop to confess," he said. "But as you know I didn't want to risk having him tell me to postpone my mission. Hanging around here I'm not going to get any more righteous than I am now," he laughed, "so I might as well go. That's what the spirit told me."

I believed he was right, although I felt that there would have been no danger in going to the bishop since the spirit would surely have told the bishop the same thing. Still, Walter had already been ordained an Elder, so I didn't want to contradict him on spiritual matters.

"Now the place I'm taking you is the most spiritual place I've ever been outside the holy temple. It's as good as confessing to the bishop. No, better, really."

I was proud of him that he so earnestly wanted to make himself worthy for his mission, and I felt touched that he wanted to share his spiritual growth with me and make amends to Heavenly Father.

"Here it is," he said, pulling the car off to the side of the road. Not too far from where we pulled over, but not visible from the road, there was a large, flat stone as big as a table or altar.

"Isn't it amazing?" he asked. "See, it's just like the rock where Jesus prayed at the Garden of Gethsemane. I found it by chance, and I come here sometimes when I want a special, spiritual place to pray. I've never taken anyone here before."

"It's wonderful," I said. "Thank you for sharing this with me. I won't tell anyone."

"Can't you feel the spirit?" he asked.

I was standing there next to him in the dark with a gentle breeze moving the upper branches of the trees. The moon and stars were

shining down on our little altar. It was the most calm, peaceful, spiritual feeling I'd ever felt. "Yes, I feel it," I said, taking his hand.

"That's why I come here," he said. "Now, will you kneel with me?"

"Of course," I replied.

We each knelt across from each other on opposite sides of our rock altar and bowed our heads. Rather than folding my arms, it seemed more appropriate to clasp my hands together over the altar as Jesus did in the paintings of him praying at Gethsemane. Walter put his hands around my hands. It was dark and we were alone instead of surrounded by people in white and mirrors to eternity, yet still I imagined that we were kneeling at the altar in the Celestial Room of the temple.

Walter began praying aloud. "Our Dear Father in Heaven. Forgive me. Please forgive me for my weakness and for what I have done. Grant me the strength to serve Thee and to do Thy will. Grant me the strength to keep myself clean and pure so that I will be worthy to feel Thy spirit and lead people to Thee in the years to come. Please send down Thy love generously upon us, upon me and upon this precious daughter of Thine. In the name of Jesus Christ, amen."

And forgive me, too, I thought to myself as I repeated Walter's amen. I felt so much better and lighter and cleaner for having repented with Walter like that. He was right—I didn't see how it would have been possible for a confession to the bishop to be more purifying than that. Walter didn't even know the extent of what I had to repent of, yet the spirit had moved him to bring me to this special place to share his repentance with him. It was a sign that he was already becoming more receptive to the promptings of the spirit as to what he needed to do to bring people closer to the Lord and to the gospel. I was sure he would make a fantastic missionary.

He held my hand as we stood up and walked back to the car. Just before we got in, he held me in his arms. Nothing sexual, just a hug. We got back in the car and started driving back.

"This has been a very special evening for me, Jill," he said.

"For me too," I said. I couldn't help but feel like this was the sort of spiritual experience that eternal companions should share.

He drove me to my house and walked me up to my door. At the door he gave me a gentle kiss. Not a kiss of passion but of sweet affection.

"Will you write to me while I'm on my mission?" he asked.

"Yes, I will."

Characters in *Saturday's Warrior*

The Wendells

Kathy

Rex

Jill

Joy

Jared

Brother Wendell

Sister Wendell

Rex's Friends

Jake

Paige

Ben

Andy

Other Cast Members

Walter

Laura

Linda

Charlene

Pinky's niece

Directors

Pinky

Grace
(Jake's mom)

IV. Brigham Young University

Lynn

18. SUNDAY AFTERNOON

I WATCHED THE SECOND HAND slowly make its way around the clock face. For all of the bright, enthusiastic people running it, Sacrament Meeting in a BYU student ward really wasn't any more interesting than the Sacrament Meetings put on by the worn-out, tired families back home. And here of course Sacrament Meeting had the added fun of being mandatory, and I don't mean just "earn your stars in heaven" kind of mandatory. I mean more like "if you don't show up for church regularly, then don't bother to come back to school next semester" kind of mandatory. At BYU, your bishop was always watching, and an "ecclesiastical endorsement" from him every year was a requirement for continuing enrollment.

I shifted around in my uncomfortable wooden chair. The speaker had just gotten to the crying part of her story. I wished I were instead attending my Physics lecture that was held in the same building during the week. I felt like a real jerk for being so indifferent to the girl's spiritual joy in finding the one and only true gospel, but she'd already told essentially this same story in a couple of Fast and Testimony meetings, and I really just wanted to get home and out of these uncomfortable nylons.

The girl giving the talk was something of a celebrity or hero to our ward because she was a convert. She demonstrated the wonderful effects that the only true gospel has on people's lives when they join the world's fastest-growing religion. She was an inspiration to the rest of the ward who didn't have to find the true church because we were raised in it. I sincerely wanted to be happy for her. Yet I also wanted to go home.

I looked back up at the clock. I couldn't even console myself with the thought that there were only five or ten minutes left to go since in fact the speaker had already gone over time. I started looking around the room at the other students. Some of them, mostly girls, looked to be on the verge of tears, hanging on the speaker's every word in rapt attention. I marveled that this level of interest seemed to come so naturally to certain people when no matter how much effort I put into it, I couldn't seem to work up the enthusiasm for this sort of thing that Heavenly Father surely wanted and expected from me. Other people, including almost all of the boys, were dozing or doodling on their programs or had on the kind of glazed expression that seemed appropriate temporally if perhaps wrong celestially.

Finally she came to the "in the name of Jesus Christ, amen" part, which meant only one more droning hymn and one more elaborate prayer. After that there would be only two more hours of meetings, each only a little more painfully dull than the last, and each with an attendance sheet to pass around and sign.

After the usual eternity, we were set free for another week. My friends and I stepped out of the science center where our ward's Sunday services were held and into the autumn afternoon sunlight.

Immediately Wendy challenged Lavyrne to a quick race, and they sprinted off to be the first to touch the wall of a building about a hundred yards away. The two of them were always racing each other like that—best friends with a bit of a fun, competitive spirit. It was kind of a ridiculous image to see them doing it in their Sunday dresses and shoes though.

Of course even sitting reverently in church neither one of them looked particularly natural in a Sunday dress. This highlighted something of a sore spot for me about the church, namely that being the only true church on the Earth for everyone, it was necessarily a one-size-fits-all church. Yet, like most one-size-fits-all items, it fit some better than others. I certainly wasn't much more at home in the standard pioneer-gingham Sunday attire than Wendy or Lavyrne. I was dying to get back into my comfy jeans.

Some of the other girls fared a little better in their Sunday best. My older sister April, who was the RA on my floor this year, always found a way to look nice. Amy, my best friend from my high school days, seemed to do as well in a dress as in jeans. Lavyrne's roommate Trisha was kind of overweight, so I couldn't really tell if church dresses looked better or worse on her than anything else. My own roommate Janie seemed to have been born to wear a pioneer dress, and in fact looked ill at ease in her version of weekday clothing.

The only one who looked fabulous in a Sunday dress, however, was Cindy. Cindy was stunningly beautiful. She had a gorgeous face and body, and her shimmering long blond hair had just the right amount of natural curl to it. She had such a flair for putting together the perfect look that she somehow managed to find dresses that fit into the category of appropriate for church yet looked sophisticated and even sexy on her. Cindy happened to be Amy's cousin, so after years of planning with Amy that we would room together at BYU, when it finally came down to it she chose to room with Cindy, leaving me with the luck of the draw. I ended up sharing a room with Janie, a few doors down from Amy and Cindy, along the same hall.

Cindy was walking along at a slight distance from the rest of our group because she was accompanied by her latest love-interest Hyrum, who was a handsome, muscular slugger on the BYU baseball team and a returned-missionary. He wasn't in our ward, but he had shown up near the end of our service to see Cindy. Apparently after attending services at his own ward, he actually attended an additional church meeting in our ward just to spend time with Cindy! It was a different experience having a girl like Cindy as a part of our little circle of friends since I'd never really been friends before with anyone who attracted so many highly-desired boyfriends so easily. Interestingly, it turned out that despite this unusual quality, she was a nice girl and fun to hang out with.

The only other girls in our group that had boyfriends were April and Amy. Amy was dating a guy named Jake whom she had met in her *Book of Mormon* class and who lived in Orem with his mom. April was still seeing Andrew, who had been her boyfriend throughout high school.

Andrew was planning to enter the Missionary Training Center at the beginning of the next semester. (He was setting off a little older than the usual nineteen years old because he had been delayed for health reasons.) Everyone predicted that he would soon pop the question and give April a big rock to keep her company during her upcoming two years in which she would be acting as that beloved archetype of LDS young-womanhood: the girl waiting for her missionary. We all liked to tease her about how quickly after Andrew's departure she'd be writing him a "Dear John letter" and getting engaged to someone else, as the stereotype goes.

As we walked along a little farther, we caught up with Wendy and Lavyrne. April snuck up on Lavyrne and tapped her on the left shoulder while approaching her on her right side. That little game of getting the person to look the wrong way was one of the jokes Lavyrne and Wendy liked to play on people. April was one of the few people who could successfully pull that trick on one of the two of them. April was so feminine and petite that she looked like a pixie next to these big, athletic girls, yet she got in on their in-jokes with ease. It was kind of like how she'd made several close friends among the girls on the softball team in high school even though she wasn't very interested in softball herself. I figured that April just had a way with people, which was what made her such a good RA.

When we got back to the room, I immediately started peeling myself out of those awful nylons and donning something reasonable. Janie gave me a bit of a disapproving look for this because in truth our Sunday duties weren't quite over. After dinner we were scheduled for another exciting round of reading out of church manuals in the form of "Family Home Evening." And Janie felt that one should respect the sabbath by dressing reverently the entire day.

Janie put on some religious music—the only thing allowed to be played in our room on Sunday according to the rules she set for us—and started preparing the lesson for Family Home Evening. I was lucky enough not to have a calling this semester, but Janie was called to be the "mom" of our Family Home Evening group.

Family Home Evening is supposed to be the weekly devotional held by the family at home in the evening, hence the name. Here at BYU we're obviously not with our families nor are we at home, but that's no excuse for getting out of holding a meeting! So the ward randomly assigns people a group of boys and girls to be their "family" so that there's no danger of missing out on the blessings that come from regular doses of Family Home Evening.

Even though normally Family Home Evening would be held on Monday nights, logistics require the BYU student families to meet on Sunday evening instead. Monday night would be inconvenient for the times when people have tests or big assignments due on Tuesday. A Sunday meeting couldn't possibly interfere with school work since we're not supposed to be working on Sunday in the first place. Additionally on Mondays it would be difficult to find a place to meet. Most of the time the girls' dorms were off-limits to boys and the boys' dorms were off-limits to girls, but on Sunday afternoon there were special visiting hours. Every other Sunday the boys could visit the girls' dorms and on the opposite Sundays the girls were allowed in the boys' dorms. Of course the doors to the rooms containing opposite-sex visitors must remain open. And to give the devil a little less lee-way, we ate up a good chunk of this dangerously tempting time-bloc with a wholesome episode of Family Home Evening.

I looked up from my page of Latin homework that I was clandestinely reviewing to see what Janie was up to, aside from humming along with the Mormon Tabernacle Choir. Astonishingly, she appeared to be making some flannel story-board characters.

"What are you doing?" I asked.

"I'm preparing our Family Home Evening lesson, silly," she replied.

"Okay, but why are you cutting out pictures of Noah's Ark for a flannel story board?"

"It's one of the suggestions for this week's lesson in our Family Home Evening manual," she said, pointing to the page.

"Um, I hate to be a wet blanket here," I said, "but I would suspect that that suggestion is intended for families with children under five years old."

"Oh, I know that," she said, "I just thought it would be fun." And with that she went back to her humming and handicrafts.

Or more likely it was her way of demonstrating what a good mom she would make in a real family, I reasoned. Janie was fond of reminding us all that one of her (real-life) older sisters had married a guy she had met as a "brother" in her BYU Family Home Evening group. Janie was pretty clearly headed along this same path as she openly flirted with the short, chubby, freckle-faced boy who was our

Family Home Evening Group's "dad." Our beloved Family Home Evening parents weren't an established couple yet, but the guy was starting to look interested. As distasteful as attracting a man using a baby story board may seem, it's hard to criticize what works. Janie had one more serious prospect than I did.

Actually I generally found Janie's stories about her family to be kind of disturbing. She was the third-to-youngest in a family of eight children, all of them girls except the very last one. So when she wasn't explaining what tricks an older sister had used to land a husband (or "eternal companion" as Janie liked to say), her stories usually revolved around her younger brother, the boy of the family. She loved to recount how he had been raised to be the perfect gentleman, so when the family went to church on Sunday, it was the boy who got out of the car first and held the door open for every single one of his older sisters. Then he would rush ahead and open the door to the church building for them as well. It was kind of cute in a way, but in a way I felt sorry for her.

Once Janie had finished preparing her lesson, we set off with our friends to our local cafeteria, the Cannon Center, for dinner.

At dinner, Trisha was gushing over the latest letter she had gotten from her missionary in Brazil. Missionaries are supposed to stay focused on spiritual matters at all times, so three of the four pages of the letter were devoted to describing discussions he had taught and other spiritual matters such as how well the Holy Ghost was helping him to learn to speak Portuguese. But there were enough sweet nothings in it to keep Trisha's attention. In fact Trisha was corresponding with three different missionaries, one in Japan, one in Brazil, and one in Idaho. It wasn't clear to me precisely how she had met them or if they knew about each other. By coincidence, Janie seemed to be wondering the same thing, so she asked Trisha how she had found three missionary pen-pals like that.

"Why, do you want one?" asked Trisha. "All three of my missionaries know other guys in their missions who would be happy to have a girl back home to write to. That's basically how I met them myself—it was a friend-of-a-friend thing."

It sounded interesting. Corresponding with missionaries would be a pleasant and simple way of lining up some future prospects if they were guys who were coming back to BYU. I was about to ask for details myself when Wendy and Lavyrne broke into a rollicking chorus of *Will I Wait for You?* from *Saturday's Warrior*. They were practically rolling over each other laughing by the time they got to the final line: *"Like a faithful girl waits for her missionary..."* At that I figured it would be better to ask Trisha privately later rather than suffer that sort of teasing. April was already blushing as Wendy was punching her in the shoulder laughing heartily at her own joke.

After dinner, Janie went straight to the mirror to redo her hair and make-up. She fired up her curling iron and took off her glasses to do her eye make-up. She then spent about twenty minutes re-curling the entire front part of her hair and puffing it up and spraying it. She had perfected the technique of getting that "bangs to heaven" look that was so popular at BYU.

Family Home Evening passed without incident. Bizarrely enough, no one besides me seemed to think it was at all incongruous that Janie was holding up a flannel-covered board and sticking pictures of animals to it to illustrate the story of Noah's Ark, as if none of us had ever heard the story before. The little smiles exchanged between our "mom" and "dad" were actually kind of cute even though to be honest I found that I normally didn't like Janie very much.

In my opinion, none of the guys in our Family Home Evening "family" were very cute. Still, girls at BYU can't afford to be picky. The girl-to-boy ratio was such that all three floors of our wing of our dorm building were paired with only two floors of a corresponding boys' dorm wing to make up our ward. The bottom floor of the boys' dorm was grouped with some girls from Heritage Halls, the all-girls dormitory complex. Our FHE group of course bore out the same ratio. I looked at the guys in our group again, but none of them interested me in the slightest. They certainly didn't interest me enough to inspire me to fight so many other girls for them.

When Janie and I arrived back at our dorm after Family Home Evening, we found that our friends had already started a game of Hearts in Lavyrne and Trisha's room. Janie was incensed to see it because playing with face cards was already a sin in and of itself, and hence doing it on a Sunday was beyond the pale. I of course joined right in.

At last a relaxing and pleasant moment with friends. With me, Amy, Cindy, April, Trisha, Lavyrne, and Wendy all playing, we had enough girls that we had to play with Wendy and Lavyrne's special double-deck rules. Janie seemed to want to teach us a lesson by going off somewhere and refusing to participate, but since it was too easy for the rest of us not to notice that she was gone, she came back into the room periodically to remind us that she wasn't playing.

On one of her visits to the card-playing room, Janie repeated her standard refrain of how we should play the game with "Rook" cards instead of standard playing cards. To me this idea made no sense whatsoever. The two main arguments Janie gave against playing with standard playing cards were that playing with them gave the "appearance of evil" (which we should avoid) since playing cards are also used for real gambling, and that playing cards were evil because they were derived from Tarot cards, which were associated with the occult. But in my mind a bunch of girls innocently playing hearts appeared about the same—no more or less evil—whether the cards were regular playing cards or Rook cards, and since Rook cards were obviously derived from standard playing cards, they were ultimately derived from Tarot cards just like the face cards that were supposedly so evil.

Eventually Janie decided to go to bed for real and stop bothering the rest of us. Cindy noticed Lavyrne's tennis racket up on a shelf and suggested that it would be funny to set it up prominently in Janie's window, or rather Janie's side of our window. Apparently there was some story going around that there had once been a prostitution ring at BYU in which the girls advertised their availability by displaying tennis rackets in their windows. Opinion was divided in our circle as to whether it was a true story or an urban legend, but either way everyone agreed that it would be funny to see Janie's reaction to being signed up by her friends to this new profession. Lavyrne and Wendy, who lived for pranks, were particularly partisan to the idea. So I agreed that I would take the racket and set it up at the end of our game.

Looking around the room I could see that the contrast between Trisha and Lavyrne as roommates wasn't nearly as unpleasant as the contrast between me and Janie. In fact it was kind of funny. A glance at their posters was enough to get the idea. Trisha's half of the room was covered with giant posters of various boy heartthrobs such as you would find in magazines for teenage girls. I prided myself on not recognizing any of them except the seventies-era poster of Donny Osmond which matched a pillowcase I had had with his picture on it when I was a kid. Lavyrne's side, by contrast, was covered with posters of race cars and exciting sports scenes, including one of a baseball player hitting a home run, probably in a World Series or something. Over the bed, she had a similarly exciting action shot of Martina Navratilova on the tennis court.

I don't remember how the subject came up, but at some point in the game I got started on my pet subject of how annoying it is that everyone has to dress up in these same, same, same, bland, ugly dresses every Sunday. My friends had heard this lecture before, so they responded as usual that if I were really so concerned about the obligatory conformity, I should fight it by doing something truly non-conformist. I told them that I would love to except that the BYU dress code was very strictly enforced.

"There are plenty of non-conformist things you can do without breaking the dress code," April pointed out. "For girls, as long as your skirt's not too short and you're wearing a bra, almost anything else is allowed."

"You should do something crazy with your hair!" suggested Amy helpfully.

"Yeah, you could shave off part of your hair!" said Wendy, starting to get interested in the idea.

"That would be so cool if you shaved off all of the hair on exactly half of your head," said Lavyrne.

"It would be cool because it's me and not you," I said laughing.

"Hey, you're the one who's always on about the conformity here," Cindy pointed out.

"I know how to cut hair, and I have all the equipment in my room," said Amy, ever helpful.

I was understandably hesitant, but the idea kind of intrigued me.

On the following hand, the non-trading one, by chance I was dealt an exceptional set of cards. It was almost all hearts, both very high and very low, which would allow me to easily avoid getting any points (and of course the goal of the game is to avoid getting points), but at the same time it might allow me to get all of the points, that is to "shoot the moon", which would give every single other player the double of all of the points in the round. I had never shot the moon before, but this time I was tempted to go for it.

I was normally a very conservative player, so it was difficult for me to stay calm to avoid tipping everyone off as to what I was up to. At first nobody noticed. They continued chatting as usual, April absently giving Lavyrne a foot-rub as some of the girls sometimes liked to do for each other. It became clear pretty quickly what I was doing, though, given the cards that I was playing.

About midway through the round, I realized that I had almost all the cards that it took to ensure that I could take all of the points, but that Wendy had one card that allowed her the choice of possibly taking a Queen of Spades—a huge number of points—or of leaving it to me. She realized this as well, and agreed to drop the card at the right moment provided that I went through with getting the lovely haircut that the girls had planned for me.

I was nervous, but my choice was clear. With my timid playing style, I undoubtedly would never attempt to shoot the moon again, so in a sense it was a once-in-a-lifetime offer. Plus on some level I wanted to bravely become the most non-conformist girl in our dormitory, but I was too shy to do it without getting my friends to push me into it. Normally the other girls would have seen a deal like this as cheating, but they were excited enough by this new project to allow me my fun of shooting the moon and were happy to see my daring repaid by the fact that that round put me over the edge to win that night's match.

Amy ran and got all of her hairdressing implements, Cindy grabbed a chair for me, and we all went to our floor's communal bathroom. Amy parted my long, straight blond hair down the center and pulled the right side out of the way with a large hair clip. Next she took the left side and with a scissor cut it off in bunches almost to the scalp.

Then she took the electric razor and shaved off the remains. All of the other girls in our group stood around me gasping and giggling.

When Amy was finished, I decided to take a shower to wash off the hairs that were still sticking to me, and the rest of the girls turned in for the night. Getting in bed I remembered that I hadn't grabbed the tennis racket to put in the window as planned. But this new prank was sufficient to get everyone to forget about the other one.

19. MONDAY MORNING

I WOKE UP TO the most incredible feeling of dread. In those few moments of re-orientation while reaching consciousness, the full force of what had happened last night hit me. I ran my fingers along the side of my head, feeling the faint stubble on my fingertips and hardly believing what I had done.

"Ah, well, what's done is done," I sighed to myself, getting out of bed.

I grabbed my hairbrush and went to look in the mirror on the closet door. As I stood there brushing the remains of my hair—the right side—to a glossy sheen, I had to admit that it was rather striking as a look, although strange.

Just then Janie got back from her shower and saw me. She gasped, and her eyes opened wide behind her thick glasses.

"Oh, my heck!" she exclaimed, horrified. "What did you do to your hair?"

"The other girls talked me into it," I meekly replied. I then immediately started mentally kicking myself for feeling apologetic in the face of her self-righteous attitude. "I think it looks kind of cool, though, don't you? Why always follow the crowd when you can start a new trend?"

"You're not going to start a new trend like that, you look like a freak!"

"Now, Janie, is that really a Christlike attitude?" I asked her in a tone of mock-sweetness.

"Humph!" she sniffed, "I'll never understand you feminists. If you were really so proud to be a woman, you wouldn't be ashamed to look like one!"

"So you're saying that this hairstyle makes me look like a man?" I asked.

"You look like a lesbian!"

"Okay, now you're saying nonsense," I said calmly but firmly. "You don't even know any lesbians. I have no idea why you would imagine that they would do their hair this way."

"Whatever!" she said, and she finished dressing, grabbed her bag, and stormed out.

I realized that unfortunately I couldn't stay in the room forever myself, so I grabbed my toothbrush and headed off to the bathroom. I survived a few stares, but the smiles from my friends encouraged me. Wendy and Lavyrne both high-fived me when they saw me walking down the hall behaving as if nothing were amiss. I started to feel proud to be brave enough to go against the grain! Just in case, though, I grabbed a hat before heading out of the dorm.

The hat turned out to be helpful when getting my sack lunch at that cafeteria—no sense bothering to rock the cafeteria ladies' world.

I took off the hat again walking up to campus, but I didn't make it past the humanities building before the stares and strange looks got to me. I ducked in and headed straight for the ladies' room. There I combed the hair from my right side over to a ponytail just below my left ear. Like that you could hardly see that anything was strange at all.

I was sad to see that I couldn't bring myself to really go against the grain, but at least I had tried a bit more than the others. I figured I could keep doing my hair to disguise the shaved part like that whenever I was on campus for a few weeks until the left side grew out long enough for me to cut it all to match.

I came back out of the bathroom. Now that I looked essentially normal again, it seemed like everything had returned to normal. People passed by walking to their classes and chatting with each other without noticing me.

Walking along, I passed the bronze statue of a young family. It showed a father and mother who looked not far from my own age, conservatively dressed, looking down at a little girl and holding her hands. The mother reminded me of the pictures representing an idealized young woman that appeared on all of our church materials and manuals in the Young Women's organization and on the golden medallions that we earned by setting and keeping goals.

The statue appeared to show the idealized culmination of the goals we had set in Young Women's. I of course intended to start a family one day, yet somehow I couldn't feel any sort of affinity with the people represented by this sculpture. Once my hair grew back I might be able to make myself look like the young mother, but I actually felt more natural kinship with another favorite BYU bronze sculpture, the Indian. He stood there day after day in his loincloth looking down at the students passing by, physically present among them without fitting in as one of them.

I had set off extra early and had plenty of time before I needed to get to class, so I headed into the university bookstore. For fun I went and checked out all of the various styles of CTR rings. I remembered having a CTR ring as a kid when it was just a cheap little thing they gave to all of us to help us remember to "choose the right." Since then some enterprising person had realized that many people had fond childhood memories of CTR rings, and hence a nicer version of the same ring could be marketed to adults. A lot of my friends had them. They were kind of cute, but I wasn't sure if I wanted one myself or not.

To cross the bookstore to go out the exit by the library, one had to pass through the chocolate department. In fact the chocolate department was right in the middle of the store, and all of the possible paths to go anywhere seemed to pass through it. A strong and irresistibly delicious smell of chocolate saturated the entire region of the candy counter. Amy's boyfriend Jake had joked that it was because Mormons aren't allowed any real drugs that they wildly overdo it on the minor ones that are allowed, like chocolate. This time I managed to escape the siren call of the chocolate counter without buying anything, but I wasn't always so lucky.

Walking out the door I passed a distribution stand for the school newspaper, the *Daily Universe*. The cover story was about a devotional that one of the General Authorities had given at BYU. I wished that I could instead pick up a copy of the more lively independent weekly, the *Student Review*, but unfortunately they were forbidden from distributing on campus at all. One had to go all the way out to the border of campus to one of the entrances to pick up a copy.

I headed to the Eyring Science Center. When I arrived, the class before mine still hadn't let out yet, so I milled around the entry area looking at the various displays in the display cases as I normally did while waiting. One of the displays was about Philo T. Farnsworth, inventor of television. Farnsworth was a source of pride to Mormons in general because, like the author Orson Scott Card, he was a Mormon who had produced something of value recognized outside of Mormon circles. Of course at the rate that the church was growing, there would certainly be many more such examples in the future.

Physics class eventually started, and after that I had Humanities. All in all, the rest of the day was pretty uneventful considering the secret of my strange hair.

In the evening I finished my homework early since I had some free time to get work done on Monday afternoons. I decided to go see if any of my friends were up to anything interesting.

Amy and Cindy's door was partially open, which was the signal that they weren't busy and that it would be okay to come in and join them. I came in and took a seat on the bed. They were talking about Amy's boyfriend Jake.

It turned out that Jake had just found a better-paying job and was considering moving into a studio apartment in Provo instead of commuting in on his motorcycle from his mom's house in Orem. Getting a studio apartment meant necessarily moving into housing that wasn't "BYU-approved" which was against the rules.

Normally it was difficult to get away with living in unapproved housing because you needed to be a member of an official LDS ward to get your ecclesiastical endorsement for continuing enrollment, and your ward is determined based on where you live. But Jake could continue to officially reside at his mom's house and attend her ward even though in reality he would be living somewhere else.

"Guys," I said getting up to close the door, "you really need to close the door if you're going to discuss this sort of thing. Remember that Janie has told us in no uncertain terms that if she ever got wind of any of us breaking the rules she would immediately turn us in to the Honor Code Office. She certainly wouldn't hesitate to turn Jake in if she hears this."

"You're right, Lynn, of course, we weren't thinking," said Cindy.

"And Jake's mom is okay with this plan?" I asked Amy.

"Of course," she replied, "you know she lets him do whatever he wants."

Jake's mom was something of a "jack Mormon." According to Amy's stories, Jake's mom drank, smoked, swore, and regularly had boyfriends spend the night. But she'd lived her whole life in the heart of the Mormon corridor, immersed in the Mormon world, and was nominally a part of it. Therefore she would periodically be persuaded to clean up her act and repent and start attending church again. It never lasted long though, according to Jake.

Jake's home bishop and ward were really pleased to see Jake grow up to be a faithful enough Mormon to be worthy to attend BYU given the home he had grown up in. Lately Jake's bishop had been pressuring Jake to commit to going on a mission, but he was still undecided about it.

Jake's mom was apparently indifferent as to whether Jake should go on a mission or not. As Amy said, she essentially let him do whatever he wanted. Amy had once heard Jake's uncle make a disapproving comment about Jake going on a road trip to Las Vegas the previous summer to go to some casinos, and Jake's mom just responded by laughing and saying, "Well, you know, Jake's always been a naughty boy."

I found that in my few seconds of inattention the conversation had already turned to Cindy's new baseball-player hunk Hyrum and the date she had planned with him for Saturday night.

"It's going to be so romantic!" she gushed. "He's planning to make dinner for me at his apartment, and get this—he just told me today that it turns out that all of his roommates will be away for the whole weekend!"

"Wow, he works fast," said Amy, "sounds like a job for Aunt Julie."

Aunt Julie was Amy and Cindy's maiden aunt who lived in Provo not far from BYU campus. She was a really nice lady, and close with both Amy and Cindy. Also her proximity was particularly convenient because whenever Cindy or Amy wanted to spend the night anywhere other than in their own dorm room, they were officially "staying at Aunt Julie's house."

"Are you sure that that's what he has in mind?" I asked. "This one's a returned-missionary, isn't he?"

"Yes, but he's an *athlete*," Cindy explained. "All of the guys on the sports teams are the same. I should know."

Sports were important enough to BYU culture that the athletes tended to be treated with a bit of indulgence. They were also one of the few segments of BYU culture where non-members were non-trivially represented, as the university was interested in recruiting students that would be star players for their teams, possibly at the expense of other desirable qualities. So while the athletes perhaps had to avoid getting too out-of-hand, the administration wasn't following them around looking to punish every indiscretion.

"I know that this is none of my business," I said, "but aren't you worried that you may be jeopardizing your chances of getting married in the temple someday?"

Cindy paused as if she hadn't really thought about that before. Then she said "Oh, come on, everybody does it."

"And besides," said Amy, "if you can't get a temple recommend right before your marriage, you can always get married outside the temple and then get sealed in the temple a year later."

"To be honest with you," I said, "I don't think that everyone is doing it. If you two confided in our other friends the way you confide in me, Janie isn't the only one who would be shocked."

"Really? You think?" asked Amy.

"Oh, yes," I said with certainty. "In fact—you guys are going to laugh when I tell you this—but just the other day I was part of a confidential conversation like this one with Janie, Trisha, Wendy,

Lavyrne, and this girl named LaBella, who's a friend of Trisha's from another dorm. At one point, they all started talking in hushed tones about what happens after you get married. They were pussy-footing around the idea of sex without anyone being willing to say the word. But without directly stating what they were talking about, they were quite unanimous about the fact that the whole business seemed nasty and distasteful, but that it was a necessary evil that comes along with the joys of marriage and family."

Cindy looked shocked. "What is with them, are they crazy?" she asked.

"Maybe, I don't know," I said, "but I get the impression that for a typical BYU student premarital sex is unthinkable."

"Well what did you say to them when they were saying all that?" asked Amy.

"I was pretty embarrassed, but I told them that I didn't think it would be so terrible, and that we've been counseled by the church leaders that physical intimacy is a vital part of an eternal marriage."

"Did any of them change their tune when you said that?" asked Amy.

"No," I said. "And that's why I think that they were being perfectly sincere and not just saying that to pretend to be holy. They all admitted that they liked kissing boys, however, except Lavyrne, who seemed disgusted by even that."

"Well I feel very sorry for them and for their future husbands," said Cindy. "If they have no sex drive at all, kneeling with their eternal companion at the altar of the temple isn't going to magically change that."

"It's true," remarked Amy. "Having a sex drive is inconvenient now since doing it is against the rules and everything, but this part of your life is pretty short compared to how long you're going to be married."

"And since those girls are planning to stay 'virtuous' until marriage, their poor sap husbands won't even know what they're getting into until it's too late!" said Cindy laughing.

Actually I had to admit that Cindy and Amy had something of a point, so I stopped feeling jealous of those other girls for having so much less of a struggle with this issue than I did.

"You know, Lynn, talking to you about boys like this reminds me of when we were in high school," said Amy. "Remember how we used to refer to them with code letters, like Y and Z?" She laughed. "Wouldn't it be funny if Y and Z had come to BYU?"

I forced a bit of a laugh in response. In fact I didn't think that that would be even remotely funny, and I wasn't too keen on being reminded of it.

"Yeah, I'd love to have seen those two, after all that Amy has told me about them," said Cindy.

"I have one more question about this date, though, if you don't mind," I said, changing the subject. "If you're not so concerned about sinning, and you're not worried about the fact that you're breaking the Honor Code, aren't you at least worried about getting pregnant?"

"A little, but not too much," said Cindy. "What I usually do is have the guy pull out before the end."

My eyes widened. "Isn't that a little dangerous?" I asked.

"Well, I guess so," said Cindy. She turned to Amy and asked "What do you do with Jake?"

Amy had spent the night at Jake's house a few times, but before this moment I wasn't sure whether or not they had actually gone all the way. Cindy's question cleared up that point pretty neatly.

"Rubbers," said Amy.

"You and Jake went out and bought some rubbers?" I asked.

"Jake did," she replied. "What happened was that of course at first we weren't planning to go all the way, so you know we weren't— ahem—prepared," she said smiling, "but since we were at his mom's house at the time, all we had to do was dip into his mom's supply of condoms. He felt bad taking them without asking like that, so he later bought some to replace the ones he took, and at that point figured he might as well buy some for himself as well."

"That's probably a good idea," said Cindy. "I mean, I normally wouldn't buy a condom since it's like planning to commit a sin. But to be realistic, I am planning it, and I'm not going to change my mind, so I might as well be prepared."

That seemed like a bit of an ironic use of the Boy Scout motto to me, but maybe it wasn't. "I have to agree," I said. "I'm certainly not going to advise you to commit a grave sin, but if you're going to do it, there's no sense in putting yourself at risk."

"I'm with you," said Amy. "I can get you a condom from Jake's supply before Saturday night, no problem. I can pick one up on Friday." Then she changed tone a little bit and said, "Oh, that reminds me, there's one more thing I was meaning to tell you guys. It's not about this."

"What is it?" asked Cindy.

"Jake's uncle is lending Jake his cabin this Friday night, and Jake was planning to have some of his old friends from high school go up there for a sleepover, and we're invited. You can come too, Lynn."

"Sounds like fun," said Cindy.

"I don't know about this," I said. I was a little leery about what the outing might entail considering the conversation we had just been having.

"Oh, it's not all about sex, Lynn," Amy said laughing. "It's a tiny cabin, and everyone will be sleeping in sleeping bags in the living room, so there's no danger of anything happening."

"You should come with us, Lynn," said Cindy. "I'll bet Jake's friends are cool, and it will make a welcome change for you from swapping secrets with Janie and Trisha and those guys."

This was one of those situations where it was pretty clear that the right answer as in "choose the right" would be to say no. But in fact it did sound like fun and a welcome change. "Oh, all right," I said, hoping I wouldn't regret it.

20. FRIDAY EVENING

T HE WEEK SPED BY, and the next thing I knew I was getting ready to go up to Jake's uncle's cabin with Cindy and Amy. Cindy and Amy's Aunt Julie lent us her car, and Cindy drove us up following Jake's map.

When the three of us finally found the cabin, Jake was already there with his three friends: two guys and a girl. I hardly noticed the rather ordinary-looking guys next to the girl all decked out in goth. Her black hair and eye make-up, pale skin, black lips, black nails and silver rings and ankh pendant seemed pretty typical goth to me (although I've never been knowledgeable about it), but aside from being all black, her outfit seemed atypical. She was wearing kind of a flouncy (black) skirt over black stockings and black boots, and over a black leotard top, she had a cute little tight black jacket. To top it off, she had on a wide-brimmed hat with the brim folded up on one side—in black again as you might guess.

Her outfit struck me as really cute and reminded me of how goth culture can be kind of internally conformist yet still give a lot of leeway for individuality. I immediately wanted to make friends with her, so as I approached to take a seat, I took off my hat to reveal my own non-conformist side.

The left side of my hair was slightly longer than stubble at this point, but the stark half-and-half thing was still startling.

"Wow, cool hair!" said the guy I soon learned was called Rex.

"Thanks," I said, affecting an air of cool confidence. "With all of the infinite possibilities, I was tired of always doing variants on the same old same old."

We then proceeded with the usual introductions. The goth girl was named Paige, her boyfriend was named Ben, and the other guy introduced himself as Rex.

Settling into a worn armchair, I took a look around the room. The decor was unbelievable. There were antlers everywhere. Every wall had a series of plaques with antlers mounted on them. The stands of the lamps were also made from antlers. Aside from the antlers, though, the room was pretty standard. There was a set of comfy but sagging couches and chairs, covered with blankets, and a round rag rug in the center of the varnished wood floor. Some faded striped curtains parted to show a mountain landscape that was quickly being lost to the darkness outside.

"What's with all the antlers?" I asked to no one in particular.

"You know it's my uncle's hunting cabin," Jake replied.

"Ugh, it's awful!" said Paige. "What kind of person thinks dead animals are decorations?"

"My uncle, I guess," said Jake, smiling.

"At least there's not a whole deer head," said Amy. "That would really creep me out."

"Ah, Mormons and Mormon culture!" interjected Rex playfully.

At that I started to sink into my chair. I was trying to decide whether to criticize or defend Mormonism when Paige mercifully settled the question with a dramatic raise of her eyebrow.

"What about Mormons and their culture?" she asked. "Just because some of them are provincial rubes, doesn't mean they all are."

I breathed a sigh of relief. That was more or less what I wanted to say about Mormons myself.

Ben looked annoyed though. "Let's not start this again," he said. "Anyone for some brewskis?"

"Sounds interesting," I said.

"Lynn, you know brewskis are beer, right?" asked Cindy.

At this I could feel myself flushing red. I realized that of course "brewski" was a word for beer—I just wasn't familiar enough with the lingo to be quick with it off the top of my head like that.

"Ummm..." I stammered, panicking, and frozen as to what to do next. Should I be the biggest dork on the planet and admit that I didn't realize he was talking about beer, and then tell everyone that of course I couldn't sin by drinking beer...? Or should I sin and drink beer just to save face...?

Amy put a comforting smile on her face and turned to me. "It's okay, Lynn. Janie's not hiding in the closet. Nobody here is going to tell your bishop if you try a beer."

In a sense Amy's statement was a relief because she gave me an excuse for my hesitation—worry about getting caught—but it didn't get me completely out of my bind.

"I see that what we need here," said Rex, "is a little bit of scripture study." And with that he got up to grab a triple-combination off the mantle. I was really starting to dread where this might be going in terms of the ridicule ahead for me. Jake was distributing cans of beer

to everyone else and opening some bags of chips as Rex searched for the right page.

"Here it is," he said, and began to read. "*Doctrine & Covenants*, Section 89. A Word of Wisdom, for the benefit of the council of high priests, assembled in Kirtland, and the church, and also the saints in Zion—To be sent greeting; not by commandment or constraint, ... yadda, yadda," he looked ahead a bit and then looked up. "See? It says 'not by commandment or constraint' or in other words, the 'Word of Wisdom' was meant to be just that—wise advice—not a commandment."

I chuckled a bit and replied, "Okay, Joseph Smith says it's not a commandment, but breaking the Word of Wisdom is still against the honor code at BYU."

"Lynn, I told you nobody here is going to tell!" said Amy, exasperated.

"And anyway being here unchaperoned with all these boys is probably a worse infraction," added Cindy.

"Ah, but there's more," continued Rex. "Let's move on to verse five. 'That inasmuch as any man drinketh wine or strong drink among you, behold it is not good.' Now why do you think he mentions wine *and* strong drink? Isn't wine a strong drink?"

"Ummm, because the scriptures are full of redundancy and repetition?" I offered.

Now he laughed, "And bad grammar and unparsable sentences. But, no, that wasn't my point. My point is that wine is listed alongside strong drinks because wine doesn't fall into the category of strong drinks. It's separate. By strong drinks here, Joseph Smith is clearly referring to hard liquor."

"Okay, I can guess where this is going," I said. "Your point is that the Word of Wisdom forbids—oops, I mean recommends against— wine and hard liquor, but says nothing about beer."

"Aha, but it doesn't quite say *nothing* about beer," he said. "Look at verse 17, where it's talking about good uses of various grains. Here it says 'and barley for all useful animals and for mild drinks.' Now, what drink is made from barley and might be considered a 'mild drink' by contrast to hard liquor, which is a 'strong drink'?"

"Postum!" shouted Paige, laughing. "He's shown us this a million times. He has this watertight proof that beer is recommended by the Word of Wisdom, so it's funny to remind him that that old Mormon coffee substitute is also made from barley."

Rex looked a little annoyed. "Yeah, but even if Postum existed back then—which it probably didn't—it's a hot drink, and therefore against the Word of Wisdom."

"But here 'hot drinks' refers to coffee and tea," I protested.

"Not according to the *Doctrine & Covenants*," said Rex.

Ben grabbed the book from Rex and said, "Okay, enough scripture study, we're here for a little fun." With that he set the book back up on the mantle and turned to me. "You see Lynn, ol' Joe Smith wants you to enjoy a beer with your friends—hell, if he were here he'd be happy to pour you one himself."

"I care about 'choosing the right' too," said Paige getting into a minor sofa pillow-fight with Ben, "as much as these guys get on my case for it. But it's right there in black and white that beer's not a sin. Different people interpret things differently, but the highest authority is the scriptures."

This seemed somehow wrong. This appeared to be the sort of peer pressure that I was supposed to be on the lookout for. Yet their reasoning seemed pretty sound. Plus it might be fun to take the opportunity.

"Okay, okay," I said chuckling, "I can't think of a counterargument, so I guess I have to take my beer."

"Cool!" said Jake, handing me a can of beer. "You've got to watch out for that Rex, he's a sly one."

"Yeah, beware of later tonight when he shows you the scripture that says it's not a sin to do the nasty," Paige said, laughing.

"Is there a scripture that says that?" asked Amy, surprised.

"Sadly, no," said Rex.

"You've looked for it too, haven't you?" asked Cindy with a knowing smile.

"Of course," replied Rex. "Oh wait, maybe there's one. Will you indulge me?" he asked looking at Ben as he reached for the triple combination again. Ben rolled his eyes in response.

I began to sip my beer cautiously. It had kind of a strange taste, not particularly good. I grabbed a handful of chips to go with it. I glanced up at Rex flipping through the book. Not a bad looking guy really. A little nerdy perhaps. Thin, not too athletic, glasses, dark hair a little longer on top than that of the average BYU guy...

"Do you guys want to watch a movie?" Jake asked. "I've brought *The Life of Brian*."

"Aww, can't we just hang out for a while?" asked Paige. "Do we always have to relate to each other by staring at a screen?"

"I think we need some entertainment," Cindy said, "otherwise scripture-boy here will turn our little party into a Sunday school lesson."

"Hey, I'm just finding you the good parts that they don't quote you at church," said Rex, still paging through the book in search of the right scripture.

"Oh I know a good one," I offered, "If you look at the facsimiles in the *Pearl of Great Price*, one of the hieroglyphs is a picture of a penis!"

Amy burst out laughing, "That's right! That's my all-time favorite scripture."

"Great, you guys are encouraging him," said Cindy, laughing. "Now we'll be scripture-chasing all night! You can take the kids out of Happy Valley, but you can't take Happy Valley out of the kids," she said shaking her head.

"Here, I've found it," said Rex.

"Okay, I'll show you the penis picture after," I said, as Amy giggled.

"Okay," he said, "but first *Doctrine & Covenants* section 132, verse 62: 'And if he have ten virgins given unto him by this law, he cannot commit adultery, for they belong to him, and they are given unto him; therefore he is justified.'"

"Does it really say that?" asked Jake. "I mean, it seems kinda cool, but I'm not sure what the heck he's talking about."

"Duh, it's the scriptures," said Cindy, "It's not supposed to make sense."

"But wait, it gets better," said Rex, as he continued reading "'Thus saith the Lord, if a man taketh ten virgins, and giveth pleasure unto them, blessed is he above all men in my sight,'" and at that he doubled over laughing.

"It does not say that," said Paige in mock-exasperation.

"No, but it should," said Rex, regaining his composure.

"My turn!" I said, "let me show you guys the picture of a penis!" Rex handed me the triple-combination, and I quickly flipped to the circle of hieroglyphs of facsimile #2. "There it is," I said, pointing it out to Rex with the tip of my fingernail. Amy giggled.

"That's pretty hard to see," he said, "I could draw a better penis than that."

"Yeah, but it's funny because it's in the scriptures!" said Amy.

"True," he said smiling, "as scriptures go it's not too bad."

"Okay, is Sunday school over yet?" asked Cindy, "Can we watch *The Life of Brian?*"

"That movie is all full of religion too, you know," said Rex.

"Yeah, but the movie is *funny!*" said Cindy.

"You didn't find our scripture selections amusing?" asked Rex, laughing.

"Reality check here," said Cindy, "Monty Python has a lot better writing than the *D & C.*"

I was a bit taken aback by Cindy's off-handed comment there. It seemed blasphemous to suggest that a comedy troupe's writing was better than Heavenly Father's. Yet she kind of had a point. I went back to sipping my beer as Jake started up the movie.

I'd already seen this movie once at a friend's house, so I knew what to expect. It appeared that everyone else had seen it as well, so rather than silently watching, the group continued in commentary and conversation. All the while, Jake and Amy were becoming more and more intertwined on one couch and Paige and Ben were doing the same on the other.

When Cindy got up to get everyone another round of beers, I agreed to a second one. The first one wasn't so great, but it seemed there was no harm in it. I tried not to be too visibly embarrassed during the nude scene.

It was pretty late when the movie ended. It wasn't so late that we couldn't have continued hanging out, but Jake and Amy seemed anxious to go off to the bedroom. Somehow it had been silently decided that they would take the one bedroom, and the rest of us would sleep in the living room. So we took the cue to start unrolling our sleeping bags. The gentlemen gallantly allowed Cindy and me to set up our bedding on the two couches, and Paige didn't object, so Rex, Paige, and Ben set up their sleeping bags on the floor. Paige set hers up right next to Ben's, but she made a big show of the fact that she was zipping herself into her own individual sleeping bag for the night. After a brief flurry of getting ready and few good-nights, we were off to sleep.

As soon as the first morning light started coming into the window, I silently padded off to the bathroom to brush my teeth and hair (what was left of it), and wash my face. I brushed the long side of my hair until it was gleaming, and put a dangly earring in on the short side. I put on a bit of mascara and lip gloss and my change of clothing. I examined myself in the mirror. It was kind of a cute outfit, but I wished I had brought something better.

When I got back to the living-room, everyone else was still asleep, so I got my copy of *Hamlet* out of my backpack that I had to read for my Humanities class, and snuggled myself into the corner of the couch to read.

I paged past the introductory material and started skimming the list of characters. Then my gaze began to wander around the room. Paige and Ben looked pretty funny cuddled right up next to each other in their two individual sleeping bags, with Ben squeezed against Paige like two spoons in a drawer. Cindy was sleeping with her back to me and her long blond hair partially draped down the couch cushion.

Then I looked over at Rex, innocently asleep with the soft morning sun barely lighting his face. I had an incredible urge to go over and touch him. I wondered what would have happened if I had opened

his sleeping bag during the night and had slipped in to cuddle him. I wondered if he would have wanted me to.

Rex started to stir, so I went back to pretending to read *Hamlet*, gazing past the book in a manner that I hoped was subtle. Still facing away from me, he stood up and stretched. I followed the line of his arm from wrist to shoulder, and could make out the form of his shoulders and back through his light t-shirt. Within a second I had taken in almost involuntarily the striped boxers, the contours of his leg muscles, down to the shape of his feet and toes. As quickly as I could, I firmly planted my eyes back on the page, but the words there were a meaningless blur.

Then while grabbing his backpack, Rex turned around and saw that I was awake. "Good morning," he said brightly. I looked up from my book and replied "Good morning" with my cheeriest smile. Then he went off to the bathroom to get ready for the day.

I closed my book, absently putting one finger in to save my page as I gazed out the window at the mountain landscape. I indulged myself in a little mental replay of the earlier image. I noted that it

was interesting that he was wearing a t-shirt and boxers as underwear and not temple garments. Clearly he wasn't a returned-missionary. I supposed that that was reasonable since he was a friend of Jake's from high school, and hence probably just a freshman. Actually from what Rex had said earlier, it seemed he might not even be a member of the church, although he clearly had some knowledge of Mormonism.

Paige then woke up and started getting out of her sleeping bag. She had on a long, silky black nightgown that I hadn't noticed the night before. It seemed to have an elegant line to it, but it somehow didn't look right in the morning light, as if it would be better set off by moonlight or candles. She got up and went straight to the bathroom and knocked on the door.

"Just a minute, I'll be done shaving soon," came Rex's reply from the other side.

"Rex, I have to pee," said Paige, "Can you go shave in the kitchen? I can lend you a mirror."

"Okay," he said coming out, still in his t-shirt and boxers.

"Seven people in this house and one bathroom, and you have to do your whole morning beauty routine," said Paige teasingly as she grabbed a make-up mirror with a stand out of her bag and handed it to him, then slipped past him into the bathroom.

"Half-shaved," laughed Ben, now awake, "in honor of Lynn, no doubt!"

"Why not?" asked Rex, smiling at me, "everyone should do something original now and then. For today, though, I think I'll just finish shaving as usual." He took his things over to the kitchen sink.

Still cuddled in my little niche, I was annoyed with myself for having nothing witty to say. I consoled myself with the thought that at least my hair was amusing.

As subtly as possible, I moved myself to the opposite corner of the couch so as to have the kitchen in my natural line of sight when looking up from my book. It was a deliciously intimate scene. I was tempted to try to memorize every contour and movement of his back and legs. But with so many others in the room, I could hardly get away with staring, even if it were polite to do so.

Cindy then started to wake up as well, and she and Ben took their turns in the bathroom. Rex also took a turn to get dressed as Jake and Amy came out of the bedroom and started making pancakes for everyone. I jumped up to help set the table.

During breakfast, Paige asked me if she could interview me for a piece she was doing on unconventional students for the *Student Review*. I told her that I wasn't all that unconventional, but since she was having some difficulty finding enough unconventional BYU students to fill up her article, I agreed to meet her for lunch at her house on Tuesday and gave her my phone number.

Amy, Cindy, and I set off right after breakfast so that Amy could get back to town in time for her shift at the nail salon, and I needed to get down to business on reading *Hamlet*. Rex seemed to give me a particularly friendly smile with his goodbye, but it was probably just my imagination.

When I got to my room, I found that Janie was in there with her ironing board all set up and a huge pile of ironing she was working on. It looked like a bunch of men's shirts, so I didn't ask her about it because really I didn't want to know. The Jesus-flavored pop music she was singing along to didn't seem terribly conducive to appreciation of Shakespeare, so I just said hi and dropped off my things and took my copy of *Hamlet* to the study room at the end of the hall.

My sister April was there in the study room at a desk with a bunch of books open.

"Hi, what are you in for?" I asked her.

"I have a paper to write for my European History class. And you?" she asked.

"I have to read and understand Hamlet by Monday morning," I replied.

"Do you have the Cliff's notes?" she asked.

"I'm hoping it won't come to that," I said. "I always liked studying Shakespeare in High School. Of course back then we spent more time on each play."

"Do you have to write a paper on it?" she asked.

"No," I replied, "but we'll have an essay test in a week or so where we'll be expected to use examples from the text."

"That's not so bad then—you don't have to understand the whole thing, just some examples," she said smiling and returning to her books.

I settled into one of the couches and started reading. I tried to go as quickly as possible yet still get the idea of what was going on. The first part seemed to be about some sentinels who had seen the ghost of the king or something like that.

After less than one scene, my mind began to irresistibly wander to the image of Rex stretching and of our entire morning scene. I looked out the window of the study room. The room had a window with an interior view overlooking the large, high-ceilinged lobby. The lobby had rows of couches full of students variously chatting or engaging in public displays of affection. As usual there was someone playing the piano surrounded by fresh-faced students singing with him. Then I noticed Andrew looking up at me and waving. As soon as he saw that I saw him, he began pointing at his watch and making some sort of incomprehensible gesture that I took to mean that I should go get April.

"April, Andrew is downstairs signaling to us," I said.

"Oh, yeah, lunch," she said. "I lost track of the time. Do you want to come with us?"

"Sure," I said, and we went downstairs.

April greeted Andrew with a peck of a kiss on the cheek, and we all set off.

As we all walked together, I couldn't help but notice the contrast between this couple and those that were shamelessly making out in the lobby, or worse Amy and Jake, spending the night together like that. It's true that temptation can be fierce and difficult to overcome, but it was inspiring to see some young lovers who had the force of will necessary in order not to jeopardize their future temple wedding nor his mission plans. In fact they had the breezy, laid-back attitude of an old married couple already, not even bothering to hold hands as they walked along.

Since Andrew wasn't living in the dorms, we wouldn't be having lunch in the cafeteria, but since we were passing that way, April and I stopped in to get our mail.

Even though I hadn't checked my mailbox for a few days, there was only one envelope in it. I was pleased to have at least gotten something until I saw the return address: "Honor Code Office." My heart dropped. Standards. What could they want with me?

"What is it, Lynn?" asked April.

"I got a letter from the Honor Code Office," I said.

"Well don't keep us in suspense," Andrew said, "open it up."

I opened the envelope and took out the letter. It was as bad as I feared. It said that an interview with an Honor Code Official had been scheduled for me. It gave the time, date, and location, but not the reason. I showed it to April and Andrew.

"It's probably nothing," Andrew said, "Just remember to act repentant and deny everything." He chuckled.

"Andrew!" said April. "Well, come to think of it, that's probably good advice."

"Except that you have to admit to at least one small thing that you can repent of," Andrew continued as we started off again towards town. "The best thing to do is admit to whatever they already know you did, and don't give them any additional information. Do you know what they're calling you in for?"

"No," I said. I started to go over in my mind what it could be. Did they know about the trip to the cabin? And the beer? I didn't see how that could be possible since the letter had clearly been mailed before any of that had happened. Had Janie perhaps tipped them off about it in advance? That didn't make any sense since Janie knew about Cindy and Amy regularly spending the night "visiting their aunt" since the beginning of the semester and had never said anything, so I didn't see why she would suddenly turn me in for it.

"Have you confessed any sins to your BYU bishop?" asked April.

"No," I said, "and anyway, it's not like the bishop is going to go tell the Honor Code Office."

Both April and Andrew looked at each other.

"Think," said Andrew. "Have you done anything or been involved in any activity that *someone else* might have confessed to a bishop or to the Honor Code Office?"

"I don't think so," I said. "How do you guys know so much about the Honor Code Office anyway?"

April started blushing and they both looked kind of embarrassed at that. I started to get the picture. Sometimes those couples who aren't making a big display in public are the ones that are doing the most in private. I regretted having asked that. It was their business anyway.

"It seems like the Standards office tends to get wind of things that are confessed to the bishop, especially if it's something serious or that involves multiple people or if the repentance process seems not to be proceeding well enough," said Andrew. "The professor in the religion

class that April and I are taking this semester was practically bragging about it in fact."

"Really?" I asked.

"Yeah," said April, "At one point he recounted this story—I can't remember what the context was—about how they nabbed one student who had seduced a few of his fellow BYU students. Even though it was clear from the story that it was consensual, the prof called the guy a 'predator.' He never went to the bishop to confess himself, but the girls were of course asked to admit who they sinned with as part of their repentance process. The happy ending to the tale was that the girls all repented, and the 'predator' got expelled."

"I don't know if the story was supposed to be uplifting or what, but even being the righteous guy I am, I found it a bit chilling," said Andrew.

"So the moral is that—whatever you've done—if they start pressing you for additional names, don't be hesitant as if you have something to hide. Just start listing people who aren't BYU students. Preferably out-of-state," said April with a smile.

I was really surprised to hear my sweet, always-righteous older sister basically advising me to mistrust and work against the BYU authorities. It didn't seem like her at all, yet she didn't seem to be wholly joking.

"Anyway, don't sweat it," said Andrew, "it's probably nothing."

It was pretty hard not to sweat it, though, after that unsettling story they had just told about their religion professor. Fortunately the climate in some of the other departments was a bit different. One time when only a few students were around, my Multivariable Calculus professor recounted a tale of how one of the other professors had a beard (which is against the dress code) and no beard card for it. Apparently it was quite easy to get an official BYU "beard card" by lying to a doctor and saying that shaving would give you a rash. The professor in question however, being a devout Mormon, didn't want to lie about his reasons for not shaving. It was just because his features were such that he looked fine with a beard and terrible without one, not because shaving would give him a rash. The consequence of not getting a doctor's note and hence not getting a beard card was that he couldn't get a school ID card and check books out of the library. The other Math professors responded not by turning him in but rather by checking books out of the library for him.

I was still pretty worried about my interview with Standards as we arrived at Taco Bell, but I reasoned that I hadn't done anything really bad, so I would probably be okay. And since I didn't even know what it was about, I figured that there was no sense worrying about it before the appointed interview on Monday.

After lunch, April set off with Andrew to do some shopping they had planned at the mall. I parted company with them because I wanted to get down to business on reading *Hamlet*.

It was such a beautiful crisp, sunny fall day that I decided to do my reading outside on campus. A spot near the "Tree of Knowledge,"— a funky white abstract sculpture that looked vaguely like a tree and vaguely like an open book—seemed appropriate.

This time I figured I'd start with the introductory material. That would undoubtedly clue me in to the important things to notice in the play since I wouldn't have time to read it as thoroughly as I would like. So I started in on the explanation of Hamlet's situation with his mother and with his dead father and some stuff about revenge, and then unfortunately my mind started wandering again.

I started to think about that verse that Rex had read from the *Doctrine & Covenants*: the verse about ten virgins being given to someone. What was that all about? It must have been some sort of polygamy thing. Then I chuckled a little to myself at the joke verse he had followed up with. What a light-hearted attitude he had towards something as embarrassing and forbidden as sex! In my mind I saw him again standing there at the sink shaving in the half-light of morning. I imagined walking up behind him and running my fingers down his back.

It struck me as very bad that I was getting nowhere on my reading. I tried to focus on the paragraph in front of me, but I found I was just reading it over and over without understanding it. I was distracted by this burning sensation, and not exactly in the bosom. I took a deep breath and swallowed hard. I figured it was hopeless to continue, so I headed back to my dorm room.

Luckily, when I arrived Janie wasn't there, but I didn't know where she had gone or for how long. I set myself up in bed under the covers as if to take a nap so as not to get caught *in flagrante delicto* as it were.

Then I stopped holding back and let my imagination go. I walked up behind him, slowly put my arms around his nearly-naked waist from behind and gently kissed his neck, just below the ear. Actually, I thought, that might not be possible given the height difference. Might there be a fortuitously-placed footstool in Jake's uncle's kitchen? Sure, why not? It's a fantasy...

I then allowed my mind wander farther into dangerous territory. Such a terrible and powerful desire to taste the unknown.

When it was over, the usual guilt and shame began to set in. Part of it was the realization that I was too weak and perverse to avoid committing grave sins and wanting to commit graver ones. Another part of it was the thought that I had somehow overstepped my boundaries and misused another person. Perhaps he would be disgusted if he knew what I had imagined for him. After all, I was just a nerdy girl who had had a few dates in high school, but never a serious boyfriend. Perhaps my fantasies were all I would ever have.

I thought about what would happen if I were ever in such a situation for real. In various seminars and devotionals for youth they have told us many times to plan in advance in order to be ready to stop and step away before going too far. I had planned in a sense. I knew what I should do. And yet I also knew what I would do.

On the bright side, after taking care of this little problem I found I was better able to concentrate on my reading. I read the entire introductory section so I knew what the main points were, and from there I figured out which scenes were the key scenes to read thoroughly. There was some cool stuff in there. Before I knew it, Janie arrived back at our dorm room with Trisha and Lavyrne gathering our friends to go to dinner.

Cindy wasn't at dinner with us because she was off on her big date with Hyrum. I'd missed seeing her set off all decked-out and gorgeous, but I'd seen her all done up for dates before, and it was a sight to behold. I was looking forward to hearing about it the next day.

21. SUNDAY MORNING

CINDY SEEMED QUIET and withdrawn at lunch on Sunday and also later at church. I couldn't help but notice that Hyrum didn't come by to meet her at church and walk her home this week. On the way home, she was kind of shuffling along looking at her feet rather than being her usual cheery self.

From talking to Amy at church I understood that Cindy's date hadn't gone well, but I didn't have the details. Amy suggested that I come to their room after church to help her cheer Cindy up.

I went back to my room and got changed, and then I went over and knocked on Amy and Cindy's door. Cindy was in her bathrobe with a mud mask on her face and cucumber slices over her eyes. She was reclining in bed with about a million small pillows—their whole collection—carefully arranged to prop her up in a comfortable position. Amy was sitting in a chair doing Cindy's nails. They had some Beatles music playing softly in the background.

"C'mon in, Lynn," said Amy as I pushed open the door and then closed it behind me. "We've decided that what Cindy needs to cheer her up is a day at the spa."

"Spa Amy," said Cindy, giving a little smile.

"That's a good idea," I said. "Where'd you get the cucumber?"

"Oh, we bought it at Albertson's this morning," said Amy. "I know we're not supposed to be buying things on Sundays, but Heavenly Father doesn't mind if we sometimes make exceptions for emergencies like this."

"Or so we thought," interjected Cindy.

"Why, what happened?" I asked, sitting down at Cindy's desk.

"Oh, nothing," said Amy, "it's just that on our way home from Albertson's we saw Hyrum walking in our direction, and he crossed over to the other side to avoid us."

"He didn't even look at us," said Cindy, "except maybe to give a little sneer at our shopping bags."

"Wow, that must have been some awful date you guys had!" I exclaimed.

"Yeah, you could say that," said Amy.

"Here's what happened," said Cindy, starting in on her story. "First of all, he didn't really cook me dinner as he said he would, but rather he ordered us some pizza and served it on paper plates." Amy laughed at that. "That actually didn't bother me since it was about what I had expected. We had a nice conversation during dinner, and then moved over to the couch to watch some TV. He closed the curtains so that there wouldn't be any glare on the TV screen, so he said, but it was already getting dark out, so I knew it was just so that nobody could see in." At that I kind of chuckled.

"Now remember that we knew in advance that all of his roommates would be gone all weekend when he invited me over, and we all know what that means. So I wasn't the least bit surprised when he started making the moves on me as soon as we were seated in the couch. And I don't have to tell you that it wasn't long before things were pretty hot and heavy, and he was down to his g's."

"To his what?" I asked.

Amy laughed. "You don't know much, do you Lynn? His Jesus jammies! He's a returned-missionary you know!"

"Oh, you mean his temple garments," I said.

"Exactly," said Cindy. "It's too bad that people have to wear those—they're really not attractive." It was hard to imagine Cindy someday trading in her pretty bra-and-panties ensembles for standard-issue garments, even for the eternal rewards of a temple marriage.

"And usually they remind you of religion exactly when you least want to be thinking about religion," added Amy.

I was thinking that that latter point might be exactly why Heavenly Father might want those who had gone through the temple to wear them, but I kept that thought to myself.

Cindy continued her story. "Naturally at that point I figured it was time to get out the condom Amy had given me. All I did was set it on the coffee table, but that was all it took. It completely freaked him out. He sat up and moved to the edge of the couch with his back to me and his face in his hands. I didn't know what to do. Then he said 'You mean you thought I was planning to... You came here with the idea that we were going to...' Both his sentences just kind of drifted off like that as if he couldn't bear to say it. I said, 'Well, yeah. I mean, that looked like the direction you were going, right?' And then he said 'You know a lot of girls fight back. A lot of nice girls say no.'

"And then he was quiet for a really long time. And then without looking at me he said 'This is wrong. The spirit is telling me that you shouldn't be here. I think you need to go, now.' So I started putting my clothes back on. What else could I do? And as I was leaving, he pointed to the condom and said 'and take that with you.'

"And that was it. No goodbye. He certainly didn't walk me home. I walked myself to Aunt Julie's house in the dark." Cindy seemed to be on the verge of tears behind her cucumber slices.

"Wow, what a jerk!" I said. "Sure I understand if he's concerned about not committing a grave sin. But he started it. I don't see how he can get angry with you for just going along with it."

Of course Hyrum's real fault was inviting her there in the first place. But still it was kind of disturbing to hear that when it came right down to it the Holy Spirit had essentially told Hyrum to hurt Cindy. The more I thought about the situation the more it confused me, to the point where I almost started feeling sorry for Hyrum—like he was maybe as bad off as my no-sex-drive dorm-mates or worse—so I tried to put it out of my mind.

"Well, you know, men are rats," said Amy laughing a bit, "men are fleas on rats—men are amoebas on fleas on rats!" That was something Amy liked to say for fun. It was probably a quote from a move or something, but I wasn't sure which one. "Anyway," she said, "That's what spa Amy is for."

"And I know you'll find someone better in no time," I said.

Even with her eyes covered, Cindy seemed to catch on that my tone was a tiny bit glum thinking of my own prospects. "Hey, what about you?" she asked. "Jake's friend at the party the other day seemed to notice you, and he wasn't too bad."

"You're just saying that to make me feel better," I said. Of course it did make me feel a little better. If Cindy had noticed, then maybe it wasn't just my imagination after all.

After that Cindy and Amy went on talking about some beauty stuff that I wasn't really listening to, and then in short order it was time to get ready to go to dinner.

Going back to my room, I was absently humming the song *Across the Universe* that had been playing in Cindy and Amy's room. Upon arriving, I immediately got a dirty look from Janie. Just as I was humming the music to the line *"Nothing's gonna change my world,"* she cut me off by putting on her own music, which apparently she had forgotten to turn on earlier. I remembered that of course Janie did not allow secular music in our room on Sunday, and apparently that included humming. I was drowned-out by the sounds of primary children singing *"I know what a prophet does and I can name some too. They're men on Earth who talk to God the way I talk to you..."* I wasn't too thrilled about it, but I supposed I had no choice but to keep the rest of the sabbath day holy.

On Monday my classes went reasonably well. We discussed *Hamlet* in my Humanities class, and I discovered that I had picked up on some of the interesting points, yet unsurprisingly there was quite a lot of cool stuff I hadn't noticed or gotten to in my reading. Of course I was a bit distracted during my classes thinking about my interview with Standards.

The interview was in the administration building, which was a funky 60's-style building which had the shape of a narrow X, like a chromosome, when viewed from above. I handed my letter to the receptionist and took a seat in the waiting room. Some other kids were also there waiting, undoubtedly for the same sort of interview. They all looked perfectly normal, so I couldn't imagine what they might have been called in for, yet their eyes were studiously fixed on the walls or on their own shoes, and they had looks on their faces that could be either read as guilty or apprehensive.

I looked up at the wall myself and noticed that Joseph Smith's famous quote "Teach them correct principles and they will govern

themselves" was displayed there. I could hardly fault the prophet's wise words, yet it struck me as shockingly ironic to find this particular quote here in the realm of temporal punishment for misbehavior. I began to wonder what the Honor Code Office meant by posting that. Were they trying to set people at ease by suggesting that there wouldn't necessarily be any real punishment? Or perhaps they felt that kicking people out of school fell into the category of "teaching principles"? Finally I figured that they were playing mind games with us and trying to break our brains by presenting us with the most blatantly false true message possible.

I was still contemplating this strange message when my turn came up and I was ushered into an office. An almost too-friendly smiling man shook my hand and greeted me as "Sister Hanson." Even though I'd been accustomed to this use of "Brother" and "Sister" as titles all my life, I still found it a bit annoying, like baby-talk.

He started in on some random small talk about how my classes were going that was clearly intended to either set me at ease or put me off my guard. I answered his questions as reasonably as possible, but couldn't help noticing that the diplomas on the wall behind him indicated that he was some sort of psychiatrist.

Finally he got down to brass tacks and asked me if I knew why I was called in for an interview. I honestly replied that I didn't.

"Sister Hanson," he said, "have you committed any sins lately that you think you should confess to your bishop?"

"We are all sinners," I replied, "But I don't think I've done anything that would require going to the bishop." I thought about the beer and about the fantasies about Rex, but by my reckoning those transgressions slipped in just under the line of sins that one goes to the bishop about.

"Sister Hanson," he said in a calm and faux-loving manner, "we're a little concerned because of what you've done with your hair."

What a relief! That was all that it was, my hair. Fortunately my hairdo, while unorthodox, was not actually against the dress code.

The Honor Code Officer could see the relief on my face as I spilled out my explanation. "Oh, that!" I said. "What happened was that I had been complaining to my dorm-mates about all of the superficial conformity here at BYU and how the gospel doesn't require it. My friends said that if I was so opposed to conformity that I should do something really different as an experiment, so my friend who does hair did this to me. But it really isn't me to do something to make myself stand out like that, so starting from the very first day I've been combing my remaining hair over and putting it in a ponytail on the opposite side so that people wouldn't notice—just like I have it done right now."

This explanation seemed to reassure the official. "That's good to hear. It's true that it's not against the rules to do your hair like that, but we were worried that it might be a sign that you had fallen in with a bad crowd or something. You haven't taken up with any new friends outside of the church have you?"

"No, none that I know of," I said, half-wondering if Rex counted as "outside of the church" or if one could actually say that I had taken up with him.

Then he got a bit more serious and asked, "This doesn't have anything to do with your sister April, does it?"

"What?" I asked, genuinely surprised. "April is as conformist as the next girl. I don't see how this could have anything to do with her.

I mean, if she's been doing something with her boyfriend, I don't know anything about it. She hasn't confided in me, and frankly, it's none of my business."

"Of course," he said, sitting back and smiling. "It looks to me like you're a fine, upstanding student." He got up to shake my hand again as he started ushering me out. "It's a welcome break in this job to get to meet a good kid every now and then," he said with a wink. "Sorry to have wasted your time."

I felt a tremendous sense of relief as I walked back to my dorm. It turned out that it was nothing after all. But as I was mulling it over in my mind, I got to wondering how the Standards office had known about my strange haircut in the first place, considering that—as I correctly told the officer—I had been hiding it from day one. Then the solution came to me: Janie. By the time I arrived back at my room I was furious.

Janie was innocently sitting at her desk doing homework.

"Janie! Did you turn me in to Standards?" I asked angrily.

Janie paused for a bit. Then without looking up or putting down her pencil she said "I told you from the very beginning that I'd turn you in or anyone else if I caught you breaking the rules."

"But I didn't break the rules!" I shouted at her. "This haircut is not against the Honor Code or the Dress Code!"

She finally looked up with an expression of indignation on her face. "Even if there isn't a specific rule about it, you're supposed to avoid the appearance of evil. And anyway, if it were perfectly okay they wouldn't have contacted you about it."

At this point was afraid of what I might do or say if I stayed there with her, so I threw down my things and stormed out.

I paced back up to campus, mulling over all of the obnoxious things Janie had ever said to me and how much I hated her. Pretty quickly it started to annoy me that there was no place to go to be alone. Then I realized to my further annoyance that it was dinner time and that I was starting to get hungry. I didn't feel like going back to socialize with everyone, but I'd already eaten one meal out just this past weekend, and I didn't want to be wasting all of my spending money eating outside of my paid meal plan all the time. I thought about skipping dinner entirely, but I didn't even have any snacks in my dorm room in case I regretted it later. So I headed back.

After getting my dinner tray in the cafeteria, I saw Wendy and Lavyrne eating at a table far from where Janie was sitting, so I sat down and joined them. They were eating with a girl I didn't know, but they didn't mind my joining their table like that. I had meant to just join in whatever conversation they were having, but they noticed right away that I was upset, and asked me about it. I ended up spilling the whole story about Janie turning me in to the Honor Code Office because of my haircut.

Both Lavyrne and Wendy thought that it was pretty scummy of Janie to do that, and they agreed that it was unfortunate that a free-spirit like myself would have to room with a rigid, prissy, goody-goody like Janie. Even the other girl I didn't know agreed. The advised me to talk to April to see if she could arrange to have me switched to another room.

When I got back from dinner, I went straight to April's room. She was at her desk doing homework, but she was willing to take a break to chat.

I told her that I couldn't stand to share a room with Janie anymore, and asked if it would be possible to trade rooms with someone. She said that I could probably trade rooms between semesters if I could find somebody who would be willing to trade with me.

"Oh, great," I said, "who would possibly be willing to room with Janie?" After thinking a minute, I said "Well, maybe Trisha. She seems to get along pretty well with Janie. And it would be cool to get to room with Lavyrne."

"Yeah," April agreed kind of wistfully.

"I can't believe she thought it was okay—even right—to turn me in to the Honor Code Office for something that wasn't even against the rules!" As kind of an afterthought I added, "You know, they asked about you."

"Really?" she asked, surprised. "What did they ask? What did you tell them?"

"Nothing, and nothing," I replied. "The guy just asked me if my haircut had anything to do with you, and I replied that I didn't see how it could possibly have anything to do with you, which is the truth."

April paused for a bit and then said, "Actually, Lynn, there's something that I haven't told you about."

"I kinda suspected as much," I said playfully, "but whatever your secret is, you only need to tell me what you feel comfortable telling me."

"The thing is that I've had a run-in with Standards myself. They said that my repentance is sufficient that I can finish the school year as long as there are no further incidents. But if I want to get my ecclesiastical endorsement to come back next year I have to enroll in Evergreen."

"Evergreen, what's that?" I asked. But as soon as I said it, I remembered that I had heard of it in passing. "Oh, never mind, I know," I said. That was the name of the church's organization to help people overcome homosexual tendencies.

The funny thing was that I hadn't suspected, but as soon as she said it, it made sense. She'd had this one boyfriend for years—the only boyfriend she'd ever had—and she had never seemed very passionate or excited about him. She was willing to talk about him when the girls were all giggling about the boys they liked, but mostly he was like a buddy to her. On the other hand, I recalled more than one case where she was ferociously, jealously attached to a female "best friend."

Then I remembered the series of graphic novels she had written in junior high and high school. The female main character had a male love interest, but her attachment to him was kind of vague and theoretical, whereas the interactions between the two female leads were written with feeling and tenderness.

"Does Andrew know?" I asked.

"Yes, of course. I think he knew before I did."

"Do you know what you're going to do?"

"Well, first of all I'm going to transfer to another school," she said. "Actually, I'm not sure how I feel about the church at this point, and I don't know if I want to be cured or not. What I do know is that I don't want my education to depend on this choice. I want to make the right decision for my life, so I don't want my hand to be forced. I want to go to another school so I can step back and see everything from a more reasonable perspective. I need some time to get my head on straight about all of this."

"Maybe I should transfer too," was my immediate reaction.

"Don't be silly, Lynn," she said, "your life doesn't have to revolve around me. Attending BYU has always been your dream."

"Honestly, I'm starting to think it was unwise of me to have always been dreaming the same dream instead of having lots of dreams and then choosing among them."

"Well, I don't want to make your decisions for you, but I've already sent away for information from other universities and such," she said, motioning to a bookshelf which in fact contained quite a large pile of colorful brochures, "and you can look through it whenever you like."

"I just might take you up on that," I said. Then I paused and thought about it a bit. "Do you really think that Mom and Dad will let you transfer to another university like that?"

"They can let me or not as they please," replied April. "All I know is that next Fall I won't be here. Either they'll help me find something else or I'll help myself."

I couldn't help but admire her courage and determination. It was crazy though to admire what was essentially determination to sin, when everyone knows that the most courageous act should be to listen to your leaders and obey. I now had a some new things on my mind in addition to the Computer Science homework that I had planned for that evening, so I bid April goodnight and went back to my room to study.

Back in my room, I sat at my desk and said as little as possible to Janie while doing my homework. Fortunately the logic of the programs described in my textbook was appealing enough to keep me interested. I had this nagging thought in the back of my mind that I didn't want to have dwelling too much in the foreground.

With most temptations to sin, the degree of temptation wasn't all that different from one person to the next. Sure it varied, but homosexuality was an extreme case because it seemed that it wasn't at all tempting or even appealing for the average person, whereas for a certain set of people it tended to be their primary struggle. In April's case, even though I hadn't noticed it before, I was struck with the powerful impression that it was something that was a part of her and always had been. I was glad to have a distraction from the question of why the Lord would create people in this way only to send them to a therapeutic reconditioning to mold them into something else.

When Janie decided that it was lights-out time, out of politeness I replied with a "goodnight," but that was about it.

22. TUESDAY MORNING

ON TUESDAY I had my lunch interview with Paige. I started my school day as usual by swinging by the cafeteria and getting my meal plan breakfast and lunch as sack meals so that I would have some food to bring to share. After spending the morning in my Latin and Multivariable Calculus classes, I set off for Paige's house.

It turned out that she lived off-campus in a house that she and a group of other girls were renting. That sort of set-up appeared a lot more fun than the dorms, especially since she had her own room.

Paige's room was full of candles on various foreign-looking candle-holders that appeared perhaps to be from India or at least from Pier 1 Imports. The candles weren't lit as there was daylight streaming in through the window past the Indian-print cloth that served as a curtain. She was playing some soft music in the background that was at once mournful yet kind of funky.

For lunch Paige had set out some whole-wheat bread and cheese and fruit. Despite this apparent penchant for natural food, she was willing to partake in the cookies and chips from my sack lunches when I offered. Then we both took a seat on some of her many floor-pillows to continue eating and discuss her article.

I started by telling Paige that my friends had suggested my strange hairdo after hearing me constantly complaining about all of the conformity at BYU. I wanted to try to make myself sound brave and/or heroic in this story, but ended up explaining honestly that I couldn't stand all the dirty looks I was getting, and after less than a single morning of it, I took to doing my hair so as to cover the shaved half whenever I was on campus.

"It's interesting how similar your experience is to a story I heard from another student," said Paige. "This other student told me that one day—just to be different—he went around campus wearing a rainbow-colored beanie with a propeller on top. I would regard that sort of thing as silly but inoffensive. Yet apparently some girl on campus looked him straight in the eye and gave him such an accusing look that he ended up just taking the hat off and never wearing it on campus again."

"Yeah, that's definitely similar," I agreed, laughing. "The desire was there, but like me he was too chicken to buck the social pressure."

"I think in my story I might take the angle that while there's a lot of conformity at BYU, it's essentially enforced by social pressure, just as it might be at any other school," said Paige.

"Well, I wouldn't go that far," I said. "The dress code here is strictly enforced as part of the Honor Code, and that contributes to a prevailing attitude that a conservative appearance is a sign of good character."

"Did you get the impression that people were making moral judgments about you based on your unusual haircut?"

"In a word, yes."

"How so?"

"Well for one thing, my roommate called the Honor Code Office on me for it, even though I wasn't breaking any rules. And then the Honor Code Office, instead of telling her not to worry about it, called me in to have a talk with me."

"Really? How interesting," she said, scribbling furiously in her notebook.

"Actually, I'd really prefer that you not mention that in your article, if possible," I said. "The Honor Code guy let me off without even a warning, and I'd hate to go out of my way to make trouble for myself but making it look like I went straight to the press about the incident."

"But this is important to the story," Paige protested. "How about if I change your identifying personal information and then let you read the article before it goes to press?"

"Okay," I said.

"You know, you should consider joining the staff of the *Student Review*. We have a lot of fun, and I think you'd fit right in."

"You think so? I'm not sure I really have anything to contribute," I said.

"Sure you do," said Paige. "I mean, I don't know you that well, but it seems to me that you have an interesting point of view. We're always looking for good articles, and we need people with other skills as well such as illustrations, page layout, and selling ads."

I wasn't sure I'd be much help on illustrations, layout, or sales, but I thought perhaps I could come up with a reasonable article or two. "Sounds like fun," I said. "Maybe I could try my hand at writing an article."

"Cool! Our next meeting is on Thursday evening. If you come, I'll introduce you to the other people who work on my page, and we'll see if we can get the page editor to give you an assignment. Here, I'll write down for you the address of the building where the meeting is held."

At this point our little interview appeared to be wrapping up, which was a bit of a disappointment because there was one more topic that I kind of wanted to discuss with her, and I wasn't sure quite how to bring it up. Fortunately she seemed to be thinking the same thing.

"Actually, there's one other thing I wanted to ask you about if you don't mind," she said, handing me the paper with the address.

"Fire away," I replied.

"Well, I was wondering what you thought of my friend Rex."

"Why?" I asked, "Did he ask about me?"

"No," she said, "but he seemed like he might be interested in you, so naturally I was wondering what you thought of him."

"What can I say?" I asked. "Sure, he seems cute and fun, and I'd be happy to get to know him better if he's interested."

"So you don't already have a boyfriend?" she asked.

I laughed, "Not at present."

"Good, that's what I was hoping you'd say. I know that he doesn't have a girlfriend either. And it turns out that he's coming back into town in a few weeks for his sister's wedding, and—"

"Oh, he's not a BYU student?" I interrupted.

"Oh, no, he attends Stanford. You didn't know that?"

"Ah," I said disappointed. "That's kind of far away. Do they have a particularly good program in his major or something like that?"

"Probably, but actually I think he was more on the 'get the hell out of Utah' track," Paige said chuckling. "There's one thing I ought to tell you about him though: He doesn't believe in the church anymore—he's an apostate."

"Really?" I asked.

"Yeah, it's too bad, too, because he's such a nice guy. To tell you the truth, I don't think he's really prayed about it very hard. Otherwise he'd have a testimony of the truthfulness of the restored gospel." She was fiddling with her various silver rings while saying this, and I noticed for the first time that one of them was a CTR ring.

"Hmmm," I said, kind of nodding.

"I've talked to him about it, and it seems to me that he was just really chafing against the rigid rules of the church, kind of like you and me."

"Ah, yes, I can relate to that," I said.

"Anyway, I was thinking that you might be a good influence on him. You could show him that it's possible to be a free spirit and reject some of the petty aspects of Mormon culture without throwing out the church as a whole."

"I see," I said. So that was it. Missionary work. I had been hoping that Paige had been interested in befriending me just for my various qualities, the way I had been instinctively drawn to try to make friends with her. I didn't want to be too cynical about Paige's motives though because she seemed so cool. Granted it was starting to look like she was taking an interest in me more because of her hope of bringing her wayward friend back into the fold than anything else. Still I figured I might as well go with the flow since it meant potentially a fun friend and a cute boyfriend, and I could hardly argue with that. "Well, that sounds reasonable," I said, not sure I really agreed with what I was saying.

"Cool, I'll give you his phone number," she said taking back the paper with the *Student Review*'s address on it. She flipped the paper over and wrote "Rex Wendell" on it with a phone number and then handed the paper back to me.

"Um, listen," I said, "I'm really shy, and I don't think I could just call up someone I don't really know just like that."

"Oh, come on, of course you can!" she said encouragingly. "Like I said, he's a really nice guy, and I'm sure he'd be happy to hear from you."

"I don't know," I said. "Maybe we'll talk about it again at the meeting on Thursday."

"Okay," she said.

"Well, I have to go to a class soon," I said, getting up and gathering my things. "Thanks for having me over."

"You're welcome, and thanks for your help on my article. See you Thursday."

"See you," I said, as she showed me out.

My next class was my *Book of Mormon* class. On my way to class I thought about what Paige had said about Rex.

First I mulled over the fact that he was an apostate. Normally I would be willing to date a non-member in the absence of other possibilities, but I wasn't sure if it was a good idea to date an apostate. Those who have had the truth and rejected it are the only ones who go to "outer darkness"—the Mormon equivalent of Hell. On the other hand, I wasn't versed enough in theology to be sure whether it was possible to become a son or daughter of perdition and get sent to outer darkness without first having been through the temple.

Then I thought about what Paige had said about how Rex would have a testimony if he had prayed hard enough. I knew that in my own case I had prayed fervently and sincerely my whole life for a testimony. I'd occasionally had a warm feeling about it, but nothing like a sure knowledge as we were supposed to receive. I couldn't help but feel like maybe I had something in common with him.

Bizarrely, it struck me as almost courageous that Rex's response to this problem was to walk away and reject the church entirely. I had never met anyone who had done that. As far back as I could remember we had always given thanks in our prayers for the fact that we were born into the only true church on the face of the Earth. Imagine giving up that blessing and facing the eternal consequences!

Rex seemed like a perfectly normal, well-adjusted guy. He didn't seem to be buffeted by the power of Satan or something like that as I had always heard about apostates. I couldn't stop wondering how it had happened and what had gone through his mind. It didn't appear to be from lack of knowledge of the scriptures. On the contrary it looked like the problem was the opposite, namely that these books that we have always held up as the greatest and most profound books of all were in reality too simple and foolish for him. It couldn't be possible, but I couldn't deny that impression.

With such thoughts swimming around in my head, I was in no position to enter my *Book of Mormon* class with the right spirit.

In *Book of Mormon* class, the professor opened by calling on one of the students to give the prayer, as usual, and as usual, I was glad not to have been called on since I never felt particularly inspired to come up with something appropriately spiritual to say to our Father in Heaven in front of all of those people. Then we had our usual quiz.

My *Book of Mormon* professor was new, and had an innovative new teaching style which was that instead of giving a syllabus at the beginning of the semester, he would pray every morning for the spirit to guide him as to which chapter of the *Book of Mormon* he would teach us that day. Then we were to reread the same chapter as homework in order to be ready for a quiz on it the following class period. Today's quiz was on the "Lord of the Vineyard" allegory from Jacob 5.

The "Lord of the Vineyard" chapter was an elaborate allegory in which a landlord and his servant were grafting different branches from one olive tree to another. It was meant to describe how God and Jesus moved parts of the House of Israel around and intermingled the House of Israel with other peoples at different times. It was really quite difficult to follow without a diagram, which fortunately the professor had prepared for us and had distributed during the previous lecture.

The chapter was kind of amusing if read with the right (or perhaps wrong) attitude since it was full of things like "And it came to pass that a long time passed away, and the Lord of the vineyard said unto his servant: Come, let us go down into the vineyard, that we may labor in the vineyard. And it came to pass that the Lord of the vineyard, and also the servant, went down into the vineyard to labor. And it came to pass that the servant said unto his master: Behold, look here; behold the tree." Basically it read like a faux King-Jamesian version of a paper where the student was trying to stretch one page of material into three pages. Of course in that respect it wasn't much more extreme than the rest of the *Book of Mormon*. Also it was kind of funny that they were growing nothing but olive trees considering that it was a "vineyard."

Luckily the quiz was pretty basic. If anything I had over-studied for it. After that we moved on to that day's inspired chapter, Alma 17.

It was a good thing that I had learned the *Book of Mormon* in seminary, otherwise it would be tricky to follow the stories out of order like that. I suspected that after this first semester the professor—however spiritual he was—would be asked to teach the book in sequence. But having studied it I could say from experience that it was only slightly more reasonable read in order than read at random.

The professor started the lesson by having the entire chapter read aloud by the class. He went around the room and had us each read a verse, and after each one he would pause to add some commentary.

As usual it was difficult to stay focused on the plodding and monotonous prose. I picked up a little bit around verse 14 where it got into a not very politically correct description of the "Lamanites" (Native Americans). "...a wild and a hard-hearted and a ferocious people; a people who delighted in murdering the Nephites, and robbing and plundering them; and their hearts were set upon riches, or upon gold and silver, and precious stones; yet they sought to obtain these things by murdering and plundering, that they might not labor for them with their own hands. Thus they were a very indolent people, many of whom did worship idols, and the curse of God had fallen upon them because of the traditions of their fathers;" etc.

Then it went on in the same style to tell the story of Ammon, a Nephite (i.e. ancient righteous white person), who became a servant to the king of the Lamanites. Apparently some bad Lamanites scattered the king's flocks just for the fun of it, and the other servants were worried that the king would kill them. Ammon saw his opportunity to impress everyone, so he gathered up the flocks and cut off the arms of all of the bad guys with his sword.

I kind of wondered why the spirit would have prompted the professor to teach us this particular story since it wasn't clear that there was any sort of lesson—spiritual or otherwise—to be learned from it. It seemed that it might just be that the professor had a fondness for exciting battle stories in which the good guys defeat the bad guys. He had already taught us many such stories from the *Book of Mormon* so far that semester.

I was pretty glad when that class ended and I was free to go to my Computer Science lab. Correcting the compilation errors and bugs in my program wasn't terribly thrilling, but it beat reading the *Book of Mormon* by a pretty fair margin.

After dinner I got out my *Book of Mormon* homework to see if I could make heads or tails of this story we were supposed to study for the next quiz. I couldn't get past the overwhelming impression that the story was completely pointless and what little interest there was got mired in the gluey, repetitive prose. The "Lord of the Vineyard" chapter from the other day hadn't struck me as any more insightful than this one.

Since I knew that this book was the most correct book on Earth and was the cornerstone of our religion, I felt an urgent need to find something of value in it. I instinctively turned to the part about the visit of our Savior, Jesus Christ to the New World, near the end of the book.

I went to 3rd Nephi and read through the chapter summaries until I got to the one where Christ arrives, chapter 11. I started skimming it. Jesus arrives in glory and lets the people touch his wounds. Then he says some things about repentance and baptism. Then Jesus starts giving the sermon on the mount, essentially straight out of the *New Testament*.

Reading the beatitudes, the phrase "blessed are the cheese-makers" involuntarily came to mind, and the following line about how it's not meant to be taken literally but rather refers to all makers of dairy products in general. The thought of it made me laugh to myself.

One idea struck me however: The *Book of Mormon* was supposed to have been prepared by Heavenly Father specifically to be of value to us in these latter days. Yet being omniscient, He knew that we would have access to the *Bible*. So why was so much of this book copied directly from the *King James Bible*? Realistically I had to admit that a comedy troupe's parody gave more insight into the life of Christ than this book did.

I knew that after the visit of Christ to the New World there was supposed to have been four hundred years of peace and righteousness in which the curse of dark skin was lifted from the people. I went to

4th Nephi to see if that part contained any beautiful spiritual insights. I found that the entire four hundred years amounted to less than a chapter's worth of vague mention. I hadn't remembered that part as having been so short, but then again I couldn't say that I remembered any particular stories from that part either. Before the chapter ended, instead of the entire populace being righteous white people, the people started becoming wicked again and dividing up into the white (Nephite) population and the wicked dark-skinned Native Americans (Lamanites) in anticipation of the ending in which there would be more violent battle scenes where all of the white ancient Americans were killed before the arrival of the explorers and settlers from Europe.

I had always been taught that the Lord's ways are mysterious and that we can't expect to understand them. Yet I felt that there should be some explanation as to why the most important scripture for our day should be so full of gory war stories and copied *Bible* chapters and so devoid of original spiritual insight.

Then I allowed myself to ask the one most forbidden question of them all: What if it's not true?

It was hard for me to ask myself this because I had been trained that doubting the truthfulness of the gospel is itself a sin. Yet I couldn't escape seeing this as the only possible conclusion.

Once I allowed myself to ask this question, the answer became painfully clear. All my life I "knew the church was true" because I had been trained to know it was true. I had no evidence. A "burning in the bosom" on the part of a few million people out of the billions on the planet did not constitute evidence for such an elaborate and nonsensical story.

I felt like I needed to get out and walk around to think. I had been so lost in my own thoughts that I had hardly noticed Janie at her own desk reading her own copy of the *Book of Mormon*, although perhaps not gaining quite the same insights from it as I was. I told Janie I was going for a walk. She admonished me to be careful out walking in the dark like that, and to be sure to be back before curfew. I promised to be careful, and I set off along the long and curving path back under the bridge and back up to campus. It was starting to get dark out, but the path was lit.

I started to worry that perhaps I was trying to convince myself that sin and its price don't exist because of my selfish desire to act on my sexual attraction towards Rex. Perhaps Satan and his temptations and lies were encouraging me to deceive myself. I worried about the eternal consequences if it turned out that my conclusion was wrong.

But then I reasoned that if it were true that God existed and had created me with this capacity to analyze things and he set up all of the evidence to point to this church being false, he could hardly punish me for reaching that conclusion. Either God is a just and loving God and won't punish me for solving His puzzle in the only way that makes sense, or He isn't in which case I have no reason to trust that I would get to Heaven for following this religion or to trust in anything else that people say God said. This looming eternity of punishment and reward that I'd based so many of my life's decisions on so far started to seem so absurd that I could no longer take it seriously, much less fear it.

With this thought, I began to feel light and excited. I caught myself running. I had a tremendous sensation of stepping out into the sunlight to see that there's a whole world out there after having lived my life in a tiny, dark cellar. I felt free. I was free of the weight of petty, pointless rules and of trying to fit myself into a world-view and a culture that were too small and limited to hold me.

I found that I wanted to talk to someone about this incredible jumble of thoughts and feelings. I thought of my usual confidantes Amy and Cindy. They were wrong for this discussion, though, because for all their rule-breaking they believed in the church inasmuch as they had any interest in the question at all. April also came to mind, but after what she said about needing time to think things over and get her head on straight about these same sorts of questions, I figured that it might not be appropriate for me to jump in and start pressuring her in a particular direction.

The one person I really wanted to talk to about it—the person I imagined would understand—was Rex. I had the paper with his phone number in my pocket. I was sorely tempted to call him. It was clear though that it was a ridiculous idea. I could just imagine what his response would be: "You say you're not sure if the church is true anymore? That's nice. Who did you say you were again?"

I figured I'd better head back. On my way back I asked myself if it would be reasonable to continue believing in Christianity after rejecting Mormonism. I dismissed it immediately. If the stories of Jesus and his magic tricks were any more reasonable than the claims of Mormonism, it was clearly just a question of degree. I had fundamentally no more reason or evidence to believe in Jesus than in the prophet Joseph Smith.

When I arrived back at my room, Janie had already started getting ready for bed, so I decided to do the same. After our nightly routines we said goodnight and turned out the light. But all of the thoughts in my head made it impossible to sleep until very late.

Wednesday morning I had to really fight to tear myself out of bed in time for my morning class after having gotten so little sleep. The day was kind of a crazy blur to me, partially because of lack of sleep, but mostly because of my epiphany from the night before.

Everything I saw around me, it was as if I were seeing it for the first time. I had this indescribable, giddy sensation realizing that my whole world was different yet everything in it was the same. Today the faux-Mayan glyphs all over the outside of the library looked like a joke to me. The same went for the garment lines that I could see through the white shirts of some of the students, as if it were somehow reasonable for a religion to choose your underwear for you. Then when the statue of Brigham Young himself caught my eye with his full beard, I almost laughed out loud thinking about the fact that a male student attending Brigham Young University would have to have a "beard card" in order to have the right to have a neatly-trimmed beard or even a day's growth of stubble. Brigham Young, with his long beard—and even Jesus himself for that matter—wouldn't be admitted.

The whole day I was walking around in a daze, with my mind slowly untying all of the knots it had been tied up in all of those years. In high school it had been almost painful to force myself to look away from all of the evidence presented in History class about how the Native Americans had migrated to the New World across the Bering Straits and to convince myself that I "knew" that the *Book of Mormon*'s explanation of them coming by boat from Jerusalem in 600 B.C. was "true." That brain blemish was now gone. The stress of having to believe in a "special creation" for each species and having to believe that after the universal flood apparently-related creatures were inspired to migrate together to their correct continents—it melted like butter. The odious obligation of looking the other way when faced with scholarly interpretations of the hieroglyphs that Joseph Smith's "translated" to give the *Book of Abraham* was no longer required of me.

Some more recent knots came undone as well. I no longer had to chalk it up to divine mysteries when supposedly beloved children of God didn't fit into His supposed divine plan. I thought particularly of April. If God existed and loved her, then why did He create her gay only to plan nothing but torments for her if she stayed in the church? I thought of the less extreme cases as well such as myself and Rex, who just weren't cut out to wrap our minds around all of the contradictions without protesting.

Eating dinner with my dorm friends that evening, I was a bit withdrawn and pensive. I liked my dorm-mates and thought they were fun, but I couldn't help but feel like it might be interesting to have the opportunity to meet a more diverse group of friends with more varied backgrounds and beliefs.

Fortunately after dinner Janie went off to a friend's room to work on some crafts for Relief Society Homemaking Meeting, leaving me alone with my thoughts. It was starting to sink in that I didn't belong in this place. Part of it was the feeling that I was missing out on a big part of the university experience by choosing this homogeneous and restrictive institution. But another part of it was the realization that my discovery from the previous night—although fundamentally unintentional—made me an apostate, and hence no longer worthy or welcome to attend. To be admitted to attend school the next year, I would have to pass an ecclesiastical endorsement interview at the end of this year. Theoretically I could repent of other transgressions, but not of just not believing. I would no longer be able to pass the interview without lying.

My only reasonable course of action was to go to April's room and start looking through her stack of university brochures. I was just getting up to go when the phone rang.

"Hello," I said, answering it.

"Hello? Is this Lynn?" asked a voice that I recognized only too well, "This is Rex."

"Oh, hi," I said brightly, "it's nice to hear from you."

"Listen, I hope you don't mind that Paige gave me your phone number."

"Oh, not at all," I said. "In fact she gave me your phone number too."

"Yeah, she said you were asking about me," he said.

Yikes, I wasn't sure how to respond to that. Paige was the one who had brought up his name, but I was afraid he might take it wrong if I corrected him on this point. On the other hand, I hoped my supposed inquiries wouldn't make me appear too anxious or desperate in his eyes. I decided to go with something non-committal.

"We were talking about her article, and your name came up," I said.

"Well, anyway, as she may have mentioned, I'm coming back into town in a few weeks. I was thinking it might be fun to get together."

"Sure, sounds great. Do you have any particular plans in mind?" I asked.

"Not really," he said. "Maybe go to Jake's uncle's cabin again. Unless you have some other ideas?"

"Actually, I was kind of hoping that during your visit you would have some time to discuss something with me," I said. I was nervous about bringing this up, but I was dying to talk to someone about it. "Paige said that you used to be a member of the church but that now you don't believe in it anymore. I'm starting to think that I don't believe in it either, and I don't know anyone else who would understand."

There was a bit of a pause on the line which led me to believe that perhaps I had made a mistake in springing that on him just like that.

"Wow," he said, "I don't know what to say. I hope that you don't think that with my little scripture game the other day I was trying to pressure you to change your beliefs."

"Oh, no, no, it's not that at all," I said.

"I'm sorry, maybe that came out wrong," he said. "What I meant to say was that I'd be happy to take the time to talk to you about your reasons for leaving the church, and mine."

"And what I meant to say was that you seem like a fun guy, and I'm sure we'll have a great time, and it doesn't have to be any more heavy than necessary."

He laughed. "Okay, cool, sounds great either way. The first evening I'm free will be the night of the tenth. I'll see with Jake if it's possible for him to get his uncle's cabin for that night if that's okay with you."

"Absolutely," I said.

"Wonderful," he said, "I'll be in touch with the precise details."

"Okay. I'll talk to you later. Bye."

"Bye, Lynn," he said, and I hung up the phone.

As the initial shock of what had just happened subsided, I found that I was nearly hysterical with delight. I was surprised to discover that I could have such an intense physical reaction to a voice on the phone, but there it was, the same urgent burning sensation as before.

I still wanted to go consult April's university brochures, but I didn't feel I could go immediately because I was too excited to sit still. I decided to go on a little walk around the outside of the dormitory.

I started to wonder what Paige would think of this new development. I supposed she would be pleased that Rex and I had a date planned— as she had clearly intended—but she might be upset to learn that the religion question had kind of gone in the opposite direction than what she had been hoping for. I completely understood that Paige was just motivated by concern for her friend's welfare. But I felt like Rex's instinctive live-and-let-live attitude more closely matched my own inclinations. I figured that when I saw Paige on Thursday I'd just tell her about the date and then later deal with the religion question if and when it came up. Hopefully she would still be willing to be friends with me just as she had maintained her friendship with Rex.

When I felt that I was sufficiently calmed down off my happy cloud, I went back into the dormitory and headed for April's room. As she let me in, I noticed that by coincidence she had out all of her brochures and apparently had been going through them herself.

"Hi April," I said, "I was wondering if I could look over some of that material you sent away for."

"Of course, be my guest. I was just looking over them myself."

I picked one up at random. It was MIT. It looked nice, but I imagined I wouldn't get in.

"So you're really thinking of transferring?" she asked.

"I'm not just thinking about it," I said, "I've decided. I have to leave too. It's not about you, it's not about Janie, it's about me. I just don't belong here, no matter what I dreamed as a kid."

"I agree," she said.

I ran my fingers through the short hairs on the left side of my head, and started going through the pile more systematically. I started with the University of Minnesota and the University of Wisconsin. Both were good schools where we would have in-state tuition (because of an agreement between Minnesota and Wisconsin). They also had the advantage and disadvantage of being not too far from Mom and Dad.

I saw that April also had a bunch of information about different types of financial aid, which would certainly be helpful since we might be on our own after Mom and Dad found out we were leaving "the Lord's University."

There were some brochures from various west-coast schools in Washington and California, including Stanford. I figured that on the strength of not even one date yet it might be a bit early to be thinking about showing up on his doorstep, but at least I put that one in my not-entirely-ruled-out category. April had information on a bunch of east-coast schools as well that looked interesting. In addition to the big state schools, she had some brochures for a smattering of smaller liberal-arts colleges, some of which I had never even heard of. I found that she had even gotten information about how to join the Peace Corps and also some brochures for work-study programs in Europe.

"Do you see anything that interests you?" she asked.

"Lots of things," I replied. "There are so many possibilities."

CHARACTERS IN BYU

Girls in the Dorm

April

Lynn

Amy

Cindy

Wemdy

Lavyrne

Janie

Trisha

Others

Jake

Paige

Ben

Rex

Andrew

Interlude
Gratuitous Love Scene

Lynn

2 3 . F R I D A Y E V E N I N G

"**Y**OU WON'T NEED to contact me," I said.

"What if there's an emergency?" asked Janie.

"Like what?"

"What if your mom calls and needs to get a hold of you?"

With my back to her I rolled my eyes. "Look, I don't have the number off the top of my head. Cindy is right down the hall. If there's an emergency, she can give you her aunt's phone number."

I grabbed my backpack and stepped out. I was hardly dressed for my little outing, but I couldn't get all dolled-up as if for a date and risk Janie getting suspicious and turning me in to Standards again. I had no intention of coming back to BYU after this year, but it would be inconvenient to get expelled and wind up not being able to transfer my credits.

Cindy and Amy's door was open, so I stepped in. "Are you ready to go?" I asked.

"Yeah," said Amy, "but you're not. Look at this hair!"

The short part had grown out sufficiently that I was able to cut it all to match, but I didn't really know what to do with it. Quick as a flash Amy worked in some gel, and with a few strokes of her magic hairbrush she had me looking as if I'd cut my hair that way on purpose and not just on a lark. Then she looked me over and added a few dabs of make-up.

Looking in the mirror I was stunned by the difference her contribution made over what I had done for myself. I began to think maybe I was wrong to think that poring over beauty magazines was a boring waste of time, but on the other hand it was probably just that Amy had a special talent that I would never attain even with years of study and practice.

Cindy excitedly saw us off as we danced our way to Aunt Julie's house.

Aunt Julie welcomed us in with her usual complicit giggles, and tried to feed us some cookies and milk as we waited. She was so like a twelve-year-old when it came to talking about boys that it made our little story about how she just liked to have slumber parties with us seem all the more credible.

In no time the doorbell rang. We answered it, and Jake and Rex greeted us. Amy immediately rushed up to Jake and embraced him and kissed him like the established couple they were, leaving me awkwardly looking at my shoes wondering what I should do.

All those phone conversations had given me the idea that I knew Rex well, but seeing him again in the flesh, it hit me that I really didn't. I'd only met him on that one brief occasion. He seemed taller than I remembered him, but it was probably because I hadn't really been standing next to him at all during that earlier visit to Jake's uncle's cabin.

Amy and Jake rushed to the back seat of the car and sat as close together as the seatbelts would allow, as I took the passenger seat next to Rex.

As soon as we were on the road, Rex turned to me and said "I'm sorry about the scheduling, setting out so late in the evening like this. My mom wanted to have a big family dinner for my first night back in town, and I couldn't get out of it. I had a hard enough time explaining why I wanted to sleep over at Jake's at my age, and I didn't want to push my luck."

"It's okay," I said.

"Perhaps I can take you out to dinner tomorrow night?"

"That would be lovely."

"We were lucky my uncle let us use the cabin at all," said Jake. "He almost didn't."

"You should tell him you want the cabin so you can go hunting," said Amy. "That would make him happy."

"Actually, that's what I told him."

"What?" asked Rex. "And he fell for that?"

"He believes what he wants to hear," said Jake.

"But he knows you've never done it," said Rex.

"Yeah, so what I told him was that you knew how to do it, and that you were going to teach me."

"What?!" asked Rex. "Jesus! Thanks for warning me! I hope he doesn't quiz me on it or something."

Rex thought about it for a bit, then smiled and said, "I know! If your uncle asks me about this later, I'll say that *I* had thought that *you* knew how to do it, and it was all a big misunderstanding."

Amy started laughing. "You guys had better watch it or he'll invite you both to go up with him one of these days and teach you both!"

"Hopefully I'll be back in California before that day of reckoning."

"Look, I'm sorry," said Jake. "It was the only thing I could think of off the top of my head when he was asking me why I want to borrow his cabin all the time."

"I'm not complaining," said Rex. "It's a fine excuse. It even explains why we have to bring these girls with us."

"I didn't tell him about the girls!" said Jake.

"After all," Rex continued still with a half-smile, "manly guys like us can't be expected to skin the carcass and cut it into cute little venison hamburgers and everything. That takes a dainty hand."

"I certainly do not know how to skin a carcass," I said.

"Me neither," said Amy.

"Hey, I thought you ladies claimed you were raised LDS," teased Rex.

"Yeah, but we're from Minnesota," Amy explained.

"Ah, well, in that case I guess we'll have to cross deer hunting off the agenda."

"I hope you're not too disappointed," I said, getting into it myself.

Rex just smiled and continued looking at the road. I supposed that he was considering a line about how I could make it up to him, but decided it was perhaps too forward at this point. It occurred to me that I had never even touched him.

I studied his face for a moment. In his glasses he reminded me of the usual nerdly guys I had known in my high school math and science classes, buried in pages of dense equations or tapping out interminable screenfulls of code under a florescent lamp. Yet he was beautiful to me, with his bright eyes and his playful smile. I looked at his masculine hand casually holding the steering wheel, and looked down at his thighs, his knees in his faded jeans. I was tempted to reach over and stroke his leg with my fingers. It seemed like it might be appropriate—even welcome—given the unspoken plans for the evening. Yet I couldn't bring myself to do it.

"It's funny the list of people we all had to lie to to get out tonight," said Jake out of the blue.

"Some of whom we wouldn't have had to lie to if they'd mind their own business," I said. I still wasn't ready to forgive Janie.

"The trials of having a Christlike roommate, huh?" asked Rex.

"On my way out she tried to get me to give her Aunt Julie's phone number. I'm sure if I'd given it to her she'd have made up an excuse to call so she could check and see if we were really there."

"Aunt Julie's cool," said Amy. "She's Mormon, but she would totally cover for us."

"Well that's good news at least," I said.

It was already dark out when we arrived at the cabin. Turning on the light, I saw the same crazy scene as last time, with antlers mounted all over the walls and fashioned into lamps and other things. The familiar row of Mormon classics from *Mormon Doctrine* to *The Miracle of Forgiveness* sat proudly on the mantle. The scriptures on the end probably hadn't been disturbed since our last visit, but they looked appropriately pious pressed against the deer-shaped bookends.

I crossed the rag rug and sat down on one of the two couches. Rex came over and sat right next to me and put his arm around me. It was all so natural that I felt foolish for having hesitated earlier. I cuddled up against him and put my hand on his knee.

Jake proceeded with the distribution of beers as Amy took a spot on the other couch. Just before taking his position to cuddle her, he dimmed the lights and put the television on softly. No one was interested in television of course, but it gave us a distraction as we discretely got down to business. It was more polite and than saying "Okay, we're going to stop having a group conversation now because it is time for everyone to make out."

I'd pictured this moment in my mind so many times over the past few weeks that I felt like I should have been ready for it. I was thrilled but nervous as if the whole scene were a bubble that could burst if I did the wrong thing. As he ran his fingers through my hair and kissed me gently on the neck, I wished I still had my long hair, though it appeared I didn't really need it. At the moment his hair was actually longer on top than mine. His felt soft, thick, and luxurious.

I'd never been much for extended make-out sessions, so I was grateful that he didn't try to immediately go into nonstop liplock. Just a few deep kisses interspersed with soft caresses.

When the program was over, Jake went and switched off the television. There was no need to continue the charade of watching it since the ice had clearly been broken. He suggested that it was perhaps time to turn in.

Amy giggled and was indiscrete enough to directly bring up the question that was on everyone's mind. "But we haven't decided on the sleeping arrangements yet."

"Well..." Jake said, looking down. Then he paused and looked over at me. I noticed Amy was smiling and looking at me as well. I looked over at Rex and saw that he was looking at me with kind of a shy but hopeful smile. I got the picture. It was my decision.

I wasn't sure exactly what to say. The silence seemed to last an hour as I tried to come up with the right way of putting it. Nobody else dared say anything at all.

"Well..." I began. Turning to Amy and Jake I timidly said "You guys took the bedroom last time... So I guess it's not really your turn anymore, right?"

"Of course you're right!" said Amy with a huge grin. Jake was smiling as well. They were giving up a valuable privilege of course, but in truth they saw each other all the time and had plenty of privacy at

Jake's house since his mom frequently worked evenings and weekends, so they were more interested in the excitement of aiding their friends in a new romance.

I hardly dared to look Rex in the eye. I slowly gathered up my backpack and then I took him by the hand into the bedroom and closed the door behind us. He went and sat on the bed and I went over and sat beside him.

"Despite what this looks like, I don't want you to feel pressured to do anything you're not ready to do tonight," he said. "I know that giving up on the church is already a big transition, so I completely understand if you don't want to take things too fast."

"Okay," I replied. "If you don't really want to do it tonight, I guess we don't have to."

He smiled in response to my little game. "That's not what I said. I merely said that whatever we do will be your call."

"Oh, great," I joked. "Is this going to degenerate into one of those 'what do you wanna do?' 'I dunno, what do you wanna do?' 'I dunno, what do you wanna do?' type of conversations?"

"Nope," he replied. "I know exactly what I want to do."

"What?"

He laughed. "I don't know if I can say in mixed company."

"Look, you're going back to Stanford in less than a week, right?" I asked.

"Yep."

"And we might not have another opportunity like this one before you go."

"Very true."

"I'm ready."

He moved in closer and put his arm around me. Interestingly, he seemed to have lost some of his cool confidence. As he stroked my arm, his hand seemed to be almost trembling.

"Listen," he said, "I have to tell you that I don't really have all that much experience."

I took that to be some sort of guy euphemism for the big V, but I didn't want to embarrass him by pressing for precisions. "That's not a problem," I said.

"But I know how to use a condom," he said.

"Well, that's the important part really. I'm sure the other stuff is all pretty straight-forward."

He seemed relieved by this little exchange and ready to spring into action.

The next logical step was clearly to remove all clothing. We were happy to forgive each other a little awkwardness in the pursuit of our mutual goal. Then began the exploration and allover kisses.

It was all so new and so astonishing. We were like two kids in a candy shop. I'd never been this far with anyone. It was a treat to run my fingers down his neck, across his broad shoulders and manly chest, down to his navel. I knew I'd signed on for the whole enchilada, but still I found myself a little hesitant to explore the nether regions for some reason.

It was wonderfully arousing to feel his touch, and particularly to see how ferociously it excited him. When it seemed to be the right moment, he turned and put on a condom.

He then turned back to me and touched my arm, again almost trembling. In his nervous grin I could see the points of his canine teeth, and for an instant he had the air of a ravenous wolf.

Despite our mutual lack of experience, we managed to fit all of the pieces into place without too much difficulty. The penetration itself was kind of an unexpected sensation—more uncomfortable than arousing really—but I figured it was an acquired taste that would surely grow on me. What was really erotic, though, was how passionately it affected him. He seemed almost to go into a state of delirium like it was the end of the world.

When it was over, he held me tightly as he caught his breath. Then he pulled out and sat up, slid the condom off and tied the end. I thought I heard him say, "Um, sorry..."

"What?!" I asked, suddenly alarmed. "It didn't break did it?"

"Oh, no, no, nothing like that," he said. "It's just that, y'know, I think it's supposed to last longer than that."

"Oh, okay," I said.

I thought about for a moment then said "Well, I wouldn't worry too hard about it. It's not like there's a panel of judges in here giving us a score or something."

He smiled but didn't look up. I sat up next to him and put my arms around him from behind. "And besides," I said, "I'm sure we'll get better with practice."

"Practice..." he repeated, laughing a little to himself. Then he turned and kissed me. "Have I died and gone to heaven?" he asked.

"You believe in heaven?" I teased.

"Well I don't normally," he replied, "but I'm always willing to reconsider my conclusions when faced with new evidence. And I can't think of any other explanation for this." He put his arms around me and squeezed.

Then he pulled away and said, "I think I will slip off to the bathroom for a moment."

He took the ends of the bedsheet and started gathering it around his waist as if he were going to fashion himself some sort of crazy diaper. Then he thought better of it and just put his boxer shorts back on.

He stepped to the door and opened it just a tiny crack and peeked out. Evidently seeing the coast clear he slipped out. I put on my nightgown and waited my turn.

As soon as he was back, I set off across the living room to the bathroom myself. In the faint light I could see that Amy and Jake were sleeping separately on the two couches. Apparently it must have been too much of a bother to try to sleep together under the circumstances.

Coming back out of the bathroom, I heard Amy giggling. She looked up from her pillow and caught my eye. I found myself giggling a little as I returned her look. She was clearly looking forward to the stories I'd have for her and Cindy later. Finally I would be the one with a story to tell.

When I got back to the bedroom, Rex was already in bed. I took off my nightgown and got in next to him. He turned towards me and pressed up against me. Resting his head on the pillow, he absently traced my breast with his fingers. I could feel his penis against my leg hardening a bit. This time I got up the nerve to touch it with my finger.

"It's really kind of amazing that it does that," I said. "Of course you probably think it's silly to be impressed by it since you've had it all your life. It must be old hat to you now."

"No, actually, I've always found it kind of intriguing." He paused. "Yet—fascinating as it is—you still get in trouble if you try to use it as a science project."

I laughed and saw he was wearing his signature wry smile as he looked back at me.

I ran my fingers down his neck and traced his arm down to his hand. I wondered if it was perhaps too early to be thinking about this in terms of love.

Love.

V. Polygamist

Joe

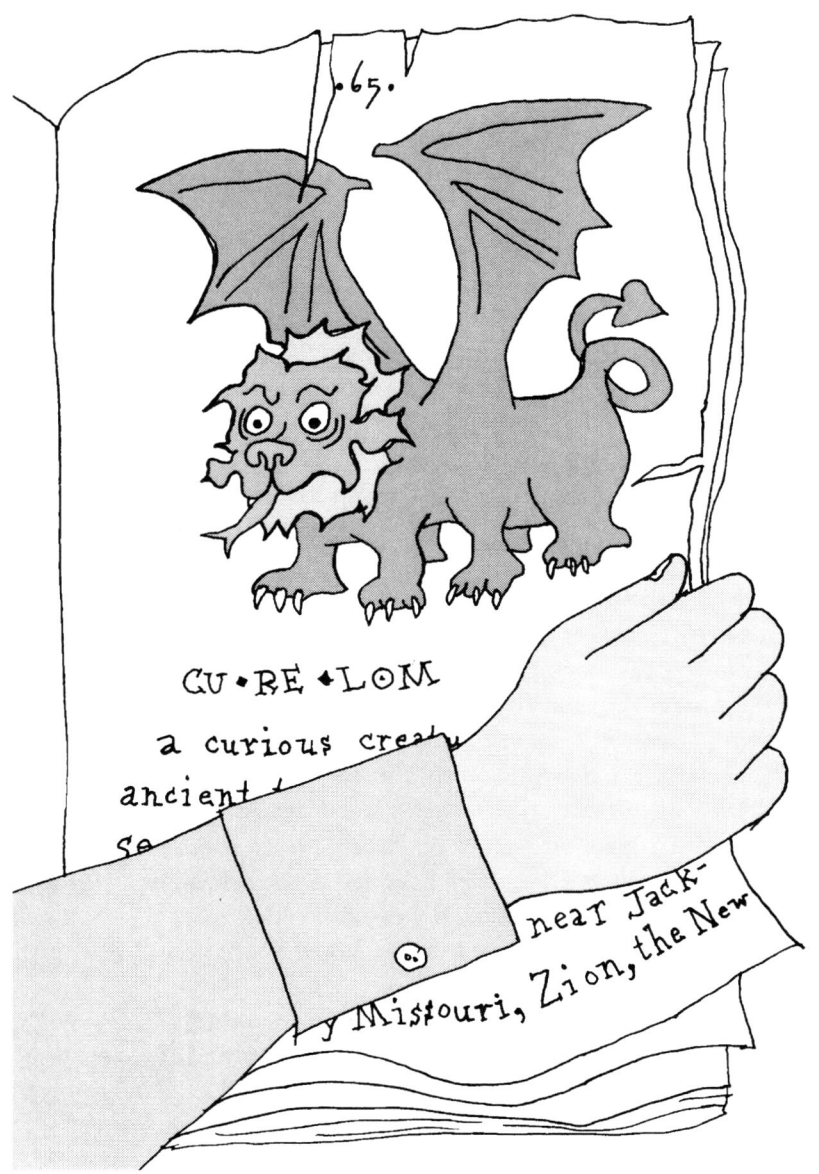

24. MONDAY MORNING

I SAT BACK IN my chair as I listened to the teacher recite the same story of Joseph Smith that he had been repeating to us all week. The handful of other students in my class looked just as bored.

The the teacher turned and asked, "Now who can tell us what year the Saints arrived in Far West Missouri?"

Since no one else responded, I raised my hand.

"Yes, Joe?"

"Please, we're supposed to be studying Biology," I said.

"Of course," replied the teacher. "And I have a special lesson for you. All of you turn to page 65 of your books."

I opened the worn, old book and turned to the correct page. On it was a brightly-colored drawing of some sort of monster with six legs and bat wings and a dragon's head.

"This is a curelom," said the teacher. "They're not common in our day, but the pioneer children used to play with them during the great trek west."

"A curelom?" I thought to myself. "That can't be right..."

Then I awoke with a start and for an instant couldn't figure out where I was. It came back to me immediately, as I saw that I was on a bus and noticed the familiar old lady I'd met earlier, on the seat beside mine. I must have just fallen asleep.

A wave of relief came over me to realize that it was just a dream and I wasn't really back there at that school. Then it hit me that it was crazy to feel relieved to find myself a bus bound for an uncertain destination. I should have felt terrified.

The envelope I'd found with the address on it was almost ten years old. I had no way of knowing if my uncle and aunt still lived there. Nor did I know if they'd be happy to see me. I knew that my father and his only brother Wes had had a terrible falling out when my parents were excommunicated from our old church for their belief in the fundamentalist doctrines, and I knew that there had been no contact between our families for years.

Yet for some reason I felt confident that I would find some way to survive. I had just the bare minimum of clothing and enough money to live frugally for a few days, and no back-up plan if I couldn't find my uncle or he wouldn't help me. But the fact that I'd gotten this far— that I'd managed to get away at all—made me feel like I was ready to face any challenge that was thrown my way in search of my freedom. It wasn't clear whether this was bravery or innocent foolhardiness...

We continued traveling all morning, and in the afternoon the bus finally arrived at the bus depot in the south of Provo. I attentively studied the local map on the wall. I was still too far away from my uncle's house in Orem to go on foot, so I figured out exactly which local bus lines I needed to take to get there, and parted with a chunk of what little money I had for the ticket.

Riding towards Orem, I dug through my old memories for anything of my uncle and his family. The only image that really came to mind was sitting on a dock with my cousin Sam, floating some toy boats in some sort of pond or lake. Then I remembered Sam's older brothers Matt and Spencer pushing both of us into the water and laughing. Typical kids' stuff. I couldn't remember anything more.

Getting off at the bus stop and walking towards the house, things started looking strangely familiar. It was definitely the neighborhood where I had visited them so long ago. But that didn't mean they were still there.

"This is it..." I thought to myself as I finally reached the house. I stepped up onto the porch and rang the bell.

A blond boy my own age answered the door. Looking at his features, I could barely make out that it was Sam.

"Sam?" I asked.

"Yes?" he asked, looking at me blankly.

"Sam, don't you recognize me? I'm your cousin Joe. Joe Hobbs."

He looked at me a minute, seeming to just barely comprehend. "Joe?"

"It's me, Sam. Don't you remember? We played together as kids."

"But we thought you were... I mean..." He seemed confused and flustered as he stood there taking all this in.

Then a voice came from inside. "Well, don't just stand there staring, Beavis! Let him in."

"Won't you come in?" asked Sam, showing me into the living room where a slightly older guy was sitting on the couch watching a baseball game on T.V. I figured it must be either Matt or Spencer. Sam went and sat by him, so I took a seat in the nearest arm chair.

"Hey Joe, what brings you to our neck of the woods?" asked the other guy.

"I ran away from home."

"Really?" asked Sam. "And where are you planning on going?"

"I don't know," I said. "I didn't have much of a plan after coming here."

"Well, you can probably stay with us until you think of something," said Sam. Seeing me looking at their bag of chips on the coffee table, he asked "You want something to eat?"

"Um, yeah, if you have something..."

So Sam led me into the kitchen and made me a sandwich which I ate immediately.

"Would you like another one?" he asked.

"Well, if it's not too much trouble..."

As I was eating the second sandwich, Sam said "Wow, you're pretty hungry."

Just then Sam's brother walked into the kitchen. Seeing him standing like that, I was surprised at how big he was, tall and broad like a wall with huge arms and shoulders. Taking another look at Sam, I could see that he was already almost as tall, and even though he was still a skinny fifteen-year-old kid like me, it looked like he might be heading in that same direction.

Getting a can marked "caffiene-free cola" out of the refrigerator, Sam's brother asked me "Do you want some pop?" I could see that there was a whole stack of cases of the same piled next to the kitchen counter.

"No thanks," I said, "could I just have some water?"

Sam got out a glass and filled it with water from the tap and handed it to me.

I then followed them back to the living room where I noticed a bunch of family portraits that were displayed next to a large embroidered wall-hanging that said "Love at Home." It was clear from the portraits that the mystery brother was Spencer. There was a picture of a young couple dressed for their wedding standing in front of a building I figured must be one of their temples. Then the individual portraits of the kids were arranged in an inverted "V" shape: first the two girls—the twins, Laura and Linda—then at the top point a guy who must have been Matt, then going down the other side Spencer and finally Sam. It reminded me a bit of the walls of portraits at my

own house, with a separate wall for each of my dad's three wives, each surrounded by the portraits of her children.

Continuing along another wall, I saw some pictures of guys in football gear that looked like more shots of Matt and maybe also Spencer, and then a really old one that was probably my Uncle Wes.

Sam and Spencer went back to watching television and paid no further attention to me, so I couldn't think of anything to do but sit in the chair and watch with them. It was a little strange since we weren't allowed to watch television at our house—we didn't even have a T.V.

After an hour or so, some people came in the door who were pretty clearly my Uncle Wes, my Aunt Felicia, and my cousins Laura and Linda. They didn't seem to notice any of the three of us at all—they just went straight for a room down the hall and closed the door.

I wanted to be polite as an uninvited guest, but my curiosity got the better of me.

"What's going on?" I asked Spencer and Sam. "What are they doing in that room?"

"Dad's giving Laura and Linda a 'father's blessing'," said Spencer.

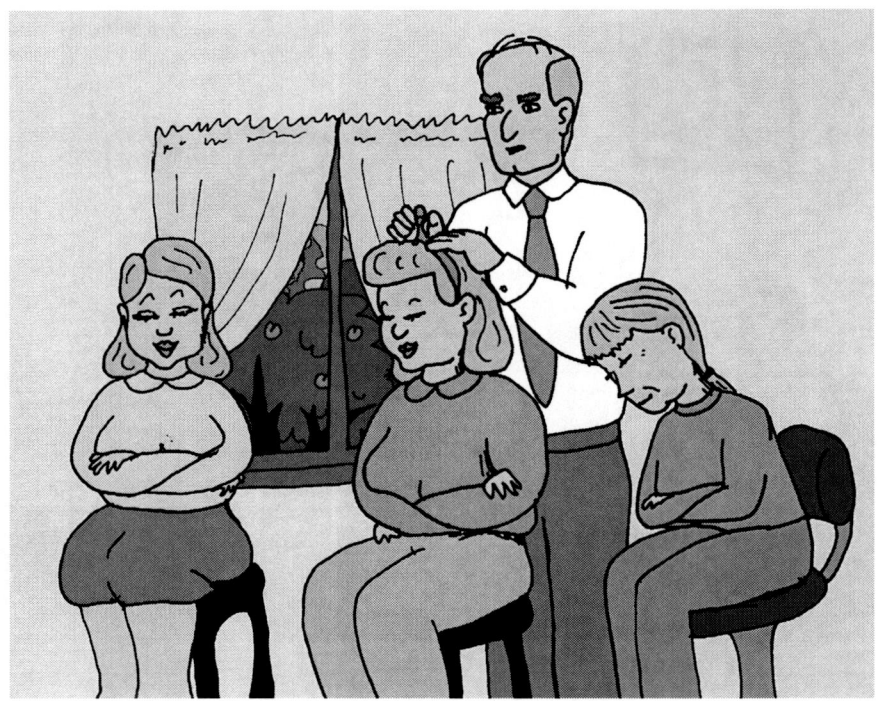

"Why'd they close the door?" I asked.

"We're not supposed to know what it's for," said Sam, starting to laugh a little, "but they were talking about it loudly enough in the kitchen earlier..."

"Dad's blessing them so that in exchange for going on missions, Heavenly Father will find them husbands when they get back." Then, after saying it, Spencer couldn't hold back a bit of a laugh himself.

"Really?" I asked. The idea kind of confused me a bit. "That's so odd. Where I come from, two healthy, voluptuous girls like that would have been married a long time ago. They'd already be bouncing babies on their laps and chasing toddlers around."

"Joe, I hate to be the one to break this to you," said Spencer, "but things are a little *different* where you come from..."

"I know," I said. "So they're going on missions?"

"Yeah," said Sam. "They held out as long as they could, but now they're almost 22 and can only stretch out college for one more year, with no husbands in sight! So they'll be setting off for the MTC in a few weeks."

Then after a little pause, Spencer chuckled and said "Hallelujah! It's a miracle!"

"What?" asked Sam.

"This proves the power of the priesthood!" said Spencer.

"What does?" I asked.

"The very day Dad decides to bless them to get married off, who should show up on our doorstep? Cousin Joe! And he can marry them both! Problem solved!" Then he laughed.

When my uncle and aunt and older two cousins finally came out of the room, my aunt noticed I was there and turned to Sam. "Sam," she asked, "is your friend staying for dinner?"

"He's not my friend," said Sam, "That's cousin Joe."

"Cousin Joe?" she asked, confused.

"You know," said Spencer, "Uncle George's son."

That caught Uncle Wes' attention. He turned and looked at me accusingly. "What are you doing here?" he asked.

"Please Uncle Wes," I said, "I ran away from home. I couldn't take it there. And I had nowhere to go but here."

"Poor thing!" said Aunt Felicia. "Of course he can't be expected to stay with those horrible people!"

"Well, he can't stay with us!" said Uncle Wes.

Then Aunt Felicia shot him a look that said that they couldn't very well do otherwise.

"Well, okay, I guess you can stay for now," said Uncle Wes, "until we decide what to do with you." And so I was left to continue watching television with Spencer and Sam.

By dinner time, it had only been a few hours since the sandwiches Sam had given me, so I wasn't all that hungry. Still, Aunt Felicia had made a pretty good casserole, and I didn't want to be rude by not eating what I was served.

The family didn't talk much while eating. It looked like Uncle Wes was eyeing me suspiciously.

Out of the blue, Uncle Wes disgustedly said, "He looks like George!"

"Oh, he does not, dear," said Aunt Felicia.

"I say he does!" said Uncle Wes.

"And he's doing it on purpose, Dad, just to spite you," said Spencer sarcastically.

Uncle Wes just grumbled and continued eating.

After dinner, the family went to the living room to have "Family Home Evening" which was some sort of home church service. It seemed that this version of Mormonism wasn't that much different from what I had left, especially when they opened by singing *"We Thank Thee Oh God for a Prophet."*

Then, after the prayer, Aunt Felicia got out a lesson book and started reading to us about Brigham Young. The story started after Joseph Smith's martyrdom with the meeting where the congregation saw Brigham Young transfigured to look like Joseph Smith so that the people would know that he was chosen to be the new prophet. Then it went on to describe how Brigham Young organized the trek across the plains with all of the handcart companies and such. All of that made it really seem like this religion wasn't very far from the one I had left behind, though it was strange that this one had rejected so many of Brigham Young's teachings and still professed to follow him.

Then, talking about Brigham Young's own westward trek, the lesson book mentioned Brigham Young's "wife."

"Wife?" asked Spencer, laughing. "You mean 'wives,' right?"

"Well, here it says 'wife'," said his mother.

"Let me look at that," said Spencer, taking the book from his mother. He quickly skimmed through the whole lesson and then looked up with an incredulous expression. "In this whole lesson it doesn't even mention once that Brigham Young had more than one wife at a time."

Aunt Felicia took the book back and started looking over it herself.

"Are they trying to pretend that Brigham Young had only one wife?" laughed Sam. "That's crazy. We've visited the 'Beehive House'. It's like a dormitory."

"I don't know who they think they're fooling here," said Spencer. Then he laughed and added "Old Breed 'em Young!"

Aunt Felicia gave Spencer a disapproving look and said, "Well it doesn't say that he *didn't* have more than one wife. It just doesn't mention it. They probably thought it wasn't very important."

"What?" asked Spencer. "He had almost thirty wives, didn't he? Oh yeah, anybody could miss that. It's no biggie, hardly worth mention." That made Sam laugh.

Then Uncle Wes sternly said "Everyone knows that polygamy was just a temporary thing that the Lord instituted in order to provide for all the widows whose husbands were killed when the gentiles persecuted the early Saints back east. Then, once the Mormons were safely settled in Utah, there weren't so many skirmishes, so men weren't getting killed and leaving so many widows, and the Lord stopped needing polygamy." Then he looked over at me as if to challenge me to disagree with him.

"Yeah, Brigham Young never emphasized polygamy," said one of the twins. "It was just a minor, temporary thing. That's why the manual doesn't bother to mention it."

"Is that true?" asked Spencer, raising one eyebrow and giving a half-smile in my direction.

"Of course Joe knows that that's true, don't you dear?" Aunt Felicia asked me.

"Well?" asked Sam.

I couldn't understand why they were so intent upon having me confirm this nonsense. Just because I couldn't stand to continue living with my family the way things were, I wasn't sure if it was right to just lie. Surely these people loved the Lord enough to prefer the truth over a lie.

"I don't know what you mean," I said. "Brigham Young always preached that polygamy is essential to exaltation, and that you can't enter into the highest degree of celestial glory and become a god one day without living the principle. He preached that the church would be in apostasy if it ever gave up polygamy. I don't understand how you can claim to follow him when he would tell you himself that your church is in a state of apostasy."

Then Uncle Wes stood up with a look on his face of the most fierce rage that I could possibly imagine. He grabbed me by the shoulders and took me to the door, then opened it and physically threw me out into the yard. I wasn't hurt, but I was a little stunned. After about a minute, the door opened again, and a hand put my backpack out on the porch, and then the door closed again.

As I went up to get my tiny sack of worldly possessions, I began to feel fear for the first time. Up until this point I had had some sort of plan. Now I really had no idea where to go.

It started to sink in that that was a really stupid thing to say. Of course these kind of Mormons hated polygamy and didn't want to be reminded that the early prophets taught it. I should have known that—it was the whole reason that Uncle Wes hated my dad so much as far as I could tell. If they wanted to live with their delusions, why shouldn't I just let them? Why take away a cherished lie if the truth meant I was no longer welcome at their table? Of course it was a little late to be deciding this now...

Night had fallen. If nothing else, I would have to find someplace to sleep, and then in the morning start worrying about the fact that I would soon starve to death or die of exposure.

I walked to the back yard of my uncle's house just because I couldn't think where else to go. The whole back yard was full of fruit trees and bushes except a portion that was fenced off for what looked like a vegetable garden. I figured I'd just have to find myself a spot sheltered by some bushes or something.

As I approached the bushes, I noticed that they were obscuring some sort of structure built of wooden pallets. It had a doorway but no door. It looked like a kind of club fort, probably Sam's. It seemed like it was probably better than sleeping outside, so I went in.

I set down my backpack to serve as a pillow and laid down on the floor. It was starting to get cold. I had taken off my jacket inside the house, and they hadn't thought to put it out for me with my backpack. I didn't have anything warmer to put on.

In addition to the cold, the hard floor wasn't at all comfortable. It was particularly hard on the bruises on my back and shoulders. Rubbing my shoulder with my hand, I remembered that last fight with my father. It wasn't the reason I had left, but it was the last straw—at that point I had already had my things packed and hidden away, ready to go.

I tried to rest for a long time, but between the cold and the hard floor, I was just too uncomfortable. Then I started feeling like I had to pee. I wondered if I should just go out and go in the bushes. There weren't really a hundred million solutions here, and if my first priority had been to keep my dignity intact I supposed I shouldn't have run away and become a vagrant...

After that, I tried again to sleep, but the cold was really a problem. I couldn't stop thinking about my home and my warm bed.

Then I though about my mother. I wondered if she was sad to see that I was gone. I wondered if I hoped she was sad about it. Then I knew she was sad about it.

And I began to think that maybe I had made a terrible mistake.

I WOKE FROM MY fitful sleep to a light in my eyes.

As I was groggily sitting up and regaining consciousness, I heard Spencer say "See? I knew we'd find him here." Then Spencer and Sam both squeezed into the tiny room, standing the flashlight up to point at the ceiling.

"Are you okay in here?" asked Sam.

"I'm really cold," I replied.

"Of course," said Sam, "I'll go get you my sleeping bag." And he got out and went back to the house.

"Listen," said Spencer, "I know we shouldn't have been joking around about polygamy like that—because it's no laughing matter—but I have to tell you that was a pretty stupid thing to say."

"I know, I wish I hadn't said it. I wasn't thinking. I just repeated what I'd been taught. Obviously I should have realized it wouldn't be the same thing you guys believe."

"That's pretty clear. Brigham Young for sure didn't say that," said Spencer.

"Who cares what Brigham Young said? I certainly don't! If I never hear of Brigham Young again as long as I live, it will be too soon!"

"Let me give you a word of advice," said Spencer. "If you want them to let you back in the house, you'd better *start* caring what Brigham Young said, and it had better be exactly the opposite of what you said he said."

"What good will that do?"

"You don't get it do you? Mom and Dad are afraid they'll lose their temple recommends if they let you stay in the house and 'preach that kind of doctrine.' That's why they wouldn't let us come look for you and we had to wait until the middle of the night."

"What's a temple recommend?"

Spencer laughed. "You really were living on a different planet, weren't you? It's the paper you take with you to the temple to prove you're worthy to enter. And one of the questions to get one is about affiliating with polygamists. So if you want to affiliate with this family, you have to not be a polygamist."

"But I'm not a polygamist! I'm just a kid. I didn't convert to that religion on purpose! And I ran away! Doesn't that count for anything?"

"Of course it does. Sam and I will get this all straightened out with Mom and Dad. We'll have you back in the house by tomorrow night. Provided you watch what you say a little better from now on."

"Thanks. I don't know how to thank you."

"It's nothing," he said, laughing a little. "Of course we can't have you living out here in the back yard like a dog or something."

As I heard Sam coming back, Spencer said to him, "He only needs one sleeping bag, Beavis—it's not that cold."

"I'm going to sleep out here with Joe," said Sam.

"Suit yourself," said Spencer. "Don't let the bed bugs bite." Then he left as Sam came in and unrolled the sleeping bags. I got into one, and Sam got into the other.

There wasn't a whole lot of room in the little club fort for two people. Stretched out diagonally I could fit okay, but that wasn't possible with Sam there, so I had to lie down on my side with my legs bent. Still, having the sleeping bag to protect me from the cold made a world of difference in terms of comfort.

"Can I ask you something?" asked Sam.

"Of course," I said.

"Aren't you afraid they'll come after you?"

"Not really. If I were a girl, they probably would, but they expect a certain number of the young guys to just fade away. I left a little younger than most, but the fact that I ran away will probably make most people back home think that I don't have the faithfulness required to become a leader, so they'll be happy enough to see me gone."

"What's it like to have more than one mom?"

"I don't have more than one mom. Only my own mother is my mom."

"Oh, I thought everyone was saying that your dad was a polygamist."

"He is," I said. "but his other two wives aren't moms to me. At best they're like aunts. It's hard to explain."

"Is that why you left? Because you knew it was wrong to live that way?"

"I don't know if it's wrong. This is what Joseph Smith and Brigham Young taught as the right way to live. I just know that I couldn't stand it. My dad's wives would always be sweet to each other on the surface while secretly stabbing each other in the back. My mom resented any attention my dad gave to the other two, and they in turn resented the particular love he had for my mom, having fallen in love with her in his youth whereas I think the other two may have been just assigned to him.

"He was supposed to love them all the same, but he didn't. His three wives were supposed to love us kids all the same too, but obviously they did everything they could to get advantages for their own kids over the others, and for their favorites among their own kids most of all. There were a million tiny kids constantly screaming and underfoot, taking and breaking things. And the stress of it all turned my once fun-loving father into a raging monster.

"We're taught that if we live the new and everlasting covenant correctly that it brings great happiness. But we must not have been living it correctly because we were lucky to squeeze out any moments of happiness at all."

"Wow, that's crazy," said Sam. "Well, I hope Mom and Dad let you stay with us. I'm going to be starting school at Orem High in the fall, and that would be cool if you could come too."

"I'd like that a lot," I said. "That's the real reason I left—more than any of that other stuff. I wanted to be able to go to a real school where I could learn things other than just religion before it's too late for me to make something of myself."

"I'm going to try out for the football team, and hopefully I'll be on it with Spencer," said Sam.

"Spencer's still in school?" I asked.

"Yeah he has one more year to go even though he's already eighteen. Mom and Dad held him back a year before starting kindergarten so that he wouldn't be the smallest in the class."

"You're joking, right?" I asked.

"No," said Sam, laughing. "I know it's pretty funny now, but when he was small, he was really small. And Dad couldn't handle the idea of his son being the little pip-squeak of the class that gets picked on by the other boys. So they started him a year late. Are you thinking of going out for football?"

"Ah, no, I'm no good at football," I said. "My older brother Helaman was really good at it. Helaman's skill at sports was one of the few things that seemed to make my dad really proud. Maybe that's why I left," I said, laughing a little. "I didn't want to be measured according to that standard."

"I know exactly how you feel," said Sam. "It seems like not one day can go by without us hearing about 'Matt the quarterback,' 'Matt the captain of the football team,' 'Matt the missionary in Africa who's baptizing everyone in sight'!" He laughed. "So I guess things aren't so different where you come from after all."

"Yeah, except try multiplying that by three, and you'll start to get the picture..."

"Wow," he said, thinking about it a little. "Well, good night."

"Good night," I said, and we both went to sleep.

In the morning, just as the light was waking us up, Spencer came out to find us. "Sam, you'd better get back in the house," he said, "Mom's looking for you." So Sam got up and went back into the house.

Then Spencer handed me a paper bag and said, "I've brought you some food for the day. It would be better if you didn't hang around here, at least for the moment. By this evening I hope to have convinced my parents that it's their missionary duty to take you in and convert you to the true church. If you're okay with that, we should be in business."

"Thank you so much."

"No problem," he said. "Now just lay low, and I'll see you tonight." Then he went back to the house.

As soon as he was gone, I knew immediately where I wanted to go. Riding on the local bus the other day, I had noticed a large brick building marked "Orem Public Library."

I'd made a note of basically how to get there. It would probably be a bit of a walk from here, but I figured it wasn't too far, and I didn't dare waste any more of my tiny remaining money on bus fare.

The walk turned out not to be too bad. It was a beautiful, sunny day. Again I felt like I should be terrified considering my situation.

But feeling the morning sun on my face, I couldn't help but feel hopeful about the future.

I walked up to the door and went straight in. I caught myself feeling almost surprised that I was allowed to walk right in like that. On some level I must have believed that I would never be allowed to get this far.

Wandering around the library, I was astonished by the number of books. I had never seen so many different books all in one place except in my distant memories and in my imagination. I knew there had been a big public library in a community not far from where I lived, but my parents had never let me go there.

I was overwhelmed and hardly knew where to begin. Then I saw the section with the science books. It was exciting to be surrounded by so many forbidden books and nothing to stop me from reaching out and touching them. Again I didn't know where to begin until a a book with a picture of an ape on it caught my eye. For a second, I was almost afraid to pick it up off the shelf, but I couldn't stop myself.

Obviously I wasn't struck by lightning or anything picking it up, and I felt foolish for allowing my irrational fears make me hesitate even a tiny bit. The book looked interesting as I paged through it a bit. There were a few others on the same shelf by the same author, Jane Goodall. I took the first one and sat down with it.

The book was the most fascinating thing I'd ever read. It was about a researcher (the author of the book) who had traveled to Africa to observe chimpanzee society in the wild. It was filled with story after story describing and illustrating the chimpanzees' social behavior. I read it voraciously, straight through, without a single pause.

As I got up to pick up the next one off the shelf, I couldn't help but be struck by the similarities between the apes' behavior and that of humans. Of course the two societies were worlds apart—these were just wild animals I was reading about—but the parallels were too extensive to ignore. It was completely absurd and self-delusional of the faithful believers to deny the connection and obvious relationship between humans and other apes.

The second book was as consuming as the first. The stories that included scenes of aggression on the part of the older males to keep the younger males in line were particularly difficult, yet in some ways it was liberating to read them.

I started thinking about how brutal our animal nature could be and how as civilized humans we needed to rise above it. Then I caught myself. That was exactly the conclusion that the religionists had drawn, and they didn't seem to have succeeded as far as I could tell. There was a famous quote from the *Book of Mormon* about how "the natural man is an enemy to God."

As I read farther, I started to conclude that instinctive social behaviors were neither all good nor all bad. The believers merely labeled the "natural man" as being all bad because they didn't understand him, and they feared what they didn't understand. It became clear to me that it was better to try to study and learn to understand the "natural man" in order to work with him instead of denying him and fighting him. Knowledge is power.

After I'd finished the second book, I got up to find the bathroom for a short pause and to wash up a bit. On my way back out of the bathroom, I noticed that one of the librarians was looking at me funny. It made me uneasy. It reminded me of the way people would look at my family the times when we would go out together in the world outside our closed community. With all of the women in their long dresses and long braids, and so many women and children with just one man, they must have known what we were, and probably wished us harm.

I wondered if maybe there was something about me that the librarian saw that gave me away. I couldn't think of anything that made me stand out as different than these other people, but I didn't know enough about this place to know if maybe I was giving off a signal that I wasn't aware of.

Then I thought that maybe she hadn't recognized me as a fundamentalist but rather as a vagrant. I hadn't had the chance to shower or wash my clothes for a few days. I hoped I didn't smell. I figured maybe it was time to go outside and eat the food that Spencer had given me.

There was a park right outside the building. I sat down under a tree and watched some kids playing baseball. Everything seemed so calm and ordinary. Back home we had been taught that these "gentiles" were so sinister, so full of Satan, and so dangerous to us. Of course I'd been one myself as a kid, so I knew it couldn't be true. But watching them laughing and playing like ordinary people made it really sink in on a gut level how wrong that teaching was.

When I was done eating, I got a drink from a drinking fountain, and then I couldn't keep myself from going back into the library. After all I'd been through to earn this reward, I wasn't about to let a sideways look from one librarian stop me from immersing myself in it.

I went back to the same shelf and read a few more books about various types of great apes and their social behavior until finally it was closing time and I had no choice but to leave.

Walking back to my uncle's house, I was really hoping that Spencer had succeeded in convincing his parents. If I didn't get some proper shelter soon, I wouldn't be able to continue like this much longer. I'd probably end up having to go to a government official and be put in some sort of institution. Or maybe I'd starve to the point where I'd break down and go back home. I didn't even want to think about such a possibility.

All I wanted to think about was going back to the library. The books I had read that day had been unbelievably fascinating, and all I had done was grab the first thing I had stumbled across. I imagined that that whole huge library was like that, and I could spend every day for the rest of my life just exploring and reading everything in sight. The last thing I wanted to worry about was a mundane survival strategy when I was this close to paradise.

I'd always been taught that the last days were nearly upon us and that all but the very righteous would be destroyed. This frightened me to no end since I knew I could never be righteous enough. But seeing a world that was so much bigger than the world of darkness and fear that I had known, I knew that I didn't ever want to go to the fundamentalists' paradise. Their suffocatingly restrictive paradise seemed as terrible as any hellfire.

I remembered how proud my father had been of my intellect and how he had always planned for me to one day become a great scholar of church history and doctrine. What a horrible, sick joke that seemed now that I'd touched the tip of the iceberg of the things I could study and learn.

I couldn't imagine going back to that limited place where I'd have to bow to the wishes of the prophet for any important decision in my life such as where to live, my choice of employment, and who to marry. I was ready to do anything to stay here in this new place.

When I got back to the house, I figured I'd better just go back to the club fort and wait. After a while, Spencer came around.

"There you are!" he said. "You're finally back."

"I was at the library," I said.

"Well, it's a green light for coming to live with us. All you have to do is renounce your parents' religion and agree to be baptized LDS."

"I can do that," I said.

"Great," he said, "then come with me." He started leading me back to the house. "Supper's already over, but Mom saved you some in the kitchen." Then Spencer set up a bowl of soup for me and some bread, which I sat at the table to eat.

While I was still eating, Uncle Wes came in and stood at the head of the table and looked at me. I just looked back up at him, not knowing what else to do.

"So," he began, crossing his arms across his chest. "Spencer tells me that when you denounced your parents' religion to join the true church, they disowned you, and now you need a place to stay. Is that right?"

"Yes, sir," I said.

"And he also said that all of that stuff you said during Family Home Evening was a mistake—because they deceived you—but now you see that you were wrong. Is that right?"

"Yes, sir."

"Okay," he said. "I guess you can stay in Sam's room with Sam. But you'll be expected to do your share of the chores, and I'd better not hear any more of that Satanic doctrine from you, understood?"

"Yes, sir."

"And you'd better be faithful at church. This is a strong LDS household, not some sort of fairy resort. One slip up—and I mean anything—and you're out on your ear. Understand?"

"I understand sir," I said, "Thank you."

When I was done eating, Sam showed me where I was going to sleep. It was Spencer's old bed from before Matt had left on a mission and left his room to Spencer. I explained to Sam that I didn't have any clean clothes and I needed to take a shower. He understood and showed me where the shower was and gave me some of his old things to wear when I was done. It was nice to finally be clean again.

As Sam and I were getting into bed that night, I said to him, "I really appreciate everything you and Spencer have done for me. Thanks."

"It's no problem," said Sam. "It's the least we could do. And besides, we're going to have fun, aren't we?"

"Of course we are," I replied. "Good night Sam."

"Good night."

CHARACTERS IN POLYGAMIST

The Hobbses

Laura

Linda

Matt

Spencer

Sam

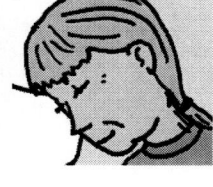

Sister Hobbs

Brother Hobbs

Joe

VI. Temple Wedding

Lynn

26. THURSDAY EVENING

IT LOOKS SO small from a distance. When you're immersed in it—living in Utah or in an LDS household—Mormonism is like a cage with one small clouded lens to look out through that distorts your every view of the world.

Then one day you step out. You leave home, or you leave the Mormon corridor of Arizona, Utah, and Idaho, and suddenly it's as if it's hardly even there. It's this tiny, unimportant thing that you can forget about for days, weeks, months, even years at a time. You can take it out of your pocket and show people if you like, as an amusing conversation piece at parties. Or you can just not even bother with it at all.

Except that if you come from Mormon stock and your family is LDS, you occasionally have to face the disorienting task of stepping back in.

Now, after more than three years apart at our respective universities and one year back together at grad school on the East Coast, Rex and I were about to step back in.

My younger sister Annette was getting married to a returned-missionary from Orem named Matt Hobbs. She had met him at BYU. The marriage would be solemnized in the Provo temple, a stone's throw from campus. So we would be traveling back to Utah Valley, "Happy Valley" as it is lovingly known, to see all of my family at the reception. At the same time Rex, who grew up in Utah Valley, would be going home.

Even with Rex's younger sister Jill back home from college for the Summer and his even younger siblings, Joy and Jared, still living at home, there would have been room for us to stay with Rex's family if we had wanted to. Like Matt's family, they lived in Orem. The thing was, though, that Rex's parents had told him directly that since we weren't married we would have to sleep in separate rooms, and they had also told him that they would require him to "respect the rules of their house," which was their code for saying that there was to be no illicit hanky-panky even when nobody else was around.

Certainly it wouldn't have killed either one of us to go three days without sex. But it was the principle of the thing, and Rex wanted to make a statement to his parents that if they were going to stick their noses in his private life like that then he wasn't going to stay with them. So even though it took a bite out of our meager grad student budget to pay for a hotel room on top of paying for our plane tickets, we managed. Interestingly, when Rex's parents offered him the use of one of their cars for the duration of our stay, he was willing to accept that. I figured that that meant that at least there would be no hanky-panky in the car.

Our flight arrived in at the airport, and from there we took the bus into downtown Salt Lake where we caught another bus south to Utah Valley.

April and her new girlfriend Susan picked us up at the bus stop. They'd only been seeing each other for four months, but already it was serious enough that they were living together. Susan was twenty-seven years old and had an eighteen-month-old daughter named Judy. And since—unlike us—Susan and April were both gainfully employed (at a magazine in Seattle), they had no trouble renting a car for the weekend.

We set up our things in our hotel room, and then the five of us went out to dinner.

When the waiter came by, we ordered a few simple dinners off the menu. It was Susan's first day ever in Utah, so she was quite taken aback when the waiter asked us for ID when we ordered beers with dinner.

"Obviously I'm over twenty-one. Look I have a child," she said, reaching for her purse and pointing at Judy in her high chair. "And I'm just ordering beer with dinner, not drinks at a bar."

"Now see here, my good man," said Rex. "I'll have you know that all of my wives are of age. I certainly take no child brides. Well, except for that one over there." He pointed at baby Judy and smiled.

The waiter gave Rex a blank look as if he didn't think that that was funny at all, so Rex just got out his ID like the rest of us so that we could have beer.

As soon as the waiter was gone, Rex laughed and said to Susan, "It shows that you've never been to Utah before. Here merely having a small child is not at all an indication that you're over twenty-one."

Susan seemed almost creeped out by the incident. "What kind of place is this?" she asked.

"Welcome to Wonderland," said Rex.

I was dying to ask April and Susan how Susan had come to have a baby, being as she was a lesbian and all. I wondered if it was artificial or natural insemination, and under what circumstances. I hadn't really talked to April since she had started seeing Susan, so I had gotten the information off the grapevine (from Mom) about her having a kid and about the two of them living together. I figured that this was one advantage of being straight, namely that if I one day had a baby, it would still be something of an intimate procedure, but people would be less inclined to want to ask too many awkward questions about it since everyone pretty much knows how it works.

I asked April "Is it different living in a house with a baby and acting as a step-parent and all?"

"Yes, it is," she replied, "it changes everything. Basically we can't just go out and do whatever we want whenever we want at the drop of a hat like I used to do with other girlfriends. We always have to take Judy into account. But it's wonderful. She's such an amazing little person. And I'm starting to feel like I'm ready to settle down," she said, taking Susan's hand and gazing lovingly at her.

Rex was making a game of making faces at the baby and making her smile. He looked up and asked April "Do you think you might consider having a baby yourself?"

"We're thinking about it," said April. "It's maybe a little early to make a final decision, but I've started reading Susan's books about how to make arrangements for anonymous-donor artificial insemination."

Rex smiled and nodded and said "Ah" as if her statement were perfectly ordinary, but he seemed vaguely uncomfortable, perhaps because of the realization that the man could be edged out of the picture so easily.

Susan then said "It's one of the joys of being in a female-only romance, that both partners get to experience the joys and pains of motherhood if they like, or if one person in the couple has more inclination to do it, you can actually choose who it will be. You guys are stuck. If you guys decide to have a kid or kids, it will be Lynn who does the hard part every time, no ifs ands or buts about it."

"Well, I guess that's the way it goes," I said. "Some biological realities are hard to work around." Rex chuckled. I turned to him and said "You're just happy because you would get the easy job."

"Hey, you don't hear me complaining, do you?" he said, smiling.

Our dinners arrived, and we continued chatting while we ate.

Then April asked me "So how are you guys going to get around if you don't have a car?"

"Oh, we'll have a car tomorrow," Rex answered. "My parents have agreed to lend me one of their cars for the weekend."

"Your parents live around here?" asked Susan, spooning some food into Judy's mouth.

"Yep," he said.

"Rex grew up here in Orem," I said.

"You grew up in Orem?" Susan asked with an air of innocent astonishment as if amazed that ordinary human reproduction might occur in such a bizarre place.

"Shh, I don't like to tell people that," whispered Rex in a jokingly conspiratorial tone.

"So are you going to get to see any of your old friends from school?" April asked him.

"No, unfortunately the ones I've kept in touch with have all wisely moved far away from here, like me."

"Maybe tomorrow morning you could drop off Rex at his parents' house to get the car, and then we'll be out of your hair," I suggested.

"I noticed you said 'drop off Rex' and not 'drop us off,'" said April. "Don't you want to visit Rex's parents?"

"I'm not terribly thrilled about the prospect, no," I said, "but I imagine I won't be able to avoid it for the whole weekend."

Rex laughed.

"You don't like them?" asked Susan, giving Judy another spoonful.

"Let's just say that sometimes they can be a little difficult," said Rex.

"Well Lynn and I can relate to that," said April. "It's not as though our parents are always super easy to deal with."

"Here's to braving the dark waters of family," said Rex raising his glass.

Susan gave a bit of a smile. "Luckily for us, we'll be braving them a bit less than you will," she said.

"Because you don't have family in town?" I asked.

"Yeah, that, and we won't even be seeing all that much of your family," said Susan.

"It's true," said April. "We got a bit of an insulting blow this morning after we arrived. If we'd been told earlier, we wouldn't even have gotten on the plane, we'd have had our tickets refunded."

"What happened?" I asked.

"Well we saw Dad this morning, and he said he'd spent the day yesterday with Matt's family," said April. "He told us he got the strong impression from them that they would feel more comfortable if Susan didn't attend the reception."

"That's awful!" I said.

"I know," said April. "But Dad told us that since this is Annette's special day, we should think of her rather than of ourselves, and quietly accept this without making a scene and ruining her reception."

"So Dad was saying that Annette didn't want Susan there?" I asked.

"No, he didn't say that," said Susan. "I got the impression that he was uncomfortable enough about the whole thing that he didn't even want to bring it up with Annette."

"We'll see what happens when we talk to him then," said Rex. "After all, we're 'living in sin' as they say, so perhaps I'll be *persona non grata* at the reception as well." He smiled.

"Nope," said Susan, "in fact we specifically asked him that. It turns out that they're okay with you—not thrilled mind you—but not offended by your existence."

"We tried to pin Dad down and get him to give us a straight answer as to why Susan in particular should stay away when the reception is an open house that Matt's family invited their entire ward to attend. But Dad just seemed to regard all these questions as painfully uncomfortable, and just kept repeating that we should think of Annette on her day."

"I am absolutely livid about it," said Susan. "Who is going to reimburse me my plane ticket? It wasn't free, you know. And have you ever flown in a plane with a toddler on your lap? It's no small task! But I did all of this willingly so I could be there for Annette on her special day. And now this!"

"Then to add insult to injury, Dad said that they would be willing to let Susan help take care of the kids during the ceremony in the temple," said April.

"Yeah, he said it like it was some sort of great kindness that the members of the family would be willing to allow someone like me take care of their kids. I didn't know what to say! Already it had taken some doing for April to explain to me that we shouldn't take it personally that we aren't allowed to attend the actual ceremony, and how it's a Mormon thing that only temple-worthy, full tithe-paying adults can attend and that it's always like that. She convinced me not to be too offended by that. But Jesus, not to even let me swing by the open house! I'm sorry, but in my book that's just going a little too far."

"So what are you going to do?" I asked.

"We haven't decided yet," said April.

"I think that you should talk to Annette about it," I said. "She has never had a problem with your orientation, and I can't imagine that she wants you excluded like that!"

"You're probably right," said April. "Still, she's so busy with preparations that I hate to bother her with our little problem. Plus, if it's her in-laws who have made the request, I hesitate to put her in a position where she feels pressured to make a big stink with them on her wedding day."

"I think what we'll probably do is just have April swing by for any family portrait obligations, and for the rest of the weekend just consider this to be a little weekend getaway with as little contact with the extended family as possible."

"That's awfully noble of you to just bow out like that," I said. "If it were me, I'd talk to Annette."

We finished our dinner and went back to the hotel. On the ride to the hotel, little Judy fell asleep in the car. Since Susan said that Judy was a good, sound sleeper, we decided that we would all go back to April and Susan's room to hang out and chat while Judy slept.

April and Susan had a few bottles of wine and light snacks in their room. They put on some familiar music from our younger days, and we all hung out and chatted about life some more.

It was late by the time Rex and I got back to our own room and got to bed.

27. Friday Morning

FRIDAY MORNING APRIL dropped off Rex to visit his family and dropped me off at Matt's parents' house to see if I could help with any of the preparations for the reception. April and Susan and little Judy set off to do some picnicking and nature-walks in the canyons.

My dad and his new wife Sharon were staying with Matt's family, as were my grandparents on my dad's side and Annette herself. None of Matt's relatives were staying there since almost his entire clan lived in the area, so those visiting from out of town had plenty of choices of other relatives to put them up. Matt himself was already living in the apartment that he and Annette would be sharing after their marriage.

On our side, we had a few relatives from my dad's family come to Utah for the wedding. They were mostly staying with my aunt and uncle who lived in Lehi. Dad came from a family of seven kids, each of whom proceeded to produce a family on that order of magnitude, so of course no one expected the whole extended family to gather every time somebody got married, which seemed like it was practically every other year with so many people. But we could always count on a few to show up.

Aside from our Uncle Adam who never married, our immediate family with only three kids was the smallest family of any that my grandparents had produced. Mom claimed that it was for health reasons that she had never tried for a fourth, and when we were kids she occasionally would make reference to her doctor's advice on the matter when she was speaking in Sacrament Meeting or in Fast and Testimony Meeting so that the other families in the ward wouldn't think that she was selfishly breaking the commandment that every family should have as many kids as their health and finances would permit. It may have been true that her doctor had given her such advice, but I also got the impression that she and Dad hadn't really wanted any more kids than that.

In Matt's immediate family, none of his siblings could attend the wedding and only one could even attend the reception. Essentially everyone's availability matched up badly because of the fact that boys set off on missions at nineteen and girls at twenty-one. Matt himself was twenty-one years old and just recently back from his mission to somewhere in Africa. He had two older sisters, twins, who were twenty-three and on missions to Chile and Australia respectively. They would be back in about six months—not soon enough to attend the wedding. He also had a younger brother who was nineteen and had set off a month or so earlier on a mission to France. Matt and his brother Spencer had just barely had a few months to see each other in the space between their two missions. That left one last sibling, Matt's youngest brother Sam. Sam was sixteen and hence too young to attend the ceremony in the temple, but at least he would be there for the reception.

At Matt's parents' house, Matt's little brother Sam let me in, and I found my dad and my grandparents still at the table finishing their breakfast.

"Lynn, it's great to see you again!" Dad said, getting up to give me a hug. Grandma and Grandpa both greeted me and hugged me as well. "Annette's waiting for you," said Dad. "She's upstairs in the bedroom. She wants to show you her dress."

In the bedroom Annette was standing on a stool modeling her wedding dress. A lady I assumed was Matt's mom was busy pinning the hem, and Dad's wife Sharon was sitting on a chair nearby watching.

"Oh Lynn, I'm so glad you could make it!" Annette said as soon as she saw me.

"Thanks, I'm glad to be here," I said. "Hello, Sharon. And I presume that this must be Matt's mom, Sister Hobbs."

"You presume correctly," Matt's mom replied, still with pins in her mouth. She stood up and turned to me, taking the pins out of her mouth with her left hand and offering me her right. "And you must be the famous Lynn that we've heard so much about."

"I guess so," I said chuckling, "I hope that what you've heard about me is all good, or at least mostly."

"Of course!" she said smiling and returning to her work.

"Wow, Sister Hobbs," I said, "This dress is gorgeous! It's amazing! And so professional! Did you really make it yourself?" It was all the more astonishing given that Annette and Matt had only know each other for six months, and had only been engaged for three. Matt's mom was a pretty fast worker.

"Thanks, Lynn, yes I did," she replied. "I made my own wedding dress once upon a time, but I haven't done a project this ambitious in a while. I'm hoping to make some more soon though when my girls get back from their missions."

"It's really elegant," I said walking around Annette and taking in the dress from all sides. "It's quite an unusual style with the simple bodice, long sleeves, and high neck, with just a single line of pearl buttons down the front. I've never seen anything quite like it."

"And it's so modest," said Sharon. "We were just talking about how crazy it is that you can't buy a dress like this even if you want to. But this is the sort of dress that belongs in the temple."

"Yeah, every single dress in all of my brides' magazines was low-cut or had short sleeves," said Annette.

"And it's really too bad," said Matt's mom, "because when you go to the temple with a dress like that, they have to add fake white sleeves and a white dickie in the neckline, and it looks terrible! So many people say, 'Oh, it's okay, it's *just* for the temple.' How can they say 'just for the temple'? The temple is the most important part!"

"I'm with you, Felicia," said Sharon. "I wish I'd thought of that before my last wedding."

"Well, all I know is you look fantastic, Annette," I said. "You're going to be the most beautiful bride."

"Thanks, Lynn! I'm so excited!"

"Is there anything I can do to help?" I asked.

"Actually there is," said Sharon.

"Lynn, in one of my brides' magazines over there we found a really cute idea for the centerpieces at the reception. They did bouquets with little silver origami animals in them," said Annette.

"We've already picked out the silk flowers," said Matt's mom. "Your grandmother has them in a box downstairs."

"And we were thinking that you could help since you know how to make little origami birds and things," said Annette.

"Did you already buy the paper?" I asked.

"No, but Dad knows a store in the mall that sells some. He can take you there and help you pick some out," said Annette.

"Okay," I said, grabbing a magazine off the top of the pile. "Is it in this one?"

"Yeah that's the one," said Sharon. "Thanks for doing this."

"No problem," I said, taking the magazine downstairs.

In the kitchen, Dad and Grandma and Grandpa had finished clearing away the breakfast things and had already gotten out the silk flowers and were starting to arrange them on little stands.

"I understand I'm supposed to do some origami here," I said.

"You got it!" said Grandma. "Oh good, you've brought the magazine back. Bring it over here, honey." I handed her the magazine and she immediately turned to the page with the picture of the centerpieces we would be making. They looked pretty complicated, and appeared to require more origami work than I could normally expect to do in the space of a few hours, but I figured I'd try and do my best.

"Annette says you know of a store in the mall where we can get the papers, right?" I asked Dad.

"Right again!" said Dad. "Let's go."

We got into the car, and no sooner had we gotten out of the driveway when he started in on the personal questions.

"So are you and Rex getting pretty serious? Are you thinking about getting married?"

"I don't know, Dad," I said, "It's kind of early to be making a big decision like that."

"Early?" he asked. "You've known him for almost five years. Annette has only known Matt six months, and they're getting married tomorrow."

"If she wants to get married to someone she's known for only six months, then that's her problem and not mine," I said, hoping that that didn't sound too mean. "You know what the situation is with me and Rex. We've only been living together for a year. We hardly saw each other at all in college when he was at Stanford and I was attending the University of Wisconsin. Now that we're back together, yes, it looks like it might be getting a little serious and yes we're talking about marriage, but nothing has been decided yet."

"Lynn, I don't know about that boy," Dad said. "If you were really so in love with him, wouldn't you have wanted to get married right away, back when you first met him, like Annette and Matt?"

"Dad, you're thinking like a Mormon," I said.

"Well, that's what I am, Lynn, what do you expect of me?"

"In my mind, the fact that he and I wanted to get back together after having tried other relationships and other experiences shows that it's a deeper bond than just some youthful infatuation that we've tied ourselves to despite possibly having grown apart," I said.

Dad took that in for a second, and said "I don't know, Lynn, I still don't like him."

"Why?" I asked. "Are you still clinging to this fantasy that I'm going to come back to the church and meet a returned-missionary who will take me through the temple?"

"You know that that's what your mother and I—well, Sharon and I—would like for you. We want you and our whole family to be together in the Celestial Kingdom someday. So of course we're not happy to see you with this apostate, this atheist, who has somehow seduced you away from the church."

"Dad, *I'm* an apostate. *I'm* an atheist. How little do you know me after all these years? Rex didn't seduce me away from the church, I made my own decision."

"If you say so, honey."

"Dad, that's so insulting," I said. "I'm trying to be respectful of your beliefs, and I wish that you could be respectful of mine."

I imagined that Rex was getting a similar grilling from his own parents at their house.

Luckily our arrival at the mall put a stop to this conversation. Our little quest for origami papers gave us something trivial to talk about so that it wouldn't be just silence.

On the ride home, I decided to get a little revenge by grilling him back.

"So, Dad, have you made any progress on arranging a temple divorce, like Mom asked you to?"

"Lynn, you know I can't do that," he replied. "They don't grant a temple divorce without a compelling reason. All of your mom's temple blessings would be canceled, and you kids wouldn't be sealed to us anymore."

"But that's what Mom wants," I insisted, "She doesn't want to have anything to do with the church anymore." Shortly after April and I left the church, Mom "found Jesus"—the Jesus of her Christian childhood, not the Mormon Jesus—and consequently left both the church and Dad.

"That's what she thinks she wants now, but she'll see things differently when she gets to the spirit world."

I decided to come at it from a different angle. "But Sharon got a temple divorce from her first husband," I said, "so now her kids aren't sealed to her anymore."

"Sharon needed a cancellation so that she could get married in the temple to me. You know that a woman can be sealed to only one man. And as for her kids, we're talking about having them sealed to us since her ex-husband was excommunicated and all."

"So what you're saying is that you're a polygamist," I said.

"No, of course not. Polygamy is not permitted by the church. I am only married to one woman."

"In this life," I said. "But in the next life?"

"You said you don't believe in the next life."

"Oh, that's a convenient response now," I said with a bit of a biting tone. "But I'm not talking about me here, I'm talking about you. What do you believe? Will you be married to two women in the afterlife?"

He sighed. "Lynn, I don't know why you are playing this little game of making me spell it out for you. You know very well how it works. Yes, there is polygamy in the Celestial Kingdom. Yes, I am sealed to both Sharon and to your mother in the temple. So, yes, I will be married to both of them in the next life."

"Do you really think that that's what Mom wants?" I asked.

"She will want it when she gets to the other side and sees the truth."

"If you say so," I said, deciding that he was even less respectful of Mom's feelings than of mine...

Then after a bit of a pause, I said, "Really, Dad, take a step back. Don't you think this whole 'eternal family' thing is a little crazy?"

"I'm not crazy for wanting to spend eternity with my family that I love."

"Okay, I'm sorry, I'll stop pestering you about it," I said.

And with that we continued in silence for the rest of the ride.

When we got back to Matt's parents' house, the door was open so we let ourselves in and closed the door behind us.

Inside we discovered that my grandparents had put all of the wedding preparation materials to the side and had set up a large display on the table of bottles of herbal pills and tonics plus a series of books and recordings that they were showing to Sam. It looked like another multi-level marketing scheme.

Sam was looking at the different items, but he didn't appear very enthusiastic.

"I don't know," he said, "That's an awful lot of money, and I'm trying to save for my mission."

"But that's the beauty of it," said Grandpa. "It's an investment in going into business for yourself, and you can earn tons more money for your future."

Dad and I just stood there shocked, taking in this scene.

"I don't even know if I could afford the starter kit unless I throw in the money I had set aside for tithing."

"Oh, no, you can't do that," said Grandma.

"But you said I would earn it back, right?" asked Sam. "I could pay back my tithing money with interest."

"Son, it doesn't work that way," said Grandpa. "The Lord will never smile on any business venture that starts by stealing money from Him."

"Maybe we could start you off with the smaller starter pack," suggested Grandma.

"Mom, Dad," my dad broke in, "He's just a kid. I don't know if it's appropriate for you to get him involved in this sort of thing." Dad had earned his money in a normal job, and had bailed out his parents financially enough times to have long ago lost patience with their business ventures.

"Well, I say you're never too young to go into business for yourself if you're ambitious," said Grandpa, "but if that's the way you feel about it, we'll just put this stuff away."

As Grandma and Grandpa were gathering up their display, Grandma said to Sam, "Now honey, if you decide that you're interested, you just come and see us about it any time you want. And that goes for you, too, Joe," she called into the living room.

I looked into the living room and saw a teenage boy I hadn't noticed before, sitting on the couch reading a thick book. He looked up from his book for a second, but went right back to his reading without saying anything. I figured that that must be Matt's little cousin. Annette had once mentioned that Matt's cousin had come to live with Matt's parents because of some "family problems" that Annette didn't seem to want to go into too much detail about.

Once Grandma and Grandpa's new business was cleared off the table and put away, I started showing everyone how to fold the little silver slips of paper into birds. I figured that it would be better to keep it simple and have everyone fold the same animal.

With so many people, it went pretty quickly. Grandma and Grandpa had a hard time of it, but Dad and Sam did pretty well, and we even convinced Joe to put down his book and come over and help us. We were getting close to the end of our pile of papers when a knock came at the door.

Sam went and answered the door. From the kitchen I could just barely see that it was Rex and his little brother Jared. "Oh, hi Jared," said Sam, "what brings you here?"

Jared seemed surprised to see Sam as well. "Oh, hi Sam," he said, "I didn't know you lived here. We're just here to pick up Lynn." He looked in and said hi to Joe.

"Rex, is that you?" I called from the other room.

"Yeah, it's me," he said, coming in. "And I've brought my little brother with me who seems to already know the household."

"These guys go to my school," said Jared. "Hi Lynn, nice to see you again."

"Hi Jared," I said. "What's up? You're hanging out with Rex today?"

"Oh, he comes with the car," said Rex. "Mom and Dad wouldn't let me borrow it unless I agreed to take this guy too."

"It's my car," said Jared. "Mom and Dad bought it for me to drive."

"And he can't possibly be bothered to bum rides off his older sisters in their car for three days," said Rex. "So I figured that since our hotel has a pool, I'd bring him along and we could all go for a swim. Maybe we could bring your friends along, too," he said to Jared. "I think there's room to fit everyone in the car if we squeeze."

"Great!" said Jared.

"Cool, yeah," said Sam and Joe, running off to get their swimsuits.

"Actually, could you go ahead without me?" I asked. "We're almost done folding these origami birds for my sister's centerpieces, and I wanted to help Grandma arrange them in the bouquets. I have a room key, and Dad can drop me off at the hotel in an hour or so."

"Okay," said Rex, and he and the three boys got in the car and left.

WHEN WE WERE DONE making the centerpieces, Dad dropped me off at the hotel, and I went to my room to grab my swimsuit and towel.

When I opened the door I was surprised to see Rex there with Jared, Sam, and Joe.

"You guys didn't go to the pool?" I asked.

"Oh, we're going," replied Rex.

Then I noticed that the four of them were all drinking beer. "Um, Rex," I said, "Where did these kids get beer from?"

"Oh, I bought it for them," he replied.

"He scored us some porn, too!" said Jared, patting his backpack and smiling.

At that I broke down laughing.

"What?" asked Rex. I continued laughing as I came in the room and sat on the bed. "What? What's so funny?" he asked.

"You're funny," I said. "Rex, I want to be annoyed with you for this, but I can't, it's just too funny."

"I don't see that it's so funny," said Rex, and he got this kind of perplexed smile on his face as if he wasn't sure how he'd managed to do something charmingly amusing by accident. The boys just looked at each other as they continued drinking their beer.

"Well, maybe it's just my perception of it," I said, going over to the bathroom where more beers were sitting in ice in the sink. "Do you mind?" I asked.

"Help yourself," Rex replied.

I grabbed a beer and opened it and came back to sit on the bed again.

"It's just that it looks to me like you're reliving your own youth," I said. "Now that you're twenty-three years old, you come back armed with your adult ID card to cast yourself in the role of hero for your sixteen-year-old brother."

"Yep, that's me," he said, smiling. "The cool older brother I always wished I'd had. Okay, so maybe it's a little silly, but I'm still young enough to remember what I wanted when I was his age."

"Yeah, but did you have to bring Sam and Joe into this?" I asked. "You're going to get us all in trouble."

"Oh, we won't tell," said Sam.

"Good boy," said Rex. "See? There's no problem."

"It's no big deal," said Sam, "I've broken the Word of Wisdom before."

"Oh, you're not breaking the Word of Wisdom" said Rex with a smile. "Has anyone got a copy of the *Doctrine & Covenants*?"

"Ha ha," said Jared, "Rex's famous proof that beer isn't against the Word of Wisdom! I'll bet you've heard this one a few times, eh Lynn?"

"I don't think any of us has a copy of the *D & C* here," I said laughing. It was true that I'd heard this little demonstration a number of times already, and I figured that I'd probably be hearing it a few more times in my life. I couldn't decide which was more ridiculous, the fact that he was so fond of showing this proof to people or the idea that one of us might just happen to have a copy of the *Doctrine & Covenants* handy.

"There's a *Book of Mormon* in this drawer," said Sam, opening the drawer and looking around, "but no *D & C*." It seemed that in Utah, hotel rooms are often equipped with copies of the *Book of Mormon* just as hotels rooms in the rest of the country typically have Gideon Bibles.

"That's too bad," said Rex.

"Is beer really not against the Word of Wisdom?" asked Sam. "I'd like to see that."

"Oh, yeah, it's cool," said Jared. "I'll show you later sometime."

I then noticed that Joe wasn't really drinking his beer, but rather was just looking at it. He seemed a little uncomfortable. He reminded me of myself in a similar situation a few years earlier.

"Joe," I said, "if you don't want to drink beer, you shouldn't let these guys pressure you into it. No one here will think any less of you."

"It's not that, it's just that..." Joe kind of trailed off. "I don't think that beer is necessarily wrong, it's just that I can't risk getting caught smelling of it. I don't want to mess things up with my aunt and uncle. They told me that I have to behave like a good Mormon kid if I want to stay with them. If they throw me out, I don't know anyone else who will take me in."

"Joe ran away from some crazy polygamists!" exclaimed Sam.

"Really?" I asked, kind of astonished.

"Yeah," said Sam, "It's really scary some of the stuff he told me about them."

"Wow, what was it like?" asked Jared.

All eyes turned to Joe. I felt bad seeing Joe get put on the spot like that, but it was so strange. I'd heard that there existed these modern-day polygamist sects — so-called "fundamentalist" Mormons — but I'd never met anyone that had had any first-hand experience with one of those groups.

"Well, you guys might not believe this, but living in a polygamist family seems normal once you've done it for a few years."

"Normal!" said Sam. "Can you believe? His dad had two other wives in addition to his mom and who knows how many kids running around, and they were all living together in one house, no bigger than my house!"

"Wow, and you were okay with that?" asked Jared.

"What could I do? I was taught in school that that was the way the Lord wanted us to live. In fact, we were taught almost nothing else in school. That was what finally pushed me over the edge. We didn't learn anything of interest. There was another kid in my community whose parents let him attend a public high school. But my parents wouldn't let me go because they didn't want me learning the evil ways of the world. I so wanted to study the things that other kid was studying, so one day I just ran away."

"It's true, he's amazing in school!" Sam piped up. "When he started in the fall, he was way behind in every class! But he's a studying maniac and he's smart. He worked twice as hard as anyone else, and by the end of the year he was helping *me* with *my* homework."

"That was very brave of you to run away like that," I said.

"Well it was a little easier for me than it might have been for someone else because I remembered what it was like to live in the outside world. You see, my parents were converts to Mormon fundamentalism. When I was a kid our family was mainstream Mormon, like you guys are."

"Were," corrected Rex, smiling.

"So when they taught us how horrible life was outside our closed community, on some level I never believed it completely. I knew I had some relatives on the outside. One day I went through my dad's papers and found my uncle and aunt's address. Then over the next few weeks I gathered provisions and waited for the right moment. It wasn't easy because there weren't many places I could hide things that the little kids in the family wouldn't get into them, but I did it. Then one day my moment came, and I left and didn't look back."

Rex, Jared, and I were so amazed by this that we didn't really know what to say.

"Wow, that's impressive," I said. The funny thing was that I remembered thinking when I was a teenager how very hard I'd had it, having to put up with oppressive LDS parents. It was an eye-opener to meet someone who was grateful to have a situation like mine because he had known something so much worse. I was almost tempted to offer to take him in myself, but of course that would be impossible, living with Rex in a tiny one-bedroom apartment on our meager teaching-assistantships.

Just then the phone rang.

"Hello," said Rex, answering it. "Oh, hi Mom... Okay, just a minute, I'll ask." He put his hand over the receiver and turned to me. "Lynn, my mom wants to know if we can come over for dinner tonight or if we have some wedding-related plans with your family."

"Nothing we can't break," I said. "We have plenty of stuff planned with my family for the rest of the weekend. We can go to your house tonight."

"Okay," he said putting the receiver back to his ear. "Okay, Mom, sounds good. Oh, by the way, we ran into a couple of friends of Jared's from school. They're here with us. Should I bring them along?" He paused, "Umm-hmm," he said and then put the receiver aside again and turned to Sam and Joe. "My mom's making her famous humongous pot of chili with corn bread. You guys want to come too?"

They both said okay, so Rex spoke into the phone again. "It's a go... Okay, sounds good... Right, we'll be there at six... Okay, see you, bye." I then called Matt's mom and told her where we'd all be that evening.

Dinner at six didn't give us all that much time for swimming, but at least we got a chance to get in the water and splash around a little bit. Joe was a quiet kid, but he seemed perfectly normal playing around and rough-housing in the water with the other boys. Despite all he'd been through, he seemed resilient enough to turn out okay.

When we got to Rex's parents' house, the three boys immediately rushed upstairs to put their backpacks in Jared's room. Rex's mother met us in the entryway and took my jacket. "Hello, Lynn," she said, "It's nice to see you again." Then she yelled up the staircase, "You boys come back down here. What is the meaning of rushing off like that without even saying hello? So anxious to get to your video games that you can't even be polite to an old lady?"

The boys came back downstairs. "Sorry Mom," said Jared. "These are some guys I know from school, Sam and Joe."

"We ran into them because Sam is my sister's fiance's little brother, and Joe is his cousin," I said.

"Small world," said Rex's mom. "Does that mean you knew Lynn's sister's fiance from school, Rex?"

"Um, I didn't know him that well since he wasn't in my grade, but I knew his two sisters. They were in the same grade as me, and they were in that play with me and Jill."

"That's nice," she said. "Well, supper's almost ready, you can go in the other room and set the table."

After this exchange, Jared noticed that he hadn't bothered to take off his jacket yet, so he took it of and laid it down on the table in the formal dining room.

We went into the kitchen and saw the humongous pot of chili bubbling on the stove and the corn bread in the oven. It smelled pretty good.

Rex got a stack of plates and bowls out of the cupboard and handed them to me. I started putting them around the long kitchen table. The table had benches along the sides instead of individual chairs in order to make it easier to fit as many people as possible. Even so, it would be quite a squeeze with nine people at the table.

When the table was set, Rex's mom told Jared to go call his father and sisters for dinner. Jared did as he was told.

Rex's dad came down and took his place at the head of the table, and Rex's two sisters took two seats at the far end of the table, one at the foot of the table and the other at the end of the bench against the wall. The three boys squeezed themselves onto the same bench with her, and Rex sat in the middle of the bench on the opposite side with me next to him. His mother came and put the food on the table and then took the last place on Rex's other side.

Of course we knew better than to touch the food before the prayer. As soon as everyone was seated and quiet, Rex's dad solemnly said, "Rex, would you like to say the blessing on the food?"

Rex looked at his dad as if he thought his dad was completely crazy and said "Dad, I've told you a million times I don't believe in God. Why do you keep insisting on calling on me for the prayer?"

Rex's dad seemed unfazed by this response. He turned to me and asked, "Lynn, would you like to say the blessing?"

"Dad!" Rex said, this time really annoyed. "Will you leave her alone? She gets enough of this kind of nonsense from her own family. She doesn't need to deal with more of it here."

At that Rex's dad looked as though he wasn't happy to have his authority as patriarch challenged. He turned to Jared and sternly said "Jared, would you like to set a good example for your older brother and say the blessing on the food?"

Jared got the hint that he'd better not disobey at this point, so he said okay and we all bowed our heads and folded our arms.

"Our Heavenly Father," Jared began. "We thank Thee that Rex and Lynn could have a safe journey to come here to visit us. We thank Thee for this food and ask Thee to please bless it to nourish and strengthen our bodies. We say these things in the name of Jesus Christ, amen."

Everyone repeated "amen," some a little grumblingly, and then Rex's mom started taking people's bowls one by one and ladling chili into them as Rex's sister Joy cut the cornbread and started distributing it, passing along the honey-butter with each slice.

I ate a spoonful of chili and then turned to Rex's mom. "Mmm, this is very good," I said. I was kind of wondering what I should call her. Sister Wendell? Mrs. Wendell? Cheryl? Surely not "mom." Both Joe and Sam nodded in agreement.

"Thank you Lynn," she said. "This is just a little something I like to throw together when I know I'm going to have a lot of people over."

Then Rex's dad turned to Jared. "Jared," he said, "How's your Eagle Scout project going?"

"Um, okay," he said, glancing over at the two other boys as if kind of embarrassed that he might be bothering to make an effort in something as dorky as scouting.

"Oh, it's coming along just great!" said Rex's mom. "It's so thrilling that we'll finally have an Eagle Scout in this family." Rex continued eating without showing any visible reaction to his mom's statement.

"Are you boys in scouting?" she asked Sam and Joe. It was a bit of a ridiculous question since participation in Boy Scouts is mandatory for LDS boys. Unsurprisingly they both said yes.

"Sam, have you earned your Eagle rank yet?" she asked.

"Oh, yeah, I got it when I was fourteen," said Sam. "Both my brothers did too. My mom pushed us really hard." Then looking around at everyone's faces it seemed to dawn on him that that was exactly the wrong thing to say.

She turned to Joe. "And what about you, Joe?"

"I've been participating," he said, "but I think I probably won't make it to Eagle." I suspected that this was because he had only just started the program when he moved in with his aunt and uncle, but Joe was too wise, discrete, or perhaps just too shy to mention that.

Rex's mom said "Ah, that's too bad," and gave him this sympathetic half-smile that seemed to indicate that Joe's response at least partially compensated for Sam's.

Jill turned to Rex and asked "What's your apartment like?"

"It's a small, one-bedroom apartment in a five-story brick apartment building," he replied.

"Rex!" his mother said. "Do you have to remind the other kids about the bedroom? You know I'm not happy with the bad example you're setting for your younger sisters and brother, living in sin like that."

"Well, I'm sorry I mentioned it, then," he said, "but I don't think anyone here is in the dark about what the situation is. Lynn and I are paying for our own apartment, and no, we're not just apartment mates chastely living in separate bedrooms."

Then she turned to me, "Lynn, aren't your parents ashamed of you for living in sin?"

"Stop it right there, Mom," said Rex. "You can say what you want to me, but you are not to address Lynn in this manner."

Then Rex's dad piped up. "Rex," he said, "I don't think you understand how disappointed your mother and I are in the example you're setting for your younger siblings."

"Ah, so you're saying it would be terrible if they followed in my footsteps and graduated from college with honors and then got accepted into a Ph.D. program in Mathematics in one of the top ranked math departments in the country?" asked Rex.

"You know that's not what I'm talking about," said Rex's dad. "Just the other day Jared was telling us that now he doesn't want to serve a mission."

"Dad," said Jared, "That has nothing to do with Rex." Joe and Sam looked silently at their plates as if they wished they weren't there, but it appeared that the conversation had passed the point of no return.

"What do you mean it has nothing to do with Rex?" his father asked him. "Your exact words were 'Rex didn't go on a mission.'"

Jared looked down as if he were ashamed to have gotten his beloved older brother into trouble.

"I can't believe it," Rex's mom said. "Five kids raised in the church and no missionaries."

"Maybe Jill or Joy will serve a mission," I offered. They both glared at me as if they weren't at all happy to have been brought into this.

"I'm sure these two will have no trouble finding husbands right away like my Kathy did," she said huffily, as if I had insulted her by suggesting that her daughters would remain spinsters long enough to end up going on missions. Then as she got up to slice the next pan of corn-bread that was cooling on the top of the stove, she said to Rex "And now because of your bad example, this past year Jared's started skipping seminary!"

"Mom, how can that be because of my bad example?" asked Rex. "I *graduated* from seminary. With flying colors, as I recall."

But his mom ignored his response. She was on a roll. "He doesn't listen anymore. He's disobedient!" From her vantage point in the kitchen she spied Jared's jacket on the table in the next room. "He doesn't put his things away!" she said, walking towards it.

Jared suddenly got an alarmed look on his face and made as if to get up just as his mother was snatching the jacket off the table.

Then something hit the ground with a loud thud and rolled. Rex's mother gasped. Rex closed his eyes for a second as if bracing himself for the shit that was about to hit the fan.

"What is this?!" she cried. "What is the meaning of bringing this into our home?! Where did this come from?" She dropped the jacket and picked up the beer off the floor and took it straight to the sink where she opened it and emptied it. "Jared, answer me right this minute!" she yelled. "Where did you get this?"

Jared looked as if he didn't know what to do. He looked at his mother and then at Rex.

"Where do you think he got it?" Rex asked calmly, without looking up.

With that, Rex's mother became furious. "Rex!" she exclaimed, "I am at my wits' end with you! I don't know what to do with you anymore! This is not the way you were raised. I tried so hard to be a good mother. I don't understand where I went wrong with you." She looked like she was about to cry.

"Mom, is it such a big deal?" asked Rex.

"It *is* a big deal, Rex," she said. "Don't you understand? These things are important. The Word of Wisdom isn't just some rubbish."

Then Rex said something he shouldn't have said. "Beer isn't against the Word of Wisdom."

That drove her into a rage. "You think you're so smart! You think you're so smart! Well one of these days you're going to think yourself right into outer darkness! You say that beer isn't against the Word of Wisdom, but the prophet says that it is! And I'm going to listen to the prophet before I listen to you!"

"Rex, you shouldn't upset your mother like that," said Rex's dad. "You keep telling us you want us to treat you like an adult. Well for that you need to act like one. Giving alcohol to underage kids isn't a very grown-up thing to do."

Rex stepped away from the bench and stood up to his full stature. He was tall, with broad shoulders. He had rage in his eyes he looked at his father, but it was clear that he didn't know what to say in response.

Rex's father continued. "Do you realize that what you've done is against the law?"

At that Rex cocked a smile. "Well it's lucky for me then that Mom destroyed the evidence."

Then Rex's dad lost his cool for the first time. "Do you think this is funny?" he asked angrily. "Do you think this is some sort of joke? You come strutting in here like you own the place, and then you proceed to do whatever you want without any regard for the rules and the values of this household. If this is how you're going to behave, I don't know why you bothered to come back here at all."

Rex turned to me. "Come on Lynn," he said. "Boys, get your things."

"Oh, no you don't," said Rex's mother. "I'm taking these boys home myself. You've done enough damage already." Sam and Joe looked like they really regretted ever having gotten into the car with Rex and Jared in the first place.

Rex turned to leave, and I followed.

His mother called after him "And I'm going to tell their parents what you did, so that they'll know to keep their boys away from you!"

Rex stopped and faced her. "Please don't do that, Mom. If you tell Sam's parents, you'll just get me into trouble with Lynn's family."

"You should have thought of *that* before making trouble, young man," she replied.

"But you'll get the boys into trouble too, and it wasn't their fault," he said.

"Oh, don't worry," said Rex's mom. "I'll make sure their parents understand that this is one-hundred percent *your fault*!"

I grabbed my jacket, and we walked out the door.

"I can't believe them!" Rex said fiercely, making a fist.

"Rex, if you're angry, let me drive," I said.

Reaching the car he took a breath. "No, no, I'm okay," he said, and he opened the car door and we both got in.

It was kind of funny that we were taking their car, considering. But it was clear that they wanted us to leave, and we couldn't very well do that without the car since our hotel was on the other side of town.

Rex pulled the car out of the driveway and started down the road. He still seemed pretty upset about what had happened.

"It's not that bad," I said. "This same exact thing happens to me all the time. Well, maybe not *exactly*, but essentially. Look on the bright side—you have only one set of wacky parents to deal with, I have two. We'll get to relive these same adventures with my other set tomorrow."

Rex said nothing. He continued staring at the road.

"It's hard for parents and their grown-up kids to hammer out a workable adult relationship," I said. "It takes time."

Rex still gave no response.

"You'll laugh about this tomorrow, trust me," I said. "Here, I've got something that will lighten the mood."

Back at our apartment we used to like to listen to *Saturday's Warrior* for the humorous irony of it. We had brought the cassette with us to Utah, thinking that if we needed to appreciate the humor of Mormonism anywhere it would be here.

I put the tape in and selected the song.

"*When he was just a little boy, things were different then...*" sang the father from the play. Rex smiled a bit.

"See Rex? It's not just you. This happens in every Mormon family. The song proves it," I said jokingly. He laughed a bit, but didn't seem entirely convinced. We listened a bit longer.

"*... The years have passed like Summer dew upon the grass,*" sang the Mormon parents.

"*The little boy that held our hand grew up so fast.
There was a time he loved us the way we love him now,
but growing up has changed it all somehow...*

"Didn't we love him?
Didn't we raise him good?
Didn't we do our best in spite of all the pain?
We would do it all again and more the same."

Then the play mom sighed "I guess we've failed."

Rex reached over and turned off the music. "Can we listen to something else?" he asked.

"I'm sorry, sweetheart," I said.

The question of putting something else on was moot, however, because just then we arrived at the hotel.

When we got to the room, we both went in and took off our shoes. Rex sat down on the edge of the bed and looked at the window.

"It was just a little bit of beer," he said.

"I know," I replied.

"It's not going to hurt them. They're sixteen years old, they're not babies."

"I know."

Rex looked up. "So you agree with me that I'm right and my parents are wrong?"

"Not entirely," I said. "It's a question of perspective."

He looked away again.

"Oh Rex," I said sitting beside him and gently stroking his back. "It'll be okay. Everything will be okay."

"I just don't understand how they can be that way," he said.

I rubbed his back some more and ran my hand down his arm. He was a beautiful creature, so strong and manly, yet reduced to a child by his parents' disapproval.

I put my arms around him and held him.

O N THE MORNING of the wedding, we determined to sleep in a little bit. We were planning to meet April and Susan at the Hobbs' house, and we wanted to wait until we were sure that Brother and Sister Hobbs were gone to avoid crossing them and dealing with whatever wrath was the consequence of Rex's mother's visit the night before.

I had put on a church-style dress for the day, which wasn't my favorite thing to do, but I was willing to make a sacrifice for a special occasion.

At Matt's parents' house, we found the people who were not allowed to attend the wedding in the temple: April and Susan and Judy, my mom and her new husband Richard, and everyone who was too young to go to the temple, including Sam and Joe, plus a bunch of my little cousins.

The house was really crowded. April and Susan were watching the little kids in the living room, and the big kids were there as well. Sam and Joe were sitting on the floor reading comic books. My fifteen-year-old cousin Jennifer and her younger sister Emily were sitting off in a corner eyeing Sam and Joe and giggling.

When Mom and Richard saw me, they both hugged me, and they shook hands with Rex.

"It's great to see you again, Lynn," said Richard. "You too, Rex."

We sat at the table in the kitchen where there were still some breakfast muffins and biscuits waiting.

"I'm glad you and April are here," said Mom. "This is a hard day for me. I'm happy for my little Annette that she's found the love of her life, but it's hard for me to imagine that today, for the first time, she's going through that horrible endowment ceremony."

I wasn't a big fan of anti-Mormon literature, but I'd read enough to have a general idea of what the temple ceremony consisted of, with its ceremonial washing, strange costumes and rituals, secret names, secret oaths, and secret handshakes.

"Yeah, it's hard to imagine doing that without being royally creeped out by it," said Rex. "That's probably why they're not allowed to talk about it. They'd all be asking each other 'What the....?' 'What's with those crazy green aprons?' 'Did that make no sense to you either?'"

Rex had all of this second-hand as well, so of course neither one of us knew for certain if our imagined impressions of what it was like were correct.

Since some of the older kids were watching the younger kids, April and Susan came in and joined us in the kitchen.

Noticing that no Mormons were present, Mom said conspiratorially, "It's so crazy that they take the *Book of Mormon* seriously, when every bit of it has been discredited. To imagine they claim that there was a metalworking society in the New World before the arrival of the European explorers!"

"Yeah obviously that sort of thing would leave evidence," said Rex. "The mines, the smelting, the steel swords and other artifacts themselves don't just biodegrade, yet how many have archaeologists found? Zero."

"And the horses," added Mom. "Scientists have shown that horses were extinct on this continent long before the supposed *Book of Mormon* times." We nodded in agreement. "And many of the real New World writings have been deciphered, and none of the New World peoples correspond at all to any *Book of Mormon* peoples in terms of the time periods or locations they lived in or the histories they wrote of themselves." We all smiled and agreed.

"Unlike the *Bible*," said Richard, "which has been largely corroborated by archaeological evidence.

This statement caused some general confusion. "But..." said Susan, "The fact that the *Bible* is thousands of years old isn't in dispute, so of course some of the historical points are accurate..."

"Yes, but the *Book of Mormon* is clearly based on nineteenth-century ideas, while the *Bible* is not," said Mom. "For example, take the fact that in the *Book of Genesis* the writer knew well before his time that in the beginning there was nothing. Scientists today have discovered that he was right when they proved the Big Bang. In the nineteenth century, it had been recently discovered that matter can neither be created nor destroyed. So Joseph Smith *conveniently* had a revelation saying that—in contradiction with the *Book of Genesis*—all matter was merely *organized*, not *created*. Then later with the Big Bang, the *Book of Genesis* was vindicated."

"Yeah, that example is a pretty funny illustration of how Joseph Smith took the ideas of the time and claimed them as 'revelations'," said April. "Like the 'Word of Wisdom' and the 'three degrees of glory,' which matched things that other people had already published around the same time period."

"Clearly the person who wrote the *Book of Genesis* had supernatural insight to have known that the world was created from nothing," said Richard. "The Judeo-Christian tradition is the only one that starts with this idea."

"One might imagine that that required special insight," I said, "if it weren't for the fact that practically everything else in the *Book of Genesis* is completely wrong."

"What do you mean?" Mom asked. "Everyone knows that the *Book of Genesis* is essentially confirmed by Science."

"Earth to Mom," I said. "The *Book of Genesis* claims that the Earth was created with green plants growing on it *before* the creation of the Sun! That's absurd! How can you possibly say that that is confirmed by Science?"

"To an observer on the newly-created Earth, with all of the strange clouds it might have appeared that there was no sun until the green plants altered the atmosphere," said Richard.

"Well if this is supposed to be given from the point of view of an observer on the Earth, then how in God's name did he witness the Big Bang?" I asked. "Besides that, that's not the only error. It claims that *all* birds and fishes were created, and then after that the land animals were created. If you believe that one can learn anything at all from the fossil record, you will certainly agree that birds did not appear before land animals. Nor did grasses appear before animals. Grasses are specifically mentioned as appearing *before* all animals—and before the Sun, by the way—when in fact grasses are a modern category of plants on an evolutionary timescale. They didn't arise until after the appearance of mammals."

"Well all of that you've just said is based on the 'Theory of Evolution,' which has been largely discredited," said Richard.

"What?!" I asked. "Never mind. Please, let's just talk about something else."

"It'll be nice to have the opportunity to see some of your aunts and uncles on your dad's side again," said Mom. "Of course I've had no opportunity to communicate with them since the divorce. But I was friends with some of them, so it will be nice for them to see that I'm not the monster that your dad has undoubtedly made me out to be."

"Don't worry," said April. "Of course they're biased to believe their own brother, but most of them are fair enough to see that there are two sides to any conflict."

"I'm sure that they imagine that it was weakness or Satan that made me leave the church, though, so it will be nice to have the opportunity to demonstrate that it was in fact logical reasoning and the love of Christ that brought about my change," said Mom. "I love to take the opportunity to witness of Christ to LDS people. For example, recently I entered into a correspondence with some friends from our old ward. I pointed out to them a list of the ways in which Mormon theology contradicts the *Bible*. They gave a couple of half-hearted responses, but after that, they couldn't answer my arguments."

"Did you actually convince them?" I asked. "I'll believe that you won the argument if they ended up changing their minds, but if you merely wore them down, it's less sure."

"I made it quite clear that Mormonism is in direct contradiction with Biblical teachings," said Mom.

"I don't know about that," I said. "The thing is that for Mormons, the *Book of Mormon* and the *Doctrine & Covenants* are on par with or perhaps even more important than the *Bible*. The teachings of the latter-day prophets are on par with the *Bible* for them as well. So if you show them that their beliefs seem to contradict the *Bible*, they will probably just conclude that they have more information than you do, and dismiss everything you say. It's kind of like how you believe in the *Old Testament*, but you don't feel compelled convert to Judaism and live the Mosaic law because you believe that you have received further enlightenment in the form of the *New Testament*.

"Oh, no, that's where you're totally wrong," said Mom. "The entirety of Christianity is prefigured in the *Old Testament*. Even if the *New Testament* had never been written, the *Old Testament* alone is sufficient to bring people to Christ. That's why Christianity is growing so quickly among the Jews. In our congregation we have a member who is an Orthodox Jew and a practicing Christian because he understands that Christianity is the culmination of Judaism."

I didn't really have enough knowledge of Judaism to effectively counter Mom's argument. Still, I couldn't help but think of all of the Jewish mathematicians in the department where I was studying, with their various degrees of practicing. I also thought of the Orthodox Jewish neighborhood surrounding our apartment building. Every

Saturday I saw them dressed up and walking to their services with their families. Admittedly with my religious background I had a hard time having warm feelings towards the strict, gender-specific dress code of the orthodox. Yet the fact that Mom managed to bring up the miraculous growth of "Jews for Jesus" every time the subject of Judaism came up in any context struck me as somehow insulting and disrespectful to my neighbors.

I was wanting to come up for air from this theological quagmire, when poor Sam made the mistake of coming into the kitchen to grab a muffin.

"Sam, do you believe in Jesus?" asked Richard.

"Yes, sir, of course I do," replied Sam.

"Do you think that Sacrament Meeting is boring?" Richard asked.

"Oh boy, is it ever!" said Sam enthusiastically, laughing.

"And Priests' Quorum? And Sunday School? Are they dull and uninteresting?"

"Ha ha, that's for sure, Mr. Winterbottom," Sam said.

"Sam, do you think that that's the way the Lord intended for you to worship Him?" Richard asked.

Sam thought about the question for a second. "I dunno," he replied. "I guess so."

"Sam, the Mormon church places way too much emphasis on this fixed liturgy, as if it were necessary for a church meeting today to be exactly the same as a church meeting two hundred years ago. But the particulars of the liturgy aren't what's important for bringing you closer to Christ. Modern Christian services use the latest ideas and technology to create a church experience that's really inspiring, and means something to you," said Richard.

Sam just looked at him blankly as if he were speaking Chinese.

"What I'm saying, Sam, is that if you come to a *Christian* church, you can get a service with an interesting sermon and modern, inspiring music that you will enjoy."

"Um, I don't know if that's really what church is all about," said Sam. "I mean, we go to the LDS church because it's the true church and Heavenly Father wants us to."

"Well you shouldn't knock it till you've tried it," said Richard. "My pastor gave me some information about a Christian church in your area that has a great outreach ministry to LDS youth." He handed Sam some sort of flyer.

Sam took it, but with a worried expression. He looked imploringly over at Joe, who was still in the living room. Joe got up and came into the kitchen and took the paper out of Sam's hand. He quickly skimmed it and then looked up at Richard. "Thanks for thinking of us, Mr. Winterbottom," Joe said, "But we're really not interested." He handed the flyer back to Richard. Sam looked terribly relieved.

Then Mom started in. "What about you, Susan?" she asked. "We've done some research for you too, and we've found a Christian church in your area that has a gay pastor. They have a great program for kids, too."

Susan and April both got this look on their faces as if they were completely shocked by her comments but had no idea how to respond.

"Mom," said April. "We're glad that you're concerned about us, but really, we'd like to make our own decisions about religion and about the way we intend to raise our children."

Completely undaunted, Mom said, "Richard and I just started taking this wonderful course at our church about witnessing to people of different faiths. They've given us instruction on how to witness to people of all sorts of religions: Buddhist, Muslim, Hindu, Pagan, Atheist, Jewish, and even LDS, to convince people to embrace Jesus."

Looking around the room, I could see that not one single person was happy to hear that except the happy Christian couple themselves.

As April began trying to reason with Mom and Richard, I turned to Rex and quietly said "This reminds me of yesterday when my grandparents were trying to get Sam and Joe involved in some multi-level-marketing scheme."

"Your grandparents crack me up," replied Rex softly.

"Well, I think it's funny that everyone in this family keeps trying to help Sam and Joe: Grandma and Grandpa by going into business with them, Mom and Richard by saving their souls for Jesus, and you by providing them with alcohol and adult materials," I said.

Rex laughed and said quietly "Well I personally think it's obvious which favor is actually useful and which two are not."

Then Mom got my attention. "Lynn," she said, "did you get that book I sent you about how evolution can't explain everything, and there are some things that can be better explained by the existence of God?"

"Um, yeah," I said.

"Well, did you read it?" she asked.

"I read the back and skimmed it," I said.

"How can you judge its contents if you don't really read it?" asked Mom.

"Well, I know that there are things that are not one hundred percent understood," I said, "that's the nature of Science."

"Spoken like a true Christian, just like not knowing all of the mysteries of God!" Mom said, smiling triumphantly.

Yeah, whatever, I thought to myself.

"Weren't you just saying a minute ago that it was proven that horses were extinct from the new world well before *Book of Mormon* times, and that the Big Bang has been 'scientifically proven'?" asked Rex. "How can you believe all of that and be so hostile towards the theory of evolution?"

"Well you know," said Mom, "the Big Bang has been scientifically proven, whereas evolution is just a theory."

"What are you talking about?" asked Rex. "The Big Bang is well supported, but evolution of species via natural selection is an observed phenomenon that can be quantifiably predicted like a well-known chemical reaction."

"Yeah," said Richard, "but scientists agree that the Big Bang has been proven, whereas the '*Theory of Evolution*' is *just a theory.*"

Now it was Rex's turn to get that perplexed look on his face, as if they were speaking Chinese.

At that point we determined that it was perhaps time to extract ourselves from the conversation. Sam and Joe had already wandered off and were preparing some sort of bundle of items. We went over to see what they were up to.

"Hey, Rex," said Sam, "Can you take us to the temple so we can decorate Matt's car?"

"Yeah, we've got cans and streamers and Oreo cookies and stuff," said Joe, holding up their sack.

"I'd like to," said Rex, "but if you guys are caught with me again, you're going to get into more trouble than you're already in."

"Oh, we're not in trouble," said Joe, "and neither are you."

"Yeah, we saved your hide," said Sam. "You should thank us!"

"Well thank you then," said Rex. "What exactly did you do?"

"We convinced your mom not to tell my mom what you did!" said Sam.

"How'd you do that?" asked Rex.

"We used psychology on her!" said Sam.

"Yeah, I noticed that she seemed intimidated by how many Eagle Scouts Sam's mom had," said Joe. "So when we were upstairs getting our backpacks, I suggested to the other guys that on the way home we should tell her how many missionaries they have in the family, too."

"We laid it on real thick!" said Sam. "We told her about how my mom made that wedding dress and how she's always making homemade bread and jam and things!"

Rex and I started laughing.

"It was all true, though!" said Sam.

"Well, except..." said Joe.

"Oh except the part where Joe said that that was why he was living with us." Sam burst into laughter. "It was hilarious! He said that he was a wayward kid, so his mom sent him to stay with my mom because she's such a whiz at straightening out wayward boys!" Sam could hardly contain his laughter enough to tell the story. "Jared came with us in the car, and we had to pinch each other to keep from laughing!"

"Yeah, and after that, your mom didn't seem to want to tell Sam's mom about how her oldest boy was so bad!" said Joe.

"She didn't want to talk to her at all!" said Sam, laughing some more. "She didn't even come to the door, she dropped us off on the curb!"

Rex was laughing too. "You guys are the greatest!" he said. "That was brilliant!"

"Thanks! You know we had a lot of fun with you and Jared yesterday," said Sam. "I hope Jared can come to the big family picnic tomorrow with my family and Lynn's family."

"Well, I'd like to help you there," said Rex, "but I'm sure my mom won't let him go anywhere with me anymore."

"Maybe Lynn could bring him," suggested Joe.

"I don't think Rex's mom is much more happy with me than she is with Rex," I said.

"I'll send my brother Matt around to get him, then," said Sam. "Woooo! Watch out, Sister Wendell! He's a returned-missionary! I'll bet you've never seen one of those at your house!" Both Joe and Sam laughed hysterically at that, and Rex and I thought it was pretty funny as well.

"So, anyway, can you take us to the temple to decorate the car?" asked Joe.

"Okay," said Rex, "I guess if you've already taken care of all of the potential glitches, let's go!"

Rex and Joe and Sam got in the car. Jennifer and Emily seemed a little sad to see them go. Watching them, I was really glad not to be fifteen years old anymore.

A little later people began arriving at Matt's parents' house from the temple to pick up their respective kids. Annette herself even swung by the house on her way to the reception. She looked fantastic in her long, white wedding dress. She had an air of serenity and contentment and didn't seem at all creeped-out or shaken, so I thought that perhaps my imagined ideas about the temple ceremony were wrong.

"Why didn't you and April and Mom come meet us outside the temple so that we could get some family temple pictures?" Annette asked me.

"Oh, I'm sorry, I didn't realize we were supposed to," I said. Being as we weren't invited to the ceremony and all, I added mentally.

"Well, it doesn't matter," she said, "Uncle Adam got some great pictures of me and Matt at the temple, and he'll take the family pictures at the reception and at the picnic tomorrow."

"Actually, Annette, there's something I wanted to talk to you about," I said. "I don't know if you know this, but after April and Susan have flown all the way out here for your special day, Dad asked Susan not to come to the reception."

"What? Why?" Annette gasped.

"Because he thought that your new in-laws wouldn't want her there," I replied.

Sister Hobbs had arrived at the house on her way to the reception as well, and Annette looked over at her apprehensively. "But the Hobbs are such nice people," she said. "They wouldn't be like that."

"Well, maybe you should talk to them about it," I said.

Annette walked up to her new mother-in-law. "Sister Hobbs?" she said.

"Please, call me 'mom' now," said Sister Hobbs with a huge smile.

"Okay, Mom," sad Annette, looking a little uncomfortable. "I wanted to ask you about something. Is it true that you didn't want my sister April to bring her girlfriend to the reception?" she asked.

"Well, um..." said Sister Hobbs.

"Because my sister is part of my family," said Annette, "and I don't want her and her family to be excluded."

"Well, of course not," said Sister Hobbs, hesitating only slightly.

"That's wonderful!" said Annette. "Then it was all a misunderstanding!"

April and Susan were in earshot for this exchange. "Thanks, Sister Hobbs," said April.

"Of course, wonderful," said Sister Hobbs, with an air of not knowing what else to say.

April and Susan took me to the reception in their car. It was held in Matt's family's local ward building in the cultural hall. The streamers and paper bells hanging from the basketball standards were perhaps less than elegant, but the centerpieces looked fabulous. The various tables were laden with different types of punch and cookies and tiny mints, and the main table had a lovely, multi-tiered wedding cake and was piled with gifts.

Upon arriving, I caught up with Rex. He told me that the boys had had great fun decorating the car. We then got in line to greet the bride and groom and the wedding party.

The interesting thing was that this trip through the receiving line would be my first opportunity to meet Annette's new husband Matt. When our turn came around, I introduced myself to him, and I introduced him to Rex. Unsurprisingly, Matt seemed to be on cloud nine, so he greeted us in a friendly manner, but I didn't get the impression that he was paying too close of attention to us.

It turned out that Matt was a big, stocky guy, just slightly shorter than Rex. However, comparing muscular Matt to mathematician Rex, I was struck by how funny it was that I had imagined Rex to be muscular. He was perhaps muscular compared to me, but seeing him alongside Matt it was clear that despite his broad-shouldered frame Rex was exceptionally thin.

When I got my turn to talk to Annette, I gave her a kiss on the cheek and congratulated her.

"Annette, I'm really impressed with the way you stood up to your mother-in-law like that," I said. "I could never do that with Rex's mom, she scares me. Of course Rex's mom is a total psycho."

Rex laughed. "No offense Rex," I said, "but your mom's a psycho."

He smiled and said "So's yours."

"I'm lucky," said Annette. "Matt's mom keeps really strict LDS standards for herself, but when it comes down to it, she's pretty tolerant of other people doing things differently."

"That's great for you," I said. "It's wonderful to be able to get along with your new family."

After that brief exchange we of course had to move along so that others would have the opportunity to congratulate the newlyweds.

Once we had finished with the receiving line, we took up a place on the sidelines to observe the room. My bachelor uncle Adam was going all around the room taking photos of everyone. My little cousins Jennifer and Emily appeared to be still following and observing Joe and Sam from a distance and giggling. Mom and Richard were going around "witnessing" to various people from Matt's ward who were politely declining their pamphlets and brochures.

"God, they're so annoying, they drive me up the freaking wall!" I said to Rex. "I mean, I can kind of understand people who say that whenever evidence contradicts the scriptures it's the evidence that is wrong. That's wacky, but at least it's consistent. On the other end of the spectrum, I can perfectly relate to those Christians that say that the *Bible* is not to be taken literally. That's reasonable. But this idea that the *Bible* and the real world evidence are in sync—well, that's just demonstrably false."

Rex laughed. "I know, but what can you do? You can't choose your parents."

In the late afternoon the open house wound down, and we began to realize that we hadn't really had any lunch, and that cookies weren't sufficient sustenance. The reception hadn't been planned as an affair that included a meal, but the out-of-town relatives who would be participating in the clean-up would need to be fed. Fortunately, somebody wisely ordered a big stack of pizzas, and we all ate them as we put things away.

When we had finished our pizza and had finished cleaning up, Rex put his arm around me affectionately and suggested that perhaps we might turn in early. I was in agreement with this plan, so we got in the car and went back to our hotel room.

3 0 . SUNDAY MORNING

ON SUNDAY MORNING, Rex and I went out to brunch with those people who weren't going to church. Mom and Richard had been planning to visit the various local Christian churches that had LDS outreach ministries, but at the last minute the adorable baby motivated them to change their plans and have brunch with us instead.

As soon as we got to our table, Mom started installing baby Judy in her high chair. Mom had even brought some puppets and started playing with Judy and making her laugh. Susan seemed a tiny bit wary at first, but in short order she seemed to pick up on the fact that Mom was motivated by genuine affection and not proselyting.

"It's so wonderful to finally have a grandchild," she sighed. Then to Susan she said "I mean, I hope you don't mind if I think of Judy as my granddaughter."

"Of course I don't mind," said Susan. "I don't object to more love for my precious little girl."

"And maybe some free babysitting to boot," said April with a smile.

"Of course, anytime," said Richard. "We would love to help out."

When the waiter arrived, all of us except Mom and baby Judy ordered a piping hot cup of coffee. Mom ordered cocoa.

"It's so weird that drinking this is considered a sin here," said Susan, holding up her coffee cup. "What an unfathomable place this is. You don't like coffee, Mrs. Winterbottom?" she asked Mom.

"I generally don't drink coffee or tea or anything else that's against the Word of Wisdom," Mom said. "The thing is that I don't want to give the Mormons any ammunition to rationalize why I left the church. They always like to say that when someone leaves the church that it was because it was too difficult, and they had a 'Word of Wisdom problem' or something. I'd rather people see that it wasn't because of weakness that I left the church but rather because of logical reasoning and Christ's love."

"Yeah, I went through a stage where I wanted to be sure that everyone understood that my reason for leaving the church wasn't because of sinful weakness," I said. "But then I moved past that. Now

I'm at the point where I no longer give a shit what Mormons think about why I left the church."

Rex laughed. "Myself, I think I pretty much started at that stage," he said. "Of course I've always had a bad attitude."

"It's true," I said, giving him a teasing smile "just ask his mom."

"Now, Lynn, I hate to pry," Mom said, "but you're really not doing yourself a favor by getting off on the wrong foot with Rex's mom like that."

"You're right," I said. "I've really got to cut it out with these snide comments about her behind her back like that."

"Damn straight," said Rex smiling.

"Hey, it's not just me," I said teasingly. "You haven't been too happy with your parents lately either."

"I know, I know," he said. "Like you were saying the other day, it takes time, but we'll get there eventually if we all make an effort."

"That's the right attitude," said Mom. "That's how I turned things around with your dad's mom when we were first married."

"You had trouble getting along with Dad's mom?" asked April, a bit surprised.

"I thought you guys were the best of buddies, you know, before the divorce," I said.

"Well we were, but it didn't come automatically. At first, since I was a new convert to the church, I didn't understand how a lot of things worked, and it seemed like I could never do anything right in her eyes. I thought she should be more sympathetic. But one day I heard her talking about her hobby of genealogy, and it sounded really interesting. Of course none of my family's genealogy had been done, so she and I had this wonderful adventure of starting from scratch and finding the names of my ancestors. We traced some lines all the way back to Adam! We had so much fun together that we couldn't help but become friends."

"That's funny, I knew that you and Grandma liked to do genealogy together, but I didn't realize that that was where you got your passion for it," said April.

"That was it," said Mom. "Of course the downside is that now all of my ancestors' names have been submitted to Salt Lake and now they've been baptized for the dead."

"What?" asked Susan. "Baptizing dead people? That's just too wacky."

"Well of course they don't baptize actual dead bodies," I said. "It's just that Mormons believe that a Mormon baptism is a requirement for getting into heaven. Luckily, if you neglect to do it yourself, your loving Mormon descendants can be baptized for you by proxy in the temple after you're dead."

"I still think it's wacky," said Susan.

"It *is* wacky," said Mom. "I don't know why I thought that was reasonable all those years. Think what I've done to my poor ancestors."

"I don't think it's such a big deal," I said. "I could see being annoyed if they were performing some sort of ritual curses on people, but all they're doing is their way of opening the door to their heaven for you. I generally don't let it bother me if some random religion wants to bless me in some way or other, even without my consent."

"Yeah, looking at it probabilistically, the worst thing it can do is increase your chances of going to some sort of paradise," said Rex.

"But I'm sure that my ancestors don't want to go to the Mormon heaven," protested Mom.

"Now sweetheart," said Richard, "you know that you don't believe in the Celestial Kingdom anyway, so why sweat it? I'm sure that if your ancestors are anything like you they have a great sense of humor. They're probably up there laughing about it over Sunday brunch, like we are."

"Of course you're right, Richard," Mom said, chuckling and giving his hand a squeeze.

"Anyway Lynn, about what I was saying earlier, it might help if you could find a common interest with Rex's mom, like genealogy."

"Oh, she's not so into genealogy," said Rex.

"Well, not necessarily that exactly," said Mom, "but you know what I mean."

"You're right, Mom, thanks for the advice," I said.

After brunch was over we went more or less straight to the big dual-family picnic in the park. With a picnic following brunch like that, that made two meals in a row for us heathens, so we weren't very hungry for the picnic food, but those who had just gotten out of church were famished and heartily dug in.

Rex and I sat down on a grassy hillside to just hang out. After getting some food, Sam and Joe, still in their white shirts and ties, took up a spot next to us. When Rex saw Sam and Joe's food, he decided that perhaps he was hungry again after all and set off to get himself a sandwich.

"What a nice day," said Sam. "It's too bad that Jared couldn't come."

"I know," I said. "He would have had fun. Plus, I don't know what we're going to do to return his car and get to the airport without his help."

Sam saw his brother Matt talking with Annette and a group of other people nearby. "Well, maybe it's not too late," he said to me. Then he called to Matt. "Matt, come over here!"

Matt noticed Sam calling him and came over and sat on the grass next to him.

"What's up, little bro?" asked Matt.

"We were wondering if you could take us to go pick up our friend Jared and bring him to the picnic," Sam said.

"I don't know if Mom wants me to leave the picnic at all since so many people came here to see me and Annette and congratulate us. Can't he get a ride from his own family?"

"Not really. It's a long story. His parents don't want to help, and somebody else is borrowing his car," said Sam.

"Ah, he's your age and he has his own car?" asked Matt.

"Oh yeah," said Sam. "Their family has four cars, and their dad's car is this cool sports car!"

"Sounds like they have a lot of blessings," said Matt coldly.

"Oh yeah," said Sam. "And they have this really big house, you should see it."

"Lucky kid, this Jared," said Matt.

"I'll say!" said Sam. "Plus his older brother Rex is the coolest!"

Joe started giving Sam a look as if silently begging him to shut up, but Sam didn't notice.

"Oh, really?" asked Matt icily. "Is this Rex the same as Lynn's boyfriend Rex?"

"That's him," said Sam. "Jared is so lucky to have such a cool older brother!"

"What's so cool about him?" asked Matt.

Joe started nudging Sam with his foot to try to get his attention, but Sam just moved out of Joe's way and ignored him.

"He's funny, like Spencer!" said Sam "And he does fun things with Jared! Just the other day, he took us all to the pool at his hotel and bought us a bunch of beer!"

"Sam!" Joe said.

"He did what?!" asked Matt. Sam seemed to realize that he had once again put his foot in his mouth. It was a lucky thing that Sam had managed to keep his mouth shut about the porn since that would undoubtedly have been worse.

"Annette!" Matt yelled, "Annette come here!"

I was starting to get a little worried. Annette took her leave of the people she was talking to and came over to sit by Matt.

"Annette, my innocent little sixteen-year-old brother here tells me that your sister's live-in boyfriend has been buying him beer."

Annette glared at me in annoyance.

"It's bad enough we had to invite those lezzies," Matt continued "and those anti-Mormon Jesus freaks! Fetch! Your whole family's like some sort of freak show!"

That seemed to irritate Annette. "*My* family's a freak show? What about your aunt and uncle who ran off and joined that polygamist cult? Oh yeah, like that's totally normal!" she said, giving a pointed look to Joe.

"Well at least we didn't invite them to the reception!" said Matt, ignoring Joe completely.

Matt looked away. Annette calmed down a bit and moved toward him.

"I'm sorry, honey," said Annette putting her arm around him. "All I'm trying to say is that you can't choose your family."

"Yeah, and once you finally get used to your own family, you get married and find yourself stuck with a whole new family full of freaks to deal with," I said.

The looks I got from Annette and Matt gave me the impression that my input here was about as helpful as Sam's.

Just then, ever the master of perfect timing, Rex arrived and said hi to everyone and sat down next to me.

"You!" said Matt, glaring at Rex, "I've got a good mind to kick your ass!"

"Matt!" gasped Annette, shocked.

"What? What's this all about?" asked Rex.

"Matt found out about the beer," I said.

"Look Matt, I'm really sorry," he said. "I know it was a mistake. My parents royally chewed me out for it the other day."

"That's why Rex can't go pick up Jared himself," I said. "His parents won't leave Jared with him anymore."

"I've learned my lesson, though, I swear," said Rex. "I won't do it again."

"Matt, please don't tell your mom and dad about the beer," pleaded Joe. "Your dad said one slip-up and I'm out on the street. I don't know who will take me in if that happens. I can't go back to my parents."

Matt calmed down a bit. "Okay, I'll let it go this time," he said to Sam. "But I'd better not hear about you breaking the Word of Wisdom again."

Quick as a flash I grabbed Rex's arm. "Don't say it!" I hissed in his ear.

Rex pulled away, laughing. "I wasn't going to," he said softly.

"So will you take us to go pick up Jared?" Sam asked Matt.

"You're really pushing your luck today," Matt replied. "Okay, let's go." Joe and Sam followed Matt to his car.

No sooner had the three of them gone when I saw another potential family flare-up on the horizon. It seemed like there was no end to the mischief that could be caused by gathering a whole extended family or two into one place.

At a distance I saw that Mom and Richard were talking to Grandma and Grandpa, and what's worse, they appeared to be showing them some papers. I feared the worst since in-laws are already danger, ex-in-laws are serious danger, and then throwing a debate over religion into the mix spelled certain doom.

In spite of myself I got up and approached as discretely as possible to try to get a better view of what was going on. Rex followed, asking me what was up, but I motioned for him to be quiet.

When I got a little better look, I saw that my fears were unfounded. The papers Mom was showing Grandma weren't Christian leaflets, they looked like some old photos and other genealogical materials.

"Look at that!" I said to Rex. "Mom and Grandma are back to doing genealogy together as if nothing had happened!"

He laughed. "It's your doing, you know," he said. "Your bad example reminded her of her own good example."

"Thanks a lot!" I said.

"Nothing brings people together like a common enemy," he continued. "You'd be surprised how much altruism is subconsciously motivated by spite for somebody else."

"God Rex, you're so damn cynical sometimes! Don't you think this might be another example of people making an effort to get along—despite their differences—for the sake of the family?"

"Sorry," he said, looking appropriately penitent. "I guess I should probably learn to tone down that bad attitude a little bit."

"Damn straight," I said, smiling at him.

Then, watching Mom and Richard chatting with Grandma and Grandpa, I began to wonder if maybe there wasn't something to Rex's idea. It was starting to look like now Mom was buying a bottle of herbal tonic or two from Grandma.

I could see Dad a little farther away, viewing his parents suspiciously, and I caught myself plotting whether maybe I could come up with a new way of screwing up that would get Dad and his parents to gang up against me, patching everything up among them in the process. Going through the temple together the other day appeared not to have done the trick. I even briefly contemplated making a big stink about God not existing in order to inspire all of the competing forces of Jesus to make friends with each other again. Then I figured that since Mom and Dad had reached some sort of equilibrium in going their separate ways, it was better not to take chances by rocking the boat.

That Rex could always be counted on to provide food for thought, even if it led to mental indigestion sometimes. To think this was the person I was considering marriage with! Still, if one thing was certain, it was that there would never be a dull moment.

When Matt got back with the three boys, we went out to the parking lot to meet him. Rex walked up to the driver's side as Matt was getting out.

"Thanks for doing this, Matt," he said.

"No problem," said Matt. He gave a bit of a smile, but I got the impression that Rex was perhaps still not his favorite person in the universe.

Jared jumped out of the other side of the car, and ran around to hug his big brother.

"I'm so glad Mom let me come here," he said, letting go. "I was so worried that you would leave before I could see you again."

"I didn't want that either," said Rex, "but we've both learned that you defy Mom at your own risk."

"It's been terrible at home," said Jared. "Dad's been snapping at everyone and Mom has been all sad, but neither one will talk about it. And yesterday Jill and Joy set off in the morning to hang out with friends and didn't come back till late. Then they left like that again today, straight from church. I think they're just avoiding Mom and Dad, but they took their car, so I was stuck!"

"I'm sorry," said Rex. "You can have your car back now. Actually it would be a big help to us if you could drop us off at the bus stop when it's time for us to go."

"Oh, I can drive you all the way to the airport!" said Jared.

"That would take you more than an hour each way. I'd hate to have you waste your time and gas for no reason like that—it's no problem for us to take the bus," said Rex.

Jared gave Rex a sort of sad-puppy look as if to say he didn't want to say goodbye so quickly.

"C'mere, you," said Rex, grabbing Jared and giving him a friendly noogie. Jared laughed as he pulled away. "I can't believe I made it through this entire über-Mormon weekend and not one single person has zinged me with one of those annoying 'brother-of-Jared' cracks!" said Rex, laughing.

"Oh, I almost forgot," said Jared, reaching into this backpack. "Mom told me to give you this." He handed Rex a paper sack.

Rex looked in it and laughed. "Cookies," he said.

"I think that must be some sort of Mormon thing," I said. "When you can't express your love in words, say it with cookies."

Rex took the sack around and started offering cookies to everyone. I had to laugh when I saw that the cookies were in the shape of little pink hearts. I had never told Rex of my own long-ago adventures with heart-shaped cookies, and didn't intend to. But for the first time I felt some small affinity with his mother.

Just then my Uncle Adam started calling everyone together. "Come on everyone. Now that Matt is back, let's all get together for one last family portrait with the newlyweds."

He made a point to call to Susan, April, and Judy as well as to me and Rex. My two sets of parents looked on warily, not sure which pair was wanted for the portrait.

"Come on, *everyone*," said Uncle Adam. "Just this once, just for fun." My parents thought about it. "Humor me!" he said.

Matt and Annette stood in the center with me and Rex on one side and April and Susan and baby Judy on the other. Then Mom and Richard took up a spot on the far end of the line and Dad and Sharon took their place on the opposite end.

"Let's see some smiles, now," said Uncle Adam. "Come on, people, for two seconds pretend like you don't all hate each other!" he said, laughing. That line made everyone smile a bit just long enough for him to snap the picture. "This one's for the history books," he said.

As our little group broke up, I noticed that some of my little cousins were doing an impromptu singing recital of the musical number they had sung in Sacrament Meeting earlier that day:

*"Families can be together forever
through Heavenly Father's plan.
I always want to be with my own family
and the Lord has shown me how I can,
the Lord has shown me how I can."*

CHARACTERS IN TEMPLE WEDDING

The Hansons

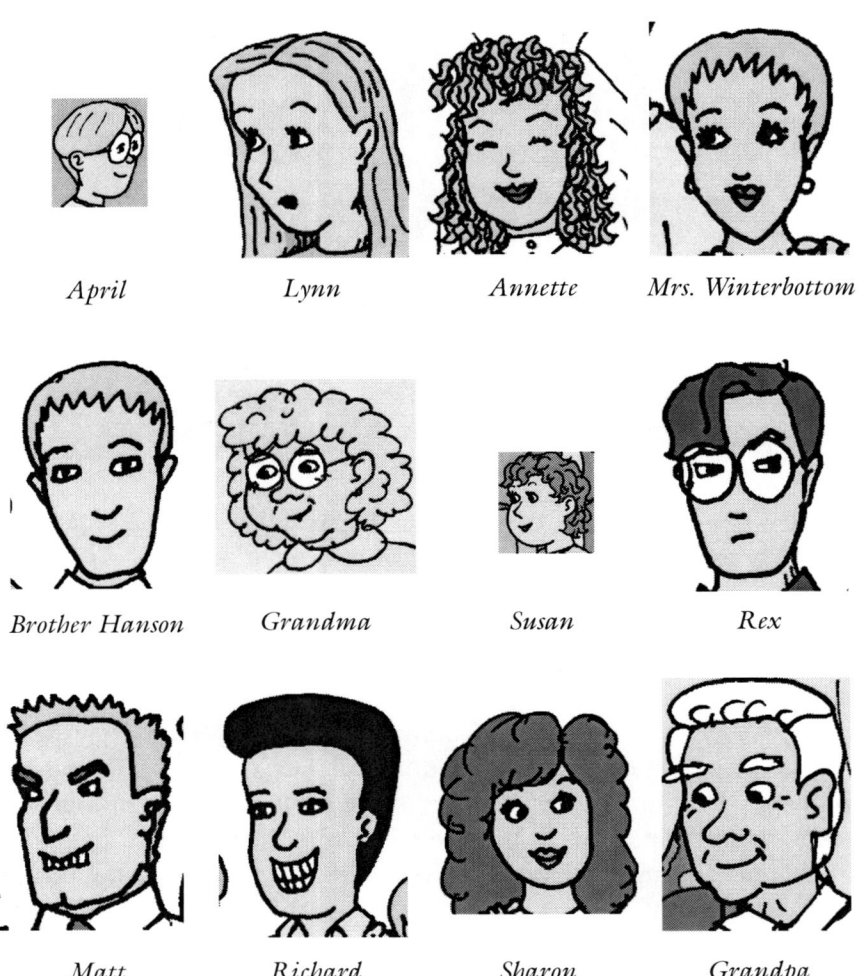

April   *Lynn*   *Annette*   *Mrs. Winterbottom*

Brother Hanson   *Grandma*   *Susan*   *Rex*

Matt   *Richard*   *Sharon*   *Grandpa*

The Wendells

Rex   Jill   Joy   Jared

Brother Wendell   Sister Wendell

The Hobbses

Laura   Linda   Matt   Spencer

Sam   Sister Hobbs   Joe

VII. Orem High

Jared

31. MONDAY EVENING

S AM WAS PRETTY LUCKY that his cousin Joe had come to live with him. The three of us were all in the same math class together, which meant that Sam got free help with his math homework every night while I only got help when they invited me over. I couldn't figure out how Joe could derive all those trig identities so easily. I mean, I could follow Joe's answers when he showed me, and so could Sam, more or less, but how the answers came to him in the first place was like some kind of miracle.

Chewing on my pencil and listening to Joe, I started wishing I had inherited some of the math talent my older brother Rex had gotten. He was a real whiz at math! He would be helping me with my homework himself if he weren't off at grad school.

We were finishing up the last few problems when Sam's mom called upstairs to us. "Sam! Is your friend Jared going to stay for dinner?"

"How 'bout it?" asked Sam.

"Okay," I replied.

"Okay, Mom," Sam yelled back downstairs.

"I just have to call my mom and tell her what time to pick me up," I said.

"Oh, yeah, I was going to ask you about that," said Sam. "How come you didn't drive today?"

"Oh, I'm being punished. I've lost my car privileges."

"What'd you do?" asked Joe, laughing.

"Nothing lately," I replied. "You guys remember when Rex was visiting last Summer and bought us all that beer and porn?"

They both laughed. "Hard to forget!" said Sam.

"Well, anyway, Mom found the porn stash just the other day. She asked me where I got it, but I didn't tell her it was left over from Rex's visit." I still felt bad that it was my fault that Mom and Dad found out about Rex buying me that beer and got into that big fight with him over it. I could see how Mom and Dad would be mad at Rex for being a bad influence on me and all especially since they knew I looked up to him. Still, I figured they should know that I wasn't the kind of guy to just blindly follow someone else's example!

"That's good you didn't get him in trouble again," said Joe. "Poor Rex."

"Yeah," I said. "I guess maybe he shouldn't have done that in the first place, but I know he was just trying to be nice in his own way."

"It was cool that he spent so much time hanging out with us, actually," said Joe.

"Yeah, it was fun!" said Sam. "He's cool even though he's bad."

"Do you guys still have the porn he bought you?" I asked.

Out of the blue, Sam said "I'm going to go see how Mom's coming with dinner." Then he left.

"What's with him?" I asked.

"Oh, he doesn't want to talk about it," replied Joe. "Here's what happened with us. Sam and I agreed that he should hide the porn with his stuff because if he got caught he might get punished a bit, but if I got caught with it there was always the chance my uncle would throw me out of the house. So Sam hid it away, but by bad luck the very next week he had an interview with the bishop scheduled. Of course I didn't ask him the details, but shortly after the interview he took the whole stash on his bike and disposed of it in some faraway dumpster."

"Man, I hate those bishop's interviews!" I said.

"Me too," said Joe. "After I realized what Sam had done, I told him that when he goes in for an interview with the bishop, if the bishop asks him questions that he thinks are none of the bishop's business, he should just answer however he pleases. That's what I do."

"Hmmmm," I said. "And what'd Sam say to that?"

"Well, he seemed to think that the bishop would use the 'spirit of discernment' to tell when he's lying. I told him that I'd never had any such problem, but Sam wasn't convinced."

"Yeah, but even if the bishop doesn't figure it out, it's still a sin to lie to him!" I said.

"That's probably true," said Joe, "but the way I see it, I've had enough problems in my life already, what with my family and all. For the moment, I'm just going to do whatever it takes to get by. When I'm old enough to support myself and I'm no longer dependent on the charity of relatives, then maybe I'll worry about my spiritual growth."

"Wow," I said. "You'd better just hope you don't get hit by a bus between now and the time you get around to repenting!"

Joe laughed. "You know, it's funny, that's exactly the same thing Sam said."

Just then Sam came back up. "Supper's ready," he said, "Let's go." I called my mom quickly to tell her that I was staying for dinner and then I went with Sam and Joe to the kitchen.

When we got to the dinner table, the places were already set and the food was already on the table. It was meatloaf and green beans and mashed potatoes. Sam's dad, Brother Hobbs, called on Sam to say the prayer, and Sam obliged.

At the end of the prayer, Sam's mom, Sister Hobbs, began slicing the meatloaf and serving it to everyone. "Are you planning to stay for family night?" she asked me.

"I'd love to have Family Home Evening with you guys," I said, stretching the truth a little bit there, "but then my parents would have to have Family Home Evening all by themselves." Actually I was kind of hoping my parents would just forget about it like they usually did.

"Oh, so you're the youngest, like my little Sam?" asked Sister Hobbs.

"Yep," I said. "My oldest sister Kathy is married, my brother Rex is in grad school, my sister Jill is in college, and now that my sister Joy has set of for college too, it's just me and my parents."

"Then you have your parents' undivided attention," she said brightly. "You're a lucky guy."

"Yeah, lucky me," I said sarcastically. Sam and Joe both laughed.

Sam's dad then asked Sam a bunch of detailed questions about how our high school football team was doing so far that season, and they continued talking about that until it was time for dessert.

For dessert Sister Hobbs brought out ice cream and a special peach-flavored cake that had a filling made from the peach preserves that she had made herself from peaches they had grown in their own yard.

"Wow, Sister Hobbs, this is amazing!" I said. "We never have anything like this at our house."

"Well, you know, we have so many jars of preserves around here that I have to always be thinking of creative ways to use them," she said. "Of course I put them in our year's supply, but the prophet says we're supposed to rotate our year's supply regularly."

"Wow, my mom's not so into all of these crafts and things," I said, thinking of the elaborate quilt I had seen Sister Hobbs working on when I arrived.

"What does your Mom like to do?" asked Sister Hobbs.

"Well, she likes to read and write in her journal," I said, trying to think of something righteous I could say. "Sometimes she makes cookies. Of course she's gone back to work since she doesn't have any little kids to take care of anymore."

"What line of work is she in?" asked Brother Hobbs.

"She's an assistant librarian," I replied.

"I wonder if I should maybe think of getting a job too since we'll be empty-nesters ourselves soon," said Sister Hobbs. "I don't know though."

"We're doing okay," said Brother Hobbs. "You don't have to go out and get a job if you don't want to, honey. I don't know what our ward's Relief Society would do without you to run the homemaking meetings." He smiled at her.

"Yeah, it'd probably wither away without Mom," said Sam sincerely.

"I guess I'm pretty lucky my husband is such a good provider," said Sister Hobbs, smiling back at Brother Hobbs.

"Oh, I didn't mean to say my dad isn't a good provider," I said.

"I'll say!" said Sam. "You should see their house! And their cars!"

"Well, it's hard to buy everything you want when you're supporting so many missionaries and paying tithing," said Sister Hobbs. In fact Sam's older brother Spencer and his two oldest sisters were all currently on missions. We didn't have any missionaries in our family, but at least I was sure my parents were paying their tithing.

We were still eating our cake when the doorbell rang. Figuring it was my mom, I ran and grabbed my things as Sister Hobbs went to answer the door. I got to the door just as Sister Hobbs was opening it, and sure enough it was Mom.

"Hello," said Sister Hobbs. "You must be Jared's mom, Sister Wendell. It's nice to finally get a chance to meet you." She smiled at Mom as she extended her hand, but I could see that she noticed Mom's pearls and cashmere. Mom was quite a contrast to Sister Hobbs who was in jeans and sneakers and a ponytail.

"It's nice to finally meet you too, Sister Hobbs," said Mom, shaking her hand.

"Won't you come in?" asked Sister Hobbs. "We're still having our dessert, cake with homemade peach-preserve filling."

"Thanks, I don't mind if I do," said Mom, following Sister Hobbs inside. Sister Hobbs served Mom a piece of cake, and we all sat back down at the table.

"We were just talking about how hard it is to support so many missionaries at once," said Sister Hobbs.

"Ah," said Mom. It seemed like she wasn't quite sure why Sister Hobbs would bring that up.

"It was a blessing that my Matt had saved up so much money for his mission before he went, and my Spencer and my twins Laura and Linda did too, but there's only so much they can save up in advance. Supporting three missionaries in the field at once is hard."

"I imagine it would be," said Mom with a nervous smile.

"You're saving for your mission, aren't you Sam?" asked Brother Hobbs.

"Yes, sir," said Sam.

"Me too," I said. Actually I still wasn't sure I really wanted to go on a mission, but I had to stick up for my mom.

"So how are your twin girls doing?" asked Mom. "I think I remember my son Rex mentioning that he knew them from school."

"Oh, they're doing wonderfully," said Sister Hobbs. "They're both such spiritual girls. Laura is serving a mission in Chile and Linda is serving a mission in Australia. Of course they haven't baptized anyone—being girls and all—but they've been instrumental in bringing so many people to the true gospel. They'll be coming home soon, and I'll be so happy to see them both again!"

Then she switched gears and turned to my mom. "And your boy Rex? What does he do?" Never mind that I had already told her that Rex was in grad school, but whatever.

"Oh he's in graduate school studying Mathematics," said Mom. "In fact he graduated from college with honors, and now he's in the Ph.D. program in one of the top-rated Mathematics departments in the country." I was really glad to hear Mom finally sticking up for Rex for once instead of always saying how disappointed she was about him leaving the church and all.

"Grad school already?" asked Sister Hobbs. "And he's the same age as my girls? He must have finished college pretty fast." In other words, he couldn't possibly have taken time off to serve a mission and be that far along in school. I was starting to get really annoyed with Sister Hobbs here.

"Yes, well, he's always been a very good student," said Mom.

"And where did he serve his mission?" asked Sister Hobbs. Now I was really mad at Sister Hobbs! Her earlier question had already made it perfectly clear that Rex had never gone on a mission! She didn't have to rub it in like that!

Mom seemed not to know what to say. "Um, you know, as I was saying, he's always been a good student. He graduated from seminary at the top of his class!"

"That's nice," said Sister Hobbs. She had such a smug smile on her face that I couldn't help but hate her.

"Well, thanks for the cake, but I guess we'd better be going," said Mom.

I thanked the family as well and said goodbye to Sam and Joe, and we got in the car.

All the way home in the car Mom was quiet. She was probably thinking some more about how sad she was that Rex didn't believe in the church anymore. She was probably blaming herself for it too after that little conversation with Sister Hobbs.

I was so mad at that Sister Hobbs! She was supposed to be so righteous! She didn't have to make my mom feel bad like that. And now I'd for sure be the one to suffer the consequences at home. Probably Rex would too on the phone. The way things were going Rex would probably never come back and visit us again.

By the time we arrived at home, Mom seemed like she was almost about to cry. I had to do something.

"Wait, Mom," I said as soon as we were out of the car. "I know you think I'm just a dumb kid, but I see what's going on here."

"What?" she asked softly.

"Look, so you don't have the same interests as Sister Hobbs. So you don't have the same kids either. So what? Heavenly Father knows you're doing your best."

"Thanks Jared, you're a good kid," she said giving me a hug. "You know I love you."

"And Rex too?" I asked.

She sighed as she thought about it a bit. "And Rex too."

32. SATURDAY

ON SATURDAY THE WEATHER was strangely warm for late October. It was like Summer again all of the sudden. I had nothing to do, so I called up Sam and Joe's house. Joe was home all by himself because Sam was at football practice and his parents had decided to go with him in order to show their support and then maybe go out do a little shopping afterwards. Joe was just sitting around reading or something, so he said he didn't mind if I wanted to come over.

We fixed ourselves some lunch, and after lunch—since it was such a nice day—we decided to go for a walk along the Provo River.

The Provo River isn't too impressive as rivers go. It isn't all that much more than a stream. But it was a nice place to hang out on a warm day. As we walked down the path along the river, we got to talking about what colleges we were thinking of applying to.

Joe seemed to notice something in the distance. "Hey look, there's Andrea Sharp," he said.

I looked up ahead along the path and saw a tall, thin girl with long hair and glasses. She was standing on the bank and seemed to be staring into the water.

"Who's she?" I asked.

"She goes to our school," said Joe.

"I don't think I've ever met her," I said.

"She's new this year. She's in my Chemistry class."

As we approached she kept looking into the water, and she didn't look up until we were practically right next to her.

"Hi Andrea," said Joe.

She seemed surprised to see us. "Oh, hi," she said.

"What brings you here to the river?" asked Joe.

"It's a nice day," she replied. "I like to come here."

"Same with us," I said. "This weather's amazing, isn't it? It's a great day to get out and get some fresh air."

She looked at me for a second and asked "Do I know you?"

"No," I said, "but Joe says you go to our school. I'm Jared Wendell."

"Oh, *you're* Jared Wendell," she said. She made it sound like she'd already heard all about me.

"You've heard of me?" I asked.

"Oh, it's nothing," she said.

"What did you hear?" I asked.

"No, no, it's really nothing."

"Tell me, I want to know!" I said.

"It's nothing, it's just that my friend Tanya mentioned that you're in her French class," said Andrea.

"And?" I asked.

"And she was saying that she has to help you all the time because you really suck at it!" Then she started laughing.

Oh, great, I thought. It was true that Tanya was better than me at French and that she helped me sometimes, but it wasn't like I asked her to help me or anything. And I wasn't the worst in the class, either, so I didn't see why she should have to make fun of me behind my back like that!

"I'm sorry!" said Andrea. She grabbed my hand and gave it a little squeeze. "I didn't want to say that, but you insisted on knowing what it was!"

"It's okay," I said, "I guess it was my fault for asking." I made a mental note for the future to beware of back-stabbing chubby girls who pretend to be innocently trying to help with French assignments.

"It looks like I've run into some well-known classmates here," said Andrea.

"Oh, am I well-known too? What class do I suck at?" asked Joe, laughing.

"Oh, no, that's not what you're known for."

"What am I known for then?" he asked.

"Oh, you know," said Andrea. "They say you were raised by polygamists and you ran away."

Joe stopped smiling. "Yeah, that's the rumor that's going around, isn't it?"

"Oh, is it not true?" she asked.

"Of course it's true," said Joe.

"I'm sorry," said Andrea. "Man, I really have foot-in-mouth disease today, don't I? I run into some classmates that I don't really know, and it takes me less than one minute to offend both of them."

"I'm not offended," said Joe, warming up a little. "I know, everyone's curious. How could they not be? So what's your question?"

"Actually there is a question I've always kind of wanted to ask you," she said.

"What is it?" asked Joe.

"Well, as taboo as the polygs are to mainstream Mormons, I've heard that the mainstream Mormons are just as taboo to the polygs. Yet a friend of mine said that you're living with an LDS family now and that you're a Mormon. That seems strange to me if you were indoctrinated from the cradle to think of regular Mormons as evil."

I knew the answer to that one. It was that Joe hadn't been indoctrinated "from the cradle" but rather Joe's family had converted from mainstream Mormonism to Mormon fundamentalism when he was a kid. So naturally it wasn't such a big stretch for him to switch back.

Joe thought about it for a long time. I couldn't figure out why he was taking so long since the answer was so simple.

"Actually, I'm going to be straight with you here," he said. "Please don't tell anyone at all, either of you, because it could get me into trouble. The truth is that I really don't believe in any of it. I don't believe in God. Practicing Mormonism is just a condition that has been imposed on me by my aunt and uncle for living with them, but I'm not really a Mormon."

I was shocked! I was absolutely floored by this revelation! I had no idea! The thing that really got me though was that Joe and I had been good friends ever since we'd gotten to know each other this past Summer and he had never given me any hint that he was anything but a believing Mormon. And now out of the blue he was telling his big secret to some random girl that he hardly knew!

"Wow, that's so cool!" said Andrea. "Me too. I mean, I don't believe in God either."

"I know," said Joe. "I hope you won't be angry with me for this, but I overheard some things you said to your friend Kim during Chemistry class."

Andrea smiled and looked down shyly. Then she looked back up at Joe. "Let's not just stand here gabbing," she said. "If we're going to have a freakishly warm October day, let's take advantage of it! let's go wading!" She took off her sandals and stepped into the water.

"Yikes, that's cold!" she said. Joe and I both sat down on the grass to take off our shoes and socks. "Oh, well, no pain, no gain," she said stepping back into the water.

Andrea was wearing shorts—cut off jeans, actually—so she was all ready to go. Joe and I were both wearing long pants, so we had to roll them up as high as we could in order to get in the water at all.

Once I was ready, I stepped in with one foot. It was like ice! I stepped back out. I couldn't believe my eyes, seeing Andrea walking around in it as if it were nothing. Joe then stepped into the icy water. He winced with pain but was willing to brave it. I went back and sat down on the grass and started putting my socks back on.

"Aww," said Andrea chuckling a little. She flashed me the most adorable sympathetic smile.

"You know, my brother Rex is an atheist," I said, hoping to say something relevant.

"And you?" asked Andrea.

"Me?" I asked. "I don't know, I guess I'm just a plain old Mormon." I laughed a little, feeling self-conscious.

"You don't really believe that stuff, do you?" she asked.

"What do you mean?" I asked.

"You know, like Jesus is magically talking to you," she said. Joe laughed.

I wasn't really sure what to say. No one had ever put it to me that way before. "Everybody always talks about feeling the spirit and stuff at Fast and Testimony Meeting," I said. "It's normal to think that the Holy Ghost is talking to you. Isn't it?" Now it looked like both of them were laughing at me.

Then she said "Well, you know, I always say that if you want to believe that Leprechauns or ghosts or Jesus or whatever are talking to you, then that's your business. To each his own."

Joe laughed. I just looked at them, not knowing what to do. "Oh, come on Jared," said Joe, "we're not trying to make fun of you. I know, *everyone* around here believes this stuff, so how could you not?"

"Wait a minute," said Andrea. "Have you *really* never thought about this question? Didn't you just say that your brother is an atheist? Didn't that make you stop and think?"

"Yeah, but..." I began. I was about to say "but I have a testimony." But I couldn't say it. I could say it to Mom and to the ward, but I couldn't say it to these guys. I slumped down and rested my chin on my hands. I thought about all of the people standing up in Fast and Testimony Meeting reciting "I know this church is true, I know this church is true, I know this church is true" until it was pounded into my head. My head was beginning to hurt just thinking about it.

Joe came back and sat down near me and started drying his feet and putting his socks back on. Andrea continued wading. She was wandering around looking into the water as if searching for something on the bottom of the river. Her hair hung down to one side as she peered through her glasses into the water. Her cut-off jeans came midway down her thighs, and I could see some reflection of her long legs in the water where she was wading a bit deeper than her ankles. She was wearing a loose t-shirt, but I could make out the shape of her breasts under it.

"Will you look at that!" she said all of the sudden. Then quick as a flash she reached into the water and pulled out something long and narrow. It was moving. It was a snake!

"Can you believe it? I would have thought that they would be hibernating at this time of the year." She said it with this calm expression as if it were the most ordinary thing in the world that she was holding up a little snake by the tip of its tail. "It must be the weather."

"What are you doing?!" I asked. "Good gracious, put it back!"

Joe looked a little concerned. "Careful, it could be poisonous," he said.

"Oh, no, no, not this one," she said, pointing at its head with her finger. "Look here." The snake looked like it was going after her finger!

"Aah!" I shrieked, "it's going to bite you!"

She looked at me quizzically. "You're afraid of a little snake like this one?" she asked, holding it towards me.

"Just please put it back!" I said.

"Okay, sorry. So much for naturalism," she sighed.

She gently placed the snake back in the water and started walking back towards me and Joe. "I love to go out looking for frogs and turtles and other little animals. It's sort of this weird hobby of mine. Normally I just observe them though, I don't catch them."

She sat down on the grass near us and started drying off her own feet and put her sandals back on. The skin of her ankles was all goose-bumpy from being in the cold water. I followed the line of her leg from her knee down to her delicate foot that was partially exposed by the sandal she was fastening. I was tempted to move closer.

"That's pretty impressive that you can catch a snake with your bare hands like that," said Joe.

"Did it take lots of practice?" I asked.

"I dunno," she said.

"At least it must take some bravery," said Joe.

At that she laughed. "Don't be ridiculous. It's a harmless, inoffensive creature." When she had finished with both of her sandals, she turned to Joe and said "Actually, speaking of bravery and of what we were talking about earlier, it completely blows my mind that you were brave enough to run away from home, but that you aren't brave enough to tell your uncle and aunt that you don't believe in God."

Joe looked surprised and confused by her statement. After a few seconds he said "The two have nothing to do with one another. Well, except that in both cases it's a question of pragmatism and survival, not of courage. And anyway, I'm not really actively lying to my aunt and uncle. The thing is—and Jared maybe you've noticed this—they don't pay any attention to me at all. They almost never address me directly. The closest they usually come is to address me and Sam together as a unit, as if I were some sort of appendage of Sam."

"Wow, that's rough," said Andrea with concern.

"Not really," said Joe. "As far as I can tell, all they care about is Mormonism and keeping up appearances in the ward. Oh, and sports. Basically, they are about the most uninteresting people I've ever met. Don't get me wrong—I'm grateful to them for taking me in and giving me food, clothing, and shelter and everything. I know that they didn't have to."

"Yeah, except that the clothes are all hand-me-downs from Spencer and Sam!" I said. "I should give you some of Rex's old clothes or mine instead—they'd probably fit you better since you're thin like us."

Joe smiled. "Anyway, it's nice of them to help me, and if on top of that they don't pester me too much about religion, so much the better. I'm not going to go have some heart-to-heart talk with them about it."

"Yeah, but you're lying to Sam about it, and Sam's your friend," I said.

"You know how Sam is," said Joe. "He is completely without guile. If I told him I didn't believe in God, he would immediately tell his parents. And besides, he wouldn't understand, and it would just upset him."

"Aha! So you admit that you're deliberately lying to Sam to keep the truth from his parents," I said.

"Well, what do you want me to do?" he asked. "My aunt and uncle are happy enough to keep me around as Sam's well-mannered shadow and private tutor as long as they feel like my background isn't generating too much gossip in the ward. But from what I know of them, I'm sure an atheist under their roof would be unacceptable. Where I'm at, I can comfortably focus on my schoolwork and on getting into college. Striking out on my own, it's not so sure I'll get there. All I really want to do is study."

"Of course you're right," said Andrea. "I didn't mean to make it sound like I thought you were wrong for not telling them. Sometimes being too honest with authority figures about who you are can have some very negative consequences. And you have to understand that it's hard for me to imagine what it would be like to go through what you've been through."

"The thing is that I can't take any opportunities for granted. As you can imagine, it's mathematically impossible for the polygamists to provide wives for all of the males born into their communities. Yet they believe that wives are necessary for salvation. So a lot of young guys end up being driven away to decrease the competition. But they get such a limited education in the fundamentalist schools that they have no skills and many of them end up drifting. Fortunately I would never be as bad off as some of them because I've always been motivated to learn on my own, but they're my friends and relatives, so I feel for them."

"So left your father and mother forever just so you could have the joy of attending Orem High?" she asked, laughing nervously. "I mean, it's not funny, of course. But I imagine there must have been personal reasons as well."

"Of course there were," he said. "My dad had three wives and tons of kids. There's no way he could give individual attention to all of us. Can you even imagine what it's like to be a face in the crowd to your own father? It's so much better to live with Sam's parents where I don't care if they ignore me."

Andrea looked concerned, but didn't seem to know what to say.

"And of course guys there can forget about getting attention from girls as well," I added, remembering something Joe had once said.

"It's true," said Joe. "I was interested in girls, but really the only romantic relationship allowed is marriage, and even if I'd wanted to marry at fifteen—which I didn't—it would have been impossible to have it arranged. Yes, they marry off fifteen-year-old girls, but to senior priesthood leaders, not to fifteen-year old boys."

"Senior priesthood leaders?" she asked, looking shocked and disgusted.

"Yes, and it's every bit as repugnant as it sounds. Grown men with wives and children marrying teenage girls. Obviously I didn't care for it at the time, but looking back on it after more than a year of living in normal society it really hits me how truly fucked-up that is."

"Wow, that's really... Oh my god, I mean..." she seemed kind of flustered like she didn't know what to say. "Um, listen, I just remembered, I really have to be getting back. I've lost track of time and my mother's expecting me."

"But you don't have a watch on," I protested. "You don't know what time it is!"

"No, really, I have to get home," she said. "Listen, I really hope you're okay," she said to Joe, taking his hand and looking him in the eye. Then she turned to me. "It was really nice meeting you, Jared," and she squeezed my hand too and gave me a pleasant smile. Then she was off in the opposite direction than we had come.

As I watched her go, I was amazed that I had never noticed her before. She was so pretty and so very different from the other girls. Her small touch was like electricity to me. I was wondering if maybe Joe liked her too, actually. But they weren't going out or anything, so it wasn't like he had dibs on her just because he had met her first.

"Way to go, you really creeped her out with that last bit," I said to Joe.

"Yeah, I really need to keep in mind how disturbing these stories can be to people who aren't familiar with this sort of thing. Let's head back," he said.

On the way back we really didn't talk at all. It's hard to just go back to having an ordinary conversation after something like that. Once we got back to Sam and Joe's house, I said bye to Joe and got in my car and drove home.

When I got home, Mom asked me if I'd had a nice time with Joe and what we'd done. I told her that we'd hung out by the Provo River. She said it was nice that we'd taken advantage of the nice weather to go get some fresh air.

I went to my room and sat down on the bed. I thought about Andrea asking me if I really believed in the church. I thought I did. It seemed to me that I had felt the spirit telling me that it was true just as everyone said I should. Still, maybe she had a point that it was kind of crazy to think that that feeling was Jesus or the Holy Ghost magically talking to me.

All of the smartest people I knew were atheists: Rex and Lynn were, and now it turned out that Joe was too, and Andrea. I didn't

know Andrea very well, but she seemed pretty smart. Maybe they knew better than I did. On the other hand, maybe Satan had control over them. But it didn't seem like it. They seemed perfectly nice and reasonable. None of them really seemed to be controlled by Satan. I figured they were probably right about this whole God thing.

It was funny because I had just the other day been telling myself that I didn't just blindly follow other people. But here it was getting to be an awful lot of really trustworthy people. And anyway, I was mostly just following along what my parents taught me by believing it in the first place.

It was kind of a relief, actually, to think that I didn't have to worry anymore about whether or not I was sinning or whether or not I was doing the right things to get to the Celestial Kingdom one day.

I would hate to end up like Sam, all ashamed to think about sex at all. I was already one step ahead of the Mormons on that subject. A while back Rex had had a talk with me about it. He told me that no matter what they told us in devotionals and other youth events I shouldn't let them make me think I was different or perverted for thinking about sex and and that sort of thing. He told me that everyone does it and that it was impossible not to. He said that if I let them convince me that there was something wrong with me for it that that wouldn't make me do it any less, it would just make me all messed-up in the head about it. So he advised me to just ignore what they say in church on the subject and not worry about it. That seemed like pretty good advice to me. I'd even gotten some condoms and had practiced putting them on just in case, on his advice.

"Jared?" Mom called, "Jared can you come downstairs please?"

Mom wanted me to help her with dinner. Mom didn't really like to cook much since we were down to just the three of us, so she sometimes had me cook dinner for the family. She said it was a good skill for me to learn for when I would be off on my own one day. Plus actually it was kind of fun to hang out and chat with my mom while we were making dinner, although I would never admit that to the guys!

We had a nice little dinner that night as usual, and the next day we went to church. I was expecting church to seem different now that I didn't believe it was true anymore, but it wasn't really any different. It was still as boring as ever! Even blessing the sacrament was just the same. I guess I should have known it would be.

33. MONDAY

O N MONDAY I was really dreading going to my French class. I waited until the very last second before the bell to go to the classroom. It was natural to arrive a little later for that class anyway because it was the class right after the period when I had seminary, which was in a different building.

When I arrived at French class, Tanya was already there of course. Her seat was right next to mine. As soon as she saw me she gave me this huge smile and said "Hi Jared." I just glared at her and turned the other way as I took my seat.

The teacher started class by saying *"Bonjour les elèves,"* and then started saying a bunch of stuff in French.

Tanya put a small folded-up paper on my desk. I opened it up. She had written "RUOK? What's wrong?"

I wrote "You're talking about me behind my back." I folded it back up and handed it back to her.

Then she wrote something and passed the paper to me. She had written *"Quoi ? Moi ?"*

"I know you did," I wrote back.

Then she wrote "Andrea told me what she said, but it's not true! I never said that!"

I wrote back "I don't believe you."

Then she wrote "You can't take Andrea seriously! She says strange things for no reason sometimes!"

It looked like the teacher had maybe noticed the note, so I quickly hid it away in my pocket. I was sure she was lying. After all, how would Andrea have known that I sucked at French and that Tanya sometimes helped me if Tanya hadn't told her?

Tanya could be pretty cocky sometimes about the fact that she always knew the right answer. She wasn't all that cute either. She wasn't really fat, but she wasn't thin. She had kind of a round face and short, straight hair all dyed black, and she wore too much dark eye make-up. And she had kind of a squeaky voice when she was correcting people.

Soon the teacher finished lecturing and passed out a worksheet for us to work on. Of course Tanya immediately started scribbling furiously on it. I turned to that day's chapter in the textbook and started looking for some of the words from the worksheet.

"Do you need any help?" Tanya asked softly.

"No," I said, "I don't need any help from *you*." I looked back down at the worksheet. I really had no freaking clue about any of it. But I figured I could get it done if I spent some time on it calmly at home. I didn't need someone else to do my homework for me. Especially not Tanya.

For the rest of the day at school, I looked for Andrea in the halls every time we switched classes. For the rest of the week as well. I saw her a few times. Every time I did, I said hi to her and she said hi back and gave me a big smile, but I couldn't think of anything else to say to her. I really wanted to get together with her and talk to her more, but there was never any opportunity.

I thought a lot about Andrea over the weekend, and I decided that I really needed to do something. I figured that maybe I could tell her that I'd realized she was right about the whole God question. That might make her warm up to me. Then maybe I could ask her out. I was really nervous about the idea of asking her out on a date, but I didn't see anything else I could do.

The next week I was determined that I would talk to her and ask her out. I saw her a few times on Monday and Tuesday and said hi to her, but she was always with other girls, and there was no way I could ask her out in front of them. Finally on Wednesday I saw her walking down the hall alone. I figured that it was now or never, so I got up all of my courage and went over to talk to her.

"Hi Andrea, can I talk to you for a minute?" I said.

"Sure, Jared," she said. "What is it?"

"Well I wanted to tell you that I thought about what you said about how God doesn't exist and all, and I've decided that I think you're right."

"That's nice," she said. She sounded like she didn't care at all either way whether or not I believed in God!

"Anyway, I was wondering if you might want to go out with me on Friday night," I said.

She thought about it for a second. "Okay," she said.

"Great!" I said. "We could go out to dinner, then."

"Sounds like a good plan," she said. "Here let me give you my address and phone number." She got a piece of paper out of her backpack and started writing her address and phone number on it. Then she gave it to me. Oh, how I treasured that little paper!

"Shall I pick you up at six-thirty, then?" I asked.

"Sure," she said with a smile. "I'll see you then." And with that she continued on to her next class.

All I could think about all day at school on Friday was my big date that night. I was so excited! Normally I was lucky to maybe say one sentence to her if I happened to pass her in the hall. And now I would be able to spend the whole evening talking to her, and maybe more, I hoped.

When I got home from school I decided to take a shower. I had already taken a shower that morning so I probably didn't really need to do it again, but it seemed like a good way to kill time until it was time to go get her.

While I was in the shower I figured it was a good time to take care of some business to decrease the danger of getting too excited during the date. I knew that there was pretty much zero chance of going all the way that night, but there was no harm in imagining it.

I got out of the shower and looked at myself in the mirror at the end of the hallway. I felt that I was a pretty handsome guy even if my opinion of it probably didn't count for anything. Luckily I'd never had any acne to speak of. Some guys had it so bad that it was disgusting even to look at them some days. I felt bad for guys like that because I couldn't imagine how they could ever get any girl to want to kiss them. Not that any girl had ever kissed me, but at least I figured it would possible for a girl to kiss me without being totally grossed-out.

I finished getting dressed and headed for the door. "Bye Mom" I said.

"Wait, let me get a look at you," Mom said. "So handsome! My baby is getting so grown-up!" I was so embarrassed! Luckily no one was around to hear that! "Have a nice time, and be sure to be back before midnight," she said.

"Thanks Mom, I will," I said, and I got in the car.

I drove to Andrea's house, and when I got there I went up to the door and rang the bell. Andrea answered the door herself. "Hi Jared," she said. She had her coat on already and was starting to walk out the door when a voice from inside the house said "Andrea, won't you invite your friend in for a moment?"

"Okay," she said. "Please come in." She went back inside the house. I followed her and closed the door behind myself. Andrea took off her coat, but she didn't hang it up or anything, she just held it. I did the same.

Andrea's dad walked up to me with a smile and held out his hand. "Hi, I'm Dan Sharp," he said, shaking my hand.

"It's nice to meet you, sir," I said, "I'm Jared Wendell."

"So what are your plans for this evening?" he asked.

"Well, I was thinking perhaps dinner and a movie."

"That sounds nice," he said. "Now Jared, you're LDS, right?"

"Yes, sir," I said. I figured there was no point splitting hairs on whether I really believed in it or not.

"Are you an Eagle Scout?"

"Yes, sir," I said.

"That's nice. Wonderful."

Andrea was rolling her eyes.

"Now you two kids have a nice time and try to be home before eleven," he said.

"Okay, Dad," said Andrea, and we went out and got in the car.

"Are you okay with just going to a diner?" I asked her.

"Yeah, that would be fine," said Andrea.

Of course I would have liked to be able to take her to a nice restaurant, but I couldn't really afford it on my allowance, and my dad didn't want me getting an after-school job because he was afraid it might keep me from doing my homework.

"What's with your dad, asking me if I was an Eagle Scout like that?" I asked.

"Oh, he's really pleased to see me going on a date with a good Mormon boy. He had just gotten done telling my mom that this was the whole reason we moved out here and that it was going well."

"Your family moved here so that you would date Mormon boys?"

"Essentially. When I told my parents I didn't believe in God and didn't want to go to church anymore, Dad completely flipped out. He blamed it on the kids at school being a bad influence on me. But apparently he's not opposed to peer pressure *per se* as long as it works in a good direction and not a bad direction. He said that if I'd grown up in Utah like he did this never would have happened since I'd be surrounded by good Mormon kids who would teach me that it's cool to go to church instead of being rebellious. Same for my younger brother and sister—he wanted to be sure to get them into a good environment before the same thing happened to them. So Mom and Dad both quit their jobs in New Jersey and found new jobs in Utah. Naturally Dad is hugely proud of himself seeing me go on a date with an Eagle Scout. Back at my old high school in Princeton I doubt that there was a single Eagle Scout in the whole school."

"I didn't really want to go for Eagle Scout, actually. It was my mom that wanted me to do it. So I guess we both have to deal with parents who want to ruin our lives and make us Mormon."

Andrea smiled at that.

When we got to the restaurant, we took a booth and ordered some hamburgers.

"You know, that's interesting that you're from New Jersey," I said. "My brother lives there. He's in grad school at Rutgers."

"Ah, that's not far from where I used to live, but I didn't go there often."

"So do you like it here in Orem?" I asked her.

"No, not at all," she said.

"Were you sad to leave New Jersey?" I asked.

"Of course I was sad to leave New Jersey! And it pisses me off all the more to know that my dad moved us here for the sole and express purpose of taking me away from my friends and ruining my life!"

"That's too bad that your dad made you leave your friends and everything. But Orem's not so bad when you give it a chance."

"Are you kidding? It's horrible! It's completely intolerable! I feel like I'm drowning in Mormon shit twenty-four-seven! Back in Princeton there wasn't a single other Mormon kid in my whole school. A lot of kids hadn't even heard of Mormonism or had heard of it only vaguely like you hear about the Amish or something.

"What's more, there were all different types of people there. Not far from where I lived there was a black neighborhood and a Hispanic neighborhood. Of course there were plenty of Jewish people there too, and in fact there were a lot of foreigners from all different countries attracted by the University. Here everyone is the same. Everyone has exactly the same background."

"Well, except Joe," I said.

"Yeah, there's that," she said.

"Even if the people aren't so interesting, at least there's the Provo River," I said.

"Yeah, it's okay," she said, "but in Princeton we had these wonderful canals. The Provo river can't compare. All along the canal there was this grassy, marshy region filled with frogs and turtles."

"Snakes too, I imagine!" I said.

"Some, but not too many," she said. "There were so many types of animals, it was amazing! Woodchucks, chipmunks, deer, rabbits, geese, ducks, swans, all types of birds of all colors, butterflies, and obviously squirrels. You could barely walk across the yard without tripping over a squirrel. They had these all-black ones there that I've learned are actually kind of unusual. One time I saw a baby opossum on the university campus! That was cool because you don't usually see them except dead on the road because they're nocturnal. Same with raccoons. But my favorites were always the frogs. During the Summer I used to go to the canal every single day and look at the frogs. It was best in the early Spring when there wasn't much vegetation yet." She looked wistful, as if imagining it.

"Ah, yeah, some of the guys used to like to catch frogs at scout camp," I said. I didn't mention the fact that I never really got into it since I always thought they were kind of gross.

"Oh, you really shouldn't catch them," said Andrea. "Amphibians are very fragile, and many of them are in danger worldwide. It's fun enough just observe them."

"Well, that was back when we were just kids and didn't know any better," I said. I figured I'd better not add the part about how one of the guys used to think it was funny to light firecrackers in the frogs' mouths. Really, I couldn't see how it would be at all interesting to go look at frogs, but it was cute and kind of exotic that she would have such an unusual hobby. "Anyway, I just mean there are animals around here too."

"I know there are animals here," she said, "and I'm starting to get to know them. But it's not like home."

I noticed her eating her hamburger and said "Even though you're an animal lover, I see you're not a vegetarian."

"Oh, I know," she said. "I'm really trying to become a vegetarian, but I can't because I'm just too damn lazy!" she laughed. "The thing is that I really hate preparing my own food, and sometimes it's hard to find a vegetarian alternative. Especially here in Utah. Back in New Jersey I was much better about it. Of course I never gave up fish or sea food."

"Why not?" I asked.

"From a health perspective fish and seafood are good for you. And from a moral perspective, to me a lobster is essentially just a gigantic bug. I just can't see killing arthropods and mollusks as being equivalent to killing mammals or birds."

"What about the fish?" I asked.

"Well of course then there's always the question of precisely where to draw the line. When I drew my line I was probably biased in the wrong direction by the fact that I love sushi!" She laughed.

"So you think that it's wrong to eat a pig and not to eat a fish?" I asked.

"Essentially," she said. "The thing is that when you step back there's really no canonical purpose to life and no moral reason for anything in the universe to exist or not. Nothing really matters in a universal, objective sense. Right and wrong are human concepts and they only have meaning in terms of the way humans perceive the universe. Therefore it's reasonable for me to define right and wrong in terms of my own human experience. So naturally I see killing a pig as wrong because it is a thinking, feeling creature I can empathize with. Swatting a mosquito, for example, registers zero for me on the empathy scale. Anyway, maybe I'm wrong, but that's the way I see it."

It seemed like she was probably right, but I wasn't sure I really understood what she was talking about. "You should study philosophy!" I said.

"Nah, I hate philosophy," she said. "Too boring! Whenever I try to read philosophy people start deconstructing things and my eyes start to glaze over. Maybe I'm a simple person, but I have to see the world in concrete, practical terms. That's just the way I am."

I never expected to hear Andrea saying that some subject was too boring or difficult for her to follow! Another something I could relate to her on! I smiled at her and reached across the table to touch her hand briefly. She smiled shyly back and looked away. She was so pretty!

"So what movie do you want to see?" I asked.

"I don't know. I don't like to go see movies in the movie theater because they're too expensive. Even if I have the money for it, I don't like to pay for extravagances that cost a lot more than they're worth. Is that weird?"

"I was going to pay," I said.

"On principle," she said, "Even if it's someone else paying."

"We could go to the dollar theater," I said. That was what I was kind of hoping to do anyway.

"I don't feel like going to an ordinary movie tonight. I'm kind of in the mood for a really old movie or maybe something foreign."

I wasn't too thrilled about that idea. I thought about some of the weird films they sometimes made us watch in French class. But I guessed that I could sit through one of them for Andrea.

"We could go to the BYU International Theater," I said. "They show foreign films."

"Oh, do you know what's playing?" she asked.

"No," I said. As if I would just happen to know what was playing at the BYU International Theater!

"Let's just rent a movie and watch it at my house," she said.

"Okay," I said.

So we went to a movie rental place and she went straight for the foreign films.

The first one she picked up was called *Women on the Verge of a Nervous Breakdown*. "I love this one!" she said.

That didn't sound too promising. It sounded like a chick-flic. Reading my expression, she put it down and grabbed another one.

"Oh, this one is really good!" she said. The film was called *The Wedding Banquet*. That sounded worse than the first one!

She put it down and picked up another one. It was called *La Cage aux Folles*. Oh, no, something French!

"Well, let's take a look at the classics," she said, putting the film down. "Oh this one is perfect! You'll love it!" she said, picking up *Harold and Maude*. I had never seen that one, but I remembered my

sister Joy once telling me it was good. Not that I usually put much stock in Joy's movie tips, but it seemed like it was the most promising choice so far, so I said okay.

"All the music is this great stuff by Cat Stevens," she said. "He's one of my favorite singers." So we rented the movie and went back to Andrea's house.

We set up the movie and sat down on the couch in the family room. Andrea's little brother and sister wanted to watch it with us, but Andrea's mom cleared them out of the room and told them to leave us alone.

I started wishing we had gone to a movie theater instead of Andrea's house after all. It hit me that if I managed to get up the courage to try to put my arm around her or something, I certainly couldn't do it there where someone from her family might come in at any moment! Sure enough Andrea's mom came by to bring us some chips just as the movie was starting.

It was okay actually since it kind of took the pressure off. I would have been too shy to try anything anyway, and this way I wouldn't end up spending the entire movie worrying about it. Maybe on our next date, I thought. The best I could do was to try to sit close enough to her that my leg was kind of touching her leg.

It turned out that the movie was really cool. I could see why Andrea would like it. The woman in it, Maude, was really eccentric and was always doing unusual and unexpected things. She was just like Andrea except that she was an old lady and not a cute girl. I figured I was kind of like Harold for wanting to go on her adventures with her and for falling in love with her.

Also she was right that the music was great!

When the movie was over, she showed me to the door. Again there was no question of trying anything with her family in the house. I was kind of disappointed by that because I wanted to kiss her so badly that I thought I might have been able to get up the courage to try, but not with her mom and dad in the next room!

"I had a great time, Jared," she said, and she squeezed my hand.

"Me too," I said. I didn't want to leave, but I figured I had to.

Driving home I was on cloud nine. I was so in love with her, and I was sure she liked me too. I figured it was only a matter of time before she was in my arms.

As soon as I got back into my own room I started to imagine all of the things I wanted to do but was too shy to try. I imagined holding her in my arms and kissing her. I imagined taking off her shirt and touching her breasts. I couldn't hold back. I imagined making love to her. Ah, it would be so beautiful if only it were true! I slept well that night and had plenty of pleasant dreams.

34. SATURDAY

THE NEXT MORNING I called up Joe and Sam to ask them if they wanted to go to the mall. Mostly I wanted to get myself a Cat Stevens album after the movie I'd watched with Andrea the night before. It turned out that Sam didn't have to go to football practice that day so they were both available. I swung by their house to pick them up and we went to the mall.

When we got to the mall, my first stop was the record store. I picked out a compilation that had on it most of the songs that I remembered from the movie.

As I was buying it, Joe asked, "Why the sudden interest in Cat Stevens?" I didn't want to tell him the truth because I didn't want to tell him I'd been on a date with Andrea. In case he liked her too, as I suspected. So I made something up.

"Joy recommended it," I said.

Sam laughed. "Since when do you listen to Joy?"

"Well, it wasn't so much that she recommended it as that she has a Cat Stevens album that she likes to play all the time, and after hearing her play it I decided I wanted one too."

"Isn't Joy off at college?" asked Joe.

"Well, yeah," I said. "I mean, she was playing it during the Summer. I just remembered now, though."

"Oh, okay," said Joe. That was a close one!

"Let's go have lunch," said Sam, "my treat!"

We started walking toward the food court. "What's the occasion?" I asked Sam.

"I'm trying to get on Joe's good side," said Sam, laughing. "He just started a new job. He's been out working all evening for the past few days. Doing so many hours like that, come payday he's gonna be in the money!"

"You're working after school?" I asked Joe.

"Yep," he said.

"When do you find time to do your homework?" I asked.

"Weekends," said Joe. "Sometimes at night." That was really unlike Joe to put money ahead of schoolwork like that. Even if he was doing it to save up for college, it still didn't seem like a good idea since it could hurt his grades.

After lunch Sam wanted to play the paper airplane game. Joe had once read a book on how to make all different types of paper airplanes, and he showed us how to make some of them. We climbed onto a high wall overlooking a parking lot not far from the mall, and the game was to throw the paper airplanes and see who could get theirs to go the farthest. I'd taken to emptying our paper recycling bin at home into the trunk of my car so that I'd always have a stack of paper on hand in case we wanted to play this game.

Sam especially loved the paper airplane game. He always won, of course. It wasn't that he was any better than us at folding the planes—we were all about the same at that—but he was a real natural at throwing them just right so that they would glide a long way. It was probably because of all the sports he played that he was good at doing that. Or maybe it was the opposite, and the reason he played sports was because he had a natural talent for that sort of thing.

Another thing that Sam liked to do when we were playing this game was to goof off and pretend that he was falling off the wall.

Actually it was kind of funny that Sam liked to hang out with Joe. Sam was a popular guy. Being on the football team, he had lots of jock friends, and of course he had plenty of pretty girls interested in him. You would normally expect a guy like Sam to just ignore Joe and pretend he didn't exist the way the rest of the Hobbs family did. But it seemed that Sam was just a genuinely nice guy.

After we'd spent a long time hanging out on the wall, Joe said that he really needed to get back and get started on his homework. So I dropped them off at their house, and then went home to listen to my new album.

On Monday at school Joe told me that he had a surprise he wanted to show me and that he'd show it to me if I gave him a ride home. After school, Joe met me out by my car. As soon as I arrived, he started getting into the car and said "Let's go."

"Shouldn't we wait for Sam?" I asked.

"Not today," said Joe. "We're not going back to the house."

He directed me to an unfamiliar part of town and had me stop in front of a kind of run-down looking house. We got out of the car and walked up to the house. Then instead of ringing the bell, Joe put a key in the keyhole and opened the door himself. I came in with him, and he led me upstairs to a grungy room with peeling wallpaper and stained carpeting.

"What do you think of my new home?" he asked.

"You're renting this whole house?"

"No, just this room. I share the kitchen and bathrooms with a bunch of college students attending UVCC. The living room too, actually, although I don't think I'll use it much. The other guys who live here are mostly returned-missionaries, wandering around the house in their garments. Yuck! I'll think I'll probably spend most of my time in my room."

"What happened?" I asked. "Why did you move out of the Hobbs' house?"

"What happened was that I did a lot of thinking about what Andrea said about how it wasn't very brave of me to keep the truth from my aunt and uncle."

"But that's not what she said," I told him. "And besides, she took it back and said you were right not to tell them."

"Yeah, but after thinking about it I realized she was right the first time. I don't need them and I don't need to cower and live a lie in order to have their help. I can rely on myself."

"Wow," I said. "So you're just going to live here by yourself now?"

"Yep."

"So that's why you got that new job!" I said.

"Exactly. My friend Tom's mom is a manager of a Mexican restaurant. I figured restaurant work would be a good choice for me because it's something that I can do in the evenings after school. So I convinced Tom's mom to give me a job. I'm not sure it's one hundred percent legal given my age, but she gave me the job anyway because she sympathized with my situation. It's mostly cleaning up, but there's some simple cooking and prep. Distasteful grunt work really, but it'll pay the rent," he said.

"But how will you do your homework if you have to work all evening?"

"I've already talked to some of my teachers about it. I explained that I might not be able to turn in all of my assignments on time during the week, but that I would do my best to catch up on weekends. They were pretty sympathetic because they know I'm a good student."

"So you just left Sam's house just like that? Sam's dad didn't throw you out or anything?"

"Well, it was a little of both, actually," he said. "Before I confronted my uncle I warned Sam that I would probably have to leave. Sam didn't understand, of course. Then when I was ready I walked right up to my uncle and told him I didn't believe in God. He was pretty surprised because normally I don't talk to him at all if I can avoid it. And then to say something like that that didn't even register in his universe confused him. So in order to be sure he understood, I told him that the *Book of Mormon* is obviously a work of fiction and a pointless one to boot."

"Wow! What'd he say to that?"

"Well, as you can imagine that got a rise out of him. He called me an ungrateful leech, and then he told me that he had always known I'd grow up to be a worthless loony just like my father."

"Oh man, that's terrible!" I said.

"Yeah, but it was about what I expected him to say, so I was ready for it. I'd already brought all of my things here, so I just calmly thanked him for his hospitality and walked out."

"So that's it? You're on your own now?"

"Yep. Now I'm working on getting myself legally emancipated. A bunch of paperwork is just what I need right now on top of my schoolwork and my work work, but being emancipated will help me

get financial aid for college. It's better in the long run because it's not as if my uncle or my dad were ever going to give me one red cent for college."

"Wow," I said, not really knowing what else to say.

"Well, anyway, I have to be getting to work now. Maybe you can come over again sometime," he said.

"Okay," I said. "Do you want me to give you a ride to work?"

"No, it's not far from here, I can walk. But thanks anyway."

"Okay, well, I guess I'll see you tomorrow," I said, and I went home.

The next day Joe and I got something of a pleasant surprise near the end of the lunch period. Andrea came over to talk to us. For the main part of lunch she normally sat with the other girls, but since she was done she stopped by.

"Joe, Jared," she said sitting down at our table, "I just wanted to tell you guys that we're having a party next week at Tanya's house on Wednesday night."

"The night before Thanksgiving?" I asked.

"Exactly," she said. "Her parents are going out of town. They're not religious, so since they both have a long weekend they just see it as an opportunity for a trip to Vegas, and they're leaving Tanya all by herself. They've specifically instructed her not to throw any parties while they're gone, so we have to be careful not to trash the place."

"Wow, sounds like a lot of fun," said Joe.

"Yeah, it's going to be great," said Andrea. Then to Joe she added, "Actually, in theory though I shouldn't be inviting you."

"Why not?" asked Joe.

"My dad told me he didn't want me hanging around with you because of your background. I had just mentioned it as a curiosity, but he seemed to think that it was a way bigger deal than I thought he would. Even though I explained to him that you had actively left that religion and wanted nothing to do with it, it seemed to make you somehow tainted in his eyes. He told me not to associate with you anymore."

"So are you planning to avoid me?" asked Joe.

"What? Are you kidding? He was just being ridiculous, and I told him so! As soon as he said that I said, 'Screw you, Dad, I'll be friends with whomever I please!'"

"You said 'screw you' to your own father?" I asked, astonished.

"Well, no I didn't actually say that, but that's what I was thinking. Anyway, I hope you guys can both come to our party, we're going to have a great time!" Then she got up and left.

I noticed that Joe was watching her as she walked away and didn't stop looking at her until she had left the cafeteria. It kind of annoyed me to think that he might be interested in her. There were so many girls in the school, I figured he could just find a different one and leave Andrea to me.

Once Andrea was gone, Joe turned to me and asked, "What were we talking about?" I guessed that by going back to our earlier conversation he was just trying to pretend that getting invited to a party by Andrea was no big deal. I played along.

"You were asking me what I was thinking I might major in when I got to college," I said.

"Oh, yeah," he said. "So have you decided?"

"Well, definitely not French," I said. "I kind of like my History class. Actually, I think it will probably be Computer Science." I had done some programming on my computer at home, and I felt like that was where I showed the most promise. "What about you?"

"I was thinking possibly Mathematics," he said. "Physics might be interesting too, though. I'll have to see how I like it when we take our Physics class next year. I like Literature, but I can't see pursuing it as a major course of study. On the other hand, maybe Philosophy. I've read some of that lately, and it seems kind of interesting."

Ha! Little did he know that Andrea hated Philosophy! I figured I was one up on him there since he liked it.

When lunch was over, I started thinking about the party and how much fun it would be. The cool thing was that I had just been wondering how I was going to get up the courage to ask Andrea out on a second date, and now I didn't have to worry about it anymore since she had come and invited me to a party instead!

It was kind of too bad that it was going to be at Tanya's house, though, of all people, but it would probably be okay. I was starting to warm back up to Tanya a little. She seemed to be making a special effort to be nice lately and not to go out of her way to make me feel like an idiot if she knew something I didn't. So I went back to letting her help me in French class on the condition that she would try to help me learn to do it and not just tell me the answers.

I spent most of the rest of the week listening to my Cat Stevens album and thinking about the party. I only saw Andrea a few times in the halls, but she always smiled and said hi every time I saw her. Other than that, nothing of note happened all week except at our Math class on Friday.

Sam and Joe and I were in our Math class as usual, and it was the part of the period when we were supposed to be silently working on our assignments and the teacher would come around and collect our homework from the previous day and give us some individual help if we needed it.

The teacher came around and took my assignment and Joe's and then stopped at Sam's desk. "Sam, where's your assignment?" he asked. He asked quietly, but Joe and I could both hear him.

"I didn't get it finished," said Sam.

"What's wrong, Sam?" asked the teacher. "You're a pretty good student. But you haven't turned in an assignment in over a week."

"I'm sorry, I don't know," said Sam, looking the other way.

Poor Sam! He couldn't do a single assignment without Joe there to help him. He probably wasn't even motivated to open his book without Joe's encouragement.

After class, Joe caught up with Sam just outside the classroom door.

"Sam, I'm really sorry I can't be there to help you with your homework anymore," he said.

"That's okay," said Sam. He didn't look at Joe when he said it. "I'm probably just going to drop out of this class anyway. My dad says I shouldn't have taken this advanced math class in the first place since all the homework cuts into my football practice." Then he turned and walked away.

Joe looked sad to see him go. They'd had so much fun together in the past year or so, but they were so different! They probably wouldn't be able to stay good friends.

That was the last time I saw Sam in that class. By Monday he had already dropped out and switched to a study hall. I didn't think that people could normally just drop out of a class like that in high school, but it was somehow arranged. It made sense though because it was pretty clear that there was no way that Sam was going to pass that class without private tutoring. And it certainly wouldn't occur to Brother Hobbs to waste good money on helping Sam learn math!

I was happy that we were having a short week that week. That meant I only had to survive through Monday and Tuesday before the day of the big party.

O N WEDNESDAY ALL of our family was arriving for Thanksgiving. We didn't normally all get together for Thanksgiving, but after the fight that Mom and Dad had had with Rex when he was visiting over the Summer, they decided that they wanted to try to make a special effort to get the whole family back together and talking again.

Jill and Joy were both attending Caltech, and would be arriving together during the day on Wednesday. Kathy and her husband Bob and their kids had already arrived the day before, but they were staying with Bob's family in Provo. Bob was an only child for some reason even though he was raised Mormon, so his family agreed to have their big family dinner on the day after Thanksgiving so that Bob and Kathy could have Thanksgiving dinner at our house.

Rex and Lynn were coming in on a late-afternoon flight and wouldn't be arriving at the house until after the time I had planned to be at the party, so I knew I wouldn't see them until the next day. This time they agreed to stay at the house with the family. It turned out that the reason they had stayed in a hotel the last time they had visited here was that Mom and Dad had insisted that if they stayed in the house they'd have to have separate bedrooms. Rex wasn't happy about that because he felt like that sort of thing was none of Mom and Dad's business.

This time Mom and Dad agreed to let them share a room. It was kind of a compromise really because now Rex and Lynn were officially engaged. So Mom and Dad could say that they weren't okay with them sharing a room when they were *just* living together, but that it was okay now that they were *engaged*.

My school day passed uneventfully enough right up until Math class, which was my second-to-last class of the day. I was really excited about the party, and I knew Joe would be too. When I came into the classroom and saw him though he seemed upset.

"Is something wrong?" I asked him.

"Yeah, I just got some bad news," he said.

"What happened?"

"I just got off the phone with Tom's mother, my boss. Tom had told me I needed to call her urgently. It turns out that the person who was going to cover for me at work tonight suddenly took sick and so did the one other person who was on for tonight's shift. Every single other kitchen grunt is out of town because of Thanksgiving. So I can't go to the party, I have to work."

"Wow, that's harsh!" I said.

"I know. I'm so disappointed! It was the only fun thing I had planned for this whole holiday weekend. I tried to convince my boss to let me get out of it, but she said that she absolutely needs me tonight, and if she can't count on me, she'd have no choice but to replace me with a college student she can rely on. Obviously I need this job, so there's nothing I can do."

"That's too bad," I said.

"Can you give them my regrets when you get there, and tell them what happened?" he asked.

"Okay, no problem," I said.

I felt like an evil person for it, but I was secretly almost kind of glad that Joe wouldn't be at the party. Of course I wanted to get together with Andrea at the party myself, and it would just be that much easier if I didn't have a rival to deal with. I didn't want my friendship with Joe to be ruined by competition over a girl, but at the same time I couldn't bring myself to just step aside and leave her to him. I was in love with her!

When I got home from school, Jill and Joy had already arrived. I had to endure some pretty serious teasing from them when Mom told them that I was going to a party at a girl's house. I had told Mom and Dad about the party, but of course I didn't tell them that it was at a house where the parents were out-of-town! They would never have guessed it since to a Mormon with a big family it would be completely crazy for the parents to go out of town and leave their kid all alone on Thanksgiving weekend!

While getting ready for the party, I debated whether I should bring a condom or not. On the one hand, I figured that it was such a long shot that there was really no point in bothering to bring one. On the other hand, if by some miracle things started going my way, it would be terrible not to be prepared! Still, I worried that by bringing one I might jinx it, like how the one day you bring your umbrella is the one day it doesn't rain. In the end, though, I decided there was no harm in putting one in my wallet just in case.

As I set off for the party, Mom told me as usual to have fun and to be home by midnight.

When I got to the party, I saw Andrea and Tanya and also their friend Kim who I didn't really know all that well. Actually, looking around I realized that I didn't know most of the kids there all that well. A lot of them were kind of stoners who liked to cut class to go somewhere and smoke. I had nothing against them, but they didn't usually spend a lot of time hanging out with clean-cut Eagle Scout Mormon boys like me.

It looked like it was going to be a pretty serious party. There was a big washtub filled with ice and beers. The kitchen table was covered with bottles of all different kinds of alcohol. I was a little worried about that because I had driven to the party in my car, and I didn't want to do a lot of drinking if I would have to be driving home at midnight.

Of course I should have realized that this would be a drinking party! I'd never been to one before, though, so I didn't think of it. The only time I'd ever tried any alcohol at all was that time over the Summer when Rex bought us some beer, and that time I had only drank one. I wasn't sure what would happen if I tried drinking more than that. I decided to start with one beer and try to drink it slowly.

After grabbing a beer, I went over to talk to Andrea. She was gorgeous all done up for the party! She was wearing a nice blouse and a skirt, and she looked like she'd put on some make-up for the occasion, which she didn't normally do. She still wore her hair down and gleaming. She'd even taken off her glasses. I didn't know if she'd gotten contacts or if she just didn't care if she couldn't see or what.

"Hi, Andrea," I said. I said hi to Tanya too because she was standing next to Andrea.

Andrea said hi back, and Tanya got this exaggerated smile and grabbed me by the arm and said "Jared, I'm so glad you could make it!" It looked like she'd already started drinking. She was holding a glass of something that looked like coke, but there was probably something else in there too.

"Do you know what time Joe is coming?" asked Andrea.

"Oh, I almost forgot, I was supposed to tell you guys Joe can't make it tonight. He says he's sorry but at the last minute he couldn't get out of work."

"Oh, that's too bad," said Andrea. She looked really disappointed. That seemed like a step in the wrong direction from my perspective, but I figured that I was here and he wasn't so maybe I would still have the advantage.

"Is that all you're drinking?" asked Tanya, pointing at my beer.

"I thought I'd start with this, and maybe I'll drink something else after," I said.

"Well chug it and let's go do some tequila shots!" she said, and with that she drank the rest of what was in her glass in a single gulp. Sheesh! She was even more annoying drunk than sober.

"Not just yet," I said.

"Come on!" said Tanya. "You too!" she said to Andrea. "What kind of drinking is that? Do I need to start up a drinking game to motivate you guys to get into this?"

Andrea did as she was told and drank the rest of what was in her glass. It had been something red. If Andrea was going to drink like that, I decided I wanted to follow suit, so I drank the rest of my beer as quickly as possible. I didn't manage it in a single gulp, but I finished it up pretty fast.

"Good work! *Très bien* !" said Tanya. "You want another vodka-cranberry?" she asked Andrea.

"Okay," replied Andrea.

"Could I try one of those, too?" I asked.

"No!" said Tanya. "It's straight to tequila shots for you!"

Okay, whatever, I thought.

We followed Tanya to the table where she poured a vodka-cranberry for Andrea and then poured a shot of tequila for me and one for herself. There were some other kids around and she poured them some tequila shots too, even kids who were already holding other drinks!

"Down the hatch!" said Tanya, and she drank the shot of tequila in one gulp.

Andrea was watching me, so I drank my shot in one gulp too. Tanya immediately refilled her glass and mine.

"Um, I have to drive home later," I said.

"No you don't," said Tanya. "You can stay here as long as you want. All night, if necessary."

"But my mom told me to be home by midnight!"

"Do you always do everything your parents tell you to?" asked Tanya. "Come on, there's not going to be another party like this all

semester! If you're going to break some rules, now's the time to do it!"

I thought that Tanya was being awfully pushy, but maybe she had a point that it would be okay for me to break the rules a little bit just this once. I drank my second shot.

"That's the spirit!" she said.

Andrea walked away from the table and went off by herself. I followed her. Emboldened by the alcohol, I went to put my arm around her.

"Please don't, Jared," she said, pushing me away.

"What's wrong?" I asked. "I thought you liked me. Didn't you have fun on our date?"

She smiled. "Of course I had fun, but it's never going to happen between us. You should really just forget about me."

That was definitely not what I wanted to hear! I took her hands in my hands and said "But Andrea, you're so beautiful and you're so special to me. How can I help but want to be with you?"

She pulled her hands away. "I'm sorry, Jared, but it's just not going to work out."

Then Tanya came over to us. She had a foul expression on her face. "Who said you two could stop drinking?" she asked.

"Listen, Tanya, I'm not feeling well. I have to go home," said Andrea.

"Okay," said Tanya. As soon as Andrea was out of earshot she added "Don't let the door hit you on your way out." Then she turned to me. "Now where were we? Oh yeah, tequila shots!" She grabbed me by the arm and pulled me back to the table and poured me another shot. A bunch of other kids were standing around the table drinking tequila shots too.

I was so sad about what Andrea had said to me! I figured I might as well go with the flow and drown my sorrows. I let Tanya pour me some more shots. I couldn't tell how many.

After a number of them, I felt like I wanted to go sit down, so I went over and sat down on the couch. Tanya was right there following me.

"Had enough?" she asked.

"I think so," I said. "I think I just need to rest. I'm not used to all this drinking."

"Here, have some water," she said getting me a glass of water. I took it and drank it.

"Some people are watching TV downstairs. That would be a good place for you to rest. Let's go."

She took me by the hand and led me downstairs to the basement. It was dark except for the glow of the TV. They were watching some sort of Star Trek thing or something like that. I saw Kim sitting on the couch with a stoner guy from our school that I didn't know very well, and there was another guy sitting on the floor.

I sat down on the other couch and Tanya sat right next to me. She surprised me by cuddling up to me and putting her head on my shoulder. It felt kind of warm and nice actually. I thought maybe I'd misjudged her. She wasn't so bad. I put my arm around her.

Of course I wished it was Andrea instead. It made me sad to think that Andrea didn't want to be with me and maybe never would.

I was starting to feel a little buzzed from all the tequila. It gave me kind of a warm feeling like maybe things weren't as bad as they seemed. I tried to follow the television program, but I couldn't figure out what was going on. Even sober I never really understood Star Trek. All I ever got out of it was that there were all these women in

bizarre costumes and they all had big boobs. Why did they all have such big boobs?

I looked down at Tanya. She was wearing this low-cut blouse, and from my vantage point I could see right down her shirt. I looked over at the other couch. Kim and her stoner guy were pretty heavily making out. I didn't see the other guy anymore.

I looked back down at Tanya's chest. She rearranged her position so that she was sitting with her legs across my lap. I was starting to get a hard-on. I knew she could feel it against her leg, but she didn't show any reaction. Did she not notice? Was that possible? Did she not care?

I wondered what I could get away with. I started running my hand up under her shirt. Her only response was to cuddle up closer and put her hand on my chest. I started feeling her breast with my hand over her bra. She didn't try to stop me. It was kind of exciting. It made me want to go farther.

She was wearing a skirt which cast a shadow across her legs between her thighs. I put my hand on her inner thigh and started sliding it down until I touched her panties with the tip of my finger. I could hardly believe this was happening. It was unreal. I'd never experienced anything like it. I kissed her. I did it mostly because it seemed crazy to me to get to third base and beyond without passing first. I'd never imagined that my first kiss would be quite like this.

I started trying to move her panties to the side with my fingers to feel what was underneath. Then what happened next was kind of a blur because she took the lead. The next thing I knew she was on her back with her panties off and I was on top of her with my pants open. The other people were gone. Where did they go? And when?

Tanya got out a condom and took care of putting it in place and everything. Then she took off her bra and opened her blouse. I couldn't believe my eyes! Real live breasts right there in front of me— not just a picture! All I could think about was how much I wanted to touch and feel them.

I couldn't think straight. I was dying to slide it in. She guided me with her hand. I was suddenly overcome with a wave of the most intense pleasure I could possibly imagine. It was unbelievable! It only took a few moments. It was over almost as quickly as it had begun.

Tanya held onto the base of the condom as I pulled out, and then she slid it off and tied the end. So all of my efforts to learn to do that were wasted since I didn't have to do it myself after all.

There were some Kleenexes handy on the table, so I wiped up and closed up. I felt so sleepy. I just wanted to lie down. Unfortunately the couch was too narrow for the both of us, so I lied down straight onto the floor.

The last thing I remembered as I was falling asleep was hearing her say "I love you, Jared."

36. FOUR A.M.

I WOKE UP ON the floor. I felt really thirsty and had to pee. The T.V. was still on but not making any noise. Someone must have muted it at some point. I stood up and looked at Tanya lying there asleep on the couch. I felt confused and wanted to go home.

I went upstairs to try to find the bathroom. I saw by the clock on the wall that it was four in the morning. I was supposed to be home by midnight! I figured I was in big trouble.

I found the bathroom and turned on the light. Kim was lying there passed-out on the floor. There was vomit everywhere. The whole bathroom reeked of it. The smell of it made me a little queasy, but it also made me notice that I didn't really feel sick myself. No headache, no nausea. I didn't feel drunk anymore either. I figured I must not have drank as much as I'd thought I had.

I wasn't sure what to do about going to the bathroom. I really had to pee, and I didn't know where to find another bathroom in the house. I wondered if maybe I should just do it with Kim there on the floor. She was unconscious so she wouldn't know the difference. In the end I decided to pick her up and carry her into the living room and lay her down on the couch. Fortunately she was pretty light. I wasn't sure that that was the best thing to do—in case she had to throw up again—but I figured at least she'd be more comfortable there.

I went back and went to the bathroom and then drank about five or six glasses of water.

All I could think about was how I had to get home. I figured I was okay to drive since I really didn't feel drunk or buzzed at all anymore.

In the car on the way home I started thinking about what I'd done. I couldn't figure out if it was good or bad. It was maybe a little of both. I was happy to finally have some experience—and what an incredible experience it was! But then I thought that there might be some consequences. I wondered if maybe I shouldn't have done that, but it seemed like it would have taken an awful lot of will-power not to.

I started really hoping that I wasn't wrong about God not existing and all because I would hate to imagine what the big guy would have to say about this.

When I got home, I unlocked the door as quietly as possible. I went straight to my room and slipped into bed without making a sound.

In the morning, I got up and went to the bathroom and got dressed. The door to Kathy's old room was open, and I could hear that there was someone inside. I looked in and saw that it was Rex. He was alone and already dressed, arranging some things in his suitcase.

"Rex, I'm so glad to see you again!" I said, running up to give him a hug.

He was a little surprised, but said "I'm glad to see you, too, kiddo."

"Rex, I really need to talk to you about something," I said, taking a seat on the bed.

"Well that was fast!" he said. "I just got here and already you need to talk to me. Won't you have a seat?" he said jokingly, and he sat down next to me. "What's up?" he asked.

"Something happened last night, and I'm afraid I may have done the wrong thing."

"What happened?"

"Well, you see, there's this girl I really like," I began.

Rex chuckled. "Why do these stories always begin this way?" he asked, knowingly. "Sorry to interrupt. Go on."

"Well, this girl and her friend were having a party at her friend's house because her friend's parents were out of town. I was really looking forward to it because I figured that I could get together with the girl I liked. Anyway, what happened was that right at the beginning of the party the cute girl told me that it wasn't going to work out between us and that she wasn't going to ever be with me. But she didn't tell me why. Then she just up and left. I didn't know most of the other people at the party very well, but they offered me some beer and then a bunch of tequila shots, and I didn't feel like turning them down."

"Seems reasonable," said Rex.

"So anyway, I got a little drunk. The friend of the girl I like was encouraging me to drink. She's not very cute and normally I don't like her very much, but, well, you know, with all that alcohol and all, well..."

"What?"

"Well, I kind of had sex with her."

Rex laughed. "Put on the old beer goggles, eh? It happens to the best of us," he said putting a hand on my shoulder. "Some of them are so much cuter after a few drinks, aren't they? So what's the problem?"

"Well I'm afraid that maybe this girl is in love with me. The friend, that is, not the cute one."

"Oh, I get it," said Rex. "So you're worried that maybe the girl you like just agreed to step aside and leave you to her friend since her friend is hot for you. And now that you've done her, the cute girl will think it's a done deal and you have no further shot with her."

"No, I didn't even think of that!" I said. "Do you think that maybe she would have wanted to be with me if she weren't leaving me to her friend? And now I've screwed it up completely?"

"I don't know," he said. "I don't know these girls. Look, I'm not really an expert on relationships. Maybe we should get Lynn in here and see if she has any advice for you."

"Okay, if you think that's a good idea."

He stepped out the door and called down the stairs. "Lynn!" he said. "Lynn can you come up here?" Then he sat back down on the bed.

Lynn came up the stairs and took a seat at the desk. "Hi Jared," she said. Turning to Rex she asked "What's up?"

"My little brother has a romantic problem that he needs some help on."

"What is it?" she asked me.

I was too embarrassed to begin, so Rex told the story. "He has a girl he really likes, but she rejected him. So naturally, being a straight male, he did the obvious thing and got really drunk and had sex with her friend. Now he's wondering if maybe that was a mistake."

"Did you use protection?" asked Lynn.

"Of course!" I said. "Actually, the girl had a condom, and she took care of everything. She kind of led the way. I hardly knew what I was doing!" I hated to spell it out that it was my first time, but I thought maybe I would look like less of a jerk if I admitted how innocent I was about such things.

"So now he's worried that the girl he screwed is in love with him, and that maybe the cute one only stepped aside to give her friend a crack at him."

"While having sex, did you tell the girl you loved her or make her any promises?" asked Lynn.

"No," I said. "Come to think of it, I don't think I said anything at all the whole time."

"What makes you think she's in love with you then?" she asked.

"When it was all over, just as I was falling asleep, she whispered in my ear 'I love you, Jared.'"

Rex gave a sympathetic smile. "Poor Jared! I hate it when that happens!" Lynn gave him a look. "Kidding!" he said. "That has never happened to me, I swear."

"Hmmm," said Lynn, thinking it over. "Well first of all, I think it's unlikely that the girl you like was interested and just stepped aside for her friend's sake. I mean, that's theoretically possible, but I don't think that such a thing is part of a typical girl's code of honor. Sorry, but I would guess that she's probably just not interested."

It hurt to hear that, but she was probably right. Lynn continued. "Second, I would guess your little tryst meant a lot more to that girl than it did to you. Still, it sounds like she knew what she was doing, and you didn't actively take advantage of her. She'll be heartbroken, but—not to be callous or anything—she'll get over it. You pretty much profess your love to a passed-out drunk person at your own risk. I wouldn't recommend going out of your way to do this sort of thing in the future, but you probably shouldn't feel too bad about it this one time."

"See? I told you she's the one to go to about relationships!" said Rex.

"So, what did you say to her after?" asked Lynn.

"After what?" I asked.

"You know, like the next day," she said.

I was a little surprised. "The next day is today!" I said. "This just happened!"

"So you just slipped out during the night?" she asked.

"I had to!" I said. "I was supposed to be home by midnight! I missed curfew by like four hours! I hope I'm not in trouble!"

"Of course, I wasn't thinking," she said. "I forgot you're just a kid. I don't think you have anything to worry about as far as your curfew is concerned. I was just downstairs with your mom, and she didn't seem at all upset of preoccupied or anything like that. I think with all of the people over and the Thanksgiving plans, she probably didn't notice."

"Oh good, I lucked out then!" I said sliding off the bed and sprinting out the door of the bedroom.

"Glad we could be of help!" Rex called after me.

I went back into my own room and sat on the bed to think about what Lynn had said. I wondered if maybe she was right that Andrea just wasn't interested in me. I didn't want to believe it. I didn't want to give up hope. I was in love with her.

The phone rang. I immediately thought it might be Andrea. I got up to answer it, but Joy answered it first in the next room. She then peeked her head out the door and said "Jared, it's for you. It's a girl."

I was sure she had said it loudly enough for the person on the phone to hear. Ah, the pleasure of having the whole family home for Thanksgiving, including older sisters whose goal in life seemed to be to embarrass me. Even so, I was happy to hear that it was a girl.

"I'll take it in here," I said, and I closed my door. I picked up the phone and said hello. I heard the click of Joy hanging up.

"Hello, Jared," said a voice. It was Tanya. No luck.

"Hi Tanya, what's up?" I asked.

"What do you mean 'what's up'? You say that as if nothing had happened."

"Well, what do you want me to say?" I asked.

"Listen, I just called because you know my parents are still out of town, and I was wondering if you wanted to come over again."

"I don't know," I said. "It's Thanksgiving. I'm supposed to stay here with my family."

"Well why don't you come over later tonight when all of the festivities are over?"

"I'm not sure that I should," I said. "You're just going to try to seduce me again."

"What?" she asked. "Are you saying you didn't like it?"

I didn't have a good response to that.

"Look, if you have a problem with what happened last night, then you should come over and talk to me about it," she said.

"I don't know," I said.

"What kind of a person are you?" she asked. "So you're willing to sleep with me but you can't be bothered to waste a few minutes of your precious time on a conversation with me?"

I felt like kind of a jerk for treating her like that. "Okay, I'll come over later tonight, around nine," I said.

"Okay, see you then," she said. "Bye."

"Bye," I said, and I hung up the phone.

I thought that maybe going downstairs to help my mom prepare Thanksgiving dinner might help me take my mind off my troubles. I went downstairs and asked Mom if there was anything I could do to help.

"Oh, thank you Jared, You're such a good boy," she said. So that settled it. She hadn't noticed that I'd missed curfew by four hours.

Mom didn't really care for everyday cooking, but she seemed to like throwing herself into the all-out preparations for a special feast. So I acted as her *"sous-chef"* (Ha! I knew a French word!) stirring or chopping or whatevering anything she asked me to. It was fun, and I was right that it was a good way for me to distract myself from my problems.

While we were still working on dinner, Kathy and her husband Bob arrived with my little nephew Hyrum and baby Kira. Mom was all excited to see them and to play with her grandchildren.

Soon it was time for me to start setting the table. Jill and Joy came down to help. We had to set nine places plus a high chair for little Hyrum, so that meant putting all three leaves in the table in the formal dining room and getting some extra chairs from some other rooms in the house. Then we put on the tablecloth and set the table.

Once everything was ready, we gathered everyone up and we all sat at the table. Since it was a special occasion, Dad said the prayer himself, and it was a really long one full of all sorts of things we were thankful for. It was true that it really made me appreciate the food more having to sit there hungry and smelling it and not being able to eat it for such a long time.

After what seemed like hours, Dad finally said "In the name of Thy son Jesus Christ, Amen," and we could all dig in. We started passing the various dishes around the table and eating.

Rex turned to me. "So what are your friends Sam and Joe up to?"

"Oh, there's big news on that front! Brother Hobbs finally kicked Joe out of the house like we always knew he would. Now Joe is living in a house with a bunch of students and working in a restaurant in the evenings to support himself."

"Why did Brother Hobbs throw him out?" asked Lynn.

"It turns out Joe didn't believe in God," I said.

"And the Hobbs' don't countenance that sort of thing in their house?" asked Rex. "Wow, it's lucky for me that our parents are a little more lenient!"

"Lucky for me, too," said Jill. "I don't believe in God either."

"Me neither!" I said.

Mom looked like she was about to have a heart attack. "What? When did this happen?" she asked.

"Come on, Mom," said Jill. "You and Dad raised us to care about Math and Science and logic, etc. So how can you expect us to believe in this nonsense? We've been pretending for a while to spare your feelings because of how hard you took it when Rex left the church, but I'm starting to think it's better that you know."

"You too, Joy?" asked Dad. Joy nodded. "Well this is lovely news to spring on us right in the middle of Thanksgiving dinner when we're supposed to be thanking the Lord for our many blessings."

"Sorry, Dad, but there's nothing we can do about it," said Jill. "We'd all love for there to be a God and an afterlife and a purpose to life and all that, but you know, if wishes were fishes..."

"I don't believe this!" said Mom. "How did this happen? Do none of my children believe in the church anymore?"

"We still believe," said Kathy, putting her hand on her husband's hand.

That seemed to reassure Mom a little bit, but she still seemed pretty upset.

Then nobody said anything for a long time. After a while, Rex turned to me and asked "What about Sam? How's he taking Joe's departure?"

"I don't know, I haven't seen him much lately," I said.

"Isn't he in your math class?" asked Dad.

"He was but he dropped out. He said his dad told him to because the homework was interfering with his football practice. But I think it was also that he was having trouble doing the assignments without Joe's help."

"What?" asked Dad. "His father advised him to drop out of College Algebra and Trig so that he would have more time to play football? What kind of warped value system is that?"

"Well, at least all of their kids are still faithful in the church!" said Mom.

"Yeah, that's probably not a coincidence, actually," said Rex.

"Mom, I don't see why you think the Hobbs are this perfect family just because all of their kids went on missions," said Jill. "Every family has its problems—they're probably just better than most at keeping up appearances."

"Yeah," said Rex. "I mean, if Brother Hobbs is willing to throw his own nephew out on the street and leave him homeless just for believing differently, then that's not a very good sign in my book."

"That's not all!" I said. "It wasn't enough for him to just throw him out, he also called him a 'worthless loony'!"

"Just for not believing in God?" asked Dad.

"Yeah!" I said.

"Well how did Brother Hobbs find out anyway?" asked Lynn.

"Oh, Joe told him," I said.

"Why?" asked Lynn.

"He said he didn't want their help if he had to lie for it. He knew his uncle would throw him out for being an atheist, though, so he'd already lined up a job and a place to live before telling him."

"Wow, sounds like he's a pretty brave, resourceful kid!" said Jill.

"Well, it's not so surprising," said Rex. "We already knew he had set off on his own when he was only fifteen to escape that... well, you-know-what."

"That's awful that Brother Hobbs would do that to him," said Mom.

"See Mom? This is exactly what I was talking about," said Jill. "They're not perfect, you're not perfect, we're not perfect. I think you should just be happy with the kids you got. So we're not all Molly Mormon and Peter Priesthood." Kathy and Bob looked a little embarrassed at that.

"Anyway, we've got a lot of other good qualities," said Joy. "You should love us for who we are."

"Amen to that," said Rex.

"Well, I think it's going to take your mother and me some time to take all this in and adjust," said Dad. "But I guess you guys are the only kids we have, so we'll just have to get used to it and learn to love you anyway."

Mom looked like she wasn't entirely convinced, but she sighed and said "Of course you're right, dear."

Then Jill and Joy started telling us about all the classes they were taking that semester, and Mom went back to playing with my little nephew, and it seemed like everything was okay again.

In the evening, Rex and Lynn wanted to go visit Lynn's sister Annette and her husband Matt, who were living in an apartment in Provo. Matt was actually Sam's older brother, which was how I'd gotten to know Sam and Joe well enough to become friends with them in the first place. I told Rex not to take my car because I had plans, but I didn't tell him that it was to go see Tanya. So Rex and Lynn borrowed a different car.

When it started getting close to nine, I set off. I really didn't want to go, but I figured I had no choice. I arrived at Tanya's house and she showed me in. The place was all cleaned up. You couldn't tell there had been a party there at all. There wasn't even any residual puke smell.

I wasn't surprised to see that Tanya had chosen to wear something really sexy and revealing. I got the message that if I wanted more sex, all I had to do was ask. I didn't feel like it though, for some reason.

"Jared, we need to talk," she said, motioning for me to sit on the couch. I wondered what punishment was in store for me.

"Okay," I said.

"Jared, it's obvious that you're attracted to me," she said. "I have the used condom to prove it."

Yuck! I was hoping she didn't mean by that that she had saved it as a souvenir!

"So what's the problem?" she asked. "Why don't you want to be with me?"

I didn't know what to respond. I thought of saying "because you're mean to me" or "because you're not really all that cute," but neither of those responses seemed like the right thing to say.

"It's because of Andrea, isn't it?" she asked.

I looked away and didn't say anything.

"You know that she's seeing Joe, don't you?" she asked.

"What?" I asked.

"She's over at his house right now. I just got off the phone with her."

"What's she doing at his house?" I asked.

"What do you think?"

I didn't know what to say.

"That's where she went last night," said Tanya. "After she got home from the party she got into another fight with her parents about him. Apparently she and Joe had had some sort of date over the weekend, and her father wasn't happy about it. He chose last night to put his foot down and forbid her from seeing him again."

"And she went against her father's wishes?" I asked.

"Her exact words were 'you can forbid me all you want, but you can't stop me.' That's what she told me she said anyway. I doubt she really said it. But she really did leave home. She was waiting for Joe on his doorstep when he got home from work."

So she'd spent the night with Joe. The same night that I was with Tanya. I was devastated.

Tanya came over and sat by me and put her arm around me. "Forget about her, Jared."

I stood up and stepped away from her. "I just want to be alone," I said.

"*ça tombe bien,*" said Tanya in an unsympathetic tone.

"What?" I asked.

"It's a good thing you want to be alone, since that's what you'll be—as long as you keep choosing her over me."

I left the house and got in my car and started driving. I put on Cat Stevens' "Trouble."

"Trouble, oh trouble set me free, I have seen your face and it's too much, too much for me..."

I drove around aimlessly for a long time listening to the song over and over. Then I drove home.

When I got home, I avoided everyone and went straight to bed.

IN THE MORNING, I wanted to go talk to Rex again. Fortunately he was available for a chat just as he had been the day before.

"Well, it's official," I said. "Lynn was right. The girl I like, Andrea, she isn't interested in me. She's Joe's girlfriend now."

"Aw, that's too bad," said Rex. He gave me the most sympathetic look possible. "Well, sometimes that's the way it goes," he said.

I was practically on the verge of tears to hear such a stupid response.

"Look, I'm sorry," said Rex. "I want to be a good brother, but I know my limitations. If you want someone who's going to say something touching and profound, you should be talking to Mom or Lynn... or some gay guy maybe," he said with a small laugh. "But you know, you're just a kid. It's not like you were going to marry this girl."

"I'm almost seventeen years old," I said. "You were eighteen when you met Lynn, and now you're engaged."

Rex thought about that for a bit. "Okay, just because you're my brother and you're having a difficult time, I'm going to tell you a story that I never tell anyone. Yes, it's true that I met Lynn and fell in love with her when I was eighteen. Then what do you think happened?"

"You guys decided that you were both too young to tie yourselves to a long-distance relationship, especially since you didn't have the money to visit each other regularly or even to spend much time on the phone."

"Yep," he said. "That's the official story. And it's perfectly true! That and she was sleeping with some other guy."

"Really?" I asked.

"Look, like I said, I don't like to tell people this story, but if you think you're in a bad way, just imagine what that was like for me. There I was, this nerdy guy, taking all math, science, and computer classes, so you can imagine I wasn't meeting all that many girls. By chance I met Lynn through a friend of a friend while I was at home visiting."

"Right, she was Jake's girlfriend's friend."

"That's right. It was an intimate little gathering, the night we met," he said, looking off into the distance as if imaging it. "Jake had arranged a sort of sleepover at his uncle's cabin."

"You did it with her that first night?" I asked.

Rex laughed. "God, no," he said. "She slept on the couch and I slept on the floor. There were a bunch of us all sleeping together in the living room, so it wouldn't have been possible, even if I'd been able to convince her. But at that point she was still Mormon enough that it was a trick just to convince her to drink some beer. It was so cute the way she hesitated about it."

"I'll bet you showed her your proof that beer isn't against the Word of Wisdom!"

"Exactly!" he said. "It works every time!"

"That's funny," I said. "I can't even picture her as a Mormon."

"Well, picture this," said Rex. "In fact she had shaved all the hair off exactly one side of her head, and the other side was perfectly normal. It looked really cool, actually. She looked like someone out of Star Trek."

"Wow, that's really wild," I said. Leave it to Rex to think that it was cool to look like someone out of Star Trek.

"Yeah, I can show you some pictures sometime. That was why she had that super-short spiky hair at Kathy's reception—I don't know if you remember.

"Anyway, I figured she probably had one foot out the door of the church at least when I saw her like that. I mean, that's not exactly a 'Molly Mormon' thing to do."

"That's for sure," I said.

"Actually, she made quite an impression on me, so I called her up a few days later—after I'd gone back to California—to see if she wanted to get together again sometime. Amazingly, in that amount of time she'd already decided that she didn't believe in the church anymore."

"I can believe that," I said. "When it goes, it goes pretty fast."

"So we arranged a date for a few weeks later when I was back in town for Kathy's wedding. We went up to Jake's uncle's cabin again, but with fewer people this time. Just us and Jake and his girlfriend. This time they were the ones that slept in the living room. It was incredible. Unforgettable."

"Wow, it sounds like you were off to a pretty good start," I said.

"Yeah, and of course I wanted it to stay that way. But like you said, the distance was a problem right from the beginning. We couldn't afford to talk on the phone much, and she didn't have convenient access to email."

"That's too bad," I said.

"I know," said Rex. "It's hard to keep the passion alive with so little contact. We talked about not getting too serious for just that reason. The next semester had barely begun when she was giving me the inevitable 'let's just be friends' speech. Of course I found out through Jake that she was seeing someone else."

"Wow, they say 'absence makes the heart grow fonder' but sometimes it's more like 'out of sight, out of mind'," I said.

"I'm really glad I'm helping you to feel better here," said Rex ironically. "So anyway we ended up keeping in touch in spite of it all. You know that she was attending BYU when we met, and the next year she transferred to the University of Wisconsin. She had also  applied to Stanford where I was attending and she was accepted, but it was too expensive. Her dad refused to help her with her tuition when she left BYU, and besides, he was short on money because he was going through a divorce.

"I wished she would have been able to come to Stanford with me. I'd had a few flings since we had broken up, but nothing serious, and I would have been happy to take her back. We got together briefly that Summer, but we didn't let ourselves get too attached because we knew we'd just be separated again. At college, we both went back to seeing other people, and our respective availability never matched up again until we graduated.

"By chance we were both planning to go for a Ph.D. in Mathematics, so we had kept in touch about our grad school application process and ended up choosing the same school. Then we both went out early that Summer before our first semester there and rekindled that old flame. This time it was for good, and it was better than ever. The rest is history."

"Wow, that's a great story!" I said.

"Yep, it sure is," he said. "So anyway, what were we talking about? Oh yeah, your heartbreak. So I guess the moral of this whole elaborate story is that even if she's with Joe now, maybe you'll get together with her in four or five years or so. Or maybe you'll meet someone else."

Just then Joy popped her head in the door. "What are you guys talking about?" she asked.

"This is a private conversation, get lost!" I said.

"No, wait," said Rex. "Joy's a girl. Maybe she'd have some insights for you about how girls work."

"She just makes fun of me!" I said.

"Joy, if we tell you what we're talking about, do you promise to be nice to Jared and sympathize with his problem and not make fun of him?"

"Of course," she said.

I figured she was probably lying so she could get some dirt on me to blackmail me with later, but since Rex seemed to think she might be helpful, I agreed to tell her what was up.

So I told Joy all about how Tanya liked me and Andrea didn't, and about how Andrea liked Joe instead and how it wasn't fair since Andrea's dad liked me and hated Joe, and how she must only like him because she was mad at her dad for making her leave New Jersey so she just wanted to do the opposite of everything he said.

"I don't know about that," said Joy. "If she was willing to defy her father and run off like that, it seems like she has some of the same spiritedness that Joe has. It seems pretty natural that a girl like her would fall for a guy like him who's willing and able to fend for himself rather than put up with an intolerable situation."

Of course Joy was right, and it made me feel so much worse! "So what you're saying is that of course she would choose him over me because he's a real man and I'm just a dumb kid!"

"You're not a dumb kid, Jared," said Joy. "But you have to keep in mind that you've had a lot of advantages in life, and Joe has had a lot of hardships. Obviously that will affect the types of skills and qualities you develop. But you're still young, and you have plenty of experiences ahead of you that will help you grow."

I didn't see how that was any different from saying that I was a dumb kid, but I could see that she was trying her best to make me feel better no matter how hopeless my situation might be.

In the end, it was nice that I had my whole family around to help me through my long weekend of heartbreak, and it was also nice that everyone was making an effort to get along despite our religious differences, even Mom and Dad. I was sad to see them all leave on Sunday.

At school on Monday, when it was time for French class I went straight there instead of waiting for the last minute. I wasn't sure what to do about Tanya, so I just said hi to her as if everything were normal. She said hi back, although not as enthusiastically as she sometimes did.

"So have you thought some more about what happened Wednesday night?" she asked.

"Of course I've thought about it." Duh!

"Have you changed your mind?" she asked.

"I'm still confused about this whole thing," I said. "I think I need some more time to think it over."

"Okay," she said, smiling and sitting back in her chair.

She probably figured—correctly—that it wouldn't be long before I'd get horny enough to come knocking on her door. Maybe I was being stupid to reject her since I didn't have anything else lined up. She wasn't so bad looking, and she could be nice when she wanted to be. I figured I'd probably eventually take her up on her offer.

I managed to avoid Joe at lunch, but I couldn't avoid him in math class. Taking my seat, I said hi to him as best I could and then looked away. He seemed to understand that this was hard for me, and he seemed to feel bad because of it. I couldn't really be mad at him, though, because I knew that I would have done exactly the same thing if I'd been in his shoes.

"Andrea says you've hooked up with Tanya," he said quietly.

"Yeah, lucky me. So I suppose Andrea's living with you now," I said without looking at him.

"No, that really wouldn't work in the long term, living in that little room in that house with all those guys. My lease only allows one person."

"So she went back to her family?" I asked.

"Yeah," he said. "There's still a little friction there, but when her dad saw that she was willing to walk out rather than put up with more of his shit, it made him understand that he was going to have to make an effort to give her a little more space and privacy."

"Well that's a good thing for her anyway," I said "since he was definitely trying to control her life too much."

"Yeah," said Joe.

I tried my best to feel happy for the both of them. It wasn't easy. But as they say in French, *"C'est la vie."*

CHARACTERS IN OREM HIGH

The Wendells

Kathy

Rex

Jill

Joy

Jared

Bob

Lynn

Brother Wendell

Sister Wendell

The Hobbses

Sam

Sister Hobbs

Brother Hobbs

Joe

Others

Andrea

Tanya

VIII. Bordeaux Mission

Spencer

38. MONDAY AFTERNOON

I WAS BACK HOME FISHING. The morning sun was filtering down the canyon as I rowed my boat out to the middle of a calm lake and started preparing my lines...

Not really.

But in my mind I was already gone. Anywhere but wasting the last P-day of my mission watching the rest of the missionaries of my zone playing basketball.

At least my companion Elder Beaverton was having fun. He was doing great—he was all over the court.

Elder Beaverton was really into basketball. It always annoyed him when people would ask him about hockey, just assuming he loved hockey since he was from Canada. But I guess we all have our sports we love and our sports that we're supposed to love.

Personally I never much cared for basketball even before my knee surgery, and now of course I'm not about to do a bunch of jumping around for no reason. But every single LDS church building has a cultural hall that serves as a basketball court, so everybody's expected to like basketball since we play it all the time. It's kind of like how everybody has to be in scouts whether they want to or not.

But I couldn't really expect to have a zone activity of wrestling. Even if there'd been anyone in my league, there was no one in my weight class. Elder Beaverton was about my height, but he was more the skinny, wiry type.

Sister Bell didn't look like she was too thrilled to be hanging around watching the game either. I turned to her and said "Man, I wish we didn't have to waste our P-day doing this."

"Tell me about it!" she replied. "I'd been waiting all week to get the chance to go to the open-air market and see if I could find some fresh morel mushrooms for this recipe for *soupe aux morilles* that I've been dying to try out. But of course Sister Stein wanted us to spend all morning writing letters and cleaning and doing laundry so we'd have plenty of time in the afternoon for this," she said waving her hand dismissively at the court.

I could see why. Sister Bell's companion Sister Stein was really good. She'd played basketball in college, and she was at least as good as any of the guys.

"I hear you about this messing up the the laundry schedule," I said. "Between this and some errands I had to run this morning, I'm going to have to fly home with a suitcase full of dirty clothes. I guess it's no big deal, though, my mom'll just wash them for me when I get there."

"I don't care about the laundry," she said. "I just really wanted to try my hand at making that soup. Now I'll have to wait at least another week!"

"You really like cooking, huh?"

"Not just any kind of cooking. Ever since I was a little girl watching Julia Child with my mom, I've loved French cooking. And now here I am in France where I finally have the opportunity to try it for real, and it's just going to waste!"

She noticed my little laugh and added, "I mean, of course the point is to be doing the Lord's work, but I don't see why I shouldn't use what free time I have to learn some of the sauces and reductions and *soufflés* and such that I've always dreamed of making just right."

"I guess there's nothing wrong with that," I said. "But after two years of living here, I still don't see why some people say French food is so fancy and refined. They eat like cave-men here! Moldy cheese! Rotten grape juice! Raw meat! What's with that glob of raw hamburger meat with a raw egg floating on top? I can't believe people can just mash that up and eat it just like that! Yuck!"

Sister Bell laughed. "My last comp used to call that one the 'salmonella special'."

"Then they put a fried egg on everything," I continued. "On grilled ham and cheese sandwiches, on dinner *crêpes,* even on pizza! I'm not saying it's bad, I'm just saying that it's the kind of 'experimental cuisine' I'd expect from a bunch of frat boys, not from the country that's supposed to be some center of high culture."

Sister Bell laughingly agreed.

"I'll have a pizza," I said. "Oh, and could you slap a big old fried egg on that? Thanks."

"You know I'm not talking about *brasserie* food," said Sister Bell with a smile. "I wish I had the chance to cook something for you before you go so you can see what I mean."

"I'm mostly kidding," I said, "I know there's a lot of good stuff here."

Just then Elder Clark got a hold of the ball and broke away for a lay-up on the other end of the court. It was cool to see he could hold his own against the others despite his size. When I first met him I thought he was kind of a dork because he was so into juggling and magic tricks. He was always on about how he could juggle and ride a unicycle at the same time (though of course he wasn't allowed to bring his unicycle on his mission). But it turned out that he was a lot of fun, and his little tricks were great for getting people's attention and striking up conversations with them while street contacting in town.

I was looking at my watch and wondering when this was going to wrap up, when all of the sudden Elder West started yelling at Elder Dietrich. Elder West was saying that Elder Dietrich had tripped him. Sister Bell looked concerned.

"I did nothing of the sort," said Elder Dietrich. "It's not my fault if you can't run across the court without tripping over your own feet."

"That's not funny and it's not true," said Elder West. "I'm sick of your cheating."

"And I'm sick of your lip!" said Elder Dietrich. "Now let's get back in the game, or else I'll have to mention your bad attitude in my weekly report to the Mission President again."

So they all got back to playing, and it seemed more-or-less friendly except that Elder West was looking at Elder Dietrich like he was ready to sock him one.

"This isn't right," said Sister Bell. "Elder Dietrich is exercising unrighteous dominion."

I laughed. "Maybe, I don't know."

It was hard for me to really know which side to take. Elder West and Elder Dietrich had a feud from way back that I'd been doing my best to avoid getting in the middle of.

I liked Elder West, or Nick, as he liked people to call him on the sly. He was loads of fun back in the MTC and later when we were companions in La Rochelle. The only problem was that he was one of those guys who never wanted to do anything but goof off and break the rules. So it was always a challenge to work things out so we could get our job done right without my having to nag him and be his mother.

I'd always been pretty laid back and not real big on bossing people around and telling them what to do. So with Nick, I ended up looking the other way and letting a lot of stuff slide, and for his part he ended up following along with me a lot of the time and doing more of the Lord's work than he really wanted to, so it all sort of evened out. Things were a little easier now that I was paired up with Elder Beaverton. He was so gung-ho to serve the Lord that I never had to push him at all—if anything it was the other way around.

The main problem when I was companions with Nick was that Elder Dietrich—who was our Zone Leader then as now—wasn't nearly as willing as I was to let things slide. He kept wanting to get Nick in trouble, and me too whenever I went along with him.

Twice Nick and I ended up breaking the rules by going to the beach—it was a total accident both times (long story, don't ask)—and somehow Elder Dietrich found out about it and got us in trouble. That was when Nick started referring to Elder Dietrich as "Elder Dickhead" (not to his face, of course). And that was when I decided I wanted to try to stay out of it.

Unfortunately it looked like things were heating up on the court. Elder Dietrich and Elder West were getting a little more aggressive than you're supposed to in basketball. At one point it looked like Elder Dietrich might have shoved Elder West, who gave a ferociously threatening glare in response.

"Do something Elder Hobbs," said Sister Bell. "Elder Dietrich is really getting out of hand."

"Not my problem," I said.

As he was handing the ball off to Sister Stein, I could have sworn I heard Elder Dietrich say something about "Sister *Baleine*" and give a laugh in our direction. "Sister *Baleine*" [whale] was a nickname some of the guys had given to Sister Bell. From the look on her face, it looked like she might have heard it too.

"Look, you can see he's exercising unrighteous dominion," she said. "You know as well as I do that he only calls these stupid zone activities in the first place so that he can show off his basketball moves for Sister Stein. He's not supposed to be flirting with her at all, and he's abusing his authority as Zone Leader."

"I'm still waiting to hear what this has to do with me," I said.

"Elder Hobbs, you're the biggest guy here."

I laughed. "What, you want me to fight him? Come on, we're all missionaries here on the Lord's errand. We're not a bunch of animals."

She thought about it for a minute and said, "Well, maybe not fight him, but, you know, maybe just scare him a little."

I just laughed and shook my head.

Just then I saw Elder Dietrich trip Elder West for sure—there was no mistaking it. Elder West jumped up and got right in Elder Dietrich's face. "That's it!" he said, "You're a dead man!"

"Okay guys, cool it," I said, rushing onto the court. "Seems to me this game was almost over anyway, wasn't it? Let's just break it up and call it a day and go home."

"He threatened me," said Elder Dietrich. "You all heard it. I'm sorry, but I have no choice but to report this to the Mission President."

"Come on, cut him some slack," I said. "He's going home in less than a week. Why make a big deal over something like this?"

"I'm just following the rules," said Elder Dietrich.

"Report it all you want, dickhead," said Elder West. "This time next week, I'll be on the beach sunning myself back home in California, and you'll still be here knocking on doors."

"You'd better watch it," said Elder Dietrich. "It's still not too late for your mission to end dishonorably."

"Why you little—!" said Elder West.

"Let it slide," I said to Elder West, blocking his access to Elder Dietrich. "You'll be home soon—there's no reason to get worked up over this." Then I turned to Elder Dietrich. "And you leave him alone. How he completes his mission is between him and the Mission President now."

That broke up the fight, and everybody started gathering their things to go.

"You were fantastic!" said Sister Bell.

"All in a day's work," I said jokingly. "I don't know what this mission is going to do without me."

* * *

By the time Elder Beaverton and I got back to our apartment, it was past 18 *heures* (6 p.m.), so p-day was officially over, and it was time to get back to work.

The cool thing was that our work for the evening was hardly work. We finally had a referral for once—in fact, better than a referral, one of the local members had invited us to dinner to give the first discussion to her sister.

The member family lived a few blocks from downtown in one of the typical single-story stone townhouses of Bordeaux (called an *échoppe*). The wife, Marie-Hélène, was born and raised in Bordeaux, and the husband, Robert, was an American guy, originally from Arizona, who had served a mission to France. They'd met at BYU of all places. Marie-Hélène had converted to Mormonism as a teenager, and had left her home country on her own to study at BYU. It was a pretty lucky find for Robert in my opinion since I couldn't imagine there were many more like her back at the Y.

When we arrived at the *échoppe*, almost as soon as Robert opened the door we were greeted by his two little boys, two-year-old Benjamin and four-year-old Kevin. They tumbled on us like two cute little tornadoes. The boys knew us already since Robert was always friendly with the missionaries and let us come over whenever we wanted.

Next Marie-Hélène arrived to welcome us with the traditional French greeting of a kiss on each cheek. We weren't supposed to encourage that sort of thing, but Marie-Hélène insisted and wouldn't have it any other way. She was really very pretty, and it was a treat to listen to her speaking French so naturally, like music, the way it was meant to be spoken. And it was cute the way she pronounced her husband's name in the French fashion: "Ro-BEAR".

Marie-Hélène led us inside and introduced us to her sister Julie, her brother-in-law Jean-Pierre, and their three-year-old daughter Anne. Jean-Pierre and Julie were sitting on the couch drinking an *apéritif* of fruit juice, and little Anne was sitting sweetly between them. Our hosts offered us a seat and some fruit juice and we all started in on the usual small-talk about how much we liked Bordeaux and how cute the kids were and everything until it was time to go to the table for dinner.

Once we were seated at the table, Robert asked Marie-Hélène to give the blessing on the food.

Starting on the *entrée* [first course], a salad of *endives* and *fruits-de-mer*, Elder Beaverton steered the conversation towards the first discussion. He'd done a great job of keeping up with the earlier conversation in the other room even though he'd only been in France for six months, but giving the discussions he really hit his stride and had no trouble at all expressing himself in French. His years of learning French in High School probably helped him pick up the language so quickly even though he claimed he hadn't learned a thing back then.

The discussion couldn't have gone better. We were already up to the part about prophets when Marie-Hélène brought out the *plat principal* [main course] which was a delicious *magret de canard*.

It turned out that Julie had already started reading the *Book of Mormon* and was interested in talking about it. Robert was pretty excited to help out and join in the conversation as well although he could only do so much. He had his hands full trying to get his two rowdy little boys to sit still and eat the plates of pasta that were specially prepared for them. "Will you please eat the tasty pasta?" he implored them (in English). Little Anne watched her cousins with interest as she politely used her fork to eat the *magret* that her father had sliced up for her.

After talking about 3rd Nephi, chapter 11, of the *Book of Mormon* (the part where Christ arrives in the New World), Julie turned to her husband—who had been silent all through dinner so far—and asked him "*N'est-il pas intéressant d'apprendre ces histoires de Jésus qu'on n'a jamais connues ?*" [Isn't it interesting to learn these stories of Jesus that we've never known?]

He replied "*Si c'est pour apprendre à inviter les gens à dîner sans servir de vin...*" [If it's to learn to invite people over for dinner without serving wine...]

Julie laughed. "*Il faut excuser mon mari—il est du vieux Bordeaux et il a ses idées sur les traditions.*" [You'll have to excuse my husband—he's from an old Bordeaux family and he has his ideas about traditions.]

We just sort of laughed it off. It was always better to let those sorts of remarks go.

At that point it started to look like the little boys weren't going to sit still any longer, so Robert took them in the other room and got them started playing with their toy trains. Anne jumped up from the table to join her cousins. Her parents raised their eyebrows a bit as she ran off, but they didn't stop her.

Robert looked like he was having lots of fun playing with his sons and his little niece. Elder Beaverton was doing fine on the discussion with Julie and Marie-Hélène (who had joined in), so I let him handle it as I watched Robert and the kids.

It was cool the way little Kevin spoke perfect English to his father and then would turn to his cousin and say the same thing in perfect French. Of course Robert had no trouble in French himself, but he spoke to his kids only in English so they would learn to be bilingual. And it worked perfectly! On Kevin at least. Benjamin seemed to say only "train" and "Daddy", but he was super-cute!

By the time Marie-Hélène brought out the dessert—a fresh fruit salad—Elder Beaverton had already gotten Julie to commit to reading more of the *Book of Mormon* and to taking the next discussion. It was really a red-letter day for us—we almost never had this kind of success. It was a great note for me to be closing my mission on.

Of course no matter how satisfying it can be to make a spiritual connection with an investigator, as missionaries we can only plant the seeds and hope they take root after we've gone home. I couldn't help but envy Robert's opportunity to stay and build up the kingdom and nurture it himself in this beautiful country where the few members (compared to the number at home) needed so much help and support.

Elder Beaverton was on such a roll that he courageously decided to challenge Jean-Pierre to read the *Book of Mormon* with Julie. Marie-Hélène had brought Jean-Pierre a cup of instant coffee to drink with his dessert, and he was busy looking down his nose at it when Elder Beaverton gave him the challenge.

Jean-Pierre calmly replied "*Si ma femme veut lire votre livre, ce n'est pas à moi de l'en empécher. Mais comment pouvez-vous imaginer que je vais prendre au sérieux vos histoires d'anges et de Jésus, etc. ?*" [If my wife is interested in reading your book, it's not my place to tell her not to. But how could you imagine that I'm going to take your stories of angels and Jesus seriously?]

"*Si vous ne l'avez pas lu, comment savez-vous que ce n'est pas vrai ?*" asked Elder Beaverton. [If you haven't read it, how do you know it's not true?]

"*Bon, je n'allais rien dire, mais si vous insistez, j'ai une question à vous poser moi-même. J'ai mentionné à un collègue que j'allais rencontrer les Mormons, et il m'a dit que votre prophète-fondateur a couché avec des filles de quatorze ans et avec les femmes de ses adhérents en guise de 'mariage pluriel'. Alors, c'est vrai ? Oui ou non ?*" [Okay, I wasn't going to say anything, but since you insist, I have a question to ask you myself. I mentioned to a colleague that I was going to meet the Mormons, and he told me that your founding prophet slept with fourteen year old girls and the wives of his followers, calling it 'plural marriage'. So is that true? Yes or no?]

Oh great, I thought to myself. The anti-Mormons had gotten to him first. This sort of damage control was always a pain. Julie and Marie-Hélène looked shocked by the direction the conversation was going.

"*Bien sûr que ce n'est pas vrai !*" said Elder Beaverton. "*C'est n'importe quoi ! Ce sont les gens qui veulent nuire à notre religion qui racontent ce genre d'histoires.*" [Of course it's not true! It's nonsense! It's people who want to harm our religion that make up these sorts of stories.]

"*Et pourtant, c'est plus credible que vos histoires d'anges qui lui ont rendu visite...*" [And yet it's more credible than your stories about angels visiting him...]

I figured I'd better let Beaverton continue to handle this. From talking to some older people in my ward back home who knew a lot about church history, I'd heard a few strange stories about Joseph Smith's plural marriages, but it was a question that I didn't think was very valuable to pursue, particularly with investigators.

Then Jean-Pierre said "*Il m'a également dit que dans votre temple vous apprenez une façon secrète de se serrer la main pour entrer au paradis. Quel genre de dieu a besoin de ça pour savoir qui a le droit d'entrer au paradis ?*" [He also told me that in your temple you learn the secret handshake to get into heaven. What kind of god needs that to know who has the right to go to heaven?]

Marie-Hélène went back to the kitchen to start cleaning up. Julie stayed to listen.

"*Ce qui a lieu dans le temple est sacré. Nous ne pouvons pas en parler,*" replied Elder Beaverton. [What takes place in the temple is sacred. We can't discuss it.]

"*En plus,*" continued Jean-Pierre, "*j'ai entendu dire que vous sacrifiez des lapins et des chatons dans votre temple pour boire leur sang !*" [On top of that, I've heard that you sacrifice rabbits and kittens in your temple and drink their blood!]

"*Quoi ?! Certainement pas ! Jamais !*" exclaimed Elder Beaverton. [What?! Certainly not! Never!]

"*Aha !*" said Jean-Pierre. "*J'ai inventé ça. Donc vous avouez l'autre puisque vous ne le niez pas. Vous devez comprendre messieurs pourquoi je ne suis pas hyper-enthousiaste de voir ma famille se mêler à ce genre de choses."* [Aha! I just made that up. So you admit the other thing since you don't deny it. You must understand, sirs, why I'm not thrilled to see my family get mixed up in this sort of thing.]

"*Excusez-moi,*" I broke in, "*mais cette discussion n'est pas convenable. Je pense que c'est maintenant l'heure de remercier nos hôtes et de rentrer."* [Excuse me, but this discussion is not appropriate. I think it's time to thank our hosts and go home.]

So we thanked our hosts for their hospitality, reaffirmed Julie's appointment to take the next discussion, said goodbye to the kids, and walked back to our apartment.

Before bed, Elder Beaverton felt it would be a good idea to say a prayer together that Julie would receive witness of the truthfulness of the *Book of Mormon,* and that her husband's heart would be softened so that he would accept the truth himself or at least not stand in her way.

Getting in bed, I told myself "only five more days to go." Then *aussitôt* [just as quickly] I was already dreaming of coming back.

T HE NEXT MORNING, after Elder Beaverton and I had done our usual personal study and companion study, we set off to go out tracting. As usual, no one wanted to let us in. To break up the tedium and frustration of it, we played little games to vary our door approach such as picking a particular word we'd have to work into our opening line somehow.

The whole morning the only person who let us in to talk was an old guy who mistook us for the Amish. We would get this problem all the time because in the French version of the movie *Witness*, the word "Amish" was mistranslated as "Mormon". So a lot of times people would ask us about how we always drive around in a horse-and-buggy back home or some other crazy thing that of course we don't do. Still, it was better than getting mistaken for the *Témoins de Jéhovah* [Jehovah's Witnesses].

After grabbing a sandwich for lunch, we decided to spend the afternoon street contacting along *rue Sainte Catherine*, the main pedestrian drag that spans the whole length of the urban center of Bordeaux from the *Place de la Comédie* in the north to the *Place de la Victoire* in the far south. *Rue Sainte Catherine* and the main east-west pedestrian road *rue de la Porte Dijeaux* were good places to meet people because they were always crowded. Most people were on their way somewhere of course, but there were always a certain number of people who were just wandering around bored and were willing to stop and chat.

We were looking around for likely prospects when all of the sudden I heard a girl's voice say, "Hey, isn't that Spencer Hobbs?" I looked up and saw three girls walking towards us.

"God, Tanya, you're not going to make us talk to the Mormon missionaries here on vacation, are you?" said the shortest of the three.

When they got close enough to read our name-tags, the first one said "It is, it's Sam Hobbs' brother! Here he is, just like Jared said he would be." So I'd graduated from being "Matt's little brother" to being "Sam's big brother" without skipping a beat. I should have known I'd have to get used to that after the four-page letter my mom had written me about how Sam had heroically scored the winning touchdown in the championship game...

Walking right up to me, the first girl pointed at my name tag and said "Elder Hobbs, huh? You wouldn't by chance be from Orem, Utah and have a little brother named Sam, would you?" The short girl looked annoyed.

I smiled. "How'd you know?"

"We're from Orem too."

"In a manner of speaking," added the tall girl on her other side.

"So you're friends with my brother Sam?"

"Here, let's sit down in a sidewalk café and have a drink," said the girl. "I'll treat you guys to a glass of... whatever the hell it is you guys are allowed to drink." She laughed. Her small friend looked more irritated than ever.

"We're not supposed to be hanging out in sidewalk cafés," said Elder Beaverton.

"What? Why not?" asked the girl. "We won't make you drink beer if you don't want to."

"It's not that," said Elder Beaverton. "The Mission President thinks it doesn't present a good image for missionaries to be seen hanging out in a sidewalk café."

"Not even for a referral?" asked the tall girl.

"You have a referral for us?" asked Beaverton, showing some interest for the first time.

She laughed. "Of course not! We're not giving you guys a referral! We have few enough friends as it is! I was just curious as to whether that would affect the rule." Now Elder Beaverton was starting to look annoyed.

"Just take your name-tags off," suggested the first girl. "Plenty of guys wear suits and ties around here. Without the name-tags you'll blend right in and there won't be any danger of giving the church a bad name."

"Yeah, don't they teach you dorks anything in the MTC these days?" asked the short girl.

"I think it would still technically be against mission rules," I said. I found myself half-hoping they'd find a way to talk us into it since sitting in a café chatting with some girls from my home town was sure to be more fun than street-contacting.

"Look," said the first girl pointing to her two friends, "these two are 'inactive' members. You don't want to pass up your opportunity to use your magical missionary powers to fellowship them, do you?"

Then the tall girl smiled and said "And Tanya's a non-member who actually wants to talk to you, so that makes her like a 'golden contact' or something, doesn't it?"

"I don't think these girls are very respectful to the church," said Elder Beaverton. At that the short girl laughed.

I was kind of thinking the same thing, but on some level it seemed like that was part of their appeal. It would be nice to have a good excuse to take a break from being "Elder Hobbs" for a little while and have a conversation in English with some Americans other than missionaries. And if we managed to slip in a few points from the discussions we could probably count this as work in our weekly stats...

"Let's sit down over here," I said, walking towards the nearest café.

"I can't wait to call Jared and tell him we found you!" said Tanya.

The short girl rolled her eyes. "Will you give it a rest about Jared? You're not seeing him anymore, remember?"

I sat down at a table and took off my name-tag. Elder Beaverton looked a little shocked, but he did the same, and the three girls each took a seat as well.

The girls introduced themselves. As I had gathered the leader was named Tanya. Her tall friend was named Andrea and her short friend was named Kim. They had of course already read our names off our name-tags.

"So how do you know Sam?" I asked.

"We don't," said Kim, looking at her watch.

"She means we don't know him all that well," said Tanya. "We all went to school together, and he was friends with this guy Jared that I was kind of seeing."

"You know, I'm kind of seeing your cousin Joe," said Andrea.

"Small world," I said. I was surprised by the coincidence, but actually it seemed pretty reasonable that this odd girl—who seemed to be staring off into space whenever she wasn't talking to someone— might be seeing my cousin Joe, who was a bit of a strange guy himself.

"What do you guys mean 'kind of seeing'?" asked Elder Beaverton.

"They mean we're all setting off for different colleges in the fall," said Kim, "so we all made arrangements with our respective high school boyfriends that starting from this trip to France we would officially begin 'seeing other people.'"

I was starting to feel like I didn't really like this Kim very much.

"Anyway, it was kind of an on-again off-again thing between me and Jared," said Tanya, "so it's no big loss."

Just then the server came to take our order. I ordered a *Perrier*, Elder Beaverton ordered an *Orangina*, and the three girls all ordered beer.

As soon as the server was gone, Elder Beaverton said to them "You know, you girls shouldn't be drinking beer."

"Why not?" asked Andrea.

"Because it's not good for you," he replied. Both Kim and Tanya laughed heartily as if he'd told a great joke.

Andrea just tilted her head to the side and smiled indulgently as if humoring a child. "Where are you from?" she asked him.

"Alberta," he replied.

"Ooh, Canada! How exotic!" said Kim.

Andrea ignored her. "Do you like it here in France?" she asked him.

Elder Beaverton immediately launched into the usual speech about how blessed he was to have been called to serve among the French people because of their wonderful spirit, etc.

Before Elder Beaverton was done bearing his testimony of the truthfulness of his call to the Bordeaux Mission, the drinks arrived. That seemed to remind him that he was talking to girls that were naughty enough to order beer, so he wrapped up his discourse and went back to looking down his nose at them. Tanya paid for everything.

We all silently started sipping on our drinks.

"So you're a non-member but you grew up in Orem, Utah?" I asked Tanya.

"Yep, that's right," she said.

"Would you like to know more about our church?" asked Elder Beaverton.

All three girls laughed. Even I was kind of embarrassed that my companion would ask such a stupid question. Having grown up in Orem, Tanya for sure already knew plenty about the church.

Kim drank about half her beer in one gulp and started getting up. "Well, it was nice meeting you guys," she said.

"Kim!" said Tanya, seeming a little irritated.

"What?" asked Kim. "You were the one who suggested that we should go to the bookstore and see if we could meet some guys there. So let's go."

"But we've met some guys right here," said Andrea.

"Earth to Andrea! I mean some proper French guys. *To pick up*. Not some dorkazoid missionaries. If I'd wanted to meet some retardo Mormon guys with sticks up their butts, I would have stayed in Orem!"

"Hey now, that's a little harsh, don't you think?" I asked.

"They're not so bad," said Tanya, "in fact they're kind of cute."

Elder Beaverton started to look nervous. I wanted to say something in my own defense, but I didn't want to say anything that would sound like I was encouraging them to flirt with us.

"God, don't tell me that now you've developed some sort of perverse Mormon missionary fetish!" said Kim.

"Well there's a certain logic to it," said Andrea, adjusting her glasses. Her tone sounded a little like a professor's despite the subject. "The thing is that typical religious celibates—Catholic priests and nuns, Buddhist monks, etc.—usually make up a small, élite, self-selected subset of believers. The set of people who choose a path of permanent religious celibacy are clearly people for whom spirituality is more important than sex. It seems to me then that such people have a lower-than-average libido, and hence are not very interesting sexually.

"With LDS missionaries—at least the men—it's not like that at all. Ideally every young man is supposed to serve a mission, not just those who are less interested in sex."

"More than that," added Tanya. "In LDS culture, being a returned-missionary makes a big difference in a guy's dating prospects."

"Exactly," said Andrea. "So it's a temporary period of celibacy for which a non-trivial part of the reward is lots of sex later."

This discussion was starting to become a little uncomfortable—Elder Beaverton looked positively terrified—but we were not sure how to get them to stop talking about this.

At this point Kim finally started to seem interested in the conversation. "Considering the reward, one might even say that the male missionaries are taken from the more sexual part of the LDS population."

"Holding back their desire and letting it build up for two years," said Tanya. "A squeaky clean exterior with this tremendous sexual energy bubbling right under the surface." She said the last bit slowly and looked me straight in the eye. Then she broke out in a huge grin.

Then Kim took Elder Beaverton's hand and made as if she was going to kiss it. He pulled away and suddenly stood up. "I think we need to go *now*," he said. Then without pausing to see whether or not I agreed he grabbed his things and started walking away. My first thought was that he was probably right, so I followed.

Behind us I could hear the girls laughing as we walked away. "That was hilarious!" said Kim. "You guys were right—we should meet with the missionaries all the time!"

"Oh my goodness gracious!" said Elder Beaverton as we made our escape. "Merciful heavens! That's what we get for breaking mission rules! Satan led us right into the hands of those sinful girls!"

Luckily the whole incident had been quick and shocking enough not to have been too arousing at the time. But walking away south down *rue Sainte Catherine* I couldn't stop thinking about it.

The three girls all had bare midriffs and pierced navels. Obviously not good little Mormon girls even though they were from Orem. Andrea was tall and thin, but maybe a little strange and awkward. Kim was tough and compact. She had the perfect shape with her thin waist and full breasts, but she was a little abrasive, and didn't have quite as pretty a face as the other two.

Tanya was the most curvaceous of the three. Her movements were fluid and sensual. I pictured her face and her eyes as she said "tremendous sexual energy" and then her smile. Tremendous sexual energy.

Mmmm... Tremendous sexual energy. I had to stop thinking about that.

"Those girls were worse than the French girls!" said Elder Beaverton all of the sudden.

I tried not to laugh hearing that. So he was still thinking about it too. Plus in a backwards kind of way he seemed to be admitting that despite all of his holiness he had maybe noticed the French girls.

Then I heard him begin very softly singing to himself *"Choose the right, when a choice is placed before you..."* At that point really had to fight to keep from laughing. In priesthood, they would always teach the teenagers that singing a hymn is a good way to chase away certain types of thoughts, so I kind of had an idea of what was going through his mind.

Not that I was any better off. Tricks like that one worked a little, but not very well. There wasn't really a good solution.

There was only one bad solution—in the morning, while showering—the only real moment of privacy the whole day. During the first few months of my mission I'd tried to do as I was told and give it up, but I found that I could no more go without this than I could give up bad habits like food and water. So I just tried not to think about it too much. And even though this small release was itself a sin, it wasn't much of a consolation. It was a little like trying to live on nothing but oatmeal and carrots. It'll maybe keep you alive, but the craving for something more substantial just never goes away.

I suggested to Elder Beaverton that maybe we should turn west since we were headed straight for the university which was kind of the

wrong direction if we didn't want to be surrounded by more attractive girls our own age.

Elder Beaverton agreed. He wanted to redouble his efforts at faithfully tracting to cancel out our earlier rule-breaking and thoughts of girls.

I was willing to go along but my heart wasn't in it. I was starting to feel more burnt-out than usual—I was ready for all of this proselyting to be over. The last thing I felt like doing was using one of the usual tricks to get someone to buzz us into one of the "buzzer bats" and then knocking on all of the doors of the various apartments of people who didn't want to see us. Since Elder Beaverton was so gung-ho, I suggested that he take the lead.

Of course the few apartments where people were home at all were harried moms who wanted to be polite but saw us as an annoyance. Elder Beaverton chalked up our failure to not being sufficiently in tune with the spirit. Maybe he was right, but I was getting to the point of being too burnt-out to care.

Between buildings we passed by a pharmacy that had in its display window a large poster advertising some sort of mysterious medication.

The image on the poster was a soft black-and-white shot of a nude woman looking off into the distance with her breasts completely exposed to view. This sort of thing was typical on every commercial street. When it wasn't the pharmacies it was the tobacconists advertising magazines with topless women on the cover or just random sidewalk billboards advertising lingerie.

When I first started my mission it took some effort to train myself to look away and later to convince myself to just be blasé about it, as if I didn't notice or care. But I was getting so lazy and sloppy about everything these days that I allowed myself to follow the line of the model's perfect breast and to linger for a second, taking in the shape of it.

As we walked on I thought about how my companion had probably at that very moment been carefully forcing himself to look away. Only four more days to go, I thought, and tomorrow was the last work day...

As we were walking back to our apartment, we ran into the office elders, Elder Gladwell and Elder Young. Elder Beaverton stopped them to ask if they had any information on the transfers that were coming up.

"Not yet," said Elder Gladwell. "All we know for sure is that Elder Dietrich is going to be going on splits."

"Ah, maybe you and your new companion will get to go around with him," I said to Elder Beaverton. "Won't that be fun?"

"So we have an odd number this time?" asked Elder Beaverton. "What happened, one of the new arrivals have visa problems?"

"There aren't any new arrivals this time," said Elder Young.

"Really? Why?" I asked. For a long time now we'd been getting fewer and fewer arrivals from the MTC. So as people went home at the normal rate, the mission was dramatically shrinking. Elder Beaverton, despite being out for six months, was one of the greenest around (or rather bluest, in French terms)...

"Well, you didn't hear this from me," said Elder Young, "but the rumor that's going around is that they're thinking of eliminating the Bordeaux Mission and maybe merging it with the Marseille Mission."

The office elders always had all the good gossip!

"Well if no one is arriving, how can we have an odd number of missionaries?" asked Elder Beaverton. "I thought an even number were leaving."

"Nope," said Elder Gladwell. "Elder Cannon is being sent home early."

"What? Why?" I asked.

"Well of course they don't tell us directly," said Elder Young, "but it's got to be health-related. He was just hospitalized the other day."

"Really? What happened?" I asked.

"Not sure. It's really hush-hush. From the paperwork that's come through the office, it looks like depression or some other psychological problem."

"That's terrible!" said Elder Beaverton.

"Yeah, I don't know exactly what's up, but his companion, Elder Wilson, is pretty shaken up. He's had to meet with the Mission President a bunch of times. I hope Elder Cannon didn't try to kill himself or something..."

"Wow," said Elder Beaverton. We were both so shocked and horrified that we didn't know what to say.

"Well, it's been uplifting chatting with you guys, as usual," I said.

They laughed. "Congrats on finishing your mission Elder," said Elder Gladwell.

Elder Beaverton and I didn't say a word as we walked the rest of the way home, and said very little while preparing dinner.

After the prayer, Elder Beaverton seemed to want to talk about it. "That's really too bad about Elder Cannon, poor guy!"

"I'm sure he'll be fine once he's back in familiar territory with his family," I said, even though I wasn't really sure.

"But even if he's okay, getting sent home early is a stigma that sticks to you your whole life. People still speak about it in hushed tones years later, and even if it's for health reasons, on some level it's taken as a shameful excuse for why you weren't strong and faithful enough to 'endure to the end.'"

"It's worse if it's for misbehavior, though," I said. "Actually, that happened to my sister Laura's husband."

"Really? What did he do?"

"Well, obviously they didn't tell me the gory details," I said. "But I assume it was for sex. That's what it always is, isn't it? From what my brother Matt said in his letter, apparently this guy was a real Don Juan before he set off on his mission, crawling with hot girlfriends."

"And he couldn't kick the skirt-chasing habit, huh?"

"I guess not. And it probably didn't help that he was in the Florida Jacksonville Mission where all the girls are dressed—or rather undressed—for the warm weather."

Elder Beaverton laughed. "If that was his weakness, he wouldn't have lasted a week here in France!"

"Yeah, that's for sure! As it was, he got sent home after a year. The funny thing was that before they sent him home, he was the number one baptizer in his mission. Which makes me doubt what they're always saying about how impure thoughts keep you from being prompted to find the right people to lead to the Lord and all that. I think a lot of it is just charisma."

"He's really handsome or something?"

"That's what they say. But according to Matt's story, getting sent home in disgrace really messed him up. When he found that he wasn't getting the same attention from the LDS girls that he was used to getting, he stopped going to church and went completely inactive for years. Then my sister Laura, a year off her mission and still full of missionary zeal, found him and convinced him to start coming back to church."

"Found him? Was she looking for him?"

"Probably. She said he was her 'high school sweetheart' or something like that, but I don't remember him myself."

"So it worked out for him in the end," said Elder Beaverton. "Despite getting sent home early, he found a faithful LDS wife."

"Yeah, but it took him long enough. He's been back from his mission six years, and he only got married just last month." Plus, I didn't want to say it about my own sister, but if what they said about him was true, he probably could have done better. Matt said he used to have girls lined up around the block to date him, and Laura… Well, she wasn't exactly a dog, but…

"Wait a minute," said Elder Beaverton. "They got married last month and you're going home in less than a week? They couldn't have waited one more month so that you could be there for the ceremony?"

"Apparently not," I said. "They got married in the temple, and considering his weakness for you-know-what, I'm guessing they were cutting it pretty close with a six-week courtship." Actually, I wasn't sure I was too thrilled about this image of my innocent, returned-missionary sister being doinked by this leisure-suit-Larry who couldn't keep it in his pants to save his life. But it was her choice and the church found him temple-worthy, so I figured it was none of my business.

"Wow, I can't even imagine how my family would take it if I got sent home early," said Elder Beaverton. "You're lucky you're essentially done."

"I know," I agreed, "Thank heavens." Two years of hard work and faithful service, and all that was left was a few more days and one temple-recommend interview. It was too late to mess it up now.

O N WEDNESDAY MORNING we were having about the same luck as Tuesday morning. We were wandering around the *Place Gambetta*, thinking about finding some lunch, when we heard a familiar voice:

"Hey Tanya, look! It's your boyfriend!" Then laughter. It was Kim, followed closely by Andrea and Tanya carrying a big basket.

"Hi again, ladies," I said.

"What a coincidence!" said Tanya.

"Oh, it's not a coincidence Tanya," said Andrea, "it's destiny. I'll bet you and Spencer met in the pre-existence, just like me and Elder Beaverton." Then Andrea walked right up to Elder Beaverton and put her hand on his chest and started moving it up towards his neck as she leaned in as if to kiss him. Elder Beaverton jumped back with a shriek, and all three girls started laughing hysterically. I secretly laughed a little bit myself.

"Hey listen guys," said Tanya. "We just stopped by a really good *traiteur* to pick up some food for a picnic, and everything looked so good that we ended up buying about ten times as much food as we can eat ourselves. Wanna join us?"

"We're going to *quai* to look at the river," said Kim.

"What?" asked Andrea. "I thought we agreed we were going to the *Jardin Public*! I want to go to the *Jardin Public* and look at the turtles."

"Andrea, Andrea, Andrea," said Kim. "I hope for your sake that that's some sort of crazy euphemism for 'I want to go to the *Jardin Public* and look at the hot guys playing soccer with their shirts off'."

Andrea laughed. "Okay, that too."

"Hey, listen, we don't want to cramp your style…" I began.

"No, no, they're kidding," said Tanya. "Come along, it'll be fun!"

"I don't think this is a good idea," said Elder Beaverton.

"Oh come on," I said. "It'll be okay just this once. Besides, it's a public park. It's not like they're inviting us to their rooms. And remember—they're investigators or inactives or something, so we have a responsibility to lead them to the Lord."

Elder Beaverton didn't look convinced, but he relented and started following the rest of us towards the *Jardin Public*. "Okay, but only if we can teach you one of the discussions," he said. The girls laughed as if that was the funniest joke they'd heard all day.

"Can you teach us the one about riding on tapirs?" Andrea asked him.

"Riding on *what?*" asked Elder Beaverton.

"Nothing," said Tanya, and the pointedly at Andrea, "Nothing."

"Oh come on," said Andrea. "What's the point in hanging with the mishies if we can't have a little fun with them? They're big boys, they can handle it."

"I think she just doesn't want you to scare them off again," said Kim.

"Why not?" asked Andrea. "There are plenty more where these came from!"

"I think maybe she wants to hang with these two in particular," said Kim, "or one of them, anyway."

Elder Beaverton raised an eyebrow disapprovingly as Andrea looked us over. "Oh, okay," she said, as if she hadn't considered the possibility before. "But with all the effort they make to look like an endless series of identical clones, you can hardly fault me for thinking that one's as good as another."

When we got to the *Jardin Public*, the girls started getting out the food. It was true that they'd gotten a ton of tasty stuff. They'd also brought three bottles of wine. Elder Beaverton looked pretty shocked that they'd apparently had the idea that they would drink a full bottle of wine *each* with *lunch*, but it didn't stop him from serving himself a big plate of food, or from digging in after we'd said a quick prayer, which the girls ignored.

Fortunately they started by opening just one of the bottles. Of course they offered us some, and of course we declined.

It looked like some people were looking at us. I didn't think we were really breaking any important rules in any serious way, but still it seemed like maybe we weren't presenting a good image of LDS missionaries. Trying not to be too obvious about it, I took off my name-tag. Elder Beaverton shot me a look as if he weren't too pleased about this whole thing, but he took off his name-tag too.

Once our meal was underway, Elder Beaverton said, "Now ladies, about that discussion. I was thinking it might be prudent to start with the law of chastity."

That really set the girls laughing. They seemed pretty happy to have invited us along since Elder Beaverton was clearly the funniest guy on the planet.

"Oh! Oh!" said Tanya, "Can you teach us all how to become eight-cow wives?" Then they were falling over each other laughing. "Dammit, Andrea, now you've got me doing it!" she said. Elder Beaverton and I both laughed too. After all, it was true that that "Johnny Lingo" and his "eight-cow wife" thing was pretty cheesy...

"So what brings you ladies to Bordeaux?" I asked. "Besides looking for me, that is."

"We spent a few days in Paris," said Kim, "and we were thinking of traveling all over France, but we have such a sweet set-up here in Bordeaux, we might just stay here for the rest of our trip."

"Some of my parents' friends from Princeton own an apartment in town, and they're lending it to us," said Andrea.

"Ah, yes," said Tanya. "It is very important—no one is ever to forget—that Andrea's not really from Orem." Then in a haughty tone, looking down her nose, she said "Andrea's from *Princeton*." Then the three of them laughed.

Once we'd eaten our fill, the girls started gathering the remains back into the basket. In the end, the girls had drank just the one bottle of wine and hadn't opened the other two. Then Andrea took us to go look at the turtles. There really were turtles—actual turtles, not half-naked guys—sunning themselves on some branches in the little lake near one of the grassy islands.

I went to get my watch out of my bag, and as I was opening it up, a copy of *Le Livre de Mormon* caught Tanya's eye.

"Can I see that?" she asked. I handed it to her as I was putting on my watch and closing my bag.

"Wow, this is really wild," she said, paging through it. "It's the *Book of Mormon*, all in French!"

"Well, of course it is!" said Elder Beaverton. "Do you think we expect the French people to read the *Book of Mormon* in English?"

"Sorry, I guess I'm a little slow," said Tanya. "I hadn't thought about it." Then she said, "You don't need this do you?" and ran off with it to one of the little *passerelles* [foot bridges] to the island.

It was pretty clear what her little game was. She wanted me to chase her, and then to catch her, and then...

I wasn't about to fall into such a simple trap so easily. I casually walked to the *passerelle* where she was standing, holding the book over the water as if to drop it in. Then I stepped onto the *passerelle* and calmly took the book out of her hand.

"I wasn't going to drop it in," she said.

"I know that."

"You've gotten pretty far away from Elder Beaverton there—aren't you going to get in trouble?"

"I can still see him from here," I said. I raised my hand to signal Elder Beaverton and he nodded in response. He had moved to a park bench with Kim and Andrea where they all appeared to be having a lively conversation. He was probably doing his comedy routine known as the first discussion.

"So you read that?" she asked. "I guess you must speak French pretty well."

"My French is excellent, if I do say so myself," I said.

"Ah, I wish I could say the same!" said Tanya. "It's been my favorite class all through high school—that's why my parents gave me this trip as a graduation present—but then I've gotten here and…"

"You find you can't communicate with people?"

"*Je me debrouille* . [I get by.] Maybe a little better than I expected, but not as well as I'd hoped. I can carry on a one-on-one conversation without too much difficulty. Of course I've improved dramatically in just the short time I've been here."

"I've really enjoyed learning French myself," I said, leaning on the railing of the *passerelle*. "Actually it surprised me how much I enjoyed learning it and how naturally it came to me when I first started studying French in the MTC."

"Why did it surprise you?"

"Because I'd never done anything like it before, and I'd never really thought of myself as much of a scholar…"

"Why not?"

"I don't know," I said. "I guess schoolwork wasn't really important in my family. To my dad, football is everything and everything is football. So of course I was on the team in high school, but I wasn't all that into it, and I was never really a star. Not like my brother Matt, who was Mr. Football."

"And now Sam, too …"

"Exactly," I said. "I was always more into wrestling—I was the captain of the team—and my dad was pleased about it, but didn't care about it like with football. Then, the fact that I always got better grades than my two brothers counted for even less in his book than wrestling. So, since I was obviously no Einstein, I never put much effort into my schoolwork or really thought much about it. Then when I got to the MTC and surprised myself by being the best in the class, and later when I had such a great time reading some *Asterix* comics in French that my first companion had clandestinely purchased, I began to feel like maybe I'd been selling myself short."

"I love *Asterix* comics!" said Tanya. "They're a great way to learn French! My all-time favorite *bande-dessinée* [comic strip] though is *Jean-Claude Tergal*. It's hilarious! And it's great for learning colloquial speech and everyday customs. With a lot of comics, they make the background and the details so generic that the story could be taking place anywhere. But with *Jean-Claude Tergal*, all of the cultural cues make it abundantly clear that it's taking place in *France*."

"Sounds cool, maybe I should check it out."

"Oh yeah! The same author also did a really funny *bande-dessinée* called *'Sacré Jésus'.*" She laughed a little to herself, thinking about it. "Never mind, maybe you wouldn't like it."

I smiled a little and looked at the fish swimming in the water below. "Anyway, about what you were saying about the cultural cues—that part has been almost as interesting to me as learning the language. Not that the way they do things here in France is any better or worse than the way we do things back home, it's just that it's been an eye-opener to see the ways that things can be different and also the ways that people are always the same. I don't know if that makes any sense."

"Of course it makes sense," she said. "I know exactly what you mean. And even though—as you say—it's no better or worse than back home, I find that for some unexplained reason I love it here. I'd like to come back here someday, maybe to stay."

"It's probably hard to get a work visa," I said.

"I'll find a way. Maybe I can get a visa to teach English or something..."

I looked at her delicate hand resting on the railing and at her beautiful, bright eyes looking up at me. I was sorely tempted to move closer and put my arm around her waist. But of course that would be very much against the rules. "I'd like to come back someday too," I said. "I'd like to see this place as a normal person, not as a missionary."

Then suddenly I heard someone yelling to me. "Elder Hobbs! Hey, Elder Hobbs!" It was Elder Dietrich. He was standing on the sidewalk just outside of the high iron bars that surrounded the *Jardin Public.* As soon as he saw that I saw him, he rushed around to the entrance, followed by his companion, Elder Clark.

Elder Beaverton and the girls and I went and met him just inside the gate.

"What's going on here?" he asked. "Are you guys on some sort of date?"

"Of course not," said Elder Beaverton. "These girls are inactives, and we're fellowshipping them into coming back to church."

"That's not what it looked like from my vantage point!" said Elder Dietrich. Elder Clark just kind of stood there and looked away as Elder Dietrich continued. "This is the sort of behavior I might expect from a trunky troublemaker like Elder Hobbs here, but you,

Elder Beaverton, I'm really surprised to see you following his bad example!"

Then Kim explained "We just ran into them because we went to school with Spencer's brother Sam."

Ouch, that was the wrong thing to say…

"What?!" asked Elder Dietrich. "So now you're encouraging your friends from home to come out and visit you *on your mission*?"

"Of course not!" I said. "I'd never met these girls or even heard of them before yesterday."

"Actually, we're the three Nephites," explained Andrea with a little smile. Elder Dietrich didn't seem to think that was very funny.

"No, Elder Beaverton was serious," said Tanya. "They're inactives and I'm an investigator, and these two missionaries were teaching us the discussions. Really."

Elder Dietrich didn't look convinced. "Why aren't you wearing your *plaque*?" [name-tag]

Oops. Elder Beaverton had put his back on, but in the confusion I had forgotten.

"I have no choice but to report you guys," he said.

I then stepped just a little into his space so he'd have to look up at me. "Are you sure you need to do that?" I asked him.

"Are you threatening me?" he asked, stepping away.

"No," I said calmly, "I just think it would be very nice of you to overlook this, since we weren't really doing anything wrong."

"If you weren't doing anything wrong, then you'll have no trouble explaining this to the Mission President in your interview on Friday. Now I think we should all go." So Elder Beaverton and I followed Elder Dietrich and Elder Clark to the exit.

As soon as we were on the sidewalk, Elder Dietrich started walking southwest, back towards downtown. "Um, we were going to go this way," I said, pointing the opposite direction. Elder Dietrich gave me a stern look in reply, but then he turned and kept going.

Elder Beaverton and I didn't say anything as we walked northeast along the side of the *Jardin Public*. When we got to the corner, I suggested that we turn northwest and continue going around the park. I knew that the girls were still inside. I couldn't help but feel like if Elder Dickhead was going to label me a troublemaker anyway, it didn't really matter if I broke the rules a little or not.

As we approached another entrance to the *Jardin Public*, I turned to Elder Beaverton and said "It was very rude the way we left like that. We should at least go back and apologize to those girls and say goodbye to them properly before we go back to tracting."

"No, Elder Hobbs, don't do it. You're just going to get us into more trouble."

"You were fellowshipping them, weren't you? I'll be gone soon, but we should at least give them the contact info for the mission so that in case your efforts had some good influence on them, maybe they can meet with some other missionaries."

Elder Beaverton raised his eyebrow doubtfully, as if he thought maybe the missionaries shouldn't be spending too much time with these girls.

"You can warn the Mission President to send them some sister missionaries or something if they call, but we should at least give them our card."

"I don't know about this," said Elder Beaverton, but he followed me back into the *Jardin Public*. We found the three girls immediately.

"You again!" said Andrea. "We seem to be running into you everywhere!"

I smiled. "Sorry to have left so abruptly."

"It's okay," said Tanya. "I hope we didn't get you guys into too much trouble."

"Nah," I said.

"We just came back to give you the contact info for the local mission in case you'd like to attend church while you're visiting here in Bordeaux," said Elder Beaverton. That made the girls laugh again. Elder Beaverton was a real cut-up today.

"No really, you'll like it," I said. "Over in Talence there's this cool LDS church building that looks just like the ones back home except that it's all funky colors. Instead of being made of red brick with a black roof, it's made of the local materials—white stone with an orange Spanish-tile roof—plus the front is all decorated with turquoise tiles. It's kind of psychedelic."

"Okay, we'll be sure to bring our mushrooms when we go then," said Kim.

So I got out one of my cards, and in the white space I wrote "Meet me Friday morning at 11h at the *Café Utopia, Place Camille Jullian*," and handed it to Tanya.

Tanya looked at it and then put it in her pocket. "Okay, thanks guys," she said. "It was nice meeting you, good luck on your missions, see you around." Then we all shook hands and went our separate ways.

For the rest of the afternoon, we had no luck at all tracting. Not one single person wanted to let us in. After dinner, Elder Beaverton wanted to discuss it.

"We really shouldn't have been flirting with those bad girls today," he said. "Regardless of what you were saying the other day, I think it's because of our unfaithfulness that we haven't been prompted to find the people who are waiting to hear the gospel, and we'll be accountable to them in the next life."

"Because of our unfaithfulness?" I asked. "You're still thinking about that talk by that General Authority, what's-his-name, at the last mission conference, aren't you?"

"Yeah, that among other things."

"Just because he's a Seventy or something, he's supposedly an expert on how things work here in France."

"What about what he was saying about how the missionaries in Latin America are getting so many more converts than we are here?"

"Ray, he was talking out of his hat!"

"Don't call me Ray!"

"Sorry, Elder Beaverton, but he was talking out of his hat!"

"What do you mean?"

"If the church gets tons more converts year after year in Latin America than in Europe, how could that possibly be the fault of the missionaries? If anything, he's saying that the prophet isn't very inspired if he keeps sending all the faithful missionaries to Latin America and all the slackers to Europe. You'd think he'd mix it up a little!"

"Then how do you explain how the missionaries in Latin America are bringing so many more people to the truth than we are?"

"Get real, Beaverton! We're selling the idea that wine is a sin in *Bordeaux, France*! You know how it goes! You get to the discussion about the Word of Wisdom and how it's a sin to have a *verre de rouge* with dinner, and they look at you like you're from another planet! It takes a heroic effort to find anyone at all who is ready to hear that message!"

"You may be right."

"He doesn't remember what it's like! He doesn't even remember his own mission except in little nuggets of faith-promoting stories to tell in talks like that one! And for that oh-so-inspiring message, he got a free trip to Europe! Then he had a lovely dinner with the Mission President and his family while we went home to a dinner of warmed-over rice. We're the ones who are out here pounding the pavement every day, busting our balls for the Lord. He doesn't know jack about how faithful we are."

"Elder Hobbs, that's not a very appropriate thing to say, especially about the Lord's anointed!"

"He may be the 'Lord's anointed' but I still say he doesn't know jack."

"And why, pray tell, would the Lord anoint someone who 'doesn't know jack,' as you so quaintly put it?"

"Even if the church is perfect, the people aren't."

"And that includes you, Elder Hobbs."

"Hey, I never said I was perfect. I'm just saying that I'm not going to kiss that guy's butt and thank him for telling me I'm doing a crappy job when I know I'm not."

After our nightly prayers, as we were getting in bed, of course I started thinking that Elder Beaverton was right. I shouldn't have been breaking the rules. I shouldn't have been allowing myself to have impure thoughts. That was why I hadn't been feeling the spirit lately, and really hadn't felt it in a long time.

As far as being inspired to find people to teach, however, it didn't really matter anymore. My last work day was over. Now I just had Thursday to pack and to go around and say goodbye to some favorite local members, then Friday to have my temple recommend interview, and Saturday I'd be on the plane.

41. FRIDAY MORNING

FRIDAY MORNING I gathered my things and Elder Beaverton helped me carry them to the other side of town to the mission office. Elder Beaverton didn't have to move his own things this time—he just had to gather up his new companion, Elder Wilson, and bring him back to the apartment.

When we arrived, Elder Wilson was there waiting with his things, so I said goodbye to Elder Beaverton as he left with his new companion. Elder Wilson didn't look particularly shaken-up, despite the whole thing with Elder Cannon, so I figured Elder Beaverton would be fine with him.

The office elders scheduled appointments with the Mission President for all the guys that were leaving, and then we were free to spend the rest of the day doing whatever we wanted. Everyone wanted to go see some sort of auto show at the *Parc des Expositions* in the far north of Bordeaux, near *Bordeaux Lac*, far from the urban center of town. Everyone, that is, except me and Elder West, and of course Elder Cannon, who was to be supervised in the mission office by the office elders for the day. So Elder West was assigned to be my temporary companion for the day.

First off, Nick said he wanted to get some chocolates for his mother, so we went to a local chocolate shop. I thought perhaps it would be nice to get some for Tanya too, so I bought a box just like the one he got.

As we were leaving the shop, I was wondering how I was going to suggest to him that we might start heading towards the *Café Utopia*. I figured that he was such a rule-breaker himself that he probably wouldn't tell on me for making a date with Tanya. So I started asking him what he was thinking we might do for the day.

He stopped in front of the door of a nearby building and turned to me. "I don't care where you go or what you do," he said. "Just don't let anyone see that I'm not with you." And with that he pressed one of the buttons of the *interphone* in the doorway.

Over the *interphone*, a female voice said "*Oui ?*"

"*C'est moi, cherie,*" said Nick. [It's me, darling.]

Then as the door buzzed, he pushed it open a crack. That little devil had found himself a girlfriend!

Then he turned to me. "Please, Spencer," he said. "This is the last time I'll see her in I don't know how long. You were always cool when we were companions…"

"Okay," I said. "I'll be back here at 14h sharp to pick you up, so be ready."

I saw the look of relief come over his face as he said, "Thank you, you're a real pal."

Then I noted the address and the name on the correct buzzer as he disappeared into the building. Well, that was one problem solved…

I did my best to take side-streets to the *Café Utopia* so that I wouldn't be seen out alone. I'd picked that café because it was on a *place* that was a little bit off of the main traffic routes where hopefully we wouldn't be spotted even though it was in the middle of town.

When I arrived at the Utopia, Tanya was already there sipping a coffee. She got up to give me a squeeze, and then I took a seat beside her as we sat back down. I then gave her the chocolates. She sweetly thanked me and took one out for me and one for herself and put the rest in her bag.

"So where's your sidekick?" she asked. "I thought you guys weren't allowed to go out alone."

"Funny thing," I replied. "By coincidence, he had a date too."

"Elder Beaverton had a date?"

"No, Beaverton is already with his new comp. They've paired me up with someone else just for today. I'm flying home tomorrow, you know."

"Oh, wow, congrats!" she said.

"Thanks." Then the server came by and I ordered a *Perrier*. "So maybe we can see each other again when we're both back in Orem."

Her expression changed. "Oh," she said, "I'm not going back to Orem. My parents have moved to Atlanta. They've arranged me a great internship there for the rest of the summer. When my plane lands in Atlanta, I'm getting off and staying—I'm not continuing on to Salt Lake with Andrea and Kim."

I couldn't think how to respond. I wanted to see her again— sometime when I wasn't a missionary anymore, and would be allowed to date her without it being against the rules—but it didn't seem like this was a serious enough relationship yet for me to offer to fly all the way out to Atlanta to see her.

"Well, you'll probably be back to Orem sometime to visit friends, right?"

"Yeah, I might," she said non-committally. Looking around, she said "This place has a lot of atmosphere, with all the stained-glass windows and carvings and such."

"I thought you'd like it. I think it was once a monastery. Now I think it may be run by communists, but I'm not sure. It's been converted into a movie theater, obviously. They show a lot of foreign films here in *version originale* [subtitled], including American ones."

Then my *Perrier* arrived, and I paid for it and started pouring it from the bottle into the glass.

"What are you humming?" she asked. I hadn't really noticed I was humming until she mentioned it.

"It's this song I've had stuck in my head since yesterday. I'm not even sure what song it is. I just have this impression that it's something my sisters used to play."

"How does it go?"

I sang it to her softly: *"Something's at the gate and rushing through... All the rusty chains of time can't hold it back..."*

She laughed.

"I can only remember little bits of it though," I said, continuing with a different part of the song: *"I recall the morning you arose, shining like a star on an endless sea of sand..."*

Then she softly sang the reply: *"And the tender child in your eyes... As the compass drew us out, I took your hand..."* And with that she put her hand on my hand.

"Oh you know it!" I said, holding her hand in mine. "What song is it?"

She laughed. "You don't want to know."

"Well, we have all morning to do whatever we want," I said, "provided that no one sees that I'm with you and not my companion."

She looked me in the eye and calmly said, "Come up to my room with me."

I laughed. "And do what?"

She smiled in response and asked, "You can't really be that innocent, can you?" She put her hand on my knee.

I felt my immediate physical reaction. Arousal obviously, but also fear.

Apparently noticing my change of expression, she asked, "Are you okay?"

I couldn't answer.

"Spence, get a grip. People have sex all the time, it's no big deal."

"I have my interview in three hours."

"That gives us plenty of time," she said. "The apartment where we're staying is right nearby."

My hand was shaking as I reached for my glass to take a sip.

"What's the matter? You don't find me attractive?"

I was so surprised by her question that I swallowed wrong and started coughing. But I managed to calm my cough enough to ask her, "How can you even think that?"

I looked at her pretty eyes, her short, black hair pulled casually behind her ear, the curve of her neck leading down to a simple necklace, the line of her cleavage which was continued down by a row of small buttons that were painfully inviting…

"It's just that with this temple recommend interview, they determine whether I've completed my mission honorably," I said.

"Then what you do is you come to my room now, and in three hours when the Mission President asks you if you've had sex with anyone, you say 'no'. It's that simple."

"It's not that simple," I replied.

Her expression turned to one of sympathy. "I understand. I shouldn't—it's completely crazy—but I do. Growing up in Orem, I've seduced enough Mormon boys to know how it works. This mission is important to you. You've been preparing for it your whole life. You've worked hard and endured for two years, and you don't want to throw all your efforts in the toilet this close to the end. That's why this offer coming right now freaks you out so badly."

She understood. I could hardly believe it.

"Listen, I can see that I'm stressing you out just by being here with you right now. You go do what you need to do to prepare for your interview. I'll meet you here after."

"Thank you," I said. "We can meet back here again at 16h."

"Okay," she said. "Then we can talk about what we're going to do from there. No pressure." Then she kissed me on the forehead and left.

I was a little sad to see her go, but she was right that there was no way I'd be able to get into the right spirit for my interview by spending the morning with her. And besides, we'd have the rest of the afternoon to spend together after the interview.

I tried to prepare myself mentally and spiritually for the interview, but I found I couldn't stop thinking about what we might do that afternoon. I could see myself going with her up the stairs to her apartment, and I could picture only too vividly what would follow...

I had to get that image out of my mind. After all, even after the interview was over, it would still be a grave sin, and just waiting until after the interview was over wasn't enough for me to complete my mission honorably because I wouldn't actually be released from my calling as missionary until I arrived back home.

But then I wondered what it was I was planning to do with her this afternoon if it wasn't sex, and why I was planning to get back together with her at all. Did I really think I was going to just date her? Could I imagine that there was any chance at all that we could just court sweetly and then get married in the temple?

On the other hand, she understood how I felt and didn't try to pressure me to do something I might regret. It was clear that she had a good heart. She might be persuaded to accept the gospel. Maybe it had just never been presented to her in the right way.

Then I thought I must be off my rocker. The reason she had understood was from *seducing good Mormon boys*. How could I imagine that she might someday make a faithful mother in Zion?

On the other hand, plenty of people had had a pretty wild youth and then settled down and later gone on to be faithful adults. She and I could have a courtship that would perhaps be a bit questionable by LDS standards, then have a civil marriage and then be sealed in the temple a year later.

I knew I was never supposed to set a goal to be married outside the temple. Yet, what if we really had met in the pre-existence? What if she was foreordained to be my wife? And what if making love to her was the only way I could convince her to be with me? In that case I couldn't just judge her a sinner and deny her my best efforts to bring her with me to the Celestial Kingdom.

Even so, it seemed like maybe it wasn't the right time to be planning all this. I felt like I needed to take a walk to clear my head. I had an incredible urge to go to the *Pont de Pierre* and see the river, *la Garonne*, one more time. I knew it was a bit of a risk since it was always crowded there, but I figured I'd try to just keep my head down and hope I wouldn't be seen.

When I got to the bridge, it wasn't too crowded because it was still morning. I looked at the row of lonely lampposts as I approached. The river was low that day and flowing north. It seemed like it usually flowed north when it was low and south when it was high. When I'd first arrived in Bordeaux, I was actually a little uneasy about crossing the bridge because the railing was not even as high as my chest. But as I'd gotten used to it, I found the place kind of relaxing and peaceful, despite the crowds and traffic.

Feeling the light breeze on my face, I looked out at the water. The edges of the moving water between the feet of the bridge curled into little whirlpools here and there. I tried to drag up all the rusty memories of my former life in Orem, back when everything was so much simpler. I was so faithful then, what had happened to me?

Picturing my home and my family, my youth and my old ward, I started to feel like a good missionary again. I kept all of these pleasant images in my mind until it was time to go get Nick and go to my interview with the Mission President.

When it was my turn, the Mission President shook my hand and started asking me all of the familiar temple recommend questions:

Do you believe in God, the Eternal Father, in his son, Jesus Christ, and in the Holy Ghost; and do you have a firm testimony of the restored gospel?

Of course.

Do you sustain the President of the Church of Jesus Christ of Latter-day Saints as the prophet, seer, and revelator; and do you recognize him as the only person on Earth authorized to exercise all priesthood keys?

Of course.

Do you sustain the other General Authorities and the local authorities of the Church?

Yeah, essentially.

Do you live the law of chastity?

Other people have probably done it better, but considering what I'd given up, I felt justified in answering in the affirmative.

Is there anything in your conduct relating to members of your family that is not in harmony with the teachings of the Church?

I hadn't even seen my family in two years, and that was the way the Church wanted it...

Do you affiliate with any group or individual whose teachings or practices are contrary to or oppose those accepted by the Church of Jesus Christ of Latter-day Saints, or do you sympathize with the precepts of any such group or individual?

That was a bit of a sticky one... I only sympathized with her in as much as I wanted to bring her to the light, not with her 'precepts' so I guessed I was okay to answer 'no'. Besides, everyone knows that question is just to weed out people who sympathize with the polygamist groups, not people who associate with random individual sinners.

Do you earnestly strive to do your duty to the Church; to attend your sacrament, priesthood, and other meetings; and obey the rules, laws, and commandments of the gospel?

Yes, to the best of my limited ability.

Are you honest in your dealings with your fellow men?

I try to be.

Are you a full-tithe payer?

Obviously.

Do you keep the Word of Wisdom?

Yes, of course.

Do you keep all of the covenants that you made in the temple and wear the authorized garments both day and night?

Yes.

Has there been any sin or misdeed in your life that should have been resolved with priesthood authorities but has not?

No.

Do you consider yourself worthy in every way to enter the temple and participate in temple ordinances?

I think so, yes.

Then the Mission President signed the paper and shook my hand and said, "Good work, Elder Hobbs. The Lord is pleased with your faithful service."

And that was it. He didn't even mention the little incident that Elder Dietrich said he was going to report.

Nick had finished his interview first, so we went back out together as soon as my interview was done. As I stepped out into the light, I could hardly believe that it was over—the whole two years of it—and that that was all there was to it.

We started back to Nick's girlfriend's apartment. We didn't even make it all the way to the door—she came running up to him on the sidewalk and grabbed him in her arms and said "*Ah, mon petit Nico adorable !*" She was a really pretty girl, and they looked so happy together smiling in each other's arms.

As they rushed back up to her apartment, I yelled out the time I'd be by to pick him up again, and I hoped he'd heard me.

I was one hundred percent certain that he had just flat-out lied on the chastity question on his interview. Yet seeing them together, I couldn't help but think maybe on some level that he was the one who had made the right decision. Of course I was essentially on my way to find out myself...

When I got to the *Café Utopia*, I took a seat out front and ordered myself a *Perrier* and waited.

When it got to be 17h, I started to get a little worried. I was sure some sort of emergency had come up—she wouldn't just not show like that. I wished I'd thought to get her phone number or something rather than just arranging a meeting time and place.

The longer I sat there, the deeper my sinking feeling became. I didn't have any contact info for her. I didn't even know her last name. Why hadn't I thought to ask about this earlier?

Then I thought Sam might be able to help me find her once I got back. Then I remembered that she said she didn't really know Sam all that well, so there was no way he would just happen to have her parents' new address in Atlanta. Then I thought maybe that guy Jared might have her new contact info—he was supposed to be a friend of Sam's. But it seemed like maybe that wasn't such a hot idea considering that she said she'd had an "on-again off-again" thing with him. And since—if I understood correctly—he had been dumped specially for the occasion of her trip to France, he might not be too keen on helping me find her.

When the server girl came by to bus my third bottle of *Perrier* at 18h, behind the look of sympathy in her eyes I could almost hear her saying *"Elle ne va pas revenir."* [She's not coming back.]

I couldn't believe what I'd been reduced to. There I was— supposedly this big, tough guy—sitting alone in some frou-frou French café, crying into my *Perrier*, almost.

When it was time to go get Nick, I was dreading seeing him again. I was sure he'd be positively glowing from the afternoon of pleasure he'd just spent, and I didn't think I could face seeing that. But of course he was completely broken up after his tearful goodbye from his girlfriend. I felt like maybe he was actually worse off than I was since he was probably really in love with that girl, and now he'd be back in California and she'd still be here in Bordeaux, a million miles apart from each other.

That evening the whole group that was leaving had dinner with the Mission President and his family. I felt like I should be enjoying it, but I couldn't concentrate—I was completely in a daze the whole time.

Something's at the gate and rushing through...

I had to force a smile, and I couldn't follow or pay attention to anything anyone was saying.

All the rusty chains of time can't hold it back...

I didn't understand why I felt that way. It was just some foolish infatuation, some idle lust, wasn't it?

Memories of our former life...

I should be so happy to be going home.

I recall the morning you arose...

So much had happened since I'd been gone. Matt's wife had had a baby—I was now an uncle, and I would get to meet my new niece.

Shining like a star on an endless sea of sand...

I'd get to meet Laura's new husband, and I'd even get to attend Linda's wedding since she and her fiancé had graciously held off the wedding long enough to wait for me to come back.

Shining like a star...

There were so many reasons to be celebrating.

On an endless sea of sand...

After dinner, we had an informal testimony meeting. Actually, all the guys seemed at least a little emotional about their testimonies, so I felt like maybe I wasn't so crazy to be feeling confused and conflicted about leaving.

When it was my turn to stand up, I spoke from the heart. "I'd like to bear my testimony of the truthfulness of the restored gospel, and of the important place it holds in our lives. I am so grateful to the Lord for giving me the strength to endure to the end and to work hard and serve Him faithfully these past two years." Then I paused and said, "I only hope that I have succeeded and that my small efforts have been pleasing in His sight."

After that, I couldn't say anything more, so I just said "In the name of Jesus Christ, amen," and sat down.

As I went to bed that night, I thought to myself that there was maybe one last chance. We'd be waiting for the airport shuttle on the steps of the opera house at the *Place de la Comédie* right downtown. She knew I was leaving that morning, and she might know that that was where we'd be waiting, or if she didn't know it, there was a small chance that she might happen to walk by. I said a little silent prayer that she would be there.

In the morning, I gathered my things and waited with the other guys on the steps of the opera house. I thought to myself, 'if she comes, I'll beg her to continue on to Salt Lake at the end of her trip, and I'll find a way to send her back to Atlanta later.'

Then I thought, 'If she comes, I'll ask her to change her ticket and leave with me now, and then we can both go to Atlanta later when it's time for her to start her internship.'

Then I thought, 'If I can't convince her to change her own ticket, I'll try to change mine. Or if I can't, I'll throw mine away and stay with her in France until the end of her trip, and not worry about the future.'

Then I thought, 'If she comes, I'll do whatever she asks and follow her to the ends of the Earth...'

Then I thought, 'Now I'm being a real idiot. I'm not going to see her again. I'm going home, and I'm happy about it. And that's that.'

I got onto the airport shuttle and took a seat by the window. I watched the familiar white stone buildings and the city spires go by

of the *ville* [city] that was by far my favorite *ville* of all of the places in France I'd served during the course of my mission. When I thought about it, it was true that I was happy to be going home. But for the moment, all I could think about was all of the things I was leaving behind.

Ah, Tanya.

I'll find you.

Somehow...

CHARACTERS IN BORDEAUX MISSION

Missionaries

*Elder
Hobbs*

*Elder
Dietrich*

*Elder
West*

*Sister
Bell*

*Elder
Young*

*Elder
Beaverton*

*Elder
Clark*

*Elder
Cannon*

*Sister
Stein*

*Elder
Gladwell*

Friends

Tanya

Andrea

Kim

IX. Exmo Conference

Heavenly Father

42. SATURDAY AFTERNOON

I LOVE TO JOKE AROUND. I've got the perfect joke for just this occasion. It's an oldie, so stop Me if you've heard it:

Way back when Jesus and I were creating the world, I turned to Him and said "Hey Jesus, let's create a really gorgeous mountainous region, with lakes and rivers full of fish, beautiful canyons, waterfalls, valleys, and peaks..."

Then Jesus said "But Dad, that'll never fly! Everyone will want to live there, and it will get so crowded, it will suck!"

Then I said "I'm one step ahead of You Jesus, My boy! Why do You think I created Mormonism?"

Hahahahahahahahaha!

I'm just kidding, of course! The Mormons are My chosen people these days, so that's why I love having a little fun with them!

Now this whole idea of *leaving the only true church* is so completely nuts that I couldn't help but be fascinated when I noticed that some of My children were organizing a whole conference just for people whom I was planning on sending to outer darkness. Being omniscient and all, of course I knew it was going to happen. But that didn't make it any less entertaining to watch!

Not the conference itself, mind you—heavens, no! I avoided that like the plague! A bunch of egg-headed lectures on History, Theology, Philosophy and any other dry poindexter subject that My naughtiest children could possibly research at length! Yawnsville! It was as bad as Sacrament Meeting! Well, almost.

But there was plenty of fun stuff going on in the coffee houses and bars in the surrounding area. Here's what I saw:

I found one local coffeehouse that was buzzing with apostates, all talking about the conference and comparing notes. Lynn Hanson was sitting at a table with Andrew Denton talking about how cute April and Susan's kids were.

Lynn smiled as she was putting her pile of photos away. "I have to ask you," she said. "Whatever became of your brother David? Did he end up leaving the church too?"

"No, no one in my family has left the church but me," he replied. "In fact, David's in the bishopric of his ward and his wife is Relief Society president. Here, I've got a picture somewhere." He flipped through the pile of pictures in his wallet and showed Lynn a photo of a smiling family.

Lynn looked it over. David was maybe a little thicker at the waist and thinner on top, but still handsome. His wife was no supermodel, but she wasn't too bad. And they and their three little girls looked happy. Lynn didn't know if perhaps she'd been secretly hoping things had gone badly for him, but she didn't begrudge him his happiness. She handed the photo back.

It was too bad for Lynn that she didn't also run into Rodney Grant, who went straight from the lecture hall to a local gay club earlier that day. That would have led to some more amusing trips down memory lane!

"Well, I'd better get going," said Andrew. "I promised my wife I'd meet her after her workshop." He finished his coffee and started to get up just as Rex was coming in the door.

"Oh, just a minute, I'd like you to meet my husband, Rex. Rex, this is April's old boyfriend, Andrew Denton," said Lynn as Rex approached the table.

"April's *boyfriend?*" Rex asked, a little confused.

"I have the distinction of being the only one," said Andrew. "We were kids together."

"Oh, right," said Rex. "Now I remember. I think we met briefly when you were at BYU. God, that was a long time ago, wasn't it?"

Hardly! It was less than a fraction of a day! But I kept My response to Myself.

"Yeah. Anyway, nice seeing you again," said Andrew, going out. "Give April my best."

Rex got himself a coffee and was sitting down just as Joy and Rajendra walked in. "Oh good, you guys found the place," said Rex, waving them over. Joy introduced her new boyfriend to Lynn and then suggested that they move to a more comfortable spot in the nook with the couches. As they were taking their seats, Jill arrived to join them.

Once they were all settled in with their respective coffees, Joy turned to Jill. "You know who I thinking we might see at the conference? Your old boyfriend Walter!"

"Oh, god, Walter!" groaned Jill.

Tell me about it!

"Why were you thinking he'd be here?" asked Rex. "Did he leave the church too?"

"I don't know," said Joy. "I ran into him this morning right nearby here. I was thinking he was here for the conference, but then I didn't see him in the conference building."

"You saw him?" asked Jill. "Did you talk to him?"

"Yes, I did. He stopped me, actually. He mistook me for you! The funny thing was that when I corrected him, he remembered me immediately. I didn't think he'd ever even really met me since he was just in town for those few weeks after he got sent home from his mission."

Jill laughed. "That is so typical of him! He always knew the name of *every* girl! It was his best subject. I'll bet he's really gone downhill though, huh?"

"Not at all," replied Joy. "In fact, he was more handsome than ever, if that's possible."

"So did he ask about me?"

"Not really. He asked me to meet him for drinks later, to 'reminisce about old times'—as if he and I had shared all of these good memories together or something!" Joy laughed. "He was just trying to pick me up though, I suspect, because as soon as I mentioned bringing my boyfriend along he immediately lost interest."

"That's odd," said Jill. "I had heard that he'd married Laura Hobbs."

"Really?" asked Rex.

"Yeah, some friends were telling me that after Walter finished his MBA, he came back to Utah, and his dad started putting the pressure on him big time to give up his playboy lifestyle and settle down and become the model priesthood holder so he could take over the family business."

"And Laura got the fun of trying to settle him?" asked Rex. "Poor girl."

"Yep," said Jill. Then she turned to Rex and smiled teasingly. "Remember how you had such a crush on Laura?"

"Humph, that's not the way I remember it..." Rex replied.

"Wait a minute," said Joy, "You're talking about Spencer and Matt's sister Laura, right?"

"Yeah," said Jill.

"That's wild!" said Joy. "You know Spencer is here at the conference. I ran into him earlier and asked him to meet us at the Red Door after dinner."

"Ah, cool," said Lynn. "It'll be fun to finally meet him."

Just then Mary interrupted My enjoyment of this entertaining scene.

"Elohim," She said, "how many million times do I have to ask You to take out the garbage?"

"Can't you see I'm busy, woman?" I replied. "Couldn't You get one of Your ten-thousand sister-wives to do it?" Jesus! Just because I'm omnipotent, I have to do everything around here!

"Elo, We agreed that it's Your job," said Mary. "Now will You just do it? All Kolob is starting to stink to high heaven."

By the time I was finished with the garbage, the apostates were already done with dinner, and the lot of them had moved on to the Red Door. They were sitting at their table, and the waitress was there taking their order. Everybody ordered martinis except Lynn.

"Just a glass of juice for me," said Lynn.

As soon as the waitress was gone, Joy asked her "You're not drinking?"

"Nah, I'm the designated driver," replied Lynn.

Jill laughed. "And what trick did he use to swing that?"

"Well..." said Lynn. She kind of looked away and smiled.

"Oh, don't tell me congratulations are in order?" asked Jill.

"Pretty good trick, huh?" asked Rex, smiling.

"That's wonderful for you guys!" said Joy, "How exciting!"

"Thanks," said Lynn. "It's going to be quite an adventure."

Rex laughed. "Especially if the kid turns out to be anything like me and Lynn."

"Oh, come on, we're not so bad."

"Of course we aren't, dear," he said, patting her hand.

"And anyway, adventure is better than boring, right?" asked Lynn.

"That's why I married you," he replied.

Then the drinks were served and they all drank a toast to new life.

When Spencer arrived, he ordered himself a martini as well.

"Spence, this is Lynn," said Joy. "She's the one I was telling you about whose sister is married to your brother Matt."

"Ah, so you're Annette's sister Lynn," he said, shaking her hand.

"Hi Spencer, it's nice to meet you. I missed meeting you at the wedding reception. You were on your mission, right?"

"Yep, best two years of my life," said Spencer, laughing. "Or something like that."

"You know, we have a question for you, actually," said Joy, "about Walter Smith."

"What about him?" asked Spencer.

"Is he still married to your sister Laura?" asked Jill.

"Yeah, why?" asked Spencer.

"Well, I ran into him earlier and he hit on me. He wasn't wearing a wedding ring."

"Oh, god! Not again!" said Spencer rolling his eyes. "She never should have married that prick!"

Jill gave a wry laugh. "Still an asshole after all these years, huh?"

"Tell me about it," said Spencer. "This is for sure going to end badly and their kids are going to suffer for it."

"Has he left the church?" asked Rex.

"God, no!" said Spencer. "He's on the fucking Stake High Council, the prick!"

I didn't see why Spencer had to keep invoking Me here. As if it were My fault that the guy was a prick! Hadn't Spencer ever heard of free agency?

"So then Laura hasn't left the church either?" asked Jill.

"No, I'm the only one in my family who's out of the church."

"What's Sam up to these days?" asked Rex.

"He's in the army," replied Spencer.

Nobody knew what to say to that. They weren't even sure if it made sense to say "That's nice," in case Sam were perhaps deployed in some danger zone. Spencer didn't volunteer any more information.

So Lynn changed the subject slightly. "And your cousin Joe?" she asked.

"Oh, I just got back into contact with him again recently since I resigned from the church. I asked him if he wanted to come to this conference, but he was too busy studying for the qualifying exams, and he didn't feel like is was a good time to be distracted."

"What subject?" asked Lynn.

"Physics," replied Spencer. "Don't ask me any more than that, though. He's told me what he's hoping to do research on, but it was all Greek to me. To each his own!"

Spencer laughed and picked up his glass as he said it, so Rex jokingly took it as a toast. "To each his own!" said Rex, raising his own glass, and everyone drank to it.

"You guys were in graduate school too, weren't you?" asked Spencer. "How'd that go?"

"Oh we're done now," said Rex. "Lynn has a tenure-track position at the University of Minnesota."

"Ah, cool," said Spencer, "and you?"

"I'm not doing Math anymore," said Rex. "I've switched to programming."

"You didn't finish your degree?" asked Spencer.

"Oh, no I finished. My dissertation was good enough to earn me a PhD, even if it wasn't quite good enough to land me a post-doc at Columbia or something," he smiled at Lynn. "Anyway, I was never that passionate about Math research."

"Programming's cool," said Rajen.

"Not jealous, eh?" asked Jill with a sly smile.

"You know I wouldn't be like that. I chose what I'm doing and I'm happy with it," said Rex. Then he laughed and added "And besides, I'm still taller than she is."

They hung out and laughed together a little while longer, and then it was time for Joy and Rajen to go to a party they were invited to at the home of one of Joy and Spencer's former classmates who had moved to Salt Lake City. They invited Spencer along with them since he knew the hostess too.

In the taxi on the way to the party, they drove past Temple Square. The Salt Lake Temple looked magnificent as always, all lit up for the evening with its golden Moroni on the highest spire.

The cabbie picked up on the fact that his passengers weren't LDS. Perhaps he smelled alcohol on them. Perhaps he noticed Joy's sleeveless dress. Or perhaps he noticed Rajen's—shall We say—"ethnicity."

Whatever it was, as soon as they got to the big statue of Brigham Young welcoming people to Temple Square, the cabbie laughed as he recited the old poem "Here stands Brother Brigham, his arm out perched—his hand to the bank, his back to the church."

That one always makes Me giggle! Good old Briggy!

Soon they arrived at the party, and was it ever crowded! People were everywhere, all wasted and having a fabulous time. Joy, Rajen, and Spencer couldn't even find the hostess to greet her, but they managed to find some drinks.

Both Spencer and Joy ran into tons of old friends, and all three of them met up with some new friends they'd chatted with online but had never seen in person. Those kinds of meetings are always a delirious delight as you meet for the first time someone that you're in a sense already old friends with.

Spencer was enjoying himself immensely. He slipped off to the kitchen to find himself another drink.

In the kitchen, he heard a familiar voice. "Gina, your party is fabulous! A big success!"

The voice of his classmate Gina replied "Well, I can't take all the credit. It's the guests—they're fantastic! And just wait until the Exmo Womens' Pasta Wrestling Squad arrives!" She laughed. "You know, nobody know how to party like the exmormons!"

"It's so true! Hell, I'm tempted to finally convert to Mormonism just so that I can become an exmo!" She laughed. It was Tanya.

"Tanya! I thought I'd never find you again!"

"Spencer!" She couldn't believe her eyes. "Or should I say 'Elder Hobbs?'" she said with a smile.

"Oh god, please don't call me that!"

As if I ever did! I always get blamed for everything!

"What are you doing here?" she asked.

"I was going to ask you the same thing! I'm here for the conference. I'm out of the church now."

"I'm in town visiting friends. God, it's so amazing to see you again. Let's sit down somewhere where we can talk."

They grabbed their drinks and found a quiet corner.

"Tanya, there are so many things I want to say to you—that I've wanted to say to you for so many years."

"Me too."

"I looked for you for years, but no one was able to give me any information to help me find you—not even Google!"

"Really?" she asked. "I'm sure I've been even harder to find lately since I moved to France. I'm surprised to hear you were looking for me though—I didn't think you were all that interested."

"Are you kidding? I was crazy about you," he said. "I was ready to throw away my plane ticket right then and there and run away with you. I would have stayed in France as an illegal alien to be with you. I would have followed you to the ends of the Earth."

"I had no idea. I mean, imagine a faithful Mormon guy like you wanting to be with someone like me."

"Is that why you didn't come back after my interview?"

"That's part of it," she replied. "I'm sorry, I wanted to go see you. This will sound stupid, but I was outvoted. Kim was badgering me, saying how retarded it is to want to seduce inexperienced Mormon boys because they just come immediately and then have no clue what else they might do to make the whole thing more enjoyable for the girl."

Spencer laughed as Tanya continued. "I countered by telling her that it's fun teaching them new tricks, and I like breaking them in. Then Andrea started teasing me about how charitable and civic-minded I was, giving all those lessons *pro bono* and everything. God, I shouldn't have let them bully me like that, but I was just a dumb kid."

Hehe! I just love creating dumb kids!

"I was just a dumb kid too," said Spencer. "I've learned a thing or two since then, but now of course I wish I'd let you break me in way back then." He laughed. Then thinking about her friends, he asked "What ever happened to those two, anyway?"

"Kim works in a bank. She has a serious boyfriend now. I've lost track of Andrea. Last I saw her she was traveling across Europe as some sort of Bohemian. God only knows where she is now."

It was true! I did know! And I wasn't about to tell these guys! Hehe!

"Well, there's no sense wasting too much time on regrets," said Spencer. "We're together now." And they embraced and kissed. "I can't tell you how many times I've thought of you. I only saw you those few times, but no other girl I've met can compare. They don't have your spark, your *joie-de-vivre*."

"I know exactly how you feel," she said. Then she stood up and took his hand and led him to the door.

"Where are you taking me?" he asked.

"To the ends of the Earth."

So cute!

I could hardly believe Tanya could seduce him with such a corny line. I had to hand it to her, though—she knew her stuff! I laughed.

Ah these foolish apostates! Every one of them too weak to live up to the high standards of My true church! Oh why oh why did I create them this way?

Of course My righteous children are the ones in whom I am well pleased. But these wayward children—these beautifully flawed vessels—I think I love them most of all.

In the name of My son Jesus Christ, amen!

About the Author

Born and raised Mormon, C. L. Hanson enjoys observing Mormon culture. She is an enthusiastic participant in the LDS-interest blogging community, writing for the group blog "Main Street Plaza" and for her personal blog "Letters from a Broad." She enjoys reading new works of Mormon literature and writing book reviews. She also maintains an extensive blogroll of former Mormon blogs (called "Outer Blogness") and helps encourage community discussion by posting a weekly link round-up.

C. L. Hanson currently lives in Switzerland with her husband and two sons.

CPSIA information can be obtained at www.ICGtesting.com
Printed in the USA
BVOW02s0012230615

405592BV00019B/264/P